The Reeducation of
CHERRY
TRUONG

ALSO BY AIMEE PHAN

We Should Never Meet

The Reeducation of

CHERRY
TRUONG

Aimee Phan

ST. MARTIN'S PRESS ⚑ NEW YORK

THE REEDUCATION OF CHERRY TRUONG. Copyright © 2012 by Aimee Phan. All rights reserved. Printed in the United States of America. For information, address St. Martin's Press, 175 Fifth Avenue, New York, N.Y. 10010.

www.stmartins.com

Library of Congress Cataloging-in-Publication Data

Phan, Aimee.
    The reeducation of Cherry Troung : a novel / Aimee Phan.—
1st ed.
        p.   cm.
    ISBN 978-0-312-32268-7 (hardcover)
    ISBN 978-1-4299-6247-6 (e-book)
  1. Vietnamese Americans—Fiction.   2. Orange County (Calif.)—Fiction.   3. Refugees—Fiction.   4. Extended families—Fiction.   5. Family secrets—Fiction.
6. Vietnam—Fiction.   7. Paris (France)—Fiction.
8. Malaysia—Fiction.   9. Domestic fiction.   I. Title.
    PS3616.H36R44 2012
    813'.6—dc22

                                                    2011041346

First Edition: March 2012

10   9   8   7   6   5   4   3   2   1

For Amélie

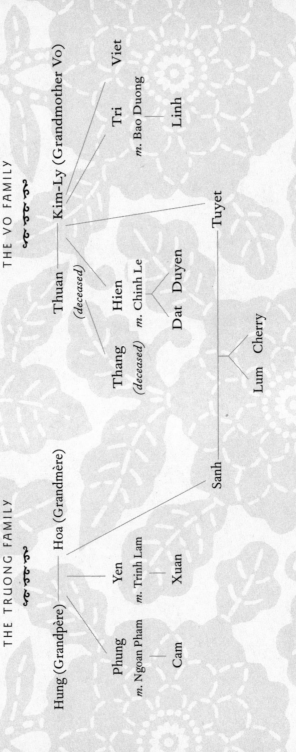

THE VO FAMILY

Thuan ——— Kim-Ly (Grandmother Vo)

Thang *(deceased)*

Hien
m. Chinh Le

Dat Duyen

Tri Viet

m. Bao Duong

Linh

Tuyet

THE TRUONG FAMILY

Hung (Grandpère) ——— Hoa (Grandmère)

Phung
m. Ngoan Pham

Cam

Yen
m. Trinh Lam

Xuan

Sanh

Lum Cherry

The Reeducation of
CHERRY
TRUONG

1978

Kim-Ly Vo
Ho Chi Minh City, Vietnam

Mother, I hope this finds you well. I think about you and our family often. I think about you every hour of every day.

I know you are angry. I wish I could explain the circumstances that forced me to do what I did, but I don't know who else could be reading this letter. I can only ask that you trust me, a difficult and perhaps impossible request. Please believe me. This wasn't my choice.

Why couldn't I tell you? Why didn't I respect you enough to tell you personally? I tried to find the words, but they would not come. How can you tell your own mother that you are abandoning her? What kind of daughter would do that?

I am not that kind of daughter. I will make this up to you. If you've taught me anything, it is that determination will help me endure and overcome even the most trying situation. This is what I struggle with now, yet I remember you and our family, and I know we will see each other again. I promise you.

Your devoted daughter

Tuyet Truong
Pulau Bidong, Malaysia

∂ꝰ *Prologue*

CHERRY

Saigon, Vietnam, 2001

CHERRY RELEASES THE GRIP AROUND HER BROTHER, steadying her trembling feet onto the hot, bright concrete. Lum jumps off his motorbike, leaving his sister to dig her fingernails into their seat, battling vertigo. After inhaling several hot muggy breaths, her eyes finally open.

Identical plots of demarcated land and bleached sidewalks surround her. Wooden beams and smooth stone piles litter the construction site. Men in bright-yellow polo shirts and black jeans crouch along the ground, planting new trees and arranging signs advertising the new housing division. Her gaze resettles on her brother. Lum is beaming.

"What do you think?" he asks.

"It's Orange County," she says.

"No," he says, shaking his head. "It's better."

They squeeze between a cement mixer and a mud-splattered orange tractor. "It's still in the early stages," Lum says almost apologetically as local contractors in hard helmets and goggles stand under a trailer awning examining blueprints. "We're going to bring in mature landscaping for the border, not like those flimsy baby-stick trees at other subdivisions. Lawns for every home. We're working on the irrigation system with a Hong Kong company." Ahead, construction workers monitor a backhoe clawing the earth and spitting piles of dirt into a white truck. Cherry shakes the dust from their hour-long motorbike ride out of her flip-flops—first the left foot, then the right.

Her brother had told them that he worked as a manager in a housing development company, but Cherry never imagined this. All these employees, the layers of responsibility. Surrounded by waist-high piles of wooden beams, they cross the lot toward a single French country-style house. She tries to keep up with her brother, but her steps feel heavy from jet lag, having only landed in Saigon fourteen hours earlier. Instead of touring landmarks or museums, she gazes at the exterior of a house that nearly replicates their parents' home in Newport Lake. Even the materials look similar, alternating between creamy stucco and stone. The bare windows reveal the progress inside: unfinished plywood, rolls of insulation, cans of paint scattered about.

"This is what you've been doing?" she asks.

"Yeah," Lum says, looking triumphant. "Are you surprised?"

"No," she says, forcing a smile. "I just thought you hated tract housing." Cherry's eyes travel to her brother, then the house, then back at him. The arched doorways, the skinny turret. Years have passed since he has been home, but he cannot ignore the resemblance.

"I was young," Lum says, an uneasy smile distorting his face. "Aren't you glad I've grown up?"

If only their parents were standing here, too, so they could see their transformed son: the responsible, successful Lum.

The construction foreman waves for her brother. Cherry stumbles across the graveled site, careful not to get in anyone's way. Her head feels dusty, heat presses on her eyes. The development walls loom so high she cannot see the rice fields and shantytowns outside of them. Near the entry gates, several crew members cluster for a cigarette break. Their eyes skim Cherry's small waist and bare legs. She asks for a cigarette; they hesitate briefly, but eventually hand one over.

"You're Mr. Truong's sister?" a man with a long mustache and a baseball cap asks, offering his lighter. "From America?"

Cherry nods, trying to downplay her struggle with the Zippo lighter.

"He's a smart man," he says. "All this? His idea."

Arms crossed, Lum looks absorbed in discussion with his colleague. His face is confident, contemplative, an expression Cherry doesn't recognize at all. Suddenly, his image doubles, then multiplies. Cherry blinks a few times and turns away.

"We're very proud of him," she says, coughing up some dust.

"Wait until you see the finished product. You'll be happy." He gestures up to a sign.

Cherry hadn't noticed it when they drove in. On a clean yellow billboard, in red block letters, her eyes take a minute to focus: THE FUTURE SITE OF NEW LITTLE SAIGON . . . THE COMFORTS OF AMERICA, IN YOUR TRUE HOME, VIETNAM.

Three months ago, the day her acceptance letter arrived, Cherry didn't open the envelope. She volunteered at the neonatal care unit at the hospital Tuesday and Thursday afternoons and her mother didn't see any reason to delay the celebration. The white manila envelope was large and thick, full of forms to fill out. Schools didn't waste extra paper on rejects.

Driving home, she passed her relatives' cars along the sidewalk and in the driveway. Her cousin Dat's Lexus sat parked in front of their neighbor's house, and he would only come for news from UC Irvine, his medical school alma mater. He also attended Irvine as an undergraduate, just like Cherry, the only school that mattered to her family.

"Congratulations, Cherry!" Auntie Hien gushed, smothering Cherry's face with one of her trademark sniffing kisses. "Do you want to specialize in pediatrics? Dermatology?"

"Anesthesiology," Uncle Chinh predicted. "That's where all the money is. Anesthesiology, like Dat, right?"

At the dining room table next to the prominently displayed acceptance letter, Cherry's mother fretted over a pristine violet sheet cake. In bright-blue piping gel, she carefully scrawled "Doctor Cherry Truong" atop the buttercream frosting.

"Your father is supposed to be back with the ice cream," her mother complained when Cherry approached her side. "I ask him to do one thing and he can't even get that right."

They waited ten more minutes before her mother decided to proceed with the celebrations. Uncle Chinh arranged the family around the cake to take pictures. Then the relatives took turns handing her envelopes full of money to use on books and school supplies. Auntie Tri reminded Cherry to smile with her teeth. In a rare slip of affection, Grandmother Vo kissed Cherry on the cheek, proud that at least one granddaughter had graduated from college, and was on her way to medical school.

"I was smart like you once," Grandmother Vo said. "But I was expected to raise a family. I never had your opportunities. Don't squander them."

As Cherry walked away, her grandmother quietly passed Cherry's mother a folded check, their slender, elegant fingers briefly touching. The tuition deposit for UC Irvine. Their discretion wasn't necessary. Of all her medical school applications, Cherry hadn't bothered applying for financial aid to UC Irvine. It was the one school Grandmother Vo had agreed to fully fund.

Her cousins Duyen and Linh sat on the staircase. They'd come straight from their shifts at the beauty salon, and were complaining about Kim, the new hairstylist whom they believed was stealing their clients. Cherry sat on the stair below them, where she had a view of the garage door, to keep a lookout for her dad.

"Are you going to call your brother?" Duyen asked, as she passed Cherry a fried vegetable cracker from her plate.

"I haven't had the chance to read the letter myself," Cherry said.

"No," Duyen said, shaking her head impatiently. "About the wedding."

In the corner of the living room, Dat and his fiancée, Quynh, sat on the dragonfly-embroidered couch, showing their aunts the proofs from their engagement photo session. Their engagement was a well-known eventuality, since they were only waiting for Quynh to finish pharmacy school. When Quynh waved, Cherry smiled insincerely and looked away. Cherry had not told Lum. She wondered if anyone else in the family had.

"We looked yesterday for the bridesmaids' dresses," Linh said. "She wanted this awful tangerine shade, but I talked her into choosing green. Green is still a nice summer color, right?" Since Quynh had no sisters, and her only female cousin still lived back in Vietnam, she had asked Cherry, Duyen, and Linh to stand in her wedding.

"The guest list is already up to three hundred," Linh continued. "They're going to have to reserve two ballroom spaces."

"Who could they be inviting?" Cherry asked.

"Their friends, colleagues from my brother's clinic, our parents' friends," Duyen said, shrugging her tanned shoulders.

"Dat doesn't have any friends."

"Cherry," Duyen scolded.

"I'm serious," she said. "Besides Quynh's friends and our family, no one likes him. Is he going to invite strangers?"

"What's your problem?" Duyen asked, giving her cousin a sharp look.

"Quynh and Lum broke up years ago," Linh reminded her. "Can't you just get over it?"

Cherry ignored her, allowing them to return to their silly debate over dress colors. She hated when they ganged up on her, pinching history between their overmanicured fingers. She looked across the living room again, where Quynh chatted with her future mother-in-law and Dat dabbed his sweaty forehead with a napkin. When they were little, people used to mistake Dat and Cherry for siblings, assuming Lum and Duyen were brother and sister. It never failed to aggravate her. Cherry didn't want to look like Dat.

"So we were thinking Maui," Linh said.

"Sorry?" Cherry asked, refocusing on her cousins.

"For your graduation present," Duyen said, softly pushing on Cherry's hip with her bare foot.

"Oh, right." Another dangling carrot toward UC Irvine. With the money they'd be saving for living expenses—because naturally Cherry would live at home—Grandmother Vo had offered Cherry and her two cousins a vacation. "Why Maui?"

"Grandmother already rented that condo for Dat and Quynh in August," Linh said.

"You want to go with them on their honeymoon?"

"The condo has three bedrooms. We already talked about it before you came and they're fine with it."

The prospect of spending two weeks tagging along on her cousin's honeymoon sounded like a punishment. This vacation was supposed to be a reward for all her hard work. She wanted to spend it with someone important to her.

The garage door opened and Cherry's father wandered in, holding a plastic grocery bag. He smiled at the guests until her mother approached him and impatiently tugged at his arm. Cherry immediately stood.

"What do you mean you got lost?" her mother asked as Cherry walked up to them. "We've been going to that supermarket for years."

"They were doing construction work on Jamboree. I had to take a detour."

Her mother peeked inside the grocery bag. "I told you vanilla ice cream," she said. "Who is going to eat all this mint chocolate?"

"Mint is Cherry's favorite," her father replied.

"It is," Cherry agreed quietly, taking the bag from him. "I love it."

The next morning, Cherry brought up the idea of going to Vietnam. Her grandmother and parents rejected it: too far, too expensive, too risky.

"You let Lum live there for five years," Cherry reminded them.

"He's a boy," her father said. "And it wasn't supposed to be for that long."

"Some playboy will target you," Grandmother Vo said, "and trick you into marrying him for a visa. I've seen it happen before, trust me. Remember that Lam girl?"

"What happened to Hawaii?" her mother asked.

"I don't want to lie on a beach and chase after boys," Cherry said. "I want to see my brother."

They finally relented, purchasing Cherry a ticket to spend a month in Vietnam. No one else wanted to go with her. Her parents had to work. Linh and Duyen claimed they didn't want to get stuck in Vietnam, like they heard had happened to others returning to the motherland. But because Cherry wasn't born there, she probably wouldn't have such trouble. No one could mistake Cherry for anything else but an American.

"Maybe you can talk some sense back into your brother," Grandmother Vo said. "Bring him back to where he belongs." She was not specific on the *where,* which was not surprising. Lum's former bedroom had long since been transformed into a guest room and Grandmother Vo's occasional abode, his clothing, posters, and CDs packed up in cobwebbed boxes in the garage.

The day before Cherry was supposed to leave, her mother had a bad dream. She normally wasn't superstitious, and even as she described it to them the next morning—the threatening Communist police officers; the dark, rat-infested jail cells—Cherry couldn't help wondering if she was making it up as she went along, recalling melodramatic scenes from an old movie she once saw on television.

"You can save the trip for another time," her mother finally concluded. "How about next summer? Daddy can ask for vacation leave, and then we can go with you."

"Why can't I still go now?" Cherry asked.

"Fine," she said. "Don't listen to me. You never do."

Later that evening, Cherry's father softly knocked on her bedroom door and tried to play peacemaker. "She is scared," he said. "She doesn't want both of her children so far away from her."

"No one's stopping her from coming with me. She's always saying how much she misses Lum. Here's her chance to see him."

"Mommy needs more time," he said. "Leaving Vietnam was difficult for her. It was for all of us."

Cherry did not press her father to elaborate. She knew better. This was all she knew of her parents' departure from Vietnam: they escaped by boat and landed in Malaysia. Her parents and brother left for America, while her father's relatives relocated to France. Then Cherry was born.

"What else do you need to know?" her mother would say. "That's what happened."

"But why did you and Dad choose America?"

"Are you unhappy here? Haven't we given you a good future? Why are you complaining?"

"I'm not," Cherry would answer. "I just want to know more. I want to know what it was like."

"Such silly questions. How is knowing how poor and desperate we were going to help you? These things will only distract you, pollute your brain. Look at the problems in your textbooks. Those are the answers you want. Those are the ones that will help you."

Aside from the afternoon tour of the housing project, Cherry has barely seen her brother. Lum's company is at a crucial stage in the project, days away from their grand unveiling to clients, and he can't afford to go sightseeing. He leaves her every morning at the house with Grandaunt and Granduncle Tran.

It's not so bad. She has a month. She likes exploring the house where her grandparents lived, sleeping in the bedroom that once belonged to her parents. Cherry's grandparents gave their house to the Trans before escaping the country. The tall, gray concrete house with creaky floors and paper-thin walls sits in a middle-class neighborhood surrounded by other homes just like it. The shady winding street crackles with women young and elderly cooking outside their front doors, trucks and scooters rattling by, and children chasing one another in overlapping, endless games of tag. At night, Cherry listens to the thumps of the water pipes constantly adjusting to the changes in pressure. She imagines one of them bursting, flooding the house, forcing them all out.

Spending so much time with the Trans, Cherry understands why Lum hasn't bothered moving out. They are his ideal parents: compulsively doting upon him, preparing his meals, and pressing his clothes, without ever questioning his comings and goings or scolding his table manners. Having lost two sons in the war—the youngest, Cherry's father's age—Lum's presence is more than enough to fill them with excited chatter at dinnertime.

In the daylight, Cherry can best recognize Grandaunt's resemblance to Grandpère, the same lion's nose and widow's peak forehead. While these features accentuated Grandpère's stern demeanor, Cherry finds them unsettling and severe on Grandaunt's face. Granduncle appears less intimidating, a chubby squat man with ice-white hair and a sneeze that can shake the kitchen table. He and Grandaunt owned a tailor shop that catered to foreigners during the war; after the Fall of Saigon, the Communist police forced their business to close. Eventually, through persistent networking with the local government, they landed a uniform contract for the primary schools in Ho Chi Minh City, which allowed them to reopen their shop.

After Grandaunt prepares a breakfast of pan-fried noodles or vegetable soup, they walk around the neighborhoods, attempting to fulfill Cherry's request to see the city her parents once knew, before the Microsoft billboards and ubiquitous Kodak photo shops. In the Cholon district, Grandaunt points out the Trans' old apartment and former friends' homes. They pass the food markets her grandmère once frequented and have lunch in Grandpère's favorite garden. They visit the cemetery where the Trans' sons are buried.

Cherry never feels more American than when they are walking. She guiltily buffers herself between her much frailer relatives, who never seem nervous as they weave through the steady cross flow of cars, motorbikes, and pedestrians, pulling Cherry through the city current.

"They won't hit you," Granduncle tries to assure her, "if you go slow enough."

"In America, we stop for pedestrians," Cherry says, eyeing a family of four sailing past on a scooter.

Grandaunt shakes her head at yet another illogical foreign habit. "If we all stopped, no one would get anywhere."

No matter. Grandaunt feels most comfortable at home, cleaning the rooms and preparing meals, and when Cherry sits with her, Grandaunt likes to tell stories. Her subject taboo is clear: nothing about the war and its aftermath (*Bad memories,* she says, *I'm too old to cry anymore*). She prefers talking about her childhood in Nha Trang with Grandpère, her sons, and the fables she learned from Cherry's great-grandmother. Her favorite is the Trung sisters, legendary warriors from the first century, who successfully drove out the Chinese (the first time anyway) to establish the country's independence. They are considered Vietnam's national mothers.

"But they were married to the same man," Cherry says.

Grandaunt waves her hand dismissively. "All marriages have their problems. Look at your grandparents. Perhaps they would have been happier with that kind of arrangement."

"You mean, Grandpère would have been happier," Cherry says.

Grandaunt only smiles. "They had a complicated marriage. Many of us do."

The Tale of Kieu, which Cherry tried to read in college, is another fable Grandaunt likes to repeat. Though the main heroine is a prostitute, her despised social position is a tragedy she is forced into. Every story ends with a lesson: everyone has choices taken away from them. Despair is pushed into our lives. We can only control how we recover.

"Like you," she says carefully, as they assemble salad rolls for dinner. "You look so healthy and strong now. Your parents must be proud."

So Lum has told her about the accident. This shouldn't surprise Cherry, although she suddenly feels self-conscious, wondering how much Grandaunt knows.

"Lum had me call every day while you were in the hospital," Grandaunt says, dipping another sheet of rice paper into a bowl of water to soften it. "I tried to get him on the phone, but he didn't want to speak to your parents."

"My parents don't know the whole story," Cherry says. "They still can't understand."

"Have you tried to make them understand?" Grandaunt asks.

Cherry falters briefly under the woman's firm gaze. "Yes."

"It doesn't matter," Grandaunt says, returning to her rolls. "He is fine now. I don't have to tell you, you can see for yourself. We have been good for your brother."

"They did ask him to come back."

"He has a life here now."

"But it's not home," Cherry says, struggling to control her impatience. "It's not America."

Instead of becoming angry, as Cherry expects, Grandaunt only smiles faintly, bemused. After spreading the mint, basil, bean sprouts, and shrimp together, she wraps and tucks it into a perfectly shaped roll.

"You know who you sound like?" Grandaunt says. "Your grandfather, when he tried to convince Bac Tran and me to leave Vietnam."

Cherry peers down at the saturated rice paper between her fingers. She held it underwater too long. It is ruined now. Folding it up, she tucks it behind the water bowl. "Grandpère wanted you to escape, too?"

"He'd already bought our seats," Grandaunt says. "He bothered us until the night they left. But the point is, he was wrong. I am glad we stayed. How could I have left my two boys before they were properly buried? And now we have your brother. Not everyone was fated to leave."

"Maybe," Cherry says, distracted. It doesn't matter what she thinks, this relative she hardly knows. Instead, Cherry imagines these two seats on the boat, empty, wasted. They mold the salad rolls in silence, allowing the chorus of children's chatter and motorbike engines from the alley to fill the kitchen.

The legend of Grandmother Vo's grudge against the Truongs was far juicier than any mundane story about how any of their parents met. Grandmother Vo always referred to them as *those relatives*, reminding Cherry and her brother every opportunity she had that their father's family had gone back on their promise to help the Vos escape, disappearing into the night to selfishly save themselves. While the Truongs lived the good life in France, the Vos endured the vengeful wrath of the Communists. They tortured Cherry's uncles in reeducation camps, killed her eldest uncle, and harassed Grandmother and her daughters, who were trying to make any kind of living they could manage, so Cherry's cousins wouldn't starve to death.

Of course, it was more complicated than that. Her father had explained that the Vos were supposed to be on the same boat with the Truong family. Grandpère, who had purchased the contraband seats from the boat captain, was unable to secure enough. He was lucky to provide for his own family. When he came home from his meeting with the boat captain, Grandpère told Cherry's mother that there were no other seats left—not even for Grandmother Vo.

Her father's explanation had never satisfied Cherry, but then again, she had no reason to push for further details—until now. Although she believed she understood both sides, she felt protective of Grandpère and Grandmère in France, who had never even met Grandmother Vo, and couldn't defend themselves against her accusations. Cherry knew she couldn't always trust her maternal grandmother, who painted herself the victim in every story. As Cherry knew firsthand, Grandmother Vo was no martyr.

But what had happened to the extra seats? Couldn't Grandpère, with all his connections, have found another boat for the Vos? Couldn't he have offered another way to help?

Her grandmother, aunts, and uncles, and even her cousins, talked as passionately about these lost years as if they had just happened. If they'd escaped Vietnam earlier, perhaps Uncle Chinh would have earned his business degree. Perhaps Linh's little brother, born prematurely in Vietnam, would have survived in America. Perhaps Grandmother Vo's heart condition would have been detected earlier. Perhaps Lum wouldn't have lost his way. Perhaps, perhaps, perhaps.

When they put it that way, Cherry couldn't help but dream with them.

After dinner, when the relatives go upstairs to bed, Cherry finally has her brother to herself. They sit on vegetable crates in the alley, smoking cigarettes and throwing the butts into the dumpster so Grandaunt doesn't find them in her herb garden. Stray dogs poke their noses into loose garbage, occasionally sniffing at their feet.

"Is this how you got so thin?" he asks, handing over his lighter.

"I don't know," she says, not mentioning that smoking is a recent habit. He still occasionally looks at her like he doesn't recognize her, startled by her company.

"Do you remember Mom's old nail salon in Tranquillity?" Cherry asks. "They gutted the shopping plaza last year. They're putting in condos."

"That was a long time ago," he says, distracted.

"We played in the parking lot," she persists. "You organized these huge games with all the merchants' kids."

Hardly a response. Cherry tries another tactic.

"Dat and Quynh are getting married."

Not even a sharp inhale or blink of the eye. Lum slowly nods.

"You already knew," she realizes out loud. She wanted to be the one to share this news with him, to observe his initial, sincere reaction.

"Of course," Lum says. "I'm in Vietnam, not dead." The muscles in his cheeks tighten, preventing her from pressing further.

They retreat to typical chatter. Cherry again complains about his busy schedule, and Lum again promises it will let up soon. After the company's big debut next week, he will have much more time to spend with her.

"You can meet Tham at the ceremony," he says. "She'll be back from Hanoi by then." His girlfriend, this Tham, slips into every conversation they've had since Cherry's arrival, but she exists only in name. She does not drop by the house, and there are no pictures of her in Lum's bedroom. The relatives never speak about her. It is difficult to take this Tham seriously.

And Cherry still finds it strange to hear him talk about another girl. "How often do you talk to Quynh?" she asks.

Lum exhales loudly. "How often do you?"

Her nose wrinkles, but he can't see this in the dark.

Lum stares at the lit embers on the ground. "She's family now, Cherry."

"You're family," she clarifies. "You could talk to her, if you ever came home."

Lum smiles. "I've been busy."

"Busy. It's too much to get on a plane to America, but you can make it to France? Twice?" Cherry tries to keep her voice even, but the resentment scratches at her throat.

He doesn't even look ashamed. "Someone from our family should visit Grandmère."

Cherry doesn't answer, stubbornly staring at her nails.

"She asks about you," Lum says. "She misses you."

Cherry fights the urge to roll her eyes. "I miss you. We all do." Her head has begun to ache, but she resists the urge to pull at her hair. "They're getting older, Lum. Mom is okay, she's always okay. But Dad. He's starting to forget things."

"C'mon," he says, looking doubtful.

"It's true."

"He sounds pretty sharp every time I call home and he passes the phone right to Mom."

"You don't know," Cherry says, shaking her head. "You haven't been home with them."

"That's right," Lum says, "because they didn't want me there."

One of the stray dogs approaches Lum, licking his hand. He tenderly looks at the mutt, caressing its flea-infested ears, and when he turns to Cherry, his eyes look large and sad. "The thing is," he says, "if I were a parent, I probably would have done the same thing. I know that now."

Her vision blurs. Her hands grasp for the sticky underside of the vegetable crate. "But it wasn't just you," Cherry says.

"I didn't mind," Lum says. "I had to take responsibility. I understand that."

"You can still come back," Cherry says. "We're still your family."

She waits for a spark in his eye, a nod, anything. But it doesn't come. Instead, he sighs. "Cherry. That family doesn't exist anymore."

The pain has seeped to her forehead. She throws her half-finished cigarette to the ground and digs the heel of her flip-flop into it, realizing how silly she must look. Lum's hooded eyes blink sympathetically. Piteously. She is tired of people looking at her like that.

Cherry's eye is drawn toward an open window in the house across the alley. Two button-down shirts hang from the window like curtains. Can the neighbors hear them? Their words barely register above whispers, but given the houses' proximity, the neighbors can eavesdrop on every word. As recent as yesterday, she sat in the kitchen, listening in on the neighbors' bickering. But despite the harshness of their voices, the screams, the taunting, their words always felt rooted in intimacy.

She rolls the back of her head against the concrete wall, then stands. "My head hurts."

"I didn't mean to give you a headache."

Standing in the doorway, Cherry watches Lum finish his cigarette. "When they sent you away," she finally says, "it hurt all of us."

"I know," he says, but she cannot see his face in the dark. She has to trust his words.

Later, Cherry lies in bed, watching a spider move across the cracked ceiling. She imagines her brother fast asleep, so comfortable with his life, confident in his knowledge. He hadn't asked what it was like for her after he left. Maybe he didn't want to know. But siblings should share each other's pain. That is part of the responsibility.

People don't realize how long it takes to heal. They never dramatize recovery time in the movies because it is slow, the rehabilitation tedious. After months of surgeries, physical therapy, and X-ray consultations, Cherry's body had begun to repair itself. Cherry's parents tried to distract her from these hospital visits by giving her anything she wanted . . . anything, except Lum's return. And when she had resumed her normal life, they couldn't understand why she looked so miserable. Her rehabilitated body was in better shape than before the accident and she had just received a Chancellor's Scholarship to UC Irvine. They never realized that a part of her wanted to feel that way. Cherry welcomed the scars on her back, the aches that vibrated along her spine. Even now, years later, she can sometimes feel a loose sliver of pain travel through her body, floating around her tissues, something the doctors will never be able to locate and remove. She hopes they will never be able to find it. As long as this abnormality lives inside her, scraping at her nerves, she remembers that while Lum suffers, so far away from home, she does, too.

Though the air feels humid, everyone pretends otherwise. Tall dandelion-colored canopies rustle over noisy oscillating fans. Guests wilt in plastic chairs, clutching portable automated fans and personal water spritzers. No one but the servers and musicians dares to step out from under the shaded tent. The guests nibble on French pastries and sip iced jasmine tea as they wait for the ceremony to begin. Granduncle wears his brown suit with a yellow tie that Lum bought for him. Grandaunt shows off a pale blue dress she's been working on for the last week. At her relatives' urging, Cherry concedes to a blouse and skirt, but soon regrets it, as the fabric sticks to her sweaty skin, perspiration spots already appearing.

The housing development's model home, the Magnolia, has already elicited approving nods and whispered speculations. The crew has transplanted roses into the garden beds around the perimeter of the house. A silky green ribbon drapes across the double doorways.

Along the aisles, journalists snap pictures and interview clients. Several prominent Asian financial newspapers and wire services are covering the debut of the New Little Saigon Community Project. As Lum stutters through his practice speech in his office trailer, Cherry smirks at his nervousness. The old Lum. But by the time he reaches the stage to introduce his boss, his voice is smooth and assertive, the suave salesman.

After a few speeches and brief applause, Mr. Pham, the chief financier, cuts the ribbon and the audience stands. The words sounded pretty (most expensive housing community project in metropolitan Ho Chi Minh City, private 220-acre golf course, twenty-four-hour guard-gated security), and the space looks idyllic, but now business can commence. The people make their way past the stage, forming a line to enter the model home.

While her relatives get in line, Cherry steals off to Lum's office trailer to avoid the outhouses. Someone is already in the restroom, so she relaxes on the sofa, enjoying the trailer's climate-controlled temperature. Cherry peers at the walls decorated with housing permits, real estate awards, and photographs of Mr. Pham shaking hands with assorted Vietnamese officials. Lum's desk is covered with miniature dioramas of the development's different housing options: the Magnolia, the Westminster, the Bolsa, and the Brookhurst.

The woman who steps out of the restroom looks like Lum's type: tall for a Vietnamese woman, graceful, with long, straight hair down her shoulders and razor-sharp bangs across her forehead. Her face reminds Cherry of the young military women she has seen around town: determined, arrogant. But instead of an olive-green uniform, she wears a long gray jersey dress.

"You must be Tham," Cherry says, standing.

Tham steps back, looking as though she's been ambushed. "Hello," she says in English, then shakes her head, realizing Cherry spoke to her in Vietnamese. "And you are Cherry."

"Did you just arrive?"

"Yes," she says. "I took a motor taxi from the train station. I was just freshening up."

They stare at each other for several long seconds, smiling, blinking. Finally, Cherry nods to Tham's slightly swollen belly. "How far along are you?"

She drapes an arm across her stomach, protective. "You can already tell?"

"I'm going to be a doctor," Cherry says.

"Well, I think you're going to be very good," she says. She thinks Cherry is pleased with her news. Cherry has a feeling that outside of Tham's family in Hanoi, she must be the first to know.

Although Tham wants to walk together, Cherry persuades her to go ahead and meet up with Lum, saying that she will see them soon. Cherry counts five minutes in the office trailer. Then she counts five more. The numeration, in sync with her heartbeat, grows comforting. Finally, she stands. Her damp eyes wash over the walls that contain a world she knows so little about.

Stepping outside, Cherry sees Lum, Tham, Grandaunt, and Granduncle standing in front of the model home. Lum has his arm around his girlfriend. He gazes at her tummy, then kisses her cheek. The four of them, plus one on the way, make a lovely picture: a family Lum has created on his own, without their parents, without her.

"We were waiting for you," Granduncle says when Cherry approaches. "Let's go inside."

They step through the French doors and sigh pleasantly at the gush of air-conditioning sliding down their skin. Elegant, neutral-shaded furniture and landscape paintings decorate the expansive space; fresh flowers and bamboo arrangements balance on marble tables and molded plant shelves. Investors clog the wide staircase, gazing up at the skylight. An ornate chandelier, capturing the morning sun, transforms the hexagonal atrium into a prism of shimmering colors. The relatives and Tham ascend to observe the rooms upstairs, while Lum and Cherry remain on the ground floor. Everything down to the detailing in the tiles looks so familiar.

Cherry fingers one of the flowers, a fresh purple lily. "So, congratulations."

Lum grins blissfully. "You, too. You're going to be an auntie."

They look at each other. "I'm sorry about last night," he says.

"I'm not," she says. "I want to know what you think."

Lum shrugs. "But there are nicer things to think about. I'm not upset that I came here anymore. I don't regret Tham or anything else that has happened here."

"But I regret it," Cherry says. "Mom and Dad do, too."

His smile fades.

"What is it?" Cherry asks. "What aren't you telling me?"

Lum's boss walks by, stopping briefly to pat her brother on the back, before moving on.

"You're probably right," Lum says, straightening his shoulders. "I don't know what it was like for them. That's the problem, isn't it? No one bothers to ask because we already think we know. It's always been like that."

Cherry stares down at his black leather loafers, which he spent a good ten minutes polishing that morning. They are already covered in the day's dust. Her brother is right, and she cannot help but feel that she is the guiltiest of all. Cherry was so determined to recover from the accident, to rehabilitate her body, that she couldn't be burdened with anything emotional. Not her brother's feelings or anyone else's. Her parents and Grandmother Vo encouraged her willful ignorance, indulged it, because they did it, too. They'd grown so comfortable with forgetting, they'd begun accepting it as the truth. But that didn't have to continue. She could start listening, learning, right now.

A group of investors walks between them, gazing around the lush atrium, happily chatting in Japanese. One of them asks Lum a question, and her brother's rudimentary Japanese answer sounds impressive. As they enter the kitchen, Lum's face remains locked in its cheerful salesman mode.

"I'm glad you came here," he says. "It means a lot to me."

Cherry listens, folding and refolding the housing brochure in her hands, while he reveals his other surprise: one of the perks of working at the company is a substantial discount on the lots. He's already purchased a corner lot, the four-bedroom Westminster, for himself, Tham, and the Trans. Cherry can have the extra bedroom when she visits, whenever that is. Cherry smiles, but thinks instead of Grandmère's house: what will happen to it, who will take care of it, with the last of their family gone?

Tham calls out to Lum from upstairs. She says his name playfully, but the certainty in her voice lingers. Cherry asks to borrow Lum's cell phone and steps outside, where several crew members are busy watering the thirsty, drooping rosebushes.

"This call is expensive," her mother says when she hears Cherry's voice.

"It won't take long," Cherry says. "I'm staying here."

"Staying where? What are you talking about?"

"Here, Vietnam," she says, struggling not to stammer. "I'm going to defer medical school for a year. I want to live here with Lum for a while. I need some time to think."

Cherry knows her mother is no longer confused because there is a cool silence on the line. She presses her ear into Lum's cell phone, but there is only transpacific static.

"You did this on purpose," she finally says.

"Mom—"

"You wanted to humiliate me."

"What does this have to do with you?"

"Don't be stupid. Everything you do is because of me." She is yelling. Cherry holds the phone away from her ear. "We sent your brother away to protect your future. Daddy made me give him up for you."

"That's not true."

"What do you think you're going to do there?"

Cherry's head feels like it's spinning. "I'm not sure yet."

"Not sure yet?" her mother repeats mockingly. "You think you can live off your brother and the Trans' hospitality forever?"

"I'll get a job."

"You? You've never worked a day in your life, all so you could study."

"I'm hanging up," Cherry warned.

"I made this mistake," she says. "I thought I was so smart and that is how I ended up with your father."

"Mom."

"You watch," she says. "You'll regret this, too."

Cherry closes the phone. A few seconds later, the phone shakes in her hand. Her parents' number appears on the caller ID. She watches it vibrate several times before it clicks over to voice mail. The phone is silent, recording her mother's message, but Cherry can imagine the words.

1980

Cuc Bui
Paris, France

. . . *Do you remember that fisherman's pathetic map? It was so old and tattered. He got it wet several times until Cambodia became Vietnam, and then all the countries bled into the China Sea. It wasn't helping anyway. We couldn't see anything but water. We still blamed him, nonetheless.*

You looked so ill during the boat ride. There weren't enough rations, and you kept giving the sardines to the children so they wouldn't starve. If I had known how much you would suffer, I wouldn't have insisted that you come with us. I hope you believe it was worth it. I think it was. . . .

Hung Truong
Pulau Bidong, Malaysia

∾ *Chapter One*

HOA

H OA STRUGGLED TO IGNORE HIM, HER EYES CONCEN-
trating on the damp towel hanging in front of her, her move-
ments quick and methodical. It was impossible: Bac Nhut was not
asleep, he was watching her. Hoa had caught the old man's eyes flutter-
ing as she adjusted her canvas partition, his mouth too delicately closed,
his head conveniently propped in her direction. Their families and
neighbors were away at the mess hall for lunch, leaving the old pervert
free to leer without witnesses.

She was not afraid of her neighbor, only repulsed. Hoa felt confident
she could defend herself from his thin, weak limbs if he dared touch her.
Sometimes she wished he would—her desire to strike him, to expose
his depravity, overwhelmed her usually complacent nature. For weeks,
Bac Nhut pretended to nap in his shanty when Hoa returned from bathing, even though she altered her shower time every day. Revolting.

Back in Vietnam, she'd tell her husband. No, she realized. In Vietnam, this wouldn't happen. They had walls back home.

In the camp, since no one was better than anyone else, they had to get along. This, even her husband had to agree. If she complained about the old man's lewd behavior, word might get back to the Malay guards and she would be branded a snitch. Punishment, gossip, suspicion. Refugees from every zone would snub her, and Hoa couldn't endure embarrassing her family like that.

She refused to look at him, though his gaze crept along her still damp arms and legs. Usually, Hoa hung up the laundry like the others to serve as makeshift walls and further protection, but today their few clothing items were clean. So she concentrated on changing her garments behind a crate of Coca-Cola bottles, dressing efficiently, calmly. He would not have the pleasure of knowing the discomfort he caused her. He should be ashamed of himself. She was not some young, thin tramp asking to be ogled. Deplorable man. At his age. Their grandchildren sat next to each other at camp school.

A long shadow grew over the sand and Hung emerged atop Zone A. Hoa smiled in relief, but ducked her head as her husband moved toward the shelter, his scowl deepening. She put on her blouse, pulling up her waist-length hair and began combing. When she peered to the side, she saw that Bac Nhut had shifted his body to face the back of his tent.

Their shelter was a four-meter-long thatched roof supported by water-rotted wooden stakes, too small of a space for Hung to properly stalk around. Not even a chair to sit on, only bamboo mats and army blankets on the soft dirt for beds. The new arrivals in Zone C had it worse—plastic blue tarp shelters barely supported by skinny tree branches. The Malaysians treated the refugees worse than their dogs. While others eventually adjusted to their new surroundings, Hung refused to do so. He stood, resting one arm on a sapling post, glaring at everything.

Hung was eight years older than Hoa, but no one looking at them would ever know. Almost sixty, Hung hardly had a white hair, while Hoa discovered more in her bun each day. His face remained soft and moist, while Hoa's complexion had dried out years before.

"How was the meeting?" Hoa asked.

"They may not have an answer until next month," Hung said. "Five of us, no problem. But with ten, they need to talk to the French delegation again."

Her comb caught in a large wet tangle at the nape of her neck. She patiently picked through it, ignoring the soreness in her scalp. "We have been here well over a year," she said.

"Do you think I've forgotten?"

Hoa took a deep breath. "I'm only saying, maybe it will be easier if we leave in groups. Perhaps the officials are right. Who wants to sponsor ten people together? Too much responsibility."

"If we traveled this far together, it shouldn't be so difficult to complete it. Please, Hoa, you know nothing about this."

Despite his age, Hung stood as tall and rigid as when she first saw him at their engagement ceremony. His puffed-up chest and thin-lidded eyes supported the impression that Hung looked down on everything around him. Hoa suspected that this was one of the reasons their immigration applications kept getting delayed. Always mindful of dressing neatly in his wrinkled slacks and sun-bleached dress shirt—rather than the tank tops and shorts the other men on the island wore—Hung felt quite proud of his reputation as a snob. He *did* think he was better.

Hoa remembered when Bac Le, who departed with his family last week for America, had suggested to Hung that he slip some money to the delegation officials. Hung's solemn lecture on the dangers of bribery embarrassed both families. The Les departed without saying goodbye.

"What do the boys think?" Hoa asked. Their sons Phung and Sanh also had attended the interview.

"So passive," Hung said. "Why did you raise such weak sons? Yen would have argued alongside me."

Hung never hid his preference for their middle son, whom he boasted inherited his strength and persistence. He regularly derided his other sons as Hoa's creations—too feminine and indecisive. They hadn't seen Yen in five years. He left Vietnam to go to law school in France and claimed refugee status when the war ended. Last month, the Truongs had an offer to immigrate to Australia, but Hung declined. He wished to seek asylum in only one country.

"Sanh was so rude to the French delegate," Hung continued. "Hardly speaking at all, claiming he's forgotten his French. The liar."

"Maybe he wasn't feeling well."

"I don't care. He knows how important this is. And the only time he spoke was to ask how their resettlement process compared to the States'. Can you believe that?"

Hoa put down her comb. "Why was he asking about the States?"

"Who knows what goes on in a liar's head? He keeps crying that he wants to leave and the French are taking too long. But if we have to wait, we have to wait. God will look out for us."

The other refugees were returning from the mess hall. The Malays probably served smelly chicken again. The Vietnamese would rather eat their rations. Soon the shelter would swim with the popping sizzles of cooking oils, the sharp aroma of contraband fish, and the relentless *snap snap* of the women chewing betel nuts. Hoa briefly shut her eyes in disappointment. She only wanted a few minutes alone. She had not been truly alone, and calm, since they left Vietnam.

That was months ago. Her prayer room—a closet, the only space that was solely hers in their house in Saigon—had probably already been cleared out by her sister-in-law, wiped clean of Hoa and the rest of the escaping Truongs. She could hardly recall this sanctuary, her thoughts cluttered by more recent, tangible memories: huddling under a plastic tarp and thin, mud-crusted blankets during the monsoon season in Zone C; paltry rations that consisted mainly of canned sardines and a scoop of rice; waking up to rat bites on her legs; dirty latrines; the taunts and insults of the Malay guards.

Still, some of their neighbors accepted this as their new home, so desperate to resettle in any place that wasn't Vietnam. They opened hair salons and noodle shops within the township, and joined church choirs. Even when paperwork cleared for immigration, some felt reluctant to leave. Their son Phung said it was because their people could acclimate to anything. They'd lived with war and displacement for centuries. Their history allowed them to make anywhere home.

"This isn't a home," Hoa reminded her husband. "Please, we have to leave. I don't care what country we go to first."

Hung lifted his hand and Hoa instinctively turned her head. He didn't finish. There were others around. The last time he struck her within eyesight of the camp gossips, he'd endured dirty looks and pointed whisperings for weeks. Hoa exhaled, calmly facing him.

"What kind of mother are you?" he spat. "So selfish about your own concerns. Do you not want to be with your son? What would God think of your behavior?"

She didn't move as he stomped out of their shelter. She'd learned not to run after him. After so many years together, she realized it was better when he left.

During the afternoons, the Vietnamese liked to go bathing and to wash laundry at Pantai Beach or at the waterfall. Hoa knew her family preferred the beach, which reminded her sons of their old home in Nha Trang. A warm breeze tossed whispers of sand along Hoa's feet. Women crouched near the shore, wringing shirts and underwear clean. Naked children stomped in the water, shrieking as the prickly waves engulfed their feet, joyously throwing chunks of dirty plastic and misshapen aluminum cans at each other.

Only immediate family could live together in the camp. Phung's family was in Zone E, Sanh's family in Zone B, and Yen's wife and son in Zone D. People could request zone transfers, but they were rarely granted. Refugees preferred to stand in line for their immigration requests. Hoa didn't like her family spread all over Bidong Island; it only spanned two kilometers in diameter, but at times could feel much larger. A day could pass and she wouldn't see one of her sons or grandchildren. Her daily trips to the beach or to their shanties made sure this didn't happen.

Hoa's feet began sinking as her steps slowed for her thoughts. Hung was mistaken. Hoa did miss Yen. Though she never flaunted it outright like Hung, Hoa also preferred her middle son. This did not mean she didn't love her other boys. She'd long ago given up her own comforts for her sons and then their wives and then their children. But Yen was special. She knew this even during her pregnancy, when the fortune-teller rubbed her belly and prophesized the child's greatness.

"He is your reward," the woman had said while Hoa poured their tea. "For all your suffering and pains, he will make them all worth it to you."

Hoa bowed her head in response. She'd only agreed to see the fortune-teller out of respect for her in-laws. But as the years passed, and more calamities fell upon their country and their family, she realized how immune her middle son was to the bad luck. Yen, whose outstanding test scores and charisma earned him a full scholarship to a French university, was now waiting for them in Paris. He was a successful lawyer, and preparing a new home for them. It was something Hoa reminded herself of, every day, something to focus on that was positive and hopeful.

Three familiar children separated from the playgroup to wade through the waves toward her. Hoa held her conical hat with both hands so the breeze wouldn't take it.

"Grandmother, look," Cam said, her dripping hands holding up a blue-tinted ghost crab. "Can we eat it?"

Hoa pretended to inspect the small crustacean thoroughly, as Cam's younger cousins, Xuan and Lum, peered behind her. Their dark, wet hair lay pasted on their deeply bronzed skin, their small breaths panting from running to her. "I don't think it's large enough, child. Throw it back in the water and give it a few more weeks to grow."

Cam stared wistfully at her prize for a slow moment before bending over and releasing the creature back into the sea. "What if I can't find it again? What if it floats all the way to Vietnam?"

That was how they kept children from playing too far into the ocean. The strong current could carry you away from your family, back to Vietnam, where the Communists would shoot you. Remembering their stretched-out weeks on leaky boats, staring out at the sea and sky that loomed larger each passing day, the children obeyed, never straying far.

"You'll find it," Hoa promised. "Now where are your parents? Who is watching you?"

"Auntie Trinh is watching us."

"Well, where is she?"

Xuan shyly raised his arm and pointed farther along the shore, identifying his mother.

Lounging against a rock, alone, her dirty feet drawing lazy circles in the sand, Yen's wife, Trinh, stared listlessly at the low waves. She wore a loose green blouse and shorts that exposed much of her legs. Her plastic white-rimmed sunglasses, which she posed in with unabashed pride, were a foolish purchase in Hoa's opinion, money better spent buying precious meat for her noodle-thin little boy. Several feet away from Trinh, a group of fishermen happily chatted while hunched over a pile of fish, gutting the fresh catch and tossing the entrails back into the ocean.

The grandchildren returned to playing in the waves with the other children, while Hoa walked toward Trinh. Of all her daughters-in-law, Hoa felt furthest from Trinh. Though she'd attempted many times over the years to welcome Yen's young wife into the family, the girl proved sullen and impossible to please. Only Sanh's wife, Tuyet, seemed to get along with her.

"Where are your sisters?" Hoa asked, standing over Trinh.

The girl barely looked up. "Ngoan and Tuyet went into town for supplies."

"Have the children had lunch?"

"We just came from the mess hall."

"Did they eat enough? They served chicken. Cam hates the chicken."

Trinh removed her sunglasses and reluctantly faced her mother-in-law. "They're fine. They've eaten enough." She reached inside her blouse and pulled out a creased gray-blue envelope. "This is from Yen."

Hoa snatched the letter from her hands. "When did you get this? Why didn't you tell us right away?"

"I'm telling you now. I didn't think it was urgent."

"How would you know?" Hoa asked. The girl could barely read.

"If it was," Trinh said, turning to face the ocean again, "he would have addressed it to your husband."

Hoa opened the envelope and squatted in the sand. She looked up at her daughter-in-law. Spoiled child. Most wives in the camp would have sacrificed a week's rations for a letter from their husband. And such a kind letter, Hoa realized, her eyes lingering upon the declarations of devotion and confessions of his sleepless nights worrying over his family.

Her son's idealistic attachment to Trinh had always baffled Hoa, and it had no doubt blossomed during their years apart. She wondered what would happen when they finally reunited. Yen wrote mostly of his work, his neighborhood in Paris, his Catholic parish, questions about the rest of the family. The last page was a letter to Xuan asking his son to take care of his mother and promising to bring them home soon.

"Anything important?" Trinh asked, more absorbed in picking off the crusty mud from her heels.

"He wants to make sure you're doing well."

"Well," Trinh repeated, her eyes returning to the children on the beach. "That's nice."

The fishermen nearby had completed their gutting and stood, whispering to one another, gaping at Trinh. Hoa cleared her throat and glared at them pointedly until they turned away.

"Why don't you cover yourself up?" Hoa asked. "It's indecent the way they look at you."

"It wouldn't matter," Trinh said, briefly looking back at the fishermen. Her sunglasses hid her expression. "It's too late."

So impudent, ignorant. They'd warned Yen about the pitfalls of marrying a country girl. Hoa realized again why they needed to leave the camp soon. She didn't know how much longer she could continue looking after this one.

The children were shrieking, but not in their usual playful manner. Hoa glanced toward the commotion. On the other side of the beach, a crowd began to form, pointing to a matchbox in the sea. Wordlessly, Trinh and Hoa shuffled their feet through the sand, their eyes never leaving the object.

As the matchbox swayed closer to the shore, everyone's suspicions were confirmed: a fishing junk. The yellowing boat was overcrowded with salt-crusted refugees—some draping their arms and legs over the splintered sides. They looked haggard, starved, relieved, afraid. The Malay soldiers on duty yelled at the boat, perched on the boulders overlooking the bay, pointing their rifles. Hoa had lived on Pulau Bidong long enough to understand their few words.

Go away. No room here. Go somewhere else. We won't take you. We will shoot.

But the Vietnamese already standing on the beach worked fast. Two men had already run back to the community center to find a United Nations worker. Others yelled instructions to the refugees on how to sink the boat.

"Hammer out the floor!"

"Rip off the sail! Throw it in the water!"

"Throw everything in the water!"

"Come closer! Keep coming, they won't shoot, they're bluffing!"

For several long, frustrating moments, the passengers on the fishing boat could only stare. Hoa wondered if they looked that dumb and stunned when their boat first arrived.

The junk swayed toward the boulders near the dock. The soldiers still pointed their guns, spitting their vicious threats. When the boat bumped against the rocks, one of the soldiers attempted to push it back with the butt of his gun. But the refugees were already pulling out of the sinking boat, weeping, trudging through the dirty water for shore. They wore rags, unrecognizable as clothing. Some of the children were naked. Once they touched dry land, their legs gave out, and they collapsed on the beach.

The soldiers scrambled after the new refugees, surrounding them, attempting to isolate the group in one area. A young woman tried to reach out to Hoa, begging for food, but a soldier shoved her back into the crowd. Several children cowered in the sand, screaming at the sight of guns pointed at them. Ignoring the soldiers' orders, some people pushed bananas and star fruits into the hands of the new refugees. Hoa dug into her pockets and found some candy she'd been saving for her grandchildren. She easily slipped into the chaos, and pressed them into the hands of the young woman, who cried out gratefully, stuffing the still-wrapped confections into her mouth.

A soldier grabbed Hoa by the back of her shirt and threw her into the sand.

"Hey!" Trinh yelled, helping a dazed Hoa to her feet. "Don't push an old woman!"

"Barbarians!" someone yelled. "They're pushing the old ladies!"

More screaming, more shoving back and forth. The same soldier stumbled in front of them, his back toward Hoa. She kicked him solidly in the shin, then quickly hid behind a taller Vietnamese man, her gaze fixed in the opposite direction.

Several UN workers arrived on the beach, pushing past the onlookers, and tried to restore order.

"You are all safe," a UN worker named Betty yelled in broken Vietnamese to the terrified new refugees. "No one is going to shoot you. But you need to be quarantined and examined by doctors. Please stay calm."

This had to be repeated several times by other Vietnamese so that the refugees finally listened to their instructions. They warily clung to one another's elbows, blinking suspiciously at the Caucasians. Betty and the other UN workers assembled the new refugees into a group to head toward the health clinic.

"Welcome to Bidong!" several people shouted as the new refugees filed past them.

"Don't be afraid of the doctors. They are very kind."

"But be careful of the Malay guards. Protect your valuables."

"Don't eat their chicken! It will make you sick. Wait until you get into camp to eat."

"You made it! The worst is over!"

After the new refugees left, the crowd thinned. The tide was growing stronger, sending most of the bathers back to their shelters. Some of the children, including Cam and Xuan, loitered behind to poke around the boat wreck. Xuan attempted to climb into the wreck, eager to reenact the earlier excitement. Cam scrambled up the rocks, pretending to be a Malay soldier, while Xuan balanced on the sea-soaked planks, pleading for sanctuary.

"Get out of here, you stinking Vietnamese," Cam growled. "Go back to Vietnam."

"I have nowhere else to go," Xuan squealed. "Please save me."

Hoa warned them not to cut their feet on the splintered wood. They leaned against the rocks, as Trinh cuddled a sleepy Lum in her arms. The children's giggling and playacting faded with the crashing waves. The first boat to arrive at the camp in two weeks, it reminded Hoa that beyond the horizon, more boats floated aimlessly in the South China Sea, their passengers desperately hoping to shore up at a refugee camp. Not all of them made it. You had to be lucky.

"They won't stop coming," Hoa said, staring out at the water, which now reflected the orange in the sky. She wondered what kind of place Vietnam would become with so many of its people escaping.

"Someone should warn them," Trinh said.

"About what?" Hoa asked.

"That it's no better here."

"We're not going to be here for much longer," Hoa said, surprising herself at how much she sounded like Hung.

"How are we so sure it will be better somewhere else?" Trinh asked. "Every new place, we assume it's going to be better. We left Vietnam for something better. I don't see any difference yet."

Yen and Trinh had wanted to marry before his departure to France, but Hung and Hoa spoke against it. In order for Hung to help pay for his education in Paris, Yen had to follow his father's conditions. No marriage, not even an engagement. If they still wanted to marry after Yen finished school and returned to Vietnam, Hung and Hoa would provide their blessing and support. This was Hung's strategy. He hoped in those intervening years Yen would meet someone, even a French woman, who would change his mind about this daughter of a drunk.

A few weeks after Yen's departure, the servant boy opened their front door and led a visibly pregnant Trinh into the sitting room. She held an envelope in Yen's unmistakable scrawl protectively over her rotund belly. Trinh was having their grandchild. Yen and Trinh had eloped a few nights before he left. Yen requested, in that beautiful, cursive penmanship Hoa had been so proud of, that his family care for his new wife and child until he could return to Vietnam.

"He outsmarted us," Hung admitted, setting the letter on his desk. They whispered in his study while Trinh remained in the sitting room, a small nylon knapsack by her feet, chatting with their youngest son Sanh.

"How can you take this so lightly?" Hoa demanded. "Your plan failed."

"It is too late to dwell on that," Hung said, folding up the letter and putting it in his desk drawer. He turned to put on his coat and hat. "There's a child now. She can take Yen's room."

"Where are you going?" Hoa asked. "To another one of your poetry readings?" Hung turned and looked at her. She'd long ago given up caring about Hung's lady companions. "Only a few weeks ago you said this girl could ruin Yen's life. Now that she's done it, you've decided to reward her?"

Hung waved a hand in annoyance. "I don't give a damn about the drunk's daughter. I am taking responsibility for my grandchild—your grandchild. Once the baby is born, she can leave, which is what she'll probably do anyway. But the child will stay with his family."

He was wrong. After Xuan's birth, Trinh didn't leave, but by that time, Hoa no longer wished her gone. She'd fallen in love with her first grandson, whose joyful chatter and boisterous laughter reminded Hoa that children were the best of them. Pure, harmless, benevolent. People only soured as they aged. Xuan, along with his older cousin Cam, kept their family smiling and hopeful, distracting them from the ugly climate festering outside their doors.

The first Thursday of the month, the camp put on a Vietnamese cultural show. After dinner, the UN volunteers erected a small stage behind the mess hall and brought out metal folding chairs from the cafeteria. On Saturday nights, they used the same space to play old film reels from Hong Kong and Taiwan. Although most of the younger people preferred to watch Malaysian soccer games on television in the community center, the cultural shows still attracted enough people that latecomers sat in the aisles and huddled around the stage.

Hoa and her daughters-in-law arrived to the show alone, the men summoned by the French delegation before dinner. Hung assumed they would return quickly. Two hours had passed since then.

That evening, the children were performing *The Tale of Kieu*. A young, beautiful girl from an educated family is cursed by destiny to a life of poverty and prostitution. Hoa had memorized verses of the epic poem in school. She wondered what would happen when they moved to France, whether the children would remember these verses she still could recite by heart.

Cam and Xuan played Kieu's sister Van, and her haggard father, Old Vuong. The children shouted their lines through decorated paper bags covering their faces, while the Christian missionaries motioned for them to look out to the audience instead of the floor.

With Lum in her lap, Hoa leaned forward in her chair, straining to hear some of the shyer children mumble their verses. She had been annoyed upon arriving at the performance that the only empty seats were located in front of Bac Nhut. He stared at her, silent, blinking his slow dumb eyes, as they exchanged pleasantries with his thankfully better-mannered children. When she and her daughters-in-law took their seats, Hoa truly believed her skin itched from the old man's eyes skimming her neck, her back, her toes. She wished she could change seats, but that would have attracted unwanted attention.

The crickets clicked in the grass. In the evenings, the high tide pushed in a warm breeze that barely relieved the humidity. Hoa gingerly pressed her limp hair bun, which sagged heavily with perspiration. The flimsy palm fronds Ngoan fanned in her direction offered little comfort.

On stage, another corrupt man had duped poor Kieu. The young girl playing Kieu raised her hands to the sky, asking again why such misfortune had fallen upon her.

"What is taking them so long?" Phung's wife, Ngoan, asked, peering behind them, her square jaw clenched, making her plump face look even more serious than it usually did. "The show is almost over."

"It may be a good sign," Trinh said, fighting off a yawn. "Perhaps the French delegation said yes."

"They couldn't have agreed so quickly," Sanh's wife, Tuyet, said.

Hoa's youngest daughter-in-law was no doubt the most beautiful of the three women, with a clear complexion, a straight, attractive set of small teeth, and large, haunting eyes. Tuyet was pregnant again, but had begun to show only recently.

"Why not?" Ngoan asked. "It's happened before. If we're lucky, we could leave as early as next week."

Tuyet shook her silky head of hair. "You've been saying that for months."

"It might be true," Ngoan sniffed. "Don't you want to leave?"

"It does no good speaking like that, especially in front of the children. You'll get them excited over nothing."

"Well, you don't want your child born here, do you?" Ngoan asked, staring pointedly at Tuyet's small belly bump. "Or is France not good enough for your baby?"

"Stop creating problems," Trinh spoke up.

"Girls," Hoa finally warned, conscious of the irritated glances from their neighbors.

The women resumed watching the show, now approaching its sentimental climax: Kieu reuniting with her long-suffering, devoted lover Kim. The children embraced flamboyantly, giggling into each other's shoulders. All the children scrambled back to the stage to sing the national anthem of the South Vietnamese government. Emotional members of the audience joined in, their deeper voices soon drowning out the children's.

Ngoan shifted restlessly in her seat, the palm fronds lying flat against her thigh. As the first daughter-in-law, Ngoan was several years older than Trinh and Tuyet, and inevitably more traditional. A matchmaker had affianced Phung and Ngoan when they were still children. Though their marriage turned out successfully, Hoa's younger sons refused the same kind of arrangements. Ngoan often complained of her younger sisters' lack of manners and parenting skills, but Hoa suspected she secretly envied their youth, their friendship, their beauty.

"I'm not the problem," Ngoan finally said during the applause. "Phung told me what your husband is trying to do."

"Will you be quiet?" Trinh asked.

But Hoa could see the uncertain expression on Tuyet's face. "What is Ngoan talking about?" she asked her youngest daughter-in-law.

"Phung saw Sanh talking to the U.S. immigration officer last week," Ngoan said.

"So what?" Trinh said, waving her hand. "It doesn't mean anything."

Hoa's eyes remained on Tuyet, who didn't respond, instead only glaring at Ngoan.

"Don't be stupid," Ngoan sneered. "We know who is always talking about America. We know where she really wants to go."

Tuyet stood, reaching her hands out for a sleeping Lum. The boy whimpered as he left Hoa's arms. "I don't need to sit here and listen to this," she said.

"Tuyet," Hoa said, touching the woman's arm, but Tuyet quickly brushed it off.

"I don't care if she's the oldest sister. She can't talk to me that way."

"Am I lying?" Ngoan asked, her voice rising.

"I'll leave with you," Trinh said, standing and waving to Xuan, who still stood on the stage. He and Cam, still in costume, waved back at the family and ran toward them.

"We're walking back with Aunt Tuyet," Trinh said to her son.

"Right now?" Xuan asked, removing his paper mask, his face crumpling in a scowl. "But Cam and I were going to play tag with the other kids."

"It's getting late," Trinh said.

"The lights won't turn off for another hour," Xuan cried, stamping his foot. "Please, I don't want to go back there right now."

"Let him stay, please, Aunt Trinh?" Cam asked. "He can spend the night with us, right, Mother?"

"We can take Xuan back later," Ngoan said.

"No!" Trinh cried, then stared at the ground. "Thank you for offering, but Xuan should leave with me now."

"I don't understand why you isolate yourself like this," Ngoan said. "Tuyet isn't the only person who can help you. We're your family, too."

Trinh glared at her. "I know what you say about me."

"Do you see this, Mother?" Ngoan asked. "They turn against me, and claim that I'm the bad person."

"Be quiet, all of you," Hoa muttered, recognizing her husband and sons' shapes approaching. She watched her boys come closer, thankful she bore males, siblings who rarely argued with one another. The children ran to embrace their fathers, while Xuan wrapped his arms around his grandfather's legs. Hoa smiled, trying to look happy.

"We missed the whole show?" Phung asked, carrying Cam in his arms.

"Of course you have," Ngoan said. "You've been gone for hours."

Disappointment was etched upon Phung's sun-worn face. The eldest child, Phung had inherited his father's height and sharp bone structure; upon appearance, he seemed formidable, even fierce. But once he spoke in that gentle, wavering voice, his true nature surfaced, as soft and pliable as Hoa. Hung saw his complicity as a weakness, an inability to stand up for himself, but nevertheless, he exploited it. Phung obeyed his father's every request: agreeing to an arranged marriage, joining the army, reporting early to the reeducation camps before anyone realized what they really were.

After two years in the prison camp with his brother Sanh, Hoa hoped Phung would return home furious, disavowing his father's terrible advice and finally emerge his own person. Sanh had, screaming at Hung about his two lost years and missing his first child's birth. This insolence had finally earned his father's reluctant respect. But not Phung. He returned even more lost than before, looking to anyone, even Hoa, to tell him what to do, how to make things better. Of all her sons, she mourned the most for Phung because like her, he could never be more than a ghost, absorbing other people's thoughts and decisions as his own.

"What happened?" Trinh asked.

"Our application was accepted," Hung said, smiling faintly, like he'd expected this news all along. "A Catholic charity in Paris has agreed to sponsor us. We leave in a month."

The children cheered. Forgetting their bickering, the women embraced. Xuan clung to his mother's waist. While Hung explained the details of their departure, Hoa tried to listen, thankful of course, but unable to tear her eyes from Sanh and Tuyet, his hand over her belly, their silent conversation, the word that she believed swirled under their tongues: America.

"I need you to be honest with me," Hoa said.

"It's nothing," Sanh said. "We only talked a few times. We're going to France."

Hoa exhaled, leaning heavily into her son's arm as they walked back to her shanty. "Are you sure?"

"Yes," Sanh said, his natural, friendly face so reassuring. Her youngest son smiled the most in their family, his ability to put people at ease his greatest strength. "I only wanted to know about other options. Now that's not necessary."

Hoa believed her son and gladly put all the nonsense about America out of her thoughts. She had so much else to think about. The Truongs were scheduled to depart Pulau Bidong in four weeks. Since immigration decreed only one suitcase per person, Hoa traded away most of her belongings accumulated at camp—the kerosene stove, sleeping mats, cooking utensils—in exchange for more durable clothes and shoes.

The night before their departure, Hung still insisted on the entire family eating dinner together at the mess hall. This was a Truong rule that had never been broken, despite their two-year stay at Pulau Bidong. It wasn't their mother-of-pearl rosewood table in their Nha Trang home or their smaller teak kitchen table in Saigon, but Hung still sat at the center, flanked by his sons and grandsons, while the females filled in the remaining seats. Horrified by the casual cafeteria-style of serving meals, Hung denounced the manners of the mess-hall workers as barbaric when compared to his devoted servants in Vietnam. Hoa had to collect her husband's meal. Though the food cooled quickly, no one could eat until everyone was seated and Hung led the family through prayer.

While the other refugees at the surrounding tables hollered their conversations, swallowed their food, and rushed out the door to watch a soccer game on the community television or to gossip on the beach, the Truongs observed slow consumption and appropriate conversation. Hoa realized it had to look strange to others—further perpetuating camp rumors that the Truongs were too arrogant for their own good.

These suggestions and accusations never deterred Hung. Since they lived in different sections of the island, he argued that dinnertime presented the only few hours the whole family could stay together. With thousands of refugees on the island, hundreds arriving and leaving at any given time, dinner alleviated any insecurity they had about each other's well-being. A full table meant everyone was still safe and well. Hoa knew Hung felt a supreme satisfaction in maintaining this family tradition, up until their last meal on the island.

"We first fly to Manila," Hung informed them over the rattling of chopsticks and passing plates. "We spend three weeks there for medical evaluations and language and culture seminars before flying to Paris." He smiled generously in Trinh's direction. "Yen will meet us at the airport with our sponsors. Sanh, I'll need your assistance tonight going over our papers."

"I can help you," Sanh said, "but there has been a change in our plans."

"What change?" Hung said, looking concerned. "The delegate said everything had been settled."

"My family is not going."

Hoa slowly looked up, her eyes turning to her husband's.

"What are you talking about?" Hung asked. "Of course you are. I have the papers right here."

"Did something happen with immigration?" Phung asked. "Why didn't you tell us?"

"My family will not go to France," Sanh said, his gaze focused squarely on his dinner plate. "I'm sorry for the change in plans, but it won't affect your departure, I promise."

"When did you decide this?" Phung asked. "Why?"

While the men interrogated Sanh, Hoa glowered at Tuyet, who, like her husband, appeared incapable of maintaining eye contact with anyone at the table. Instead, Tuyet continued to feed Lum dinner.

"What are you going to do?" Hung asked. "Stay here? You want to raise your child a Muslim?"

"We're not staying here," Sanh said. "We're going to America."

"So it's true," Hoa said to Tuyet. "This is what you wanted all along."

"Quiet," Hung said. "Tell me, Sanh."

"I don't wish to raise our children in France," Sanh said. "I think we will be better off in America."

"Better," Hung spat. "Without your family?"

"I don't expect you to agree with my decision," Sanh said. "But it is final. Once we're in America, we're going to help Tuyet's family to come over."

"So this is the Vos' decision."

Tuyet slammed her chopsticks onto the table as Lum cried out in protest. "Do not talk about my family, especially after the way you have treated them."

"How I treated them? I don't even know them, child."

"You mean they don't matter?" Tuyet asked. "Not as much as your own family? You could have bought more seats on the boat if you'd wanted to, I know it."

"Tuyet," Sanh said, trying to place a hand on his wife's arm, but she pushed it off.

"We have fulfilled our duties to you," Tuyet said. "Now it is time to help my family."

Hoa stared at her daughter-in-law in shock. No one had ever spoken out against Hung in this manner, especially in public. But Hung simply smirked at Sanh's impudent wife, regarding her as seriously as a mosquito around his ankle.

"Congratulations, Hoa. I foolishly believed your youngest son actually grew some sense after his prison time, but he is still as brainless as his mother."

"Don't insult Mother," Sanh said with a sigh. "This has nothing to do with her."

"Of course," Hung said. "It has nothing to do with the Truongs. You've made that perfectly clear."

"Please," Sanh said. "I don't want to part on bad terms."

"Families don't part," Hung said. "You're the one doing this. And I hope you understand the consequences of your wife's decision. You are going to America with a wife and two children, with no help from the rest of your family. You must live with this choice."

Hung offered his youngest son another long, proud stare, one last opportunity to change his mind, to plead forgiveness for a reckless decision, to pledge to never go against the family again. When Sanh did not reply, Hung looked down at his shrimp and vegetable stew. The family resumed eating in near silence, except for a few murmurs from Xuan and Cam, and a small laugh from Lum. Sanh avoided eye contact with his mother, working hard to swallow each bite of food he pushed through his lips.

Sanh stood once he and Tuyet had finished their dinners. "Excuse us, Father," he said. "We have a lot of work to do before leaving tomorrow. I can help you later tonight with the papers."

"That won't be necessary," Hung said. "You have so much to do. We'll be fine without you."

Hoa silently watched as Sanh and Tuyet lifted their trays, walked to the counter, and dropped off their dirty plates. Sanh carried Lum on his back and Tuyet looped her arm through her husband's. They passed through the cafeteria doors.

Hung didn't say anything when Hoa made up an excuse to leave their shanty that evening. He knew where she was going, but only casually nodded as he and Phung sorted through the papers by flashlight.

"Come back before the lights turn off," Hung reminded her.

Finally free of her husband's scrutiny, Hoa allowed her composed face to collapse, to give in to the grief that had clumped up in her stomach since dinner. Even when she closed her eyes and shook her head, she could not eradicate the image of victorious Tuyet from her mind. Hoa had never wanted to strike another person so violently in her life. She'd been deceived, they all had. Hoa realized she could trace the subterfuge back to when Tuyet first entered their lives.

After Yen and Trinh's surprise elopement, Hoa naïvely thought she'd seen the last impulsive marriage in her family. Their youngest son Sanh had been so shy around girls. Though he'd refused his parents' suggestion of an arranged marriage when he was a teenager, the older he grew, still single, not even a girlfriend, the less strenuously he objected to their mentioning the topic.

That is, until one afternoon, when Hoa returned from her morning trip to the market. Sanh stood in the kitchen, wearing his light gray suit and a polished pair of loafers. While her older sons retained Hung's tall, lean figure, Sanh's stocky body and chubby cheeks clearly came from Hoa. Yet he always took pride in his appearance, his hair neatly combed, a handkerchief in his pocket to blot the sweat from his face.

"Why aren't you at work?" she asked, dropping her baskets onto the kitchen table.

"I'm taking lunch at home," he said.

Hoa stared at him suspiciously as he helped her unpack the fruits and vegetables from her baskets. "Your father went through a lot of trouble arranging that job for you."

"I need to talk to you," Sanh said.

Hoa felt her breath drain out. She pulled out a chair and slowly sank. "Is something wrong with Yen?" They hadn't received a letter from him in weeks.

Sanh shook his head. He sat next to her, placing a clump of bananas on the table.

She pressed her hand into his. "Phung? Has he been injured?"

"No, Mother," he said, impatiently pulling his hand back. "It's me."

"What is it?"

"I met a girl. I want to marry her."

Hoa sat back in her chair, relieved. "Is that all? Then why do you look so grave?"

"We want to get married next week."

"Please don't tell me she's pregnant."

"She isn't pregnant, but we need to get married soon. I want her to come live with us."

"This is hardly a good time for a wedding, Sanh. You need a proper engagement, at least six months. We need to meet her family."

"Mother, I need your support, especially when I tell Father about this. We can't wait months, we can't even wait weeks."

"I don't understand." First Yen, now Sanh. What had she done to deserve this?

"She's a good girl, Mother. You're going to love her. She's from a respected family. Her father was a doctor in the army. But her mother isn't fair to her. I don't want her living there any longer. Tuyet needs to live with us."

"Tuyet," Hoa repeated.

She did seem like a good girl. The day after the wedding, Tuyet immediately made herself useful, demonstrating she was not beneath any household chore. She sat to tea every afternoon with Hoa, learned to cook the proper family dishes, prepared the tobacco for Hung and his visiting friends. She cared for her nephew and niece, and befriended Trinh, who was relieved to have a new sister-in-law. Even Hung had to admit that perhaps Sanh's bold decision had turned out to be correct.

"My new family is so kind to me," Tuyet would say, with a different, personalized smile for every family member who looked at her. "I thank the Lord that he brought me to you."

But now, Tuyet's face displayed no such smile when Hoa arrived at their shanty in Zone B. She did not offer tea or a seat. Instead, she avoided Hoa's eyes as she slipped past her mother-in-law, carrying Lum away.

"We weren't lying," Sanh said. "We had every intention of coming to France with you. But Tuyet's mother is sick and she needs to leave Vietnam. And we have a better chance of getting her out if we're in America."

"You could have told us," Hoa said, "before all the plans were made. Then we could have tried to stay together."

"You know Father would never go to America."

"Families aren't supposed to live in different countries."

"Well, we weren't supposed to leave Tuyet's family behind. If they were with us now, we wouldn't have to separate."

If this, if that. So many conditions conspiring to take her son away from her. How could she remind Sanh now that their loyalty was to the Truongs, and not to his wife's family? He would think she was being selfish. But Hoa had honored this tradition, placing Hung's parents above her own when she married. Why wouldn't Tuyet?

Because of Tuyet's pregnancy, their shelter was a slight improvement over the other shanties. They had a wooden roof, four walls, and a real mattress on the floor. Sanh motioned for Hoa to sit on the mattress. Despite the solid walls, they could still hear a group of older men outside, loudly chuckling over a game of cards.

"You know you could come with us," Sanh said.

Hoa laughed.

"You can," Sanh said. "It's a new beginning for all of us. You have the choice, Mother."

Hoa lowered her head, curling her hand into the thick folds of the mattress. She never considered it before, such an impossible, rash option, but the mere thought of it warmed her completely, dulling her anxieties. Perhaps America was not as bad as Hung declared. He'd always been one to react in the extreme. Look how severely he turned on Sanh, practically disowning him at the dinner table. In America, she would be the head of the family, the matriarch. How could she leave Sanh and Tuyet alone to raise the children? They were too young and naïve to live in a new country by themselves. She could offer advice, take care of the children. They needed her to do these things.

Perhaps this was the best decision. Hung could take care of the rest of the family in France. Hoa could have America.

"What am I saying?" Sanh shook his head. "Father would murder us both. He's already on the verge of killing me. Never mind, it was a stupid idea."

He moved off the bed, peering over their half-packed bags. Hoa stared at his back, unable to say anything.

Footsteps outside. Tuyet appeared at the front door carrying a sleeping Lum in her arms. This time she looked at Hoa, unable to help a small smile, her triumph so apparent. Sanh belonged only to her now.

Hoa stood. "I should leave now. It's getting late."

"You don't need to go," Tuyet said, walking in and carefully placing Lum onto the bed, where he curled into a snail.

"I have a lot to do," Hoa said.

"Please." Tuyet's face relaxed into her deceptively demure frown. "I wanted to talk to you about Trinh."

Hoa waved her hand. "Whatever Trinh needs, we'll take care of."

"It's not that easy."

"She is reuniting with her husband," Hoa said. "You don't need to worry about her anymore." She turned to Sanh, her hand reaching inside her blouse pocket. "Your father has most of our assets," Hoa said, slipping a small silk pouch into his fingers. "But I have several gold leaves of my own and these pearl earrings."

"Mother," he said, closing his eyes.

She pressed the gold into his palm, folding his fingers over it. "You have a baby coming. I want you to care for your family as best you can."

"We'll visit you," Sanh said. "This is not good-bye. When we're all settled. I promise."

Hoa looked over at her youngest grandson, still deep in sleep. She walked over to him, leaning into his lightly perspiring neck, inhaling his child sour-sweet smell.

"Be good for your mother and father," Hoa whispered into his hair, softly kissing him. Lum shifted to his other side, his cheek blooming red, sighing. "Remember you are a Truong. You are Vietnamese. Nothing will change this."

The camp lights switched off as Hoa walked back to Zone A. She slowed her pace, though that meant her rubber sandals sunk deeper into the muddy trail. The moon was only a sliver, and she worried about tripping over some brushwood or a stray piece of trash. Damp, wrinkled laundry rustled softly from strung-up wires and tree branches along the shanty rows. Refugees lingered outside their shanties, mostly men, the embers of their cigarettes briefly illuminating their bored faces.

This time tomorrow, they'd be gone. They could try to forget all of the months enduring the purgatory conditions of the island: the cramped quarters; the barely edible food; the crude behavior of their fellow refugees.

They could try to rebuild a home. Hoa could prepare proper meals again. She wondered if she could remember her recipes, the ones their cook taught her after they moved to Saigon. Could she find the proper spices and vegetables in France? Where would they live? Would Yen's home be comfortable for all of them? Wherever it was, Hoa could find her private space again. It didn't have to be too large, she could even make do with another closet, just something that was entirely hers.

These thoughts, these assurances, had made the last few weeks bearable, even exciting. Now, imagining the future, she could only see the empty space that Sanh and his family would leave behind. She wondered if this was God's punishment for leaving behind Sanh's in-laws. That was her husband's mistake. Hung should have tried harder to persuade the boat captain to sell him more seats. Then the Vo family would have come with them, and Hoa wouldn't be losing her grandchildren.

At the bottom of the hill, Hoa looked up at their shanty. Hung and Phung were still going over the paperwork, methodically examining every detail to ensure no technicality interfered with their transfer to Manila. When she entered the shelter, her oldest son would murmur to her in greeting and then the men would resume their work, ignoring her for the rest of the night. Hoa observed the hill, not moving. She didn't feel tired. She should only go in when she felt ready to fall asleep.

"Excuse me," Bac Nhut said, suddenly standing next to her, a bobbing flashlight in hand.

Hoa forced the scream back into her throat. "Hello," she said. "Good evening, sir."

"Are you walking up?" he asked. He wore a thin blue cotton shirt and wrinkled brown pants.

She turned her head to the inky sky, looking at nothing, anything. "No, sir. Thank you for the offer, it is very kind of you."

He didn't leave. Instead, he crossed his arms, wiry black hair matted on dark, cracked skin. His portable light bounced along the hillside. Where were his children? Why was he creeping around the island alone so late at night?

"Your youngest son is going to America," Bac Nhut said.

"Yes, he is," Hoa said, smoothly hiding her surprise.

"He is on the same flight as my family. We are leaving tomorrow, too."

Hoa smiled politely. "I'm glad my son and his family will have friends in America. You can look after each other."

Bac Nhut wasn't as tall as Hung. He had more pockmarks on his face. Hoa's mother once said they indicated prosperity.

He stared at her. "Your husband is wrong about the United States. The Vietnamese will be better there."

"I hope so."

"Why would you want to go somewhere so cold? Your daughter's hats will not be enough. Don't you want to be somewhere more like home?"

"I want to be with my family."

"So where they go, you go? Why don't they follow you where you want to go?"

"Would you have followed your wife?" Hoa asked.

"We would have discussed it. I listened to her. I respected my wife."

His face was inches away from her. She inhaled and looked away. "You've been drinking."

His face spread open into a ridiculous smile. "Even after drinking, dear Ba Truong, I would never humiliate my wife. I wouldn't hit her in front of strangers."

Hoa shook her head and began walking away. "Stay away from the guards," she warned. "You don't want to be locked away your final night."

"Best of fortune, Ba Truong," Bac Nhut said, staggering into an exaggerated bow. "I hope your husband's choice makes you happy."

They would take a boat to the Malaysian mainland, a bus to the Kuala Lumpur airport, and then an airplane to the Philippines. And then another airplane to Paris.

Despite all their preparation, they still scrambled to make the boat off the island. Trinh and Xuan hadn't finished packing when they came by. Ngoan couldn't find Cam's jewelry box, which she'd hidden in their shelter months ago. Still, Hung blamed Hoa several times for lagging behind.

"I can't do this all myself," Hung said. "Why did you have to bring so much junk?"

The boat captain loudly grumbled as their family finally boarded, the last to arrive. All the interior seats were occupied, so they had to sit out on the deck. Hoa searched the faces of all the passengers on board, half-hoping to be surprised. But they weren't there. The America group would take a separate boat to the mainland.

At the harbor, a group of UN volunteers saw their boat off, while most of the remaining refugees, including Sanh's family, stayed away. Cam happily waved to anyone she could (*Good-bye! Good-bye! I'll never see you again!*), while Xuan wept in his mother's arms.

"Foolish boy," Hung said, an amused smile on his face. "Doesn't he know he's finally going home?"

The last time they had seen Bidong Island from a boat was when they arrived. Back then, all they paid attention to was the land, the creamy expanse of the beach, the other Vietnamese waving to them. Now, Hoa's eyes traveled upward: the palm trees arching over the knotted green hills; the gray and brown roofs of the buildings; the vivid, clean sky.

Hoa felt fine on the boat. It was the bus that made her sick. The curving Malay roads, the potholes and dips, the freezing blasts from the air conditioner, the bursts of static booming from the bus radio. Hoa curled herself into the vinyl seat, resting her head on the cool window. She vomited in her paper bag several times, and then had to use Hung's bag.

During the six-hour layover at the airport, Hoa spread herself out on the carpeted floor to rest, though the lounge chairs—gray, soft, and new-looking—seemed luxurious. But she was afraid if she sat upright any longer, she'd grow sick again. There was nothing else in her stomach to throw up.

Ngoan regularly returned to Hoa's side with a fresh damp paper towel to press against her forehead. Phung urged her to drink water and rehydrate. The children offered to sing some songs for her, but she asked them to go play elsewhere and not make too much noise.

After a long nap, Hoa awoke to Hung sitting on the floor next to her. She slowly sat up, her hair brushing over her cheeks. Her bun had undone itself while she slept.

"Are we leaving soon?" she asked.

Hung nodded, offering her more water.

"Sanh was here," he said.

Her head swung in both directions. "Where?"

"He's gone now," he said. "He was only here for a minute. They were passing through to their gate. He didn't want to wake you since you were so sick."

"You should have woken me," Hoa muttered. The tension crept back inside her body. It wasn't something to get upset over. He simply walked by, no time to stop and chat. She'd already said her good-byes to Sanh and Lum. Still, everyone but she had the opportunity for another hug, another kiss.

Hoa slumped to the floor, wanting to sleep, wanting to wake in Paris, when all of this would be over; no more waiting, thinking, regretting.

"He won't survive there," Hung said. "He will realize his mistake."

Hoa concentrated on slow, steady breaths, in, out, as Hung's words drifted over her head, lulling her back to sleep.

1980

Kim-Ly Vo
Ho Chi Minh City, Vietnam

. . . *Sanh was very angry with me. The whole family was. Mother Truong refused to kiss me good-bye. Only Trinh was kind, she cried about how she'd miss me. If I was ever tempted to go to France, it was because of her. But I remembered you, our family, and I knew we were making the correct choice.*

After we left his relatives at the airport, my husband was so angry. He wouldn't even watch Lum so I could use the restroom. I had to take him with me. When I returned, Sanh was still glaring at me.

"I hope you're happy now," he said. "Now we've left my family, too. Now we are all alone."

I am making him sound bad. He isn't, believe me. I felt sorry for him. I truly did. Because now he knew how I felt, when he asked me to make the same sacrifice with you. . . .

Tuyet Truong
Tustin, California, USA

∽ *Chapter Two*

CHERRY

LITTLE SAIGON, CALIFORNIA, 1988

IMPROVE: HER MOTHER'S FAVORITE WORD WHEN THEY were growing up, because in America, when you improve, you get anything you want. So the only problem her mother could see was that Cherry didn't want it enough.

What was *it*? Anything worthwhile, anything her smarty-pants cousin Dat had. Certainly not what she did ask for (a Nintendo, a trip to Disneyland, a golden retriever puppy). *It* could be a stellar report card, a tidier bedroom, better manners. . . . Once the complaining started, Cherry had long since learned to stop listening. But what Cherry could hear, because it was so rare, was the occasional compliment, the surprise interruptions in her lectures. Her mother could not deny her daughter's one blessed feature, the one prospect Cherry hadn't destroyed, *not yet*: her memory.

Even at the young, useless age of eight, Cherry could impress the adults with her memory. She could parrot television and radio commercials word for word, skim a brochure and recite its contents weeks later, remember directions to a restaurant or store they'd driven to only once before. Cherry's father called her his little navigator. He claimed it was the Truong gene: Cherry's grandfather in France also possessed a photographic memory, as did her Uncle Yen and cousin Xuan. But instead of being impressed by the practical benefits, Cherry's mother declared them a waste. She preferred that Cherry focus her brainpower on more useful subjects, like her studies. The only thing worse than a dumb kid was a lazy kid. And Cherry's mother was convinced her daughter's laziness was ruining her potential.

Outside the nail salon, Cherry jealously imagined Lum roaming the shopping plaza, buying candy, reading comic books, enjoying the precious after-school hours before dinner and bedtime. The neon signs along the three-story salmon-colored strip mall flickered and brightened, signaling five o'clock. Her play time ticked away with each wasted breath.

"It's going to get dark soon," Cherry said, digging her left heel across the rose-speckled linoleum squares. Lum had been released an hour ago, probably already through several dollars' worth of tokens at the arcade. Around the corner, the other girls had likely finished chalking a labyrinth of hopscotch squares. They'd start the game without her, again. Even if she left now, she'd have to sit on the blacktop and wait until they allowed her in, which rarely happened. They knew better. They'd lost to Cherry too many times during the summer.

"Next time get your work done earlier," her mother said.

"But it's done."

"You have a social studies test tomorrow, remember?"

Cherry exhaled sharply, trying not to look frustrated, because she knew her mother hated that. "I already read over the chapter."

"What did you and your father agree on? You need to read it over twice and then I quiz you."

"She looks so sad," said Auntie Hien, blinking her spiderweb eyelashes. She usually came in on Wednesdays, the slow day at the salon, to allow Cherry's mother to practice on her nails. "Duyen will be here soon. She'll keep you company."

"She is doing poorly in her social studies class," her mom muttered in Vietnamese. "Too much playing. We have to be more disciplined with her."

"I can understand you," Cherry said. "Every word."

"Go reread your chapter," her mother said, raising her chin, a level-one warning.

Slumping in her seat, Cherry opened her textbook. She pressed her hand against the oily, fingerprinted pages, trying to refocus on the faded, uninspiring, unending blocks of print that lacked the clean precision of her math book's equations and fractions. Inevitably, her eyes wandered above the book, to the rows and rows of red and purple nail polish bottles dotting the shelf. Fifty-six from her last count on Monday. Behind the colors, a dusty black cassette player crooned a Vietnamese pop version of the Righteous Brothers' "Unchained Melody." She thought of the children in Saigon: hungry, dirty, and sleeping on the corrupt, lawless streets. *That is suffering,* her mother would remind her if Cherry ever dared complain about schoolwork. *What you are doing is a gift.*

While most of their classmates went home and watched television or played video games after school, she and her brother had to come to the salon until their mother's shift ended. When Lum turned twelve, he tried to convince their parents that they could stay at the house alone. Their father disagreed. Not until Lum's grades got better.

It wasn't supposed to be this way. When their mother announced her transfer to the recently opened nail salon in Tranquillity Buddha Plaza, Cherry and Lum celebrated. It was the newest plaza in Little Saigon, across from the Lucky Tortoise mini-mall. The new salon had large photographs of Hawaiian and Caribbean beaches on the orange walls, fancy purple pedicure stations, and a large waiting area full of year-old *Cosmopolitan* and *People* magazines.

The plaza was even better, with floor-to-ceiling windows, a two-fountain courtyard where little kids could play, and an elevator when they felt too tired from the six-block walk from school to climb the stairs. The first floor had an arcade, a Sanrio stationery store, and a bakery that sold Chinese doughnuts and pâté baguettes. The second floor offered less fun: jewelry shops, insurance companies, the nail salon. Most of the merchants' kids played together in the employee parking lot behind the building.

Cleverly enough, their mother even ruined Tranquillity. Cherry hardly ever finished her homework in time to get in any decent playing.

The store's telephone rang and her mother left to answer it. Cherry watched her mother's back carefully. Auntie Hien fanned her wet nails and flashed her teeth.

"Duyen is late," Cherry said, holding up the plastic waterproof watch Lum had won for her at last year's Tet Festival. "The ballet school is only a ten-minute drive away and her lesson ended at four-thirty. Should we call the police?"

"I think she's all right," Auntie Hien said. "Uncle Viet is picking her up. He said he also needed to pick up his friend. They'll be here soon."

"How far away is his friend?" Cherry liked to approximate the driving distance of any location from Little Saigon.

"I don't know where Khanh is."

"Khanh?" Cherry repeated, recalling the woman's spiral-permed hair and lime-green plastic earrings. "Are she and Uncle Viet getting married?"

Auntie Hien laughed. "No, they're just friends."

"Is it because Khanh is already married?"

That made her aunt laugh harder, which Cherry couldn't understand. It didn't seem funny to her. When her mother returned, Auntie Hien repeated the question, much to Cherry's dismay.

Her mom replaced the polish bottles on the display shelf before bending over at her waist, her nose nearly touching Cherry's. A level-four warning. Smelling the dried plum candies on her warm breath, Cherry instinctively tucked in her chin. "Where did you hear that?" her mother asked.

"I don't remember." Duyen had told her. She had overheard Uncle Viet and Uncle Chinh talking after the family dinner the week before.

"Tell Mommy the truth. Were you being nosy?"

"No," she said, wiggling out of her mother's intense gaze.

Her mother pulled back, eyes narrow and lethal. "You can't eavesdrop on people like that. It can get you into trouble."

"But I never—"

"Adults can say silly things. Don't mind them."

Cherry pretended to return to her reading, but when her mom and Auntie Hien walked to the back room, her gaze drifted out the window again. Some of the other merchants were closing up early, typical on slow Wednesdays. It took several minutes for them to lock their front doors and affix the security gates. The floor vibrated as the merchants walked down the circular stairwell. Only six months old, the plaza had already begun to look shabby. After its grand opening, Cherry used to walk around and count the oil stains in the parking spaces and the cigarette butts and gum splotches on the sidewalks, recording them in a graph-paper notebook for future analysis. But her mother quickly squashed that project. She didn't like Cherry touching all those germs.

Uncle Viet's Honda Civic pulled into the parking space below the window. Her uncle made a big show of hopping out of the driver's side, jogging around the car, and opening Khanh's door. Her thank-you kiss reminded Cherry of the kisses performed regularly on her grandmother's soap operas. They sauntered up the stairs, hand in hand, with Duyen following behind.

What Cherry wanted to say to her mom earlier was that it only made sense that Khanh had been married before. Khanh talked about her daughter, who lived back in Vietnam, all the time. But if she'd said that, then her mother probably would have gotten more suspicious, more mad.

Khanh looked younger than most moms—she was skinny and wore teenager clothes like leggings and short denim skirts. As a mother, Khanh was probably very relaxed. She didn't seem like a big yeller. She wouldn't care if her daughter received a B on a spelling test or wanted to sleep in for a few minutes because she kept hearing frightening noises in her bedroom the night before that prevented her from falling asleep. She'd probably be her daughter's best friend.

Uncle Viet pushed open the door, allowing Khanh and Duyen to walk ahead. The adults stopped in front of her mother and Auntie Hien to talk, waving to Cherry. Her cousin, still in her black leotard and pink tights, sauntered over to Cherry, sucking on a yum-yum pop.

Duyen sat on the table, dangling a wrapped yum-yum pop in front of her cousin. Cherry snatched it before her mother could notice. "They kissed when they thought I wasn't looking," Duyen said. "But I saw it. They used tongues."

"Gross," Cherry declared, flipping her textbook closed.

"That's what adults do, dummy. Your boyfriend is going to make you do that, if you ever have one."

Cherry wrinkled her nose as she ripped off the candy wrapper. "Is she coming to Grandmother's birthday party?" The true test of her uncle's seriousness with a lady friend was if he felt brave enough to introduce her to Grandmother Vo.

"Uncle Viet isn't that stupid," Duyen said. Her hair was pulled up in two buns, so she looked like a teddy bear. Cherry once asked her mom to do that hairstyle for her, but she said it would make Cherry's face look rounder. "Grandmother's ready to move again."

Cherry looked over to their moms, who were shaking their heads at Uncle Viet. "What happened?"

"What else? She got into another fight with Auntie Tri. She plans to move out after the party."

"Where's she gonna move to?"

They stared at each other.

"You have the extra bedroom," Duyen pointed out.

"But Grandmother likes your family better," Cherry said.

This happened every few months. Cherry's mom claimed Grandmother Vo didn't want to overburden any of her children, so she took turns living in each of their houses. It was an honor to care for one's elders. So why every time before leaving a house did Grandmother need to scream and swear at all of them? Cherry had never heard anyone with a voice like her grandmother's. Even with the door closed, under blankets and pillows, fingers stuffed in both ears, Grandmother could not be ignored.

Her mother said it wasn't fair to compare grandmothers, but Grandmère in France never screamed like that. Her mom said Grandmère never had to—she'd always gotten what she wanted. Grandmother Vo had suffered a lot in Vietnam, and though her mother never went into detail about it, she seemed to blame Grandmère and Grandpère. Though what they could have done all the way from France, Cherry never understood.

"It's not that bad," Duyen said. "She gives me and Dat money for candy when we hear the ice cream truck."

"Really?"

"She doesn't with you?"

"No!"

The pluses of living with Grandmother: Lum and Cherry could go straight home after school, since Grandmother could watch them. She let them drink strawberry milk as an after school snack, sometimes even two glasses. She'd remind them to finish their homework, but she never checked it or kept them from going outside to play with the neighbors.

The minuses: If Grandmother was in a mood, she'd assign them household chores, and then criticize their lazy, sloppy work. If her soap operas were on television, they couldn't watch their cartoons. She'd tell her grandchildren that they walked too loudly up and down the stairs, even though the steps were carpeted and she couldn't hear anything. She answered the phone with a loud *Allo?* and if the caller spoke English, she'd simply hang up. She complained of the temperature in the house, always too hot or too cold. And if she was especially cranky, she'd accuse them of neglect, too stingy to properly care for her, after all she'd done for them. She wasn't nice to anyone, not even to her own daughters, unless company visited. Weren't you supposed to be nice to your own family?

"Grandmother went through many bad times in Vietnam," Cherry's mother said.

"But that isn't our fault," Cherry said.

Her mother clicked her tongue, a sideways glance. "You are too young to criticize."

Still, even their mother was relieved when Grandmother moved out last summer, her belongings packed in two tortoise-green suitcases and carried away by the next family in line to take her in. Grandmother had wept into her flowered silk handkerchief, sniffling wet kisses into everyone's necks, like she was moving out of the country instead of a few blocks over. She promised their mother that things would be better living at Aunt Tri's house. Before getting in the car, she slipped Cherry and Lum money under her magenta scarf.

"Dat says she's probably going to live with your family," Duyen said, crunching down on her candy, too impatient to wait for the bubblegum middle.

"Other grandmothers live in retirement homes," Cherry said.

"We're not that American," Duyen declared.

Cherry and Lum's parents said they should feel lucky to have their own home, to not have to live in an apartment or duplex.

"People living above or below you, sharing your walls, no thanks," her mother said. It took their parents four years after moving to America to buy their own home. Every refugee family wanted to make the switch from rent to mortgage. Homeowners couldn't get cheated by landlords (like cousin Linh's family), or get kicked out with no notice (Uncle Viet).

When Cherry and her cousins played MASH on scratch paper, nobody wanted to live in a Shack or an Apartment. They wanted House. They dreamed of Mansion. In a Mansion, Cherry imagined they could all live together again. Each family could have its own wing, so they wouldn't argue over bathroom or kitchen privileges, and they could all come together for meals in a large dining room.

The Vo relatives all lived in apartments. Auntie Hien's family in the Oceanside Pavilion (it was a lie—the beach was at least twenty minutes away) a few blocks over, Auntie Tri's family and Uncle Viet in Brookhurst Court behind the Asian Palace Shopping Center. They hadn't lived in America as long as Cherry's family—only a few years. Cherry remembered when they all lived together in her parents' house, a family in each bedroom, the biggest sleepover she ever attended. But it grew too

crowded, her father said—too much bickering between the adults—
and within a year, the Vos had moved into their own places.

Except Grandmother. So it made sense for her to stay with Cherry's
family, since they had the most space: four bedrooms (one officially a
den), two floors, a patio backyard, concrete porch and yellowing lawn
in front. It looked like every other house on the block, except for the
color—theirs was brown and yellow, while the eleven others were vari-
ous shades of blue and gray.

Their home was within walking distance of the elementary school,
although Cherry didn't like to walk. She had to pass the park where
the high school kids hung out. They threw their cigarette butts into the
sandlot like it was their personal ashtray. The boys cut their hair so short
they looked bald, and wore gold earrings in both ears. The girls dyed
their hair orange and red. In the sun, their hair sometimes radiated blond.
Cherry thought it looked pretty, so grown-up.

"It looks cheap," her mother said. "If you ever do anything like that,
I'll cut off all your hair. I didn't raise you to look like a punk."

"Your mommy is protective of you," her father explained. "Sometimes she doesn't know how to say it in a nice way." They were supposed
to understand their mother's stress. Even though their parents were still
married, Cherry and Lum's mother claimed she felt like a single mother
because their father worked the night shifts at the water treatment plant.
Every evening after dinner, Cherry and Lum followed their mother from
door to door, window to window, to confirm they were all locked and
sealed. Bells from their old toys were rubber-banded to the door handles.
Her mother didn't want anyone to know they were home alone, without
a man.

"In the refugee camps," Cherry's mother said, "we had no protection.
If they wanted to steal something from your tent, they did, and there was
nothing you could do about it. It traumatized your Auntie Trinh from
France."

"You don't need to scare the children," their father said, then turned
to Cherry. "Just lock the doors. They can't come in unless you let them."

But after talking with the other manicurists at the salon who'd heard of some recent home invasions around Little Saigon, their mother realized deadbolts and toy bells were not enough. To keep the punks off their streets, their mom brought home a supermarket pamphlet on neighborhood watch groups and decided to form her own security system. She called every family on the block to invite them over for a potluck. Lum and Cherry helped to arrange *cha gio* and *banh beo* next to a peacock arrangement of brochures on community crime watching. Because her mother's *banh beo* was rather famous, the meeting was packed. Every family went home that evening with a red sticker of the winking dog wearing a detective's trench coat to post on their windows and front doors, their united intolerance against crime. They all agreed to keep their eyes open for anything suspicious—anyone funny looking. They wouldn't allow their neighborhood to become contaminated like other sections of Little Saigon.

"Does this mean we can go to the park by ourselves now?" Lum asked as they picked up the soggy paper plates and wrinkled cups after the meeting.

"That isn't in our domain," their mom said from the kitchen. "We can only patrol the block."

"In our old apartment," Lum said, stopping in front of the living room window, "we had a playground in the complex. And a pool, too."

"I don't remember it," Cherry said. She peered outside, wondering what Lum was glaring at. It was too dark to see anything. Some of the neighbors still stood out on the sidewalk talking, but she could only see their flashlights.

They watched the last of their neighbors leave, returning to their homes, their flashlights hopping along the black asphalt. So dark, too dark. Cherry quickly pulled the curtains closed. Lum had to be wrong. It didn't matter if the apartment had a pool or a playground. Without sunlight, nothing mattered but staying inside with the doors locked, safe from the bad people that came out at night. The neighborhood watch would help; so would extra deadbolts. But they couldn't replace their father.

* * *

The day before Grandmother's birthday party, their father announced that they planned to invite Grandmother to move in.

"Didn't we just have her?" Lum asked.

"Is this how you are going to treat us when we get old?" he asked, tapping his wooden chopsticks against the platter of ginger-smothered green beans. "Caring for your parents is a privilege, not a burden."

Something was up. Lum told her so later that night when they were supposed to be sleeping and their parents were downstairs in the family room watching *Dynasty*. He planned to eavesdrop on their parents and investigate.

"Let me come, too," Cherry pleaded.

"You're too noisy," Lum insisted.

She protested, but Lum only bossed her around when he had good reasons. He shared his toys and let her play with his friends—not like their cousin Dat, who teased Duyen with stories about Thai pirates hiding outside her bedroom window. Bullies never bothered Cherry because they knew Lum would come after them. He was the tallest boy in junior high—already five foot seven inches. Their father said it was the American cow milk.

"If only we knew this in Vietnam!" he said. "We'd all shoot up like him."

When she was younger, Cherry used to think their father was the tallest man in the world. While at a department store one afternoon, a man with a cowboy hat stood behind them in line at the register. Their father barely reached the cowboy's shoulder. The realization startled, and then saddened her. She didn't like to think of their father as short. Lum was only twelve and already taller. Cherry wondered if she would surpass him, too.

After several minutes, Lum slipped into his sister's room, a birthday morning grin on his face. "They're asking Grandmother for money."

Grandmother Vo, everyone suspected, was rich. Though she didn't have a bank account or a job, they whispered about the gold Grandmother Vo had supposedly sneaked out of Vietnam in the stitching of her clothing. Families from the neighborhood would visit their grandmother asking for—or repaying—small loans. Dat bragged he once saw

Grandmother Vo stuffing bills into her mattress. She shared with the family when she wanted to; paying for Uncle Chinh's tuition at business school, and helping Aunt Tri's family with bills when Uncle Bao was fired from his dishwashing job. There were, it seemed, benefits to living with Grandmother.

"Why do we need money?" Cherry asked, sitting up in bed.

"Dad wants to open up a bookstore," Lum said. "That empty space in Tranquillity by the arcade? He wants to buy it and sell Vietnamese books and magazines."

"What about the water treatment plant?"

"He's tired of working there. Too much overtime and they're not paying him enough. Besides, this way, he can be his own boss."

Just like their mother said. Even adults had to continue trying to improve themselves. A store of their own! Cherry relished the possibilities. An after school place they might actually like. No more polish-remover fumes or older customers fussing over them. Their father would be around.

Their parents used to talk about having their own business, but when it came to either a down payment for a house or a store, they chose a home. They talked about their own store as a faraway fantasy, like they would with dream vacations to the Bahamas or Mexico.

"Did you know your Grandpère used to manage a very fancy hotel in Nha Trang?" their father once told her. "The best resort in town. All the dignitaries came to stay there. It was a prestigious position, but he always wanted to buy his own hotel, a business he could pass down to his family."

"Could I have worked there?" Cherry asked.

"Of course," he said. "It's always better to work with family."

By the time they arrived at the party, most of the children had escaped. A stream of kids stomped down the balloon-laced staircase of Aunt Tri's second-story apartment, brushing past her family. Cherry fought the urge to hand off the tray of tofu rolls to her parents and run after them. Family parties happened this way: you could never have fun immediately.

"You must greet your grandmother first," their father reminded them. First thing after taking shoes off. No drink or food, no bathroom stop. Respect had to be paid to the guest of honor.

The heavy aroma of Aunt Tri's crispy *banh xeo* lured them through the door. Purple and blue crinkle streamers and seventeen balloons hung on the walls and ceilings. Aunt Tri had pulled back the pea-green drapes to make room for six hanging paper lanterns decorated with dragonflies and butterflies. Shiny multicolored confetti lay sprinkled over the worn orange carpet. A silver-framed black-and-white photograph of Grandfather Vo, who died back in Vietnam before any of the grandkids were born, sat in the center of the coffee table, draped in a red silk tablecloth. The remaining shelf space on the ancestors' altar was crammed with incense sticks, red envelopes, and bowls of fruit. Lum dutifully squeezed their own family's fruit bowl onto the edge of the table, pushing the incense holder against the portrait.

Uncle Bao and Auntie Tri's apartment had three bedrooms: one for Uncle Bao and Auntie Tri, one for Uncle Viet, and one for cousin Linh. Whenever Grandmother Vo moved in, Linh had to give up her bedroom and sleep on the pullout sofa in the living room.

Grandmother Vo sat on the brown-and-yellow plaid sofa, stuffed between the neighbor fortune-teller Ba Liem and her twin sister Ba Nhanh. They were the only identical twins Cherry knew and their physical similarities, down to matching liver spots on their right cheeks, frightened her. Grandmother wore a royal blue *ao dai,* a matching scarf around her neck, and caramel colored sunglasses. She liked to wear sunglasses even indoors.

Lum and Cherry fidgeted in front of her and bowed. Grandmother nodded. Lum approached her first, quickly pecking her on the cheek. Cherry repeated the gesture. The smell of menthol from Grandmother's green medicine oil slid up her nostrils, reminding Cherry of what their house would soon stink of once Grandmother moved back.

"You're late," Grandmother Vo observed, barely nodding at the present their mother placed on the coffee table. "I thought you were coming early to help your sisters cook."

"Tri called and asked us to pick up more ice," their mother said.

"Ice is so important," Grandmother said, exchanging glances with the twins. "There must have been a long line at the store."

It was as if Grandmother knew their father had taken a detour through the orange groves to relax their mother. Maybe she could smell the citrus on them. They had rolled down the windows of the station wagon, stuck their heads out, and inhaled deeply. It smelled better than the ocean.

"Ba Nhanh, your glass is empty," their father said. "Would any of you ladies like another beverage?"

"Chi Tuyet," Auntie Tri's voice called from the kitchen. "Where have you been? Get in here."

Their parents swiftly escaped to the kitchen. Before Lum and Cherry could bow and join them, the fortune-teller grabbed Cherry's arm.

"I don't know what you're talking about, Ba Kim," the fortune-teller said, sharply pinching Cherry's shoulder. "I think this one has potential to turn out nicely."

"Her Vietnamese is atrocious," Grandmother Vo said. "She has her father's accent and with her half-English, I can barely understand her."

"Let me read her palm," Ba Liem said, and then nodded at Lum, who mercifully had not abandoned his sister. "I'll read both of them."

"We've done enough of that today," Grandmother said. "This one is too young anyway."

"It's never too early to determine a child's luck," Ba Liem said. She was already rubbing Cherry's hand, making it itch. She dropped her eyelids, wrinkling her forehead, concentrating.

Cherry's gaze lingered above the couch where the Vietnam-shaped clock hung. Sometimes when she felt drowsy, the clock looked like a dragon. Four minutes passed. Cherry could hear her parents laughing guiltlessly in the kitchen with her aunts. Where were her cousins? The greasy smell of the *banh xeo* was unbearable. It would be cold by the time she'd get to eat. Ba Liem's eyes finally opened.

"Good brains," she declared, squeezing her hand in her moist grasp. "It will be her brains that secure a solid, dependable husband. Vietnamese, of course. From an honorable family. He could be a doctor or a dentist.

She will be his assistant, perhaps a nurse . . . medical maladies . . . she will have earaches in her late fifties. This may cause hearing problems."

"A nurse!" the fortune-teller's sister Ba Nhanh said, clapping her hands.

"I'll tell her mother to check her ears," Grandmother said. "Who knows how often her parents clean them?"

"It's very important to keep a child's ears clear of wax," Ba Liem solemnly said. "Wax encourages stubbornness."

Lum was next. Cherry sat on Ba Nhanh's lap as the fortune-teller pressed her thumbs into Lum's palm. This time, Ba Liem seemed to hum as well, the oracle settling inside her head. She opened one eye to peer at Lum.

"This one is murky," she pronounced. "I can't get a clear reading on him. He is too impressionable, easily influenced by his peers. He must be watched very carefully . . . his eyes are good now, but he may require reading spectacles when he is forty-two."

Both Grandmother Vo and Ba Nhanh leaned forward, as if to examine Lum with a new perspective.

"I suspected this one may be more troublesome," Ba Nhanh said.

"He doesn't do as well in school as his sister," Grandmother Vo said to the twins. "His parents say he has poor reading skills, but perhaps it's more than that."

Lum withdrew his hand. "I'm doing fine in school."

The old ladies stared at him with oval mouths.

"Impudent child!" Grandmother Vo said. "Ba Liem is honoring you with a reading and you disrespect her like this?"

"We shouldn't be surprised," Ba Liem said, nodding in satisfaction. "I will speak with his mother later. We will stop it, Ba Kim, before he gets too unruly."

The children bowed and left the elder women, determined not to return to the living room for a good while.

"Don't listen to her," Lum said, recognizing the worry on Cherry's face. "She's just saying what Grandmother wants to hear. That way she'll get paid."

Cherry hoped so. She didn't like the idea of her future laid out, with no choices of her own. And to think she'd be a nurse. She hated the sight of blood. Even the possibility of seeing it was enough to make her wince. Cherry stared at the creases in her palm, at the lines that stretched out to her fingers. They said no two palms looked alike, so no two fortunes could be the same. Then why did hers sound so common?

In the dining room, Cherry and Lum circled the buffet table carefully, determining what to fill their plates with. They could hear the clinking of chips and shouts of both luck and defeat from Uncle Viet's bedroom, where the uncles played poker. After weighing down their plates with egg rolls, beef salad, chicken curry, and scoops of fried rice, Lum left for Uncle Viet's room, while Cherry wandered down the hallway.

In Uncle Bao and Aunt Tri's room, Cherry's cousins were watching a *Paris by Night* video, her aunties' favorite Vietnamese variety show. Duyen and Linh lay side by side on their stomachs, wrinkling their good dress-up clothes, elbows planted in the mattress, fists tucked under their chins. Another girl lay in Cherry's usual spot. She looked older and had two long French braids in her hair. The girl grinned a mouthful of braces and hot pink rubber bands.

"This is Quynh," Linh said. "We're in homeroom together."

The bed already crowded, Cherry sank to the floor and sat cross-legged, her plate balancing between her knees. On the television, Rocky Lam, Linh's favorite Vietnamese singer, crooned, winking at the camera during his close-up. Behind him on the glittering neon-color-splashed stage, a bevy of backup dancers preened and sashayed in low-cut leotards and feathered boas.

"Isn't he beautiful?" Linh sighed, and collapsed to the mattress. Her pigtails bounced as she shook her head. "Mom says he's married."

"Well, he has to be at least thirty," Duyen said, rolling her eyes. Unlike Linh and their mothers, Duyen and Cherry didn't find Rocky Lam so attractive. His face and hair were too oily. He made facial expressions when singing that looked more painful than seductive.

"Thirty's not old," Quynh said. "I've got cousins who are in their thirties."

"It just means he's mature," Linh said, sitting up to smile at her reflection in the heart-shaped mirror hanging on the wall. "When I'm old enough, I'm going to be a pop singer and maybe he and I will sing a duet together on *Paris by Night*."

"Oh, yeah?" Duyen snickered. "How?"

"I'm going to take singing lessons." Linh puckered at the mirror before turning to look at Duyen.

"With what money? Your mom wouldn't even let you sign up for ballet classes with me."

"I'm going to join the choir when I get into junior high, dummy," Linh said, scowling. "Right, Quynh?"

"Yeah, choir is free," Quynh said. "My older cousins are doing it."

"You don't know everything," Linh said. "A ballet recital for a beginner's class is not a real performance. The choir sings several times a year and travels all over the county."

"You have to have a good voice," Duyen reminded her.

"I have a good voice!" Linh said. "My dad says so." Uncle Bao had been a singer in hotels in Vietnam. Now he worked at an auto garage. He said if it weren't for the Communists, he'd be famous back in Vietnam.

"Lessons don't give you everything. You have to have talent first," Duyen said. "Besides, Ba Liem said you're going to be a housewife and that I'll be the performer."

"Fortune-tellers only guess at the future," Linh said. "They don't really know."

"You had your palms read, too?" Cherry asked.

"Grandmother's having all of our palms read," Duyen said. "Why do you think Ba Liem is here?"

"My mom says you can do anything you put your mind to," Linh said.

"You're so gullible," Duyen said. "Did she read that off a cereal box?"

"I *can* sing," Linh said firmly. "And if I need lessons, then Mom will ask Grandmother for the money. Singing lessons can't cost more than beauty school."

"Who's going to beauty school?" Cherry asked.

Duyen gave Linh a hard look. "No one," Duyen said.

"You're lying," Cherry said.

"It's grown-up stuff," Duyen said, waving her hand, further annoying Cherry. "You won't understand."

Linh had turned twelve last month and Duyen was eleven, not much older than Cherry, yet they acted as if those years mattered a lot. They believed they were so mature. Cherry didn't mind not having a sister. Cousins lorded enough power.

The Vo relatives arrived in Orange County when Cherry was five. Duyen and Linh had known each other since they were babies, lived in the same house in Vietnam, and fought like sisters. Cherry knew she should love both of them, but she didn't like being treated like a baby. Cherry wanted one of her aunts to have another kid, so that the three of them could keep secrets from someone else.

Lum once tried to explain it to Cherry by pinching her arm.

"Ow," she said, rubbing the sore spot.

"You'd rather I keep that to myself?" he asked.

"Yes!"

"That's what grown-ups are trying to do when they keep secrets," he said. "They don't want to pinch you. They'd rather pinch themselves."

Cherry couldn't understand why all grown-up stuff had to hurt, why there couldn't be anything good to share. If everything worth knowing hurt so much, she wondered why people bothered talking at all.

Another singer, Melody Ngo, floated across the television screen, wearing a glittery blue evening gown.

"Turn it up," Quynh said. "This is my favorite song."

"Mine, too!" Linh said, eagerly turning up the volume to a level that hurt Cherry's ears.

Duyen rolled her eyes at Cherry again, but she turned to Linh and her new friend. The two older girls lip-synched the cheesy lyrics, forgetting the last few minutes in the room.

A loud whistle pierced their ears. Linh scooted toward the window and slid open the glass partition. The girls sat up, pressing their noses against the dusty screen.

Lum waved from the grass square next to the parking lot, surrounded by other children from the party. His tie hung on a rosebush, shirt-sleeves already rolled up.

"We're playing Frisbee," Lum said, cupping his hands into binoculars to see through the sun glare. "Come down, we're picking teams."

Four boys and four girls were eligible for teams. The younger kids were sidelined as fans because they were too short to play. Duyen's brother, Dat, demanded that he should be captain of the team opposing Lum.

"We need to keep the teams even," Dat said, his chest lifting a little.

Lum looked like he was hiding a smile. "Okay by me."

While Dat and Lum were in the same grade at school, they rarely played together.

"Why can't you be nice to your cousin?" their mother asked, after Auntie Hien loudly complained that Lum ignored Dat at school. "He's new to this country and you're his family. It's your duty to help him."

"I ask him to play lots of times," Lum said. "He always wants to go to the library."

On Dat's first day of school in America, Lum invited him to play in a game of softball at recess. But when a fly ball shattered Dat's left eyeglass lens, a new pair, his parents forbade him from playing again. Dat obeyed his parents, but because of it, he remained dreadful at any kind of sport. Running down the block was enough to get him wheezing. Still, it didn't keep him from wanting to win at everything.

After picking off the two remaining boys Huy and Johnny, Dat chose his sister, Duyen, while Lum picked Cherry. And even though Dat didn't know Quynh, he waved her over, leaving Linh to join Lum's team.

"I would have chosen you over her anyway," Lum said, welcoming their sulking cousin to his team.

They pulled off their shoes and threw them underneath the stairwell. In preparation, Cherry gingerly stepped on the sun-fried grass, allowing her feet to adjust to the prickles.

If they were going to throw any sort of object in a game, Cherry wanted the Frisbee. It was made of light, harmless plastic and didn't smash your face or other body parts when you missed a catch. She shuddered to think of Dat's broken eyeglass. The worst injury she ever

had was a sprained finger from a tetherball game and she could still recall the throbbing and aching. So many injuries could happen from
games. Their parents only allowed Lum to play sports for fun, but never
to join any school teams. They wanted him to concentrate on his studies. They didn't understand why Americans paid so much attention to
games when athletic scholarships to college were so difficult and risky to
acquire.

The tallest kid in the game, Lum easily led their side to the first vic-
tory. He stretched his long body to catch the highest throws, smoothly
turning to swing them back to his slower, unprepared opponents.

"First game doesn't count," Dat said, panting from chasing the last
throw. "That was practice."

Lum exchanged a smile with his friend Huy. "Fine."

They won the second game with Cherry scoring the winning throw.
It happened so fast, she instantly wanted to replay the moment.

"Go, Cherry!" Linh cried, giving her a high five, and Cherry felt a
thrill far greater than any test score or report card could offer.

"Out of bounds," Dat said, after retrieving the Frisbee. "That throw
doesn't count."

"No way," Lum said.

"Past the rosebushes is out of bounds."

"You never said that. And you didn't care when you threw it over
the bushes."

"Then let's do over. Rosebushes and the pickup truck are the bound-
aries."

"Forget it," Lum said. "We won that game. It counts."

"Cheater," Dat said.

"Will you quit it?" Huy said. "You're just a sore loser."

"I'm not playing with cheaters," Dat said. "I did not lose to some
baby."

"Hey!" Cherry said.

"She's not a baby," Lum said.

Dat readjusted his glasses, squinting in the sunlight. Sweat trickled
from his sideburns. No one on his team came to his defense, not even

Duyen. He had to know he was wrong. But Dat didn't care. Though shorter than most boys his age, he could be as mean as any bully.

"Does your baby sister know what they call you at school?"

"Shut up," Lum said.

"Dumb Lum," Dat sang, smiling maliciously. "Dumb Lum, Dumb Lum is wrong again."

"Shut up!" Lum stalked toward their cousin, seized him by his shirt collar, and threw him to the ground. Stunned, Dat stared at him, then looked around at the other gaping children. His face wrinkled.

"Daddy!" he screamed, bursting into tears. He pulled himself up and scrambled in the direction of the apartment. "Daddy!"

No one said anything. Cherry couldn't look at Lum, who she knew felt embarrassed. He always told his sister to ignore Dat, not to let him bother her because that was what he wanted. It was the first time Cherry ever saw her older brother push anyone down.

It didn't take long for Dat to return, skulking behind his father and Cherry and Lum's dad. The children backed away from Lum once they saw the expressions on the adults' faces.

"What happened here?" a red-faced Uncle Chinh asked. "What did you do to my son?"

"He pushed me!" Dat screamed. "Everyone saw it, he pushed me!"

"Cherry?" their father asked.

She turned to her brother.

"Don't look at Lum, look at me."

He could have waited until they returned home. Tall, gangly Lum bending over their father's knee, his hands supporting himself on the concrete, punished with humiliation, which hurt more than the spanking itself. Cherry would have been mortified if it had happened to her. She could only guess how much worse it was for Lum because he was a boy and older.

Playtime was over. Since they were not responsible enough to play outside without adult supervision, they had to go back upstairs where their parents could watch them.

While the adults, Dat, and the little kids returned to the apartment,

Huy and Johnny walked with Lum to find the Frisbee, which Dat had flung in the air during his tantrum. The girls fetched their shoes from under the stairwell.

"I hope that never happens to me," Duyen said. "Everyone in school is going to be laughing at Lum on Monday."

"Why?" Cherry asked, hopping on one foot to pull on her other Mary Jane. "Who's going to tell?"

"Dat will," Duyen said. "He'll tell everyone in their class."

"Lum should have known better," Linh said.

"I would have pushed Dat, too," Quynh said.

They all looked at her, the outsider to the family, as she laced up her sneakers.

"It's easy to say that now," Duyen said.

"I'll say it to your brother's face," Quynh said. "I'm not afraid of him."

When Lum and the boys finally came back inside, Cherry tried to put her hand on his arm, but he pushed past. She followed him as he walked through the living room and into the kitchen where their mother and aunties were preparing the cake. Auntie Tri immediately cooed with sympathy as Lum approached them, his face ruddy and moist. Mom led Lum to the balcony and they sat on the plastic stools next to Auntie Tri's chili pepper plants. She stroked his curved back as he talked into his folded arms.

Cherry stood between the glass door and the refrigerator, wanting to hear what they said, but not wanting Lum to accuse her of spying.

"He called me that name! I thought you said he would never do that again. You promised!"

"He won't," their mother said. "I'll talk to Auntie Hien. Why do you let it bother you so much?"

"It bothers me," Lum said. "It does."

Cherry pressed her forehead against the sliding glass door, waiting for them to see her. A hand tapped her shoulder and she tipped her head back. Auntie Tri knocked on the glass door. Her mother and brother looked over with their matching hooded eyes, those eyes, their father would say, that threatened to weep at any moment.

"It's time for cake," Auntie Tri said.

While Auntie Tri and Lum left for the living room, their mother held Cherry back, her nails digging into her arm.

"How could you let this happen?" she furiously whispered. "Why weren't you watching your brother?"

"I was," Cherry argued.

"You're supposed to protect each other," she said. "He would never let this happen to you."

Her mother left Cherry in the kitchen, where she rubbed her arm. Once she heard them beginning to sing "Happy Birthday," Cherry patted her eyes with a dishrag hanging from the oven, and swung open the door.

After Grandmother Vo blew out the candles and the cake and punch were served, most of the guests departed, leaving behind only family and the old twins to help Grandmother open presents. Uncle Viet, Grandmother's youngest child, but the only boy, went first. He swaggered up to Grandmother Vo, a shiny silver box in his palm, and kissed her twice on each cheek, declaring her the best mother in the world.

Sitting on the armrest of the sofa behind Auntie Hien and Auntie Tri, Cherry could hear everything they said.

"Who gave him the money?" Auntie Hien whispered.

"Probably his bookie," Auntie Tri said with a snicker.

"He couldn't have won anything."

"It was a loan. Another loan Mother will end up paying for."

While Cherry's father and uncles all had mustaches, only Uncle Viet grew his past his lip line. Cherry's dad once said if Uncle Viet ever took the time to look for a job the way he did to shop, he could afford all the clothes Grandmother bought for him. Today, Uncle Viet wore a peppermint gum–colored suit and sunflower yellow dress shirt. Lum said Uncle Viet dressed like a homo. But Cherry knew Uncle Viet had Khanh as well as other girlfriends, who Grandmother Vo disapproved of. She thought Uncle Viet was too young to be married.

Because Grandmother Vo liked to save wrapping paper, opening presents took longer than it should. Her fingers slipped under the Scotch tape, seeking a clean drag and peel, never ripping, not even wrinkling, the paper. With Uncle Viet's gift, though only the size of a deck of cards, she seemed to spend even more time caressing the wrapper, savoring the moment.

An emerald pendant necklace. Emerald was their grandmother's favorite stone. But if Cherry remembered correctly, Grandmother already had five necklaces just like this one.

"It's beautiful," Grandmother Vo exclaimed, weeping. She put her tear-moistened hands upon Uncle Viet's face and kissed him again.

Auntie Hien's family gave Grandmother a new humidifier. Grand-mother smiled blandly, unsure of its purpose, even after Uncle Chinh and Dat tried to explain its function several times.

"We'll set it up in our home for you," Uncle Chinh said. "You'll see."

Cherry immediately looked to her parents. They motioned for her and her brother to retrieve the gift from the table.

They walked over to Grandmother Vo's chair. While Cherry pinched the hem of her dress, Lum silently offered the family present. After the ritual unwrapping, Grandmother held the pale green and pink fabric in her hands and looked at their mother.

"It's for a new dress," Cherry's mother said.

"I can see that," Grandmother Vo said.

"We were in that store last week and you stopped to look at this fabric. You thought it was so pretty."

"Yes, of course," Grandmother Vo said. "Pretty for one of the children, perhaps, but not for an old woman like me. I would look ridiculous in these colors." Her hands petted the fabric like it was a small puppy, if she liked puppies. "Duyen," she called out, waving for their cousin to come over. She held the fabric under Duyen's chin and smiled. "Hien, what do you think?"

Auntie Hien reluctantly looked at Cherry's mother before smiling back at Grandmother Vo. "It's lovely."

Grandmother nodded in satisfaction. "Maybe some new *ao dais* for the girls on their grandfather's death anniversary in March. It will be a gift from their grandmother. Ba Liem's daughter is an excellent seam-stress, correct?"

Of course, Auntie Tri and her family were last. Auntie Tri was not only the youngest daughter, but also the child who had most recently aroused Grandmother's anger. But Auntie Tri had prepared. Linh presented their grandmother with mother of pearl earrings and a matching necklace. The twins cooed as Grandmother Vo tried them on. Linh held a small oval mirror for Grandmother to study her reflection. Auntie Tri and Uncle Bao must have put the purchase on a credit card.

"It's nice you can spend money on your mother's birthday," Grandmother Vo said, tilting her chin at the mirror. "Too bad you can only do it on special occasions."

"Mommy, we love you," Auntie Tri said. "We will always spend money on you."

"Dear, if that were true, then I wouldn't be moving out, would I? But that's all right. You're young. You have a daughter of your own who needs your attention."

She placed the pearls back into their velvet box and set it next to her pile of presents.

"And since we are all together today as a family, this is a good time to talk about family matters."

While Grandmother Vo took a long sip of tea, the relatives impatiently adjusted in their seats.

"As most of you know, the Nguyens have finally paid back their loan, and I've been debating what to do with the money. I certainly don't want to put it in a bank, but I don't want to let it go to waste, either. Money is not for hoarding, but investing. You've all been so helpful offering suggestions, thank you for that. I've discussed it with Ba Liem and Ba Nhanh, and since I want to help all my children, I've decided you should all share the money in the new business."

Cherry's parents smiled, squeezing each other's palms. Cherry placed her hands on theirs, trying to still them.

"Mother, thank you," Cherry's mother said. "We promise, we will work very hard to return your investment. And of course my sisters and brothers can work in the bookstore. We'd be happy—"

"I'm not talking about a bookstore, Tuyet. You didn't let me finish. I considered Sanh's idea, and while it seemed promising, I can't see how it would properly involve your brothers and sisters. That's your husband's dream, not the family's. Anyway, I can see from your children, that perhaps this isn't the best time to start such a time-consuming project."

"What's wrong with the children?"

"I heard what happened outside to Dat," Grandmother said. "Lum should be ashamed of himself. Ba Liem was right in her predictions about him. If he can hit his own cousin, that means he really is out of control and needs more discipline."

"It was a misunderstanding between children," their mother said, her arm wrapping around Lum's waist, who looked like he was going to throw up. "And Lum apologized—"

"It still happened," Grandmother said. "These children have become too alienated from their own cousins. I cannot condone this, even if we are living in America, where they treat family like strangers. Now, I've enrolled your sisters in that cosmetology seminar. . . ."

Cherry stared at Duyen, who was still sitting next to Grandmother, but she wouldn't meet her gaze. Grandmother continued to talk. Auntie Hien and Auntie Tri would attend the same cosmetology program their mother graduated from, only they would specialize in hair. After they graduated from the eight-month course, they'd open a beauty salon in an open space at the Asian Palace Shopping Center. Grandmother thought the expensive real estate in the indoor mall was worth it. More customers would come there. Uncle Viet was taking a bookkeeping course at the community college and could manage the business. As for Cherry's mother, she could have a nail station in the salon.

"Being in business for yourselves will bring in a lot more income for the family," Grandmother Vo said. "And you will have to work together to accomplish that."

Cherry's mother turned to her sisters, her cheeks sucked in. "I didn't know you were even interested in beauty school."

"Why not?" Auntie Hien asked. "You think you're the only one who can work?"

"We took care of Mommy for years while you were away," Auntie Tri said. "Why should you get all her savings?"

"I sent you money every month after we came to America," Cherry's mother said.

"Out of guilt!" Auntie Hien sneered. "You think a few dollars makes up for everything you put us through?"

As her mother and aunts descended into another argument, Cherry's father stood. He walked across the living room and out the door, saying nothing to excuse himself.

Only Grandmother Vo smiled knowingly. "You see?" she said. "How can I turn over so much money to your husband when he is this selfish? Just like his father. That is why I will move into your home, Tuyet. It's clear your family needs me more than anyone else right now."

Lum and Cherry went outside to find their father. The sun had set, the air cool and gray in the parking lot. Cherry shivered, wishing she had brought a sweater. Dad stood by the station wagon, smoking a cigarette.

"Grandmother's coming with us," Lum said.

Their father, continuing to puff, didn't say anything. Cherry wasn't sure where he got the cigarette, since he didn't smoke regularly, only at parties or when he had a bad day at work. This wasn't the time to remind him about the statistics of tobacco and cancer.

"Maybe a beauty salon is better," Cherry said. "Dad, didn't you say we should work with family?"

"Shut up, Cherry," Lum said, staring at their father.

"Go help your grandmother," their father said, with a nod to Cherry. "I'll bring the car around."

She turned around and stepped away, slowly, heel first, toe last, heel, toe.

"I'm sorry, Dad," Lum said. "I didn't mean—"

"You stupid, stupid boy. Do you want to prove to everyone that you're worthless?"

"Dad—"

"Is it all you're good at?" he asked. "Destroying things?"

Cherry walked faster, turning the corner of the apartment building, determined not to hear her father's words, and ran straight into the rosebush. The thorns dug into her elbows and kneecaps. Cherry tried to untangle herself, grabbing fistfuls of branches, pulling back, but the thorns snagged at her dress. Twisting away, she stared at her palms, already prickling with bright dots of blood. She panted, struggling to calm herself, determined not to cry. That would only make her mother angrier. She started to count. After twenty seconds, maybe forty-five, the initial pain would subside, and Cherry wouldn't need to cry.

Voices lingered above her head and Cherry looked up to the sky. Uncle Viet and her mother stood on the balcony. She couldn't hear what they were saying, their voices were too soft, but that didn't matter. She could see their faces. He was clearly trying to calm her down. When Cherry began walking again, her shiny shoes clicking along the sidewalk, their chattering stopped. They peered down the balcony. Knowing what they wanted, not wanting to be pinched, Cherry pretended not to see them.

1983

Cuc Bui
Paris, France

. . . It must have been the cooking and how loud we are. Not that they weren't loud with their wooden shoes and constant dinner parties. But we won out, eventually. They moved away. I thank God they did. Eight people living in Yen's apartment? We could do it in Saigon, but that was because we felt comfortable leaving it whenever we wanted. We were always doing things in the city, going places to eat, visiting friends. It was our country. In France, all we want to do is stay inside. It is so cold here.

When the neighbors moved out, first upstairs, then downstairs, the land-lord suspected we wanted the apartment house for ourselves. He tried to raise the price of rent on the downstairs unit, but Yen talked to him. Doesn't he remember my son is a lawyer? We are fortunate to have the whole building to ourselves. While we can pretend this is our own house, we know the truth. We do not own it. We are only tenants.

When I was a student, I dreamed of living in Paris. Our teachers in French school spoke of the historical architecture, the meticulous gardens, the wide pedestrian boulevards. Vietnam's imitations in Hanoi and Saigon could not compete. But to tell you my true feelings? What I can never admit to the children? I am too homesick to appreciate the original inspirations. We

walk down the Champs-Élysées or through Les Tuileries, and I long for Sai-gon. I do not care that it contained cheap replicas. It was home. . . .

Hung Truong
Paris, France

◛ *Chapter Three*

HOA

PARIS, FRANCE, 1985

C AM AND XUAN KNELT IN THE CORNER OF THE STAIR-
well, dusting up their good church clothes. They whispered to
each other, giggling. Xuan scraped a stick against the painted wall.

"What are you doing?" Hoa asked. The children peered over their
shoulders. They didn't realize their grandmother had been watching.
Hoa liked to prop the front door open while cooking to let out some of
the oily smoke.

"We're looking for Jerry," Xuan said.

"I haven't seen him all week," Cam said. "Do you know where he is?"

Hoa certainly did. She'd tossed the dirty rat by his tail into her garbage sack a few nights ago. Phung's poison had finally worked on the
disgusting creature, but not before the rat had inflated nearly twice its
size gorging on fruits and crumbs left on the kitchen counter and dining table. Rats had disease, especially those in the city. Hoa found it on

the kitchen floor, barely alive, and after giving it a good bash with her bamboo broom, Jerry finally expired.

"He must have left," Hoa said. "Gone to a new home where he'll get more food." She noticed the children's pale, bare feet. "Where are your socks and shoes?"

They grudgingly scrambled from the floor. Xuan balanced the stick against the corner of the wall.

"We're leaving soon," Hoa said. "You might as well put your coats on, too."

Cam climbed the stairs to her parents' apartment on the top floor, but Xuan lingered, wandering into Hoa's apartment. Hoa turned off the stove and examined her freshly deep-fried shrimp toasts. The toppings were vibrant speckled pink and the edges felt crunchy. After the toasts completely cooled, she'd wrap them in aluminum foil. Hoa turned to find Xuan standing in front of her, pulling at his starched shirt collar.

"Can I stay here?" Xuan asked. "Mom said not to come up for a while."

After Hoa nodded, Xuan brushed past her to the living room and turned on the television. Yen and Trinh were arguing again. She could hear their muffled words through the building's flimsy walls and floors. Xuan twisted the volume on the television louder, his face lit with the bright cartoon characters on the screen.

"Don't sit so closely," Hoa reminded him. "Your eyes will go bad."

Xuan tucked a pillow under his arm and snuggled into the frayed green sofa, which used to belong in his apartment upstairs. Yen and Trinh had bought a new couch last year, so Hung and Hoa inherited their old one. Most of their apartment's furnishings consisted of castoffs from their children or donated items from the Bourdains, their sponsor family. Yen had offered several times to buy his parents a bigger bed to replace the lumpy twins they currently used. But Hung and Hoa preferred their separate sleeping arrangement. They kept such different hours—Hung reading late at night, Hoa getting up early to prepare the family meals—that it was more convenient. They also didn't want Yen to commit to another major expense. He was, after all, still supporting his parents—taking care of their rent, utility, and food bills.

Hoa had decorated the apartment with Asian grocery-store calendars and Vietnamese music posters she collected from her shopping trips to the 13th Arrondissement. Color photographs of Ha Long Bay, Nha Trang, and Da Lat brightened the hallway. When she could afford to, Hoa wanted to frame the pictures instead of tacking them up with pushpins. The wood floors were covered with Oriental rugs the Bourdains had given as Christmas gifts over the years. Though Hoa wouldn't have personally chosen those patterns, she appreciated their function. Wood floors stung her feet at night.

"Hoa," Hung called from the bedroom.

Hung stood behind the closet door in front of their only full-length mirror, wearing his dress shirt and slacks, a navy-blue tie dangling around his slightly hunched shoulders. She stepped in front of him, reaching for both ends of the tie.

His eyes shifted up then down as she worked. "Didn't you wear that last week?" he asked.

"I wore the dark-green *ao dai* last Sunday. This one is light green. The pattern is also different."

"Well, they look very similar."

Hoa tugged on the knot, harder than usual, but Hung didn't notice. The man who insisted that his wife not dress like a European, with knee-length skirts and bare arms, now felt dissatisfied with the clothes he did permit her to wear. Hung didn't even enjoy the idea of his daughters-in-law dressing in Western clothes, until Yen convinced him it would be more practical for them. Her husband finally agreed, but held on to Hoa's dress code as his final condition.

Hung sniffed a few times, turning his head to the door. "What's that smell?"

"I made shrimp toasts," Hoa said.

"We just had breakfast."

"They're for the Bourdains." Hoa frowned at his glare. "What? I told you last night I was going to make them."

"Where are we going to put them during Mass?" Hung asked. "They'll stink up the entire church."

"I'm going to wrap them. They won't smell. And Mr. Bourdain enjoyed them so much last time—"

"He was being polite, woman. Of course he had to say something kind."

Hoa did not agree. She'd watched Michel Bourdain gobble up four pieces the last time she brought the Vietnamese appetizer to his home. She knew when people liked her food and when they didn't. But she knew better than to argue about this with Hung.

"I don't want to go to their house empty-handed," Hoa said. "We go to their home for brunch every month. It's only polite that we bring them something as well."

"You take care of it then," Hung muttered. "I want nothing to do with it." He waved her hands away, straightening the tie himself as he walked out of the bedroom.

Hoa gathered the rejected ties Hung had strewn all over his bed and replaced them in the closet. She picked up his pajamas and socks from the floor and dropped them in the wicker laundry hamper. Hesitating in front of the mirror, she adjusted her dress, which admittedly, was getting a bit worn, especially at the sleeves. Would the Bourdains mistake this dress for the one last week? She could change her white silk pants for her black ones, but she didn't have any thermal pants to match with the black. And she didn't like the idea of going out on a brisk autumn morning without her thermals.

The cold. Her first impression of France when they arrived five years ago. Yen, the Bourdains, and other members of the Catholic charity had greeted them at the airport gate, their faces as bright and animated as the hand-colored banners and balloons they held. But Hoa didn't pay attention to these things, or the dizzying, frantic French they sang to the jet-lagged, exhausted travelers. Instead, she focused on the puffy coats their bodies were stuffed in.

When Hoa hugged her beloved Yen, who was chubbier than she remembered, pinching his arms and shoulders for proof, she pulled back, briefly lifted his coat lapel, and dropped it, stunned. How many pounds must it weigh? Then she looked at their feet, encased in thick, rubber boots, planted solidly on the cold, shiny linoleum. Hoa examined her own paper-thin clothes and sandals. She remembered the woolen hats in her suitcase, the ones she traded for back in Pulau, but they were buried too deep to dig out on the floor of the airport.

No one else seemed to be as distracted by the weather as Hoa. Hung burst into tears as he clung to Yen. With his mother's prodding, Xuan kissed his newfound father, but quickly hid behind Trinh's legs when the Bourdains starting snapping pictures. Later, when Hoa would look through the photographs, she'd only see how her teeth seemed to be chattering through her unnatural smile.

Outside, someone from the charity tried to shield Hoa from the wind as they pushed the Truong family into a cab, but Hoa still felt it, the slick air snaking through her inadequate garments, sliding up her thin back and wrapping around her bones. During the cab ride through Paris, she rubbed her face against Hung's shoulder for warmth. Would she be able to walk in such European coats and boots? She was not as strong as she used to be.

Yen's apartment was located in the 5th Arrondissement, where he said some Vietnamese immigrants had lived for years. Many of the newer refugees had settled in the 13th Arrondissement, farther from the city center.

"It's ugly over there," Yen said, his Vietnamese tinged with French so Hoa had to listen carefully. "Ugly, but cheap. Tall square buildings, like in the Soviet Union. I think they'll leave eventually. Move somewhere nicer when they can save up money."

Hoa only had to assume the someplace nicer was Yen's neighborhood, which was pretty tree-lined streets dotted with three- and four-story apartment buildings. Some of the houses had small iron-fenced gardens in front, brown and skeletal this time of year, but Yen's did not. Instead, the front space contained a metal bench and an empty stone washbasin, which Yen explained was a birdbath. They could fill it with water for the sparrows in the summer. Hoa didn't understand why people would want to attract bird droppings, remnants of which littered the ground along the building's front door.

His apartment stairwell was narrow, so only one person could fit going up or down. They struggled to squeeze their belongings up the stairs. The stairwell smelled of dust, stale perfume, and incense.

Hoa's body relaxed as the apartment's heat enveloped her limbs. She wiggled her toes, feeling them again. The bright-yellow walls were bare except for a small metal crucifix hanging by the window. The living room had a dark-green sofa, an unvarnished wood dining room set for four, several folding chairs, an inflatable mattress, and a pile of blankets and pillows in the corner. Down the hall, they could see a small bedroom with a twin bed and a fire escape outside its window. Another bedroom with a few cardboard boxes on the floor gave access to the single bathroom. The kitchen, with one broken burner, could fit only two people in its floorspace. Yen admitted he rarely cooked at home.

"It's yours, Mother," Yen said, swinging his arms around her, a hug so deliciously warm. "I was saving it for you."

At the church, the Truongs took up an entire pew, which Hoa didn't mind at all. She hated shaking hands with strangers during the peace greetings halfway through the Mass. Some strangers, who perceived her as such a cute, old Oriental lady, actually had the gall to hug and kiss her twice on the cheeks. She realized it was French custom, but Hoa was not French. One old woman, probably older than Hoa, once patted her head. Had Hoa not been in a church, she could have reacted more appropriately.

Several rows ahead, the Bourdains sat in their usual pew. It wasn't officially reserved for them, but no one ever seemed to sit in their spot, even in summers when the Bourdains were away at their vacation home in the south. During the sermons, which Hoa couldn't understand anyway because the priest spoke so quickly, she'd observe the backs of the Bourdains' heads. The father, Michel, was completely bald, not a single hair on him. Hoa had previously only seen Buddhist monks that hairless, but his was God-given. And poor Petit Michel, still a child, Hoa could already tell by the inordinately large forehead what would happen to his hair. Émilie's hair, curly and shorn close against her head, as usual, looked impeccable. Hoa never thought short hair looked good on a woman until she met Madame Bourdain.

At the end of Mass, Hoa usually stayed behind to offer a prayer to Mary while the rest of the family waited outside with the Bourdains and chatted with parishioners. Hoa enjoyed the solitary five minutes alone in the cavernous church. It meant more to her than the entire Mass, her time alone with the Lord. But lately, Trinh had been joining her, sometimes even praying longer than Hoa. She couldn't understand it. Trinh hadn't even been born Catholic. She was baptized as an afterthought during Xuan's ceremony, more to please her new family than to answer a true conversion of faith.

"She's more devoted to God," Yen had said, after Hoa sourly noted that Trinh took almost twenty minutes after one Mass for extra prayer. "How can you not like that?"

Hoa had no problem with her new commitment to Catholicism, it was the way Trinh chose to express this recent dedication. Praying loudly enough for everyone in their pew to hear her. Nodding and responding to the readings, as if the priest were speaking only to her. Weeping during the sacrament of Eucharist. At their last visit for reconciliation, Trinh took nearly an hour in the confessional so the priest was unable to meet with others waiting in line behind them.

Hoa quietly gave her prayers, closing her eyes, concentrating on her words. She humbly requested the usual: safety and happiness for all of her sons, their wives, and her grandchildren, especially for Sanh's family whom she could not watch over; the patience to endure the hardships to come; and warmer weather in Paris. After crossing herself, she slowly opened her eyes and tilted her head to the left.

Trinh's head was still bowed, nearly touching her knees, her fingers clasped together, choking her white rosary in prayer. Hoa stood.

"We'll be waiting for you outside," she said as she gathered her handbag and coat. Hoa did not wait for or expect a response.

The first week the Truongs arrived in France, they barely left the apartment. Yen had saved two weeks of vacation leave for his family's arrival. During the days, the women cooked meals from the ingredients they could find from the Chinese grocery stores, while the men sat in the living room and exchanged stories. At night, the wives slept in the bedrooms with the children, and the men stayed up late playing *tien len* at the dining room table.

Hoa didn't realize until Ngoan brought it up at the grocery store that Trinh and Yen had yet to sleep in the same room together. Since arriving in France, Ngoan had attempted to make a fresh start with Trinh. With Tuyet gone, they now only had each other as sisters.

"We can take a walk around the neighborhood if you and Yen want some time alone," Ngoan said, as they rummaged the shelves looking for rice flour and cornstarch to make *banh cuon*. Hoa, a few steps ahead of them in the aisle, examined the contents of a can of asparagus.

"A walk sounds nice," Trinh murmured. "We should all go."

Ngoan shook her head, believing Trinh didn't understand. "But don't you and Yen want to be alone?"

Trinh fussed with her mittens, a pair she borrowed from Yen, too large for her bony fingers. "There is no rush. We now have all the time we could possibly want."

Several weeks later, Yen took Trinh to a weekend retreat in Provence with some of the senior associates from his law firm. Yen confirmed that only spouses were invited, so Xuan would be staying home with the family. Early Sunday morning, they returned while Hoa was feeding the grandchildren breakfast. Trinh immediately walked toward Xuan, knelt in front of him, and clutched him in an embrace more appropriate for a year's absence than only two nights.

"Did you miss us?" Trinh asked, practically smothering the poor child, her voice cracking with sobs. "Did you miss me?"

And though Hoa knew the boy had enjoyed a fine weekend (Phung and Ngoan had taken the children to a play park a few blocks away where the children swung on the swings and scrambled on the jungle gym for hours), Xuan nodded, imitating his mother's tears, and asked her never to go away again.

*   *   *

The Bourdains lived in the 16th Arrondissement in a recently reno-vated estate surrounded by lawns and gardens larger than the structure itself. It was rumored the grounds were once owned by the mistress of a French aristocrat.

When the Truongs had their first brunch at the Bourdains' new home, Hoa admired the pillar structures and oval windows on the front veranda and told Émilie that they reminded her of their old house in Nha Trang.

"Really?" Émilie asked, her forehead creasing in disbelief. "How is that?"

A French architect who worked with Hung's grandfather had de-signed their home in Nha Trang, but Hoa couldn't find the words in the language to explain. How to say architect? Pillars? After a few confus-ing phrases that only seemed to deepen Émilie's forehead creases, Hoa turned to Hung to translate.

Hung shot her a scornful glance once he realized what she wanted him to say. "Why do you need to talk about that old house? We haven't seen it in years."

And without waiting for her response, Hung turned to Émilie and smiled. "My wife is getting sentimental, Madame Bourdain, please for-give her. Your house, of course, is the most beautiful house we've ever seen."

Hoa may have had trouble conjuring the phrases, but had no difficulty understanding Hung's affected French. He wouldn't even look at her again, too busy folding lavender chicken into his mouth. That home had been his grandfather's greatest achievement. Hung used to recall the details of the house room by room, telling his grandchildren that one day they'd go back and see it for themselves.

Usually, sponsors cut ties once the refugee families settled into their new homes and jobs. But the Bourdains refused to fade from their lives. They seemed genuinely disappointed when one of the Truongs was un-able to attend monthly brunch. Though they spent every summer on the Riviera, the Bourdains always called upon their return to the city, asking to arrange their next meeting.

Hoa was sure the Bourdains never meant to disrespect or disparage the Truongs in any way. They'd done so much for their family. But that, Hoa realized, was part of the problem. They owed their immigration from Pulau, adjustment to Paris, the support of their parish, and the arrangement of Phung's first job to the Bourdains. There were only so many times a person could express gratitude before the words became grating to say and hear.

The Bourdains had met Yen during his first year in France at an Easter luncheon celebration hosted by their parish. Michel was interested that Yen was from Vietnam, since his father had been a naval officer stationed in the former French colony. When they learned Yen was struggling to arrange for his family's immigration, the Bourdains volunteered to assume responsibility as sponsors.

"Our ancestors caused such injustice to your people," Michel had said at the Truongs' welcome party during a toast to a crowd of his closest friends and business associates. "We never should have left you with the Communists. We abandoned you then, but we will not do it again. We are honored to help the people of our former colony."

Hoa didn't understand the toast until after the party, when Phung explained it at home. Ngoan was seething: "Do they think we enjoyed their control?" she asked. "Do they think they were so much better than the Communists, the Americans?"

Hung sternly told his family they needed to forget their countries' past differences. "France may once have been our colonizer, but now it is our grandchildren's country," he said. "We need to respect their new home."

Since Hoa ate quickly, she waited for others to catch up by noting any changes in her brunch companions. The men looked relatively the same, only healthier with fuller diets and paler because of the country's dearth of sunlight. Ngoan had chopped off her hair the first year they moved to France, finding the bob more practical, and had kept it short ever since. Hoa and Trinh, on the other hand, preserved their long hair. But while Hoa always wrapped hers in a clean, discreet bun, Trinh never pulled hers back, allowing it to swing past her waist, no matter how tangled and wiry it became in the summertime.

During the first year, the men—who'd attended French school in Vietnam—often engaged in conversation with the Bourdains, while the women, freshly enrolled in language classes at the Vietnamese Community Center, would smile and nod their heads. By the time Hoa and her daughters-in-law had learned enough to understand most of what they were saying, it seemed too late to enter the dialogue. Their end of the table was hardly acknowledged. Only Trinh was bold enough to occasionally enter their discussion of current events, though often it embarrassed Hoa and the other Truongs, especially if Trinh misunderstood the conversation and said something of little logic.

"The Africans ought to live in Paris rather than La Courneuve," Trinh announced in the middle of the men's discussion of recent skirmishes between Algerian youths and the police. "If they lived in a better neighborhood, they would get along with the rest of society."

"Yen should control his wife's tongue a little better," Hung privately grumbled to Hoa. "She sounds like a foolish woman, offering opinions on things she knows nothing about."

"Madame Bourdain talks all the time," Hoa said.

"Émilie has an education. She earned her privilege to speak."

While Trinh followed her husband's advice to stay quiet on political matters at the brunch table, she found other topics that interested her. During one Sunday sermon, the priest spoke of miracles. For the next few weeks, Trinh would bring home books from the local library on Catholic miracles, especially Lourdes, the sacred Virgin Mary sanctuary located in southwestern France, only a train ride away. At brunch that afternoon, Trinh asked the Bourdains if they'd ever visited the sanctuary.

"It's been years," Émilie admitted, as she signaled for the housekeeper to bring out more coffee. "Petit Michel wasn't even born yet. It is beautiful. I hear they've remodeled and restructured the baths so that it is available to everyone."

"Everyone?" Trinh repeated. "Not only those with physical handicaps?"

"Yes," Émilie said. "Our friends the Martins went last year and took baths."

"Why do people need to take baths in Lourdes?" Cam asked, tugging at Ngoan's sleeve as her mother picked at the uneaten pile of roasted carrots on her plate.

"They're special baths, dear Cam," Émilie said, smiling at the girl. Émilie had a special affection for Cam, since her own daughter, Joan, had died as an infant. "The water was blessed by the Virgin Mary many years ago when she came down to visit three special children. Now, people go to Lourdes to bathe in that spring. Miracles happen in those waters. Those whose legs were crippled now walk. The blind can see."

"The miracles don't happen all the time," Michel said, shifting in his seat. He exchanged a glance with Yen, who sheepishly smiled back.

"No," Émilie conceded. "It's not only the water. You need to have faith when you bathe in it."

"It sounds like salvation," Trinh said, whose eyes had never left Émilie. "We should go. Yen?" She tapped her husband's hand with her linen napkin. "We should go to Lourdes."

Yen nodded. "Sure," he said. "Maybe in the summer."

Trinh frowned. "But summer already ended."

Émilie shook her head. "It's overcrowded in the summers anyway. The lines can last all day. We could go next month, before the pilgrimage season ends. Michel's office owns a time-share nearby where we can stay."

"That's very kind of you," Hung spoke up. "But it's too generous."

"No, it isn't," Michel said. "It sounds like a wonderful idea. Émilie and I have wanted to go back for years and this is a perfect opportunity. Let us take you, our treat."

The Truongs all looked to the patriarch, waiting for his reaction. Hung took a long time wiping his mouth with his linen napkin. "It's a very kind offer," he finally said, standing. "Thank you for such a tremendous gift."

The men shook hands, Michel throwing over his other arm to pat Hung on the back. The gesture reminded Hoa of dinners they hosted in Nha Trang, friends and colleagues from Hung's hotel who needed favors from her husband. Now Hung was on the other side of the handshake.

The children finished their plates and quickly excused themselves to play in Petit Michel's room. As the men were about to step out for cigars Michel had recently purchased in Spain, Hoa suddenly remembered what was in her handbag.

"Excuse me, I brought a little treat," Hoa said. She picked up her purse from the floor and opened it on her lap. The aluminum foil felt cool as she struggled to unwrap the shrimp toasts onto her soiled plate. She stood and nodded as she presented the plate in front of Monsieur and Madame Bourdain. "They may be a little cold," she said apologetically.

"Thank you, Madame Truong," Michel said, his blond mustache widening with his smile. "You are so kind. But I'm afraid I must pass. The last time I ate them, I did feel a little ill."

"A little!" Émilie said, looking both aghast and amused. "He complained of it all week. You have to remember our French stomachs, Madame Truong. They can't handle the spices and oils that your people use all the time."

Hoa's eyes dropped as Michel handed the plate back to her. Twelve cold shrimp toasts, misshapen by their travels in her handbag. She knew what Hung's face wanted to tell her. She did not need to acknowledge it.

Another hand reached over and grabbed one of the shrimp toasts from Hoa's plate. "I'll have one," Ngoan said. "I can never pass up something Mother has made."

Hoa smiled, her shoulders relaxing. She began rewrapping the rest, when Ngoan put out her hand to stop her.

"Leave them out," Ngoan said, not caring that she spoke Vietnamese at the table. "It's the best thing I've had all day."

Although Hoa didn't work like Yen and Phung, or volunteer at the community center like Hung, she kept herself busy and productive. In the mornings, she and Ngoan made breakfast in her ground-floor apartment. Hoa would prepare for Hung and Phung thermoses of crabmeat soup or baguette sandwiches for lunch, while Yen usually ate at cafés with his colleagues. The children were fed and Trinh walked them to the elementary school eight blocks away.

Ngoan still worried about allowing Trinh to take the children to school. Trinh had the habit of getting lost on the metro, and she hadn't really improved in the last five years. But Hoa assured Ngoan they'd be fine, since no public transportation was involved.

"Trinh needs to feel like she's contributing," Hoa reminded her. "She doesn't like to cook or clean. This is what she can do."

"Anyone can walk," Ngoan grumbled.

"Exactly," Hoa said. "Even Trinh." So far, she hadn't managed to lose the children.

After the house was empty, Hoa proceeded to clean each apartment. None of the family bothered to lock the doors inside the building anymore. Hoa liked this part of the day, organizing her children and grandchildren's belongings, holding and dusting the items that mattered to them. She felt hopeful when she found a technical college brochure on Phung's dresser and disappointment when she later emptied the crumpled paper out of the wastebasket. She knew when Cam had tired of her coloring books and had moved on to reading chapter novels. Or when Xuan outgrew his fear of murderers lurking on the fire escape and dismantled the barrier of pillows and stuffed animals along his bedroom windowsill.

The only area Hoa avoided was Hung's desk in the spare room. He specifically requested she not come near it when he was away from the apartment. He had been the same way about his study in their house in Nha Trang, which irritated Hoa. The entire study, which was a pleasant space—good windows with afternoon sun—would collect dust and he wouldn't care. Hung and Hoa shared the spare room, half of it his office, the other half her knitting and prayer space. Though Hung hardly kept anything on the desktop, Hoa couldn't help but linger over that corner of the room. The items of significance, his journals and letter correspondence, which he'd carried over on the boat and protected all those months in the refugee camp, lay secure in one of the three drawers on the right side.

There was no padlock. Hoa easily could have read all she pleased. But she knew that Hung would find out. It had happened once, early in their marriage. Hoa did not ever wish to incur that level of wrath again.

Still, she felt free to privately speculate about the journals and letters. She assumed they contained information about his business dealings, correspondence with the educated elite of Nha Trang, scholars that included both French and Vietnamese women. It no longer bothered Hoa that Hung once kept mistresses. When she first learned of these poets and artists, she had been pregnant with Yen. Hung's older sister assured her that continuing to bear sons secured Hoa's status as his only wife. Now, Hung was frankly too old and tired to indulge in such frivolous relations, but it irritated her that he kept such tangible evidence of his indiscretions. Sometimes, she walked past the room and saw him reading these letters. While she was busy cooking and cleaning for their family, he was reminiscing about his shameful past.

Hoa truly didn't want to know any more of Hung's thoughts. She knew enough of his stubbornness, his denigrating opinions; to read them in print would give them more significance than they deserved. He never hid his disappointment concerning the kind of wife she turned out to be. *If my father only knew before he died,* Hung would say to her on difficult days, *he would have driven that matchmaker out of Nha Trang.*

While Hoa cleaned, Ngoan and Trinh left to pick up groceries for dinner. Ngoan had favorite grocers spanning the arrondissements, though she preferred the open-air markets, which reminded her of Saigon. She had grown up on a sugar plantation and still relished buying the freshest produce available. Hoa usually stayed home. She did not like to go out unless the rest of her family was with her.

When Hoa did leave the house, she preferred remaining either in the 5th or 13th Arrondissement, where other Chinese and Vietnamese immigrants frequented. She remembered when Yen took the family to the Eiffel Tower for the first time. On the balcony, a small blond boy, cheeks sticky with chocolate ice cream, stared open-mouthed at Hoa. When Hoa grinned at the child—she was only trying to be nice—his face crumbled and he burst into tears. After Yen exchanged words, apologies, and much laughter with the boy's father, he finally explained the confusion to his mother.

"He was scared of your teeth," Yen said. "He's never seen a woman with black teeth before."

Just a little boy. He did not know and probably would not care how many hours Hoa's mother spent soaking those teeth with red sticklac and betel nuts so they would look that dark. It was fashionable back then to have lacquered teeth, *the darkest in all of Vietnam,* her mother would proudly say. With a lacquered smile, suitors knew you came from a respectable family. During their matchmaking ceremony, Hung complimented her teeth; one of the few compliments he ever gave her. Since the Eiffel Tower, Hoa tried to smile as little as possible. When her children weren't around to help and she was forced to speak with native Parisians, she kept her head low, lips close together. No one had cried or laughed at her since.

When the girls returned from the markets, Hoa would prepare a simple lunch of leftovers. Afterward, if it were either a Monday or Thursday, she'd sit at the dining room table and write letters to Sanh and his family. She used three sheets of paper: one for Sanh, one for Lum, and one for Cherry. For Tuyet, she included her name on Sanh's letter, but Hoa rarely thought of her daughter-in-law. She spent most of her time on Cherry's letter, the granddaughter she'd only seen three times. Hoa wondered if the five-year-old girl could tell how much she was loved by the words Hoa carefully printed on the paper. Tuyet's mother and family had recently arrived in America, and Hoa was ashamed to admit she worried what the Vo relatives would tell the grandchildren. She prayed that her son would have enough sense to protect the children from such unpleasant memories.

On the other days, Hoa crocheted or knitted, skills she picked up from another grandmother at the community center. She embraced the new hobby, appreciating its substantial results: sweaters, scarves, and hats, but mostly blankets, one for every Truong. When she noticed during morning cleanups that one was fraying, she'd begin another. There was always a blanket waiting to be replaced.

At three o'clock, Trinh left to pick up the children from school and Ngoan and Hoa started dinner preparations. The children and men came home. The house once again bulged with her sons' stories and Cam and Xuan's laughter. Full of food and exhausted from the day's activities, her family slept, the walls and ceilings leaking their snores, mumbles, and bed creaks, and Hoa felt secure knowing she could hear every sound.

* * *

A few days after brunch, Émilie called to say that Michel had reserved a time-share for the last weekend in October. Lourdes was a five-and-a-half-hour train ride away on the TGV. They would leave on Friday.

Although Phung and Ngoan were staying home, Cam begged to go to Lourdes with the rest of the Truongs.

"Why do you care about Lourdes?" Ngoan asked. "You don't even like going to Mass in your own neighborhood." But she eventually agreed to allow Hoa to watch Cam over the holiday.

One morning, Hoa noticed during her cleanup that Yen's desk in his dining room had been cleared. In the kitchen next to the wastebasket, Hoa found his lamp, desk clock, assorted files and folders, pens, and calendar carelessly tossed into a stained fruit carton.

After staring at it for a moment, Hoa emptied out the fruit carton and restored Yen's belongings to the desk, trying to recall as best she could their original arrangement. The next day, Hoa found the desk cleared again, this time with Yen's things thrown in the corner of his bedroom.

"Trinh needs to use the desk for prayer space," Yen explained to his mother that evening. "She wants to buy a Virgin Mary statue when we go to Lourdes and she is trying to decide where it should sit."

Hung and Hoa's apartment contained the only prayer altar in the house. Yen had a metal cross on the wall and Phung and Ngoan kept a small portrait of Jesus on a coffee end table. Since the church was close to their home, there wasn't even a need for rosary prayer in the apartment.

"Don't you need a desk for your work?" Hoa asked.

"I'll get another desk."

"This is ridiculous. We don't leave for two more weeks. Can't you use your desk until then?"

"Trinh really wants the space now."

Hoa stared at Yen. Over the years, she'd tried her best to stay out of her sons' relations with their wives. She loved them and respected their judgments, grateful they hadn't inherited their father's methods in marriage. But they'd gone too far to the other side. She couldn't understand how all three of her sons could have such weak dispositions to their wives, especially smart, industrious Yen.

"Mother," Yen said. "I appreciate your concern, but Trinh can have the desk. I want her to have it. She's endured enough because of me."

It wasn't until the next morning that Hoa understood. After breakfast, Hoa watched from the window as Trinh led the children across the street. On the sidewalk, Trinh and the children appeared to be engulfed by French businessmen and women hustling past them on their way to work. With Cam walking slightly ahead, it looked for a moment like Trinh and Xuan were alone in the crowd. No matter how much Yen tried to fill their future with desks and trips to Lourdes, Trinh and Xuan would always remember and would serve as a reminder of those five years when he wasn't there.

Despite the frosty bite in the air, the baths at Lourdes attracted lines that looped throughout the grotto. At the basilica's central kiosk, Yen read that the average wait time for general entrance was three hours.

"That's too long for me," Michel said. "Besides, I only came for the procession."

The line for parents and children was significantly shorter, promising only a one-hour wait for each child and accompanying parent. While the men went into town for some coffee and reading, the women and children went to the baths.

Shuffling along in line, Hoa yawned. She was still recovering from the train ride from Paris. Hoa disliked traveling. After half a decade of living in France, Hoa had little interest in traveling beyond Paris. What was the difference? The French were French. If Paris was the largest and most diverse city in the country, she saw no reason to subject herself to anything outside its city limits.

But this, she recognized, as she observed the small children in wheelchairs inching ahead in line with them, was worth the hassle. The morning sun had stained the clouds pink across the snow-capped Pyrenees Mountains, adding temporary warmth to the gray sky. Hoa had never been to a sanctuary before. The Virgin Mary didn't appear in too many places in the world and it was a lucky coincidence she had in France.

While the children happily chatted with a blind boy from Switzerland, Trinh related to Émilie all the facts she learned from her well-worn Lourdes guidebook, which detailed every apparition Saint Bernadette experienced. It was a poor, sick French girl's relentless loyalty and vision that had transformed Lourdes into the most visited pilgrimage shrine for Catholics and Christians to this day.

"She didn't care what others thought of her," Trinh said, "even when the priests were threatening to silence her. She believed the Blessed Virgin was speaking through her."

"I wish I had more faith when I was younger," Émilie said. "It could have saved Joan."

"Didn't your daughter die of leukemia?" Trinh asked.

"We trusted science," Émilie said. "We weren't attending church every Sunday, because we were at the hospital. All the drugs they forced into our daughter killed her, and not peacefully. The doctors took our little girl and squeezed every ounce of happiness out of her. All I remember is her crying on the day she died."

"We can be saved here," Trinh said. "Our children and ourselves."

Émilie smiled. "But Trinh, you're healthy."

Trinh leaned forward. "You can't see it," she whispered. "But inside, I'm broken. I've come here to heal myself, so the Holy Mary can give me back my virginity and I can be whole again."

Émilie stepped back, smiling nervously at Trinh. Hoa didn't blame her. Leave it to Trinh to embarrass herself once again, even when Madame Bourdain was showing such compassion by confiding in her. As Émilie called for Petit Michel so she could rebutton his peacoat, Hoa dug her fingers into Trinh's arm.

"Be careful what you say," she fiercely whispered to Trinh in Vietnamese. "They don't always understand your sense of humor."

Trinh's expression didn't change as she smoothly pried Hoa's hand off of her. "I wasn't being funny, Mother Truong," she said. "Not at all."

After an hour, the women and children stepped into a bare dressing room with a small bench in the corner. Hoa offered to go last. She didn't want to disrobe until the rest had all gone into their cubicles. Cam flashed her grandmother a mischievous smile as she skipped behind the curtain, unabashed about her nakedness. Hoa disliked undressing in front of anyone. She clung her *ao dai* to her chest for as long as she could before a volunteer gestured that her bath was ready.

She walked into a cubicle with stone walls and no windows. The large rectangular bathtub was filled with slightly gray water. She clung to the volunteers' arms as they slowly coaxed her arms to relax, to release. Hoa closed her eyes as the cold spring water swathed her legs, back, breasts, shoulders. She took a small breath as her head immersed. Her eyes opened. The volunteers blurred, transforming into celestial spirits from underneath the water. A chill tickled down her spine and she wondered if this was what a miracle felt like. This was a remarkably different cold, one she found quite welcoming.

Hoa didn't know who to confide in. She was afraid to bring this up to Yen, who looked so happy at dinner, eagerly reciprocating all of Trinh's hugs and kisses. If Phung or Ngoan were here, she would have consulted them first. Hung remained her only option.

"I think something is wrong with Trinh," Hoa announced to her husband. Outside the sanctuary, countless rows of gift shops unfolded along winding roads, like unending legs of a spider. The Bourdains and Yen's family were among the many tourists milling through the shops, perusing identical assortments of prayer cards, rosaries, apparition medals, and Mary statuettes. Hung and Hoa rested on a bench near the entrance of the basilica.

"She's sick?" Hung asked, his eyes squinting as he continued to read his magazine from the dim streetlamp light.

"No," Hoa said. "Not like a cold. Like in her head. She's not right." Hoa recounted in detail what she witnessed at the baths.

"So she's crazy," Hung said, turning the page. "Haven't we always known this?"

"Maybe," Hoa admitted. "She hid it better before. But I think she's getting worse. Yen is so busy with work. I worry about Xuan."

"At least she's crazy about religion. She could be crazy in more destructive ways. Unless she becomes physically dangerous, I've told Yen to encourage her religious path. What harm can come from more faith?"

Hoa sat back. "Yen has talked to you about this?"

"Of course," Hung said. "I'm his father. He came to me for advice on how to deal with his wife. Why?" Even in the night, Hung's smirk was obvious. "Were you expecting him to ask you?"

The children ran up to Hung and Hoa, showing off their new glow-in-the-dark rosaries. Yen and Trinh followed behind carrying two shopping bags full of plastic water bottles shaped in the image of the Virgin Mary with screw-on caps that looked like blue crowns. Trinh said pilgrims filled them with holy water from the taps in the sanctuary's Mass-abielle Spring.

"Are those for gifts?" Hoa asked.

"They're for us," Trinh said. "So we'll always have miracle water whenever we need it."

At the pilgrimage in the grotto, Hoa realized she'd never been surrounded by so many Catholics. They all held long, white candles and chanted the Ave Maria. At one spectacular view from the hillside, the procession resembled a dazzling, golden snake slithering its way toward the basilica. At the stone archway, Hoa and Xuan stared up at a row of weathered, rusted crutches. There had to be at least twenty of them teetering majestically above, irrefutable proof of the sanctuary's healing power.

"It is a miracle," her grandson murmured, such wonder in his voice, his eyes so full of trust, that Hoa couldn't help but also believe.

Their last morning in Lourdes, Trinh and Xuan returned to the sanctuary to collect more holy water in the Mary bottles and to recite the morning rosary, while the rest of the group relaxed at the château.

"Are you sure you don't want to go, Grandmère?" Xuan asked as he pulled the knitted cap Hoa had made for him over his head.

"I am," Hoa said. "But say a prayer for your grandmère. She is tired from all our activities yesterday."

A few hours after they left, the sleet-gray clouds that had loomed over Lourdes all weekend finally sank to the ground, followed by a drizzle of rain that grew heavy on the roof.

"I expect they'll be coming back soon," Émilie said, peering out the window. "I hope they'll stop to pick up an umbrella."

Hoa occasionally looked up from her crocheting to the clock next to the fireplace. If they didn't come back within the hour, she'd go to their bedroom to pack up their belongings to save them time. They couldn't afford to miss the train.

As Hoa finished her last row of stitching, she heard the front door open. Trinh staggered into the living room, her hair and dark-blue coat clinging to her wet skin, dripping a small puddle onto the marble floor. Her bags of Mary bottles were equally soaked. She dropped them to the floor.

"Is Xuan here?" she asked, her eyes scanning the room.

Hoa put her blanket down. "Wasn't he with you?" she asked.

Trinh's hands came up to her cheeks, then over her mouth. She was shivering. She should have a blanket. Hoa should wrap the blanket she was crocheting and put it over Trinh's shoulders. But instead, Hoa asked again. "Trinh! Where is Xuan?"

Her daughter-in-law's eyes finally focused on Hoa. "I don't know," she whispered.

Hoa shouted for Yen and Hung to come downstairs. Émilie called the authorities. After Hoa told the men what happened, Yen reached for Trinh, gently eased her on the sofa, calmly stroked her shoulders, and asked her to tell him where Xuan went.

The girl bent forward, eyes closed, strips of hair pasted on her cheeks. "He ran away from me. He yelled at me to leave him alone, and then he ran away."

"Where were you?" Yen asked, slipping his hands into hers.

"We were at the grotto," Trinh said. "We were supposed to be praying. I looked for him." She pushed Yen's arms away, burying her face in her hands. "I walked down every street. I looked for him, I yelled his name. He wouldn't answer."

Yen and Michel put on their coats. When Hung started for his coat, Yen told him that he didn't want his father to slip in the rain.

"Stay with Trinh," Yen said to his parents. "Look after my wife."

Émilie went upstairs to check on Petit Michel and Cam, who were playing in his room.

Hung glared at Trinh. "If something happens to Xuan," he muttered in Vietnamese, "your life is over."

"If my baby is hurt," Trinh shouted, "I will take care of that myself." Pulling herself off the sofa, she grabbed her bags from the floor and stumbled out of the room.

Hoa wanted to wait. There was no need to panic yet. Hung stood by the window, glaring at the mountains. After several distracted attempts at crocheting, she looked up at the clock. Only twenty minutes had passed. So much could happen to a little boy in twenty minutes, let alone the hours that had passed when they hadn't known their grandson was lost. She turned to look at her husband.

"I told you," she said, unable to control the shrillness in her voice. "You had to wait until something terrible happened? Well, here it is!"

"Who could have predicted this?" Hung yelled. "If you were so worried, why didn't you go with them? If this is anyone's fault, woman, it is yours."

She couldn't sit in the same room with the man. Hoa stalked through the kitchen, the dining room, the study, the family room, trying to find areas to clean, but the château's housekeeper had already gone through the house earlier that day. Hoa scowled when she realized she could still hear Hung muttering to himself in the living room.

What could have happened? Trinh and Xuan never argued with each other like Ngoan and Cam did. When his parents bickered, Xuan was always quick to take his mother's side, loyal to the parent he'd always known. Whatever happened, Trinh should have been strong enough to control and protect her child. Parents' wishes held value in their old country, but not here.

Though she didn't want to, Hoa felt compelled to check on Trinh. She knocked on their bedroom door, once, twice, and after no answer, opened the door herself. None of the lights were on, but Hoa heard water splashing in the bathroom.

Pressing her hand against the bathroom wall, Hoa flicked the light switch on. In the bathtub, Trinh huddled naked, shivering in a shallow pool of water. Her long, dark hair was plastered over her face like a soggy helmet, her thin lips white. Next to the tub on the tile floor was a pile of empty plastic Mary bottles, their vivid blue crowns unscrewed and tossed aside.

Hoa lunged across the slippery bathroom floor, falling to her knees. Reaching for the hot-water knob, Hoa twisted the fixture as far as she could. Trinh wouldn't stop trembling. She tried draping a towel over her shoulders, but Trinh shrugged it off, letting it fall into the water.

"I don't want that water," Trinh said, batting at the fixture as Hoa used her hands to swirl the waters together. There were goose bumps all over Trinh's slender body. "It's not pure; I want the holy water."

"Foolish girl," Hoa admonished. "You're going to catch pneumonia." Hoa's voice clanged off the bathroom tiles, making her sound angry rather than frightened. "How long have you been sitting here?"

"I need more holy water," Trinh said through chattering teeth as Hoa removed her from the tub and wrapped her in another towel. "There's not enough, I need to go out and get some more."

"Are you trying to save yourself?" Hoa demanded to know. "Or are you trying to die?"

Though Hoa was smaller than Trinh, she managed to maneuver the girl out of the bathroom, her arms wrapped around her waist, and drag her to the bed.

"I can feel their hands on me," Trinh said while Hoa draped the sheets and duvet over her. Trinh struggled, kicking her feet against the linens. "Get them off of me."

"No," Hoa said, wiping away the tears on her cheeks. "They're my hands."

The girl's legs finally relaxed, allowing Hoa to tuck them in the duvet. Trinh's eyes sprang open, but she wasn't looking at anything. "Why did you all leave me?"

"What are you talking about?" Hoa asked. "We didn't leave you. We took you with us."

Trinh shook her head, slowly at first, then harder and harder, until she was rocking the bed, so that Hoa tried to hold her still, for fear that she'd hurt herself.

"You left me," Trinh sobbed, pushing Hoa's arms off. "Every night with those men."

Those men. Those men. The realization of who Trinh was talking about gripped Hoa solidly by the throat. Those men. Hoa knew. She wanted to believe Trinh was wrong, that it wasn't possible, that she was paranoid, but the scattered memories, the whispered innuendo, and Trinh's words came together so forcefully, and settled upon Hoa's skin so thoroughly, that she couldn't deny it. Finally. The Malay guards, who smiled and elbowed one another, their lascivious gestures, when Trinh slumped past them in the mess hall. She never acknowledged them or spoke of them, so Hoa never said anything, either. *Watch over my wife.* Yen had said it so many times they'd forgotten to listen. Hoa pulled the blue-and-yellow duvet up to her face and cried. She did not try to touch Trinh again, but she wanted her daughter-in-law to know she was there, sitting with her, and she knew.

"We watched a man die today," Trinh said, her eyes drifting closed.

"Where?" Hoa asked.

"In the grotto," Trinh said, "right in front of Mary."

Watching Trinh struggle into slumber, Hoa realized what she must have looked like as a child, as vulnerable and innocent as any of her own sons, but now with nightmares they could never imagine. When Trinh had finally fallen asleep, Hoa wiped her face, slipped off the bed, and walked into the bathroom.

The water in the bathtub was still running. She twisted it off. Hoa sat on the toilet and watched the water, both holy and ordinary, swirl down the drain, on its way to the sewers.

Her reflection in the mirror was unforgiving. The bright, pale lights along the bathroom's low ceiling seemed to pry open every wrinkle and liver spot on her face, exposing Hoa as a meaner, uglier version of herself. She was only fifty-seven years old. Why did she look so much older?

Her eyes wandered to the Mary bottles still scattered on the floor. She knelt down, gathering the bottles into her arms, ready to drop them in the wastebasket when she spotted the sleeping Trinh on the bed. If they left for Paris this afternoon, they wouldn't have time to stop at the grotto for more holy water.

Hung appeared at the bathroom door. He glanced at the sleeping Trinh and then at Hoa, who unflinchingly stared back at him.

"Yen called," Hung said. "Xuan slipped and sprained his ankle. He's fine. They'll be back in an hour." His head nodded in Trinh's direction. "What happened to her?"

"Nothing," Hoa said. "Leave her alone."

After he left, Hoa looked down at the bottles collected around her chest. She spotted something behind the wastebasket. Gently dropping the bottles on the toilet seat, she crawled across the floor. It was a Mary bottle still full of holy water. It had probably fallen there, a forgotten casualty of Trinh's frenzy. Hoa carefully held it in her hands.

On the tile floor, Hoa lined up the empty Mary bottles so they were all standing upright. Holding the full bottle, she unscrewed the blue crown cap, and poured a small drop into each one, until every Mary had her own portion of holy water. She then placed one of the bottles under the sink faucet, filled it to the brim with tap water, and screwed on the blue crown cap. Hoa repeated this for every bottle.

After she was finished, Hoa sat on the bed next to Trinh, holding one of the Mary bottles, scrutinizing it. As she traced the Virgin Mother's serene, plastic face with the pads of her thumbs, Hoa realized Trinh would never be able to tell. Her hands trailed Mary's long robes and her folded reverent hands. It was only water.

Trinh's head lolled over on the pillow, her eyes blinking open. After Hoa told her that the men had found Xuan, Trinh's face crumpled up. Her shoulders shook with new tears. "You can't tell Yen," she said.

"I won't," Hoa said.

"If you tell Yen," Trinh said, her eyes wet, but clear and alert for the first time since Hoa found her, "I will die. I promise."

"I won't," Hoa said again.

1980

Kim-Ly Vo
Ho Chi Minh City, Vietnam

. . . I wonder what my children will think of our former country now that we are here. Lum's memories are already fading, and this new child will know nothing. Vietnam will just be a place his parents talk about. He will be an American. Did I tell you this second child is going to be a boy? I had the same feeling with Lum.

I know the child being an American is beneficial, but still it worries me. Shouldn't he know his family's history? I'm probably acting foolish. You can tell me if I am. Many parents in Vietnam must envy my position. Our children have the opportunity to be educated in a free country. They can become doctors, engineers, lawyers, whatever we'd like.

But I could never forgive myself if he were to grow too spoiled to remember the past. His parents and family have sacrificed too much for him to be here. He should know this. I will tell him. . . .

Tuyet Truong
Tustin, California, USA

❧ Chapter Four

KIM-LY

LITTLE SAIGON, CALIFORNIA, 1992

WHEN KIM-LY AGREED AT THE LAST MINUTE TO GO TO the beach with her family, she could tell by their eyes glancing at the clock and the collective exhales in their chests that they felt burdened. Having Grandma along meant less space in the minivan. They'd have to bring the large sun umbrella, Kim-Ly's preferred nylon lounge chair, and the velour blanket. Kim-Ly also insisted on carrying along a large tote bag of her books, a personal Walkman, and cassette tapes; the extra boogie board and boom box would have to stay in the garage.

The location on the beach was another negotiation. Since her children insisted on going to Huntington Beach—which they claimed was more enjoyable than the less crowded and arguably cleaner Newport Beach (Kim-Ly's preference)—she requested a patch of sand that wasn't so close to the waves, surfers, volleyball players, seagulls, screaming toddlers, and radios playing obnoxious American rock music.

"That's the entire beach," her delinquent grandson Lum said. He'd turned sixteen the previous month and acquired a driver's license, which made him think he was an adult.

After finally settling upon a spot and instructing her sons-in-law on how to properly set up her umbrella, blanket, and chair, Kim-Ly watched her family strip down to their bathing suits, while she remained decent in her *ao dai* and pants. Kim-Ly did not like to tan and was annoyed by the Americans' obsession for doing so. Though her family slathered on sunscreen, she was dismayed that the children still darkened every summer as if they were Mexicans or Africans. She was most concerned with her granddaughter Duyen, whose delicate complexion resembled her own.

"Shouldn't you cover up more?" Kim-Ly asked the teenager. "You don't want to get dark before next week."

"I'll be fine, Grandmother," Duyen said. Her voice was gentle, respectful, but her meaning was clear. Kim-Ly's opinion wasn't needed.

Vung Tau, Vietnam, 1972

Kim-Ly began bringing the children back to her favorite beach after her husband died. Her sister Ha owned a restaurant right on the sand. Kim-Ly needed a break from watching the children, and barren Ha enjoyed the company. After her oldest son Thang initiated a lucrative partnership with some American officers in Vung Tau, there was more reason to make the resort town their weekend home.

On the water, Kim-Ly's daughters attracted plenty of attention. They were beautiful back then, their skin not yet sun damaged, their hair still lustrous and black. They all inherited their mother's finely sculpted face and their deceased father's lean body. The middle child, Tuyet, was especially striking, with a small, wicked grin she could use to manipulate any man. Kim-Ly watched in satisfaction as both men and women noticed—curiously, jealously—her daughters' collective beauty.

Unlike her friends who bemoaned having daughters, Kim-Ly understood their potential. For every pretty daughter, a beneficial son-in-law could be procured. She did not believe in the old-fashioned notion that a daughter left to join the husband's family, the reason Kim-Ly always preferred to select suitors whose families she could research. Never choose an eldest or youngest son. Go for the middle, typically the most forgotten. He would crave a mother who needed him and Kim-Ly could satisfy that longing. If the suitor's mother had died, that was ideal. Her daughter Hien's fiancé, Chinh, had been raised motherless.

One weekend, Kim-Ly and Ha noticed an older American military officer ogling her daughters. The man had been meeting with her son, and stayed after Thang left. The girls waded in the low tide, while the officer, Kim-Ly, and Ha sat in the shade of the restaurant bar.

"He's been watching them for over an hour," Ha said to her sister in Vietnamese. "You should ask him which one he prefers."

"Why notice only one?" Kim-Ly asked. "From here, they're only bodies."

The officer turned around, revealing himself as a thick man, large chest, gray in both his thinning hair and mustache. Like most Americans she knew, his face dripped abundantly in the humidity. "The one in the yellow is beautiful," the man said in Vietnamese.

Kim-Ly and Ha gaped at him. They shouldn't have been surprised, Kim-Ly later realized. Most American officers in the area spoke their language fluently.

"They're mine," Kim-Ly said, smoothly recovering, taking a sip from her sweaty beer.

"Your daughters?" the man asked.

She nodded.

"You look too young to have daughters."

Unimpressed, Kim-Ly smiled nonetheless. American compliments could be incredibly transparent. The trick was not to let on to their false flattery, so one could determine what they really wanted.

"Are you married?" Kim-Ly asked.

The American shook his head. "Not anymore. I was, twice. Both my fault. I should have learned my lesson about American women the first time."

"Vietnamese women are very obedient," Kim-Ly said.

He nodded. "I know."

Their eyes drifted back to Kim-Ly's daughters, who were splashing one another, shrieking with laughter. The girls had always been close. It was Tri's yellow bikini, but that morning her older sister had asked to wear it. Kim-Ly had to agree. Tuyet did look flattering in yellow.

Usually, Kim-Ly preferred driving to walking to the family's nail salon, but not with her grandson. She didn't like traveling in Lum's death trap. He had purchased the vehicle himself, he'd tell you proudly, although the automobile was nothing to be proud of. A previously owned Japanese car, with cigarette and hamburger stink in the interior upholstery, broken front seats so one had to fall inside to find the backseat.

Yet it was still more desirable than walking by herself. She'd heard a story from the twins about an elderly Vietnamese man recently accosted by some punk on a street not too far from where they lived. She had no wish to become a cautionary tale, and resigned herself to wait for her grandchildren to return from school that afternoon and give her a ride. Quynh was with them. The well-mannered young woman was Linh's friend, a positive influence, but lately, she had been accompanying Lum on more afternoons than not.

In the Deathtrap, the children were chatting about one of their cousins. Kim-Ly wanted to listen—her backseat position should have some advantages—but she was too distracted by Lum holding Quynh's hand. Kim-Ly pulled on the oppressive seat belt, leaning forward to peer over the console. Their hands were absolutely touching.

Kim-Ly kicked the back of her grandson's seat with her slippered foot. "What is this about a boyfriend?" she asked.

The children's hands released. Quynh glanced over her shoulder, a sheepish grin on her delicate face. "Jorge is not her boyfriend, Ba Vo, he is just Linh's friend."

"A Mexican?" Kim-Ly cried. "No, no, I said that only Vietnamese suitors are acceptable."

"Grandma," Cherry groaned in the seat next to her, rolling her eyes from behind her paperback book.

"Regardless, you are children," Kim-Ly declared. "I didn't allow your mothers to socialize until after they were finished with their schooling. You need to concentrate on your studies, like Cherry." She nodded approvingly at her granddaughter, who was now frowning. "I'm complimenting you, child. I never see boys running after you, distracting you. Believe me, that's a good thing."

"Grandmother," Lum said, his eyes narrowing in the rearview mirror. "Leave Cherry alone."

"What did I say?" Kim-Ly asked. "What is wrong now?"

No one answered her. Cherry sullenly stared out the window, avoiding her grandmother's gentle elbowing. Kim-Ly gave up, instead turning her attention to Lum's driving, taking note of when he jerked on the brake and forgot to signal making left-hand turns. She worried about her grandson. He was too much like his mother—impulsive and temperamental.

Dat once tried to explain it to her: "He doesn't try in school because he's too scared. He and his friends would rather pretend they failed their classes on purpose than embarrass themselves by studying. It's a shame, Grandmother. I honestly feel sorry for them."

Dat was a good, obedient boy (honor roll every semester, advanced science classes), so Kim-Ly had no reason to doubt his stories about Lum (academic probation, repeating algebra). Kim-Ly had practically raised Dat, instilling a solid work ethic from the beginning, but Lum was already ten years old when she finally arrived in America, too late to correct the mistakes of his parents, too late for so many things.

Raising grandchildren in America had proven far more difficult than she imagined it would have been if they'd remained in Vietnam. This, Kim-Ly had discussed and agreed upon with the twins Ba Liem and Ba Nhanh and other concerned grandmothers in Little Saigon. Though staying in Vietnam was no option at all, noble values could be learned growing up in constant fear of poverty, hunger, and a corrupt government. Grandchildren had no chance of ever growing up spoiled or privileged in that kind of environment. They had to behave and respect their elders. Their survival depended on this courtesy.

In America, with no fear of death, and with opportunities lying all around their feet waiting to be picked up, they had little incentive to be courteous. Kim-Ly would witness in disapproval how her grandchildren—even her favorites—could express impatience with their parents, who deserved to be treated with esteem, no matter how they had behaved in the past.

At the Asian Palace, Cherry and Kim-Ly took the escalator to the second floor, where she spied from above clusters of children running wild throughout the mall. One boy almost ran into them at the top of the escalator, and without apologizing, took off again for the filthy, time-sucking, gum-infested video arcade.

Was this the fate of their Vietnamese community? For their children to discard their ancestors' values and traditions in favor of the next bright, material object America told them to desire? The only true Vietnamese that would be left in the following generations would be the Communist victors, who certainly had their own misguided versions of history and values to tout. No, they couldn't give up on the Vietnamese children in America. If many would fall by the wayside in American culture, then they needed to focus on the few gems they could preserve.

In their family's beauty salon, on a prime corner location across from the escalators, Kim-Ly saw her gem. Sweet, beautiful Duyen smiled when she recognized them approaching her in the mirror. She wore a black smock, her hair in curlers, face artfully painted in blue eye shadow, synthetic eyelashes, and red lip liner.

Though he no longer did any business with her son, Officer Anderson kept in touch with Kim-Ly, sharing drinks at the Hotel Majestic in Saigon or having lunch at his favorite noodle shop. For over a year, he shied away from having a formal introduction to her daughter.

"I'm an old man," he'd say. "She wouldn't want me."

After Hien's wedding to Chinh, an economics student from an educated family in Saigon, she warned Officer Anderson that Tuyet would be next to marry.

"I want to secure my daughters' futures," Kim-Ly said. "There are many men who are interested in her and Tuyet wants to marry. She is ready to become a wife."

These were partial truths. She did want to secure her daughters' futures. They'd enjoyed their youth as singles with limited supervision from Kim-Ly, but now the time had arrived to become serious before people started gossiping. Kim-Ly was also concerned about her family's safety in Vietnam. The end of the war seemed inevitable and her family stood on the losing side.

"I'd want my wife to come live with me in America," he said. "I wouldn't want to live here."

"Tuyet cannot leave her family," Kim-Ly said, pausing carefully. "We'd have to come with her."

Officer Anderson slowly nodded. "That can be arranged," he said.

"You can come over for dinner tomorrow evening. We're having crab."

The next day, while Kim-Ly personally supervised her servants as they prepared the meal and cleaned the house, she speculated about what living in America would be like. She heard that women worked equally among men in all professional fields. Though Kim-Ly felt proud of the accomplishments she'd made since her husband's death (a young widow of five children, investing the money her husband left behind to provide for her family), she knew her limitations in the patriarchal country. Her best business partnerships had been with Americans, who she found to be more open-minded and ambitious.

Tuyet and Tri arrived during the first course of dinner. They skipped through the door, giggling, ignoring their mother and older sister's glares, offering no excuse for their tardiness as they slipped into their seats. While Officer Anderson told a story about his first deployment in Korea, Tri interrupted him to ask for the fish sauce.

Officer Anderson declined to stay afterward for whiskey or coffee. He had a meeting in the morning. He shook everyone's hands goodbye, barely glancing at Tuyet.

"That's a very good man," Kim-Ly told her children after he left. "He deserves your respect."

"You're a little old for him, aren't you, Mother?" Tuyet asked, laughing.

She hadn't slapped one of the girls like that since they were small. Tuyet cradled her cheek, slouching back in her chair. Her children's eyes followed her, round and bewildered, as she rose from the table and left the room.

The girl arrived with her bastard in the late morning, as Kim-Ly had instructed, a solid hour after the family had all departed for work or school. She complained that there was traffic on the freeway. She'd obviously dressed the toddler in a new outfit: a plaid blouse and lime-green leggings.

Kim-Ly did not offer tea or sweets. They sat in the family room, where Kim-Ly had made sure to turn the television volume up after hearing the doorbell.

"I don't understand why we couldn't discuss this over the phone," Kim-Ly said, leaning back in the purple corduroy recliner. "My son-in-law doesn't like strangers in the home when he is not here." This was not true. Kim-Ly knew for a fact that Sanh was woefully apathetic about the friends his children invited over in the afternoons.

"I'd thought you wanted to see your granddaughter," the girl said. "See how big she's getting? See how much she's starting to look like you?"

"I've told you before," Kim-Ly said. "That is not my grandchild. If Viet says it's not his, then I believe him."

The girl sighed. "Like I said, we can run a test. They do that. We can make this legal."

"I refuse to waste money on what everyone knows, even you," Kim-Ly said. "Why don't you go back to your family? They're in Houston, right? They have a responsibility to you."

"Viet's family is responsible for me," the girl said, her large silver hoop earrings swinging as she shook her head.

"That's a lie," Kim-Ly said. "Viet said you've had many boyfriends and any one of them could be the father. You've only targeted our family because Viet has felt pity for you."

"It's not pity," the girl said, laughing, revealing the slightly blue molar in the back of her mouth.

"Viet has a new girlfriend," Kim-Ly said. "A good, respectable girl. He wants nothing to do with you and your bastard child anymore."

The girl simply smiled. "You're mistaken. Your son may respect you enough not to bring me to family dinners because you've forbidden me to come, but where do you think he goes afterward?"

"It's time for you to leave," Kim-Ly said, one hand pressing against her chest. "You're raising my blood pressure."

"Your blood pressure is fine," the girl said. "I doubt you've ever felt faint in your life. But I have. Did you know that? Last week, I almost fainted. I wondered why, so I made an appointment with the doctor. And she told me, 'Congratulations, Tam, you're pregnant again.'"

Kim-Ly stared at her, watching as the triumphant smile split across the slut's overpowdered face. No wonder the girl had been so confident walking into the house this morning.

"What do you want?" she finally asked.

"I'm going to need twice as much every month," the girl said. "At least until the second grandchild is born. And then, of course, you know how expensive newborns are. We may have to talk again."

Six months after the disastrous dinner, Officer Anderson called again. He'd recently returned to Saigon after being stationed in Manila for several months. He expressed concern about their family. The South Vietnamese troops had surrendered key areas in the Central Highlands, and rumors were circulating that the Communists could push farther south.

Kim-Ly told him how much her family missed him. How Tuyet regretted not being able to spend more time with him that evening. To Kim-Ly's great relief, Officer Anderson admitted he'd also thought of Tuyet while away. She suggested that the two meet for a private dinner, where Tuyet would not feel as nervous as she did when in front of her family.

Her daughter would not squander this second opportunity. Kim-Ly went to Tuyet's office at the press ministry. She didn't care that her daughter was sitting with her boss when she grabbed Tuyet by the arm and dragged her out into the hallway.

"You are having dinner tonight at the Majestic," Kim-Ly said. "You will need to leave work early to change clothes. You cannot wear that in front of Officer Anderson."

Tuyet pulled her arm away. "Who?"

"He wants to marry you," Kim-Ly said. "He wants to take all of us to America."

"That old American?" Tuyet asked, remembering, her face wrinkling into an ugly, spoiled frown.

"He is better than anyone I will ever find for you in this country. He can save our family. Do you know how many people would die for the opportunity to go to America? If you ruin this for us, there is no forgiveness for you."

Her candor succeeded. Tuyet's indulgent expression and her haughty imperiousness were wiped away by Kim-Ly's good sense. She looked scared, but finally became aware of the gravity of their situation. "Okay," Tuyet said, nodding. "I'll do it."

Kim-Ly kissed her daughter on the cheek, her eyes moist with joy. "Good girl," she said, pressing her hands into Tuyet's. "I'm going to go shopping for a new dress. Something that will look beautiful on you. Meet me at home after work, and your sisters and I will help you get ready. I love you."

That afternoon, Kim-Ly found a pale yellow silk dress designed and made in France from an importer she'd known for years. Because of their long business relationship, Kim-Ly convinced the importer to let her purchase the expensive dress on credit. At home, she had Tri try the dress on to pair the best jewelry and shoes with it. Tri spun in front of the floor-length mirror in her mother's bedroom, admiring the lush fabric.

"I bet this looks better on me than it will on her," Tri wistfully remarked.

"When it's your time," Kim-Ly said, "I'll get you your own dress. Tonight is for Tuyet."

At five o'clock, Hien arrived home from work without Tuyet. Hien said Tuyet had called her that afternoon and said she wouldn't need a ride home.

"It sounded like she had a lot of work to still do," Hien said. "She said she'd be home later. Why?"

Kim-Ly called Tuyet's office. A disinterested man said Tuyet had left the office early and offered to take a message. She hung up the phone without saying good-bye. She turned to look at Tri, who lay on the sofa next to Hien.

"Go put your new dress on," Kim-Ly said.

Duyen's eye watered as her mother dragged the charcoal eye pencil across her lower lid. Hien took a step back to look at her work.

"Too dark," Tri said, shaking her head. "She looks like a whore."

"It won't look as obvious when she's on stage," Hien said. "Without it, her eyes will sink into her face."

"Maybe we should try almond brown," Tuyet said. "Ash black could still be too severe."

The women debated as Cherry held a cup of soda out to Duyen, who sipped it through a straw. Duyen smiled at her cousin, then turned to her grandmother, who perched in a fuzzy waiting chair, and winked.

With the beauty pageant only a few days away, Kim-Ly's granddaughter still hadn't lost her composure, which couldn't be said about other girls in the competition. Ba Liem had heard from two separate sources that the Phu girl had thrown a temper tantrum after her makeup trial the day before. She threatened to take her business to the American mall in Costa Mesa if the Vietnamese cosmetology school couldn't take the job seriously.

Duyen was a finalist in the junior category of the Miss Little Saigon Pageant, the biggest community event aside from Tet in Little Saigon. Kim-Ly was thrilled, not only for her talented granddaughter, but also for the publicity it would generate for the salon as her official sponsor.

In the last three years, the family beauty salon had grown from two hairstylists (Hien and Tri) and two nail techs (Tuyet and her friend

Khanh) to four full-time stylists, three part-time stylists, six nail techs, and a full-body masseuse who worked on weekends. A year ago, they leased out the empty space next door and knocked out the wall to make room for a bigger lounge, pedicure massage chairs, and a complete row of shampoo sinks.

Kim-Ly attributed the beauty salon's success to herself. Yes, the children handled the day-to-day operations, but who delegated? Who networked in the community to encourage families to frequent the salon and spread the good word? Their business had matured into one of the two busiest beauty salons in the Asian Palace Shopping Center, and the other one had been operating for over ten years.

Of course, their success did not come without growing pains. The children resented Tuyet bringing Khanh in as the second nail tech because they wanted to keep all the profits within the family and not have to worry about billing equal hours. Hien and Tri competed with each other for hair clients, and when Viet brought in some part-timers, the girls ganged up on the outsiders.

"Viet won't schedule me any good clients," Hien accused one afternoon after Kim-Ly asked about the day's turnout. "I get five-minute trims and then have to sit there at my station and watch the part-time girls do the perms. It's humiliating."

"The clients request specific girls," Viet explained to his mother. "Is it my fault no one asks for her?"

"The girls flirt with him," Hien said. "He gives them the good clients so they'll pay attention to him."

"You answer the phone then," Viet said. "Find out for yourself. You have plenty of time to do it anyway."

In Vietnam, the children had been too frightened to bicker in front of Kim-Ly. Now, they argued in front of her all the time, sometimes forgetting she was even there.

Kim-Ly almost always deferred to Viet. As the only man, Viet lacked the petty competitiveness her daughters had leveled at one another since birth. After Thang died, Viet became Kim-Ly's last surviving son, and proved to be her only trustworthy child.

Viet turned thirty-four recently and while other mothers might have considered this an appropriate age to settle down and marry, Kim-Ly wasn't sure. He had not expressed any inclination to marry. While he liked to take girls out for dinner or dancing—Viet had always been such a social, friendly person—he confided to his mother that he often realized the relationships, after a few dates with a girl, could never work out.

Perhaps he felt wary because of his sisters' marriages. Kim-Ly couldn't blame him. Her sons-in-law had proven terribly disappointing, more concerned with preserving their pride than providing for their children. For example, the family business: Kim-Ly had made it clear that the sons-in-law should feel welcome to work at the salon under the supervision of Viet, yet all three declined the offer. She suspected bruised egos (Viet was younger than all three men), but was it any better toiling away at a water treatment plant (Sanh), getting passed over for promotions at the accounting firm (Chinh), or, worst of all, lying under broken cars at an auto shop (Bao)? In the salon, they could be with family who loved them and could watch over them (especially Bao, with his wandering eye). Alone at their jobs, they were only short, compliant Vietnamese refugees. What American would respect that?

Those macho men. That's why women had such an easier time transitioning to America than their husbands. They felt grateful for work and wasted no time dreaming or complaining. Men could be so short-sighted. Perhaps Kim-Ly's own husband would have had the same difficulty coming to America. In retrospect, she was glad Thuan died before all of this. He passed away with his dignity intact. And her eldest son, poor Thang: her smartest child, blessed with the sharpest business sense, the one who utilized his American connections in Vietnam to help their family prosper. He would have risen to the challenges of this new country. Her foolish sons-in-law did not deserve America.

While her daughters continued to hover over Duyen, debating whether she should wear her hair up or down (*Up*, Kim-Ly had suggested, *classier*), and Viet showed the new employee where and how to stock the new hair-product shipments, Kim-Ly walked to the back of the salon to enter Viet's private office, a door that usually remained locked.

Viet kept the day's earnings in a box safe under the desk. He usually waited until the register had five hundred dollars before depositing it into the safe. Kim-Ly typed a combination on the electric keypad and waited for the door to release. She pulled out four piles wrapped in rubber bands, and recounted the bills, because she knew Viet could occasionally miscalculate. Satisfied with her accounting, she slipped the four wads into the bottom of her purse. She snapped it shut.

"What do you think?" Hien asked when she returned to the salon's main floor. Duyen's hair had been arranged into a mass of sculpted curls on the top of her head.

After examining the hairstyle at different angles, Kim-Ly nodded her approval. "It looks good," she said.

Tri returned home early, a look of irritation on her face. Kim-Ly had half-expected it, although she had hoped for a different result. The delicate yellow dress designed to billow while dancing instead sagged on her daughter's body like wilted flower petals.

"Of course he got angry," Tri said. "He knows I'm not Tuyet. That was really embarrassing, Mother. People in the restaurant were gawking as that old man walked out on me."

Tri retreated to her bedroom to change. Kim-Ly called the hotel where Officer Anderson had been staying. The concierge replied that the gentleman had requested not to be disturbed that evening. Kim-Ly screamed into the telephone that she'd have the woman fired unless she connected the call. Another voice joined the line, a man who claimed to be the manager, and after again explaining the hotel policy, and again listening to Kim-Ly's threats, he hung up on her.

A few hours later, the telephone rang in the Vo household. Hien answered it, then covered the mouthpiece. "It's the American."

"I don't like to be humiliated," Officer Anderson said, once Kim-Ly grabbed hold of the telephone.

"Please accept my deepest apologies," Kim-Ly said. "Tuyet is very ill, she cannot get out of bed. I sent Tri as a dinner companion, only as a dinner companion. Tuyet can see you tomorrow. Can you have dinner tomorrow?"

"It was a mistake from the beginning," he said. "I should have realized it before. I thought a Vietnamese wife would be less trouble, but clearly that is not true."

When did she collapse to the floor? "Please, Officer Anderson," Kim-Ly said. "Tuyet can be very shy, I know this, I'm her mother. But her sister Tri, she's younger, even prettier, not so shy. She wanted to have dinner with you tonight. She begged me to let her meet you and talk with you again. When a girl is that in love, how can a mother say no?"

"Maybe this is the way you arrange marriages in Vietnam," he said. "But it's unacceptable to me. In fact, it's revolting."

When Kim-Ly hung up the phone, she realized the living room was empty. The servants had left and the rest of the family had gone to bed. Kim-Ly walked around the house turning off lights and closing doors.

She did not expect Tuyet to return home. Her daughter knew what she had done.

Within a few days, Thang learned from his contacts that Tuyet had eloped with a man named Sanh Truong, her superior in the press ministry office. Kim-Ly didn't believe the rumors that they'd been in love for a long time. Romantic fool's fantasy. She knew her daughter. She would have known if she'd fallen in love. This Sanh Truong was convenient. Tuyet didn't want to marry an old American, and so she found someone else. Someone who would do nothing for their family.

That afternoon, Kim-Ly led the servants into Tuyet's room and told them to take all the clothes, jewelry, perfumes, and cosmetics they wanted. "Make sure never to bring them back to this house," Kim-Ly said.

The Miss Little Saigon beauty pageant had three titles to crown that afternoon: Little Miss Little Saigon (girls ages nine to twelve), Junior Miss Little Saigon (thirteen to sixteen), and Miss Little Saigon (seventeen to twenty). With new sponsors saturating the Vietnamese media, this year's event boasted the biggest audience in the pageant's short history. The competition took place every spring at the Asian Palace on an open-air stage in front of the food court, where the tables had been cleared out to make room for hundreds of folding chairs.

The first pageant for Little Miss Little Saigon lasted only an hour, and most of the audience cooed at the younger girls in their sweet ruffled dresses. After the winner was crowned, audience members scattered around the food court. Kim-Ly and her dear friends Ba Liem and Ba Nhanh remained in their seats, studying the program, handicapping the upcoming contestants.

Lum disappeared during intermission and returned with Quynh and an extra metal folding chair to wedge into their row. Ba Liem tapped Quynh on the back.

"Dear Quynh," Ba Liem said, smiling at the teenager. "Why are you not backstage getting ready? You're just as pretty as any of them."

"Quynh thinks pageants are sexist," Lum said, wrapping his arms around his girlfriend's waist. "She's not going to parade around in a bikini just for cash."

"Lum!" she cried, hitting his arm. She turned to the elder women. "Dear Ba Liem, I'm not the beauty-queen type, I'm too shy. But thank you for the compliment."

Kim-Ly glared at her grandson. "Is that what you think of your cousin? You think what she's doing is demeaning? I'd like to see you try to apply yourself at something."

Lum rolled his eyes. "Relax, Grandma. I was only kidding. I'm very proud of Duyen."

"From what I hear," Ba Nhanh said, tapping Kim-Ly's knee, "Duyen's serious competitors are Kelly Thuy Phu and that Amerasian Margo Lee. The judges have been very impressed with their photo shoots."

Kim-Ly glanced behind them at the judges' table: two men, two women, all members of the Vietnamese American Community Association.

"Margo won't do better than second runner-up," Kim-Ly said. "Her family doesn't donate enough to the community fund."

"That leaves the Phu girl," Ba Liem said.

"What about that scene she created at the cosmetology school?" Kim-Ly asked.

"She apologized," Ba Liem said. "She baked cookies for the school to thank them. They think she's an angel now."

The twenty-five young women paraded across the stage, dressed in identical white *ao dais*. Most of the girls chose to wear their hair down for their first appearance, which Kim-Ly certainly worked to her granddaughter's advantage. Duyen's updo made her appear taller, important since she was actually one of the shorter contestants.

"Not all of those girls should be wearing white," Ba Nhanh dryly noted as the contestants left the stage.

"Ba Nhanh," Kim-Ly said, leaning toward the woman so their faces almost touched. "What do you know?"

"Well, I overheard one of my grandsons talking to his friends. Someone saw a group of the junior contestants at the karaoke café on Bristol last week. They were loud, they said, too loud, if you know what I mean."

"But some of these girls are barely sixteen! Who would serve them alcohol?"

"These girls have boyfriends, older men. I'm not surprised at all how easy it is for them."

Next came the swimsuit competition, Kim-Ly's least favorite. Vietnamese men could behave so repulsively, aping and hollering, imitating the Americans' guttural grunts. These were teenagers! Couldn't they save their leering for the Miss Little Saigon pageant later that evening? While most of the girls wore modest one-pieces, a few whores posed in bikinis, swinging their easy hips, naïvely assuming that showing more flesh would earn them more points from the judges. But when Kim-Ly spied one of the judges' eyes, male of course, lingering a little too long on the Phu girl's gold bikini, she elbowed Ba Nhanh in the waist.

"Who were these girls at the karaoke café?" she asked.

Ba Nhanh wrinkled her forehead, thinking. "I don't think my grandson said any names."

The contestants lined up and turned for another pose for the judges and audience.

"That Phu girl," Kim-Ly said. "I heard from my grandson that she's dating an older boy who attends college."

The twins' eyes grew wide. "Really?" Ba Liem asked excitedly.

"Yes," Kim-Ly lied. "I think we know who helped those girls get that alcohol."

Kim-Ly did not like to recall with much detail the years after the Fall, though she remembered the pain. These recollections were so crippling that she sometimes couldn't get herself out of bed, afraid her body could not stand upright.

She hadn't done anything to deserve what she suffered. Absolutely nothing. Kim-Ly supposed many Vietnamese could say this about the Communist occupation—the dark years—but she felt sure her experience was far darker and traumatic than the average Vietnamese. The wealthy in Saigon were targeted for the most humiliating punishments. Of course, she couldn't prove this. A contest of the greatest suffering was surely a silly notion, but she had no doubt that her misery, when accurately accounted, could devastate any judge.

It wasn't enough that she'd lost one stupid daughter. Fate had to rip her most precious child away, her oldest son, Thang. The government took him, along with all the other men associated with the South Vietnamese Army and the Americans. Thang and Hien's husband, Chinh, received orders to report to a reeducation camp in the jungles north of Saigon. Her youngest son, Viet, only seventeen, with no record of government employment, was mercifully spared. She didn't know what she would have done if both her sons had been taken away. Viet and Bao, Tri's new husband, a former singer at a second-rate hotel in Saigon, were the only men left in the house to protect them. Bao could barely function, revealing himself to be an unemployable, simpering coward soon after the wedding, but Viet became a source of comfort for Kim-Ly during those dark years. He held her when she wept. He listened when she could no longer contain her rage. Unlike his sisters who had husbands of their own to worry about, Viet could devote all his love to her.

The reeducation classes were supposed to deprogram the insidious propaganda the Americans had fed them over the years; to retrain them to take part in the new, unified government. But the men did not return after one month. They did not return after two months. Kim-Ly couldn't believe she'd been so naïve. Of course, they wanted money. When rumors began stirring that officers accepted bribes for the release of the prisoners (that's what they were, no need deluding themselves with more hopeful phrases), Kim-Ly and Hien immediately traveled to the camp to negotiate. The officers sneered at Kim-Ly's initial offers, asking why their men were worth so little. By the time they could gather sufficient funds—the government had already seized their home, claiming unpaid taxes—it was too late for Thang. Reading from a faded sheet of paper, the officer briskly informed Hien and Kim-Ly that Thang Vo had died from gangrene in the foot. As Kim-Ly gripped her chest in shock, afraid if she let go her body would dissolve there on those infested muddy grounds of the camp, Chinh called out to them from behind the electric fence. He was twenty pounds lighter and wore thin brown clothes. Hien's cries, both anguished and relieved, broke the hot air. Kim-Ly glanced up into her son-in-law's tearful face, but she didn't smile. She couldn't help it. It was not the face she wanted to see.

Duyen's crowning as Junior Miss Little Saigon ranked as one of the most satisfying moments of Kim-Ly's new life in America. She remembered everyone leaping to their feet, hugging each other in joy, even the surly Lum, even Duyen's likely very jealous cousins, Cherry and Linh. Chinh and Hien unabashedly wept for their daughter. Sharing this rare moment of pure, unselfish happiness with her family made it all worth it to Kim-Ly, persuading and prodding Ba Nhanh to corner the judge in the restroom during intermission, to tip the woman to very pertinent information of the Phu girl's possibly illegal, undeniably unethical misdeeds.

Only a week later, Kim-Ly was startled to hear the front door unlock as she exited the bath. She preferred to take a leisurely soak after the family had left for school and work, consuming as much hot water as she pleased.

"Mother?" a voice downstairs called. It was Viet. "Are you awake?"

She pulled on her bathrobe and walked down the hall. Viet stood on the stairs, an uncertain expression on his face.

"Why aren't you at work?" she asked, and then noticed his sisters behind him. All three of them. "Who is watching the salon?"

"We want to talk to you," Tuyet said. "It's important."

She should have gone back to her bedroom, at least to change out of her robe. Kim-Ly gripped the railing as she walked down the stairs. Sitting on the couch in the living room, a towel around her shoulders, she looked at her grown children, all still standing, peering down at her. Tuyet and Tri both had their arms crossed in front of their chests.

Viet sunk onto the sofa next to her, face level with hers. "We need to ask you about the beauty pageant," he said. "The Phus have made some public accusations."

Leaning back against the cushions, Kim-Ly tried to smile, ignoring the tightness in her chest. "What did those sore losers say?"

"They're accusing the judges of corruption," Viet said. "They were on the Vietnamese radio this morning, demanding a recall of the crown."

"You didn't have to do this," Hien said. Why was she crying? "Duyen would have won without your influence. Everyone thought so."

"How can you be so sure?" Kim-Ly asked. "I agree that Duyen deserved to win. I wanted to make sure."

"Mother," Tuyet said. "This is America, not Vietnam. Bribery is a serious offense."

Her face pinched in confusion. "What? I didn't bribe anyone."

"There is money missing from the safe at the salon," Viet said.

Kim-Ly rubbed her hands against the soft, worn couch. She could not look up with all their gazes upon her, probing, judging. She was not accustomed to this kind of insulting scrutiny. Children should not behave this way to their parents.

"Stop treating me like a criminal," Kim-Ly said. "It's my money. I can take it if I want."

"This is serious," Tuyet said. "Someone saw your friend Ba Nhanh talking to a judge in the bathroom. They were in public, Mother; of course someone was going to see them."

"The Phus are accusing us of bribing the judges," Viet said. "They are demanding to see the judges' scoring sheets."

"You stupid children," Kim-Ly said. "I did not bribe anyone."

"Mother, you just admitted you took the money from the safe," Tri said.

Kim-Ly stood, her strength returning with her indignation. "This is how you treat your mother?" she asked. "Like some thief? As if I haven't taken care of all of you since birth?"

"The pageant committee is launching an investigation," Hien said as they all watched Kim-Ly stomp up the stairs. "I hope for everyone's sake, you didn't leave any evidence."

Kim-Ly slammed the door. She walked over to her closet, pulled out her green suitcase, and threw it on the bed. Opening drawers, she tossed her undergarments, stockings, blouses, and trousers into the suitcase, swearing at each of her children: Ungrateful Hien; Follower Tri; Vindictive Tuyet; and what galled her most of all, Ignorant, Hypocritical Viet. If only he knew. Then she stopped, staring at the growing pile of garments on the bed, realizing that she was packing to leave, but that there was no child's house to go to. None of them believed her. They'd all betrayed her.

She didn't know how Tuyet had found them. They lived in a different neighborhood, a ground-floor apartment with only two bedrooms. Kim-Ly shared her bed with her grandchildren Dat and Linh. Perhaps fate was punishing her for hiring nannies to sleep with her children so she could rest peacefully.

To Kim-Ly's pleasure, Tuyet did not look any better than they did. She, too, appeared skinny. Her eyes were equally vacant and defeated. So much of the beauty that she once flaunted had withered away. Being poor had that effect on people: she looked just like anyone else. She held an infant that Kim-Ly could only assume was hers. The child must have taken after his father.

Four years had passed since Tuyet had abandoned their family, the war over, her beloved Thang buried in an impoverished city cemetery, the misery of the Communist occupation their reality. From old acquaintances, Kim-Ly knew the girl still lived in Saigon with her husband and in-laws, Catholics from Nha Trang. Kim-Ly heard the patriarch, Hung Truong, was a businessman who alienated potential partners with his religious ethics and a disdainful refusal to engage in backroom deals. Tragically naïve. Everyone knew that was the only way possible to do business in "Ho Chi Minh City" these days.

"We're only a fifteen-minute walk from this house," Tuyet said. "Isn't that a coincidence?"

Kim-Ly said nothing. While her children hugged and kissed Tuyet and her infant, overlooking her past sins, Kim-Ly did not approach, and the girl was too smart to try to force a greeting.

After a half hour, Tuyet whispered her purpose for visiting. "My father-in-law is getting a boat. He says there is room for all of us."

"America?" Kim-Ly asked, speaking for the first time since Tuyet arrived.

Her daughter tentatively smiled at her. "Malaysia first, where we can apply for political refugee status. From there, anywhere we want to go."

Tuyet visited with her son, Lum, every other day at a different time, fearful of being followed, and wanting her trips to seem as casual and unplanned as possible. Every visit brought information and instructions. What items they could bring, what food was lightest to carry and took longest to spoil. Kim-Ly offered to ask around to buy canisters of gasoline, but Tuyet assured her mother that the Truongs were taking care of that. The departure date changed with every visit, but Kim-Ly didn't care. As long as they had a departure date, she held hope for a life outside their dying country.

"It is dangerous," Tuyet warned her family on one of her discreet visits. "The police are watching for escapes. We could be caught and imprisoned."

"It's worth the risk," Kim-Ly said, holding her daughter's hand. "We can start over in America." She wanted to meet Tuyet's in-laws, these generous people who were helping to save their entire family. But Tuyet feared the large gathering would generate too much attention in the neighborhood. They couldn't have their neighbors suspecting anything.

Kim-Ly could hardly sleep at night, her mind imagining all the possible versions of their escape, which would be arduous. She certainly had no delusions about that. She also knew their entry into a new world would be difficult. She'd never been out of the country before, which on international maps appeared so small and thin compared to the other countries of the world. What would the men do for jobs in America? So many things to think about, to arrange. Kim-Ly wished they could hurry up and leave. They had so much to do to make a new home for themselves. There was little they could do waiting around in Vietnam.

Then one afternoon Tuyet and Lum did not come to the apartment. Kim-Ly became concerned when they did not show up the next day. She sent Viet out to look for Tuyet at the Truongs' home, reminding him to stay watchful of the people around him. He returned a few hours later, frustrated and exhausted.

"No one will say anything to me," Viet said. "They pretended not to know who Tuyet or the Truongs were. I told them I was her brother but they would barely look at me. Even the couple staying in the Truongs' home wouldn't open the door to me."

For the next few days, Kim-Ly could not get out of bed. She knew what had happened even though her gullible children were not ready to believe. It sickened her to think how she had been duped once again, allowing that girl into her home, trusting her, loving her. Tuyet had lied, dangling America in their desperate faces, toying with them, only to abandon them all over again. Kim-Ly was usually much, much smarter than that. Her mistake had been underestimating her daughter. She'd proven to be even shrewder than her mother.

The next week, a young boy came to the apartment with a letter from Tuyet. His family lived next door to the Truongs. He was instructed to give Kim-Ly Vo the letter on this day. He seemed relieved handing it off to Hien.

The children took turns reading the letter since Kim-Ly neither wanted to read or hear it. Then they burned the letter in the kitchen stove, according to Tuyet's instructions.

When Viet found Kim-Ly hunched in the bathroom weeping, he pulled her off the damp, grimy floor and gathered her in his arms, ignoring the stench of fresh vomit in the toilet.

"There was no more room on the boat," Viet said. "But once she's safe, she said she can still help us."

Such a good boy, so unwilling to see selfishness or evil in people. Just like his father that way. Kim-Ly didn't have the energy to tell him he was wrong. Who was she to take this only hope away from her children? If they needed to believe there was still a way to escape their lives here, if this fantasy helped them to endure, Kim-Ly would keep her mouth shut.

But she wouldn't be deluded. While she and her loyal children and grandchildren suffered, year after year, while they scrapped for demeaning jobs and sold off heirloom belongings for food and medicine for an ailing Chinh (he'd developed a congestion in his chest from the camps), the hate she felt in her heart stirred her to stay alive, determined not to allow one narcissistic, spiteful brat to destroy her family.

The investigation turned up nothing. The committee could not verify that any money had changed hands. Still, the discussions in the Vietnamese newspaper editorials and radio shows and between gossipers in the community soured much of the beauty pageant's joyful afterglow. Duyen packed her crown and the glittering *ao dais* in her bedroom closet, and seemed embarrassed whenever someone mentioned anything to do with the pageant.

"It's over," she said at a family dinner after Linh had teasingly called Duyen by her title. "I'm sick of it."

Her mother said Duyen was finished with the pageant circuit, which frustrated Kim-Ly, because she knew her granddaughter could win the senior title of Miss Little Saigon. She blamed Ba Nhanh's lack of discretion the day of the pageant. If only the old woman weren't so obvious, none of this suspicion and misunderstanding ever would have occurred. Duyen could have been proud of her accomplishment instead of ashamed.

Kim-Ly had not moved out of Tuyet's home. She didn't feel comfortable moving into her other children's homes just yet, though they'd made the obligatory offers. The twins lived with their own children, so she couldn't move in with either of them. She did have enough money for her own apartment, but the thought of living alone frightened Kim-Ly. She didn't speak English fluently (her language lessons when she first arrived to America had been miserable, condescending, and she quit after two weeks). She couldn't drive. After hearing horror stories from the twins about where Americans sent their elderly, she didn't want to move into a senior citizens' home and sit around, waiting to die.

She'd have to determine which child she felt deserved her company, and unfortunately none immediately came to mind. Following the humiliating confrontation in her bathrobe, they hadn't spoken about the missing money or the pageant again. The children probably whispered about it among themselves, but after the investigation closed, the hushed conversations faded as well.

One night after dinner, Tuyet cornered Kim-Ly in the kitchen as she prepared some tea to take upstairs to her room.

"What do you want to accuse me of now?" Kim-Ly asked while she steeped the press into the loose jasmine leaves and boiling water.

Tuyet held up a thick envelope in Kim-Ly's handwriting that was addressed to Viet's ex-girlfriend. Kim-Ly wiped her hands on her pants, squinting. The post office had stamped something red across the envelope and stamps.

"Cherry found this in the mailbox this afternoon," Tuyet said. "There wasn't enough postage on it."

Kim-Ly snatched it from her daughter's hands. "Then why didn't she give it back to me? This is my private mail." Kim-Ly flipped over the envelope and saw it had been opened.

"She thought it felt strange," Tuyet said. "I'm glad she gave it to me."

Kim-Ly opened the envelope and saw that the letter had been refolded and lay outside of the wad of cash. She suddenly remembered her granddaughter at dinner, looking sulkier than usual. She scanned the house, fuming. Sanh and the grandchildren were upstairs, likely hiding in their rooms. This was an ambush.

"Is this what you were doing with the salon's money?" Tuyet asked. "Paying off one of Viet's ex-girlfriends? Is another one pregnant again?"

Instead of answering, Kim-Ly turned and began walking toward the stairs. When her daughter pulled at her arm to stop her, Kim-Ly spun around, enraged. "What do you want from me?" she screamed. "You know everything now, why aren't you happy with that?"

"Why didn't you confide in me?" Tuyet asked, eyes shimmering—a manipulation that perhaps worked on her husband and the Truong family, but not Kim-Ly.

"Why would I want your help?" Kim-Ly asked. "The child who has betrayed me again and again?"

Tuyet shook her head, that imperious expression from her childhood once again spoiling her face. "Who brought you here? Who has always given you a place to live?" she asked. "Who has taken care of you since you've been in America?"

"That's not love," Kim-Ly said. "That's guilt. I trust the child who cared for me in Vietnam, when I really needed it. You chose to leave me there."

Tuyet raised her hands and dropped them, always the dramatic. "I never wanted to leave you, Mother. But you forced me, didn't you? You've made mistakes, too."

"I certainly have," Kim-Ly agreed, glaring at her.

"I can only hope one day you realize which children have truly been loyal to you."

"And the same for you," Kim-Ly said. "If your daughter can betray her own grandmother, she will do it to you any day now."

Walking past the grandchildren's bedrooms in the hallway, she couldn't contain the rage tickling her throat, itching at her fists.

"Are you happy?" she shrieked at their silent, closed bedroom doors. "Your unwanted grandmother is leaving. You finally get your wish."

In her room, Kim-Ly sat on her bed, her spine tall, and tried to breathe. She'd been through worse humiliations than this. There was no question she would survive this one. She picked up the telephone on her bedside table and dialed Tri's phone number. When her granddaughter Linh answered, she asked the child to hand the telephone to her uncle.

"Viet?" she whispered, in a tone so quiet and different from a few minutes before, but familiar, correct, because this was her real voice, her true voice. "Viet, this is your mother."

1984

Cuc Bui
Paris, France

. . . No son should have to grow up without his father, especially as a young boy. I feel lucky for the opportunity to have been with my boys since their births, to have raised them personally. They have grown up understanding the values every Truong should live by.

Daughters are fine to be left alone with the women. Ngoan was a good mother to Cam while Phung was away. She taught her all the necessary skills a woman should know. Cam can be willful at times, but that can help her in this new country. Whatever happens to her now, she will always have her decent upbringing to guide her in making wise decisions.

I worry for Xuan. I did the best I could for Yen's boy. But his mother is so frustrating, so stupid. You remember how she behaved on the boat, refusing to let anyone else hold him? She coddled the boy, and the other women condoned this. Too much female influence. Sometimes he listened to me, but most of the time, he would run behind his mother's legs. They complained that I was too harsh. A boy needs that.

I have warned Yen about this. Xuan needs to see his father as a man. But Yen feels too guilty. You can see it in the way he caters to Trinh's every complaint, every tear she sheds. A father should be stronger for his son. If Yen

believes it was a mistake to leave Xuan for the first years of his life, then the boy will believe it, too. He must have faith in his choices. He must make the boy understand that the decision was the correct one, the only one. . . .

Hung Truong
Paris, France

∂ℰ *Chapter Five*

XUAN

PARIS, FRANCE, 1992

Is dialogue the path to truth?

This was the bac's most popular philosophy question from the previous year. Reported in the daily newspapers, it inspired speculative editorials from the country's leading philosophers and write-in rebuttals from politicians, doctors, soccer players, and pastry chefs. The debates stretched into the late weeks of summer. Xuan remembered, because he clipped every article. The question would likely not appear on this year's bac, but his cousin Cam still wanted to go over it, not because she was studious, but because debating amused her.

"Let's talk it out," Cam said, an intoxicated smile playing on her lips, her hands carelessly wrinkling the organized clippings in Xuan's notebook. "Let's try to reach the truth."

"You'd have to be an honest person to understand," Xuan said, snatching the binder back from her, smoothing out the damaged pages. "And you're a liar."

"Ooh," Cam said, her eyes widening. With one hand, she pushed her long, tangled hair from her face, using the other hand to support herself against the toffee-colored lounge chair. "Strong words. But I can rebut. Aren't lies simply alternate perspectives of the truth?"

"'Mother, I'm going to study' is not another perspective of 'Mother, I'm going to my boyfriend's house to smoke hashish.'"

Cam's smirk faded at last, Xuan's wish fulfilled. "Michel and I are friends."

"Who sleep with each other," Xuan corrected.

His cousin peered behind her shoulder. When she realized Petit Michel was still in the kitchen, her gaze returned to Xuan. "What's with the attitude?" she whispered. "I brought you here to relax."

"I need to work," Xuan said, stuffing his books and study guides into his backpack. "So do you. The bac is in two weeks and you are wasting my time."

"Michel said he will help us," Cam said, her voice low, but determined. "He got a sixteen, remember?"

But they had been at Petit Michel's apartment—correction, the Bourdains' apartment—for over an hour and all Xuan had learned was that Petit Michel's hairline was receding, just like his father's, and despite this, Cam was openly fawning over him. A surprising, annoying revelation; he had no idea how long the two had been seeing each other, and didn't plan to ask. Xuan also had suspicions about Petit Michel's too-impressive score on the bac. It didn't seem coincidental that the richest children in the city consistently received the highest marks, securing them positions in the *grand écoles*, and further perpetuating the exclusivity of the French elite. Those who failed to possess such luck and wealth had to work even harder for their scores.

The unfairness itched at his concentration. He stood and pulled on his jacket. "I'm going to the library."

"Now?" Petit Michel asked, returning with a plate of cookies and chocolates. Like Cam, he was dressed all in black. Xuan, in blue jeans and a red sweater Grandmère knit, felt like a bright, shiny clown.

"I really should," Xuan said, annoyed how his voice turned soft, his politeness returning, just as it would for Petit Michel's parents. "It closes in three hours."

"But it's Saturday," Petit Michel said, leaning a hip against the arched entry of the living room.

"I need to work on my flash cards," he lied, reaching for his backpack.

"No, you don't," Cam said. When Xuan looked at her, she smiled with her lips. "Xuan has a genius memory."

Xuan sighed. "She means photographic."

"It's true. He reads a book only once and he'll remember chapters, footnotes, everything. It's frightening."

"Yet, I'm rusty on the seventeenth century," Xuan said, then offered a tight smile to the frowning lovers. "Thanks for the drinks."

He turned and walked out, past the furniture and décor, clear indications that Petit Michel's mother had decorated this home as well. As a child, he would marvel over the Bourdains' shiny, ornate decorations, items he was afraid to touch without his mother's permission. When no one else was looking, Xuan's mother would shove a decorative plate or crystal vase in his small, chubby hands, softly whispering in his ear, "Look at that, darling. Feel how heavy and solid that is? This is worth more than a year's rations of meals for a child in an orphanage." When Xuan asked why, his mother would shake her head and simply say, "That's the rich for you. They have the ability to do right, but they'd rather have pretty things."

Why are we sensitive to beauty?

The air felt cooler outside, and a sweetness had descended upon the boulevards. Early summer evenings were always pleasant. Xuan could walk for blocks and blocks without a jacket or sweater, even beyond the arrondissements, through the suburbs and into the countryside, where his relatives would never think to find him.

The university library was only a few blocks from Petit Michel's apartment. Xuan was tempted to take the metro to a library outside the quarter, to avoid any chance encounters with classmates—and being forced into more needless conversation—but he determined that the risk did not outweigh the extra travel time. Xuan hated wasting time. Since his first level of secondary school, Xuan consulted a daily organizer to evaluate and assign every hour of his life. He disliked how sleep occupied at least a third of his days, no matter how many times he tried getting by with less. His mother could do it—she regularly catnapped, sleeping a few hours here and there, never more than four at a time. But she was assisted by prescription pills and chronic insomnia.

If he turned left at the flower shop where Grandmère bought her Sunday floral arrangements, Xuan would be at his family's apartment house. He veered right instead, eyes fixed on the concrete, his stride pointed and brisk, hoping none of his relatives was around to spot him. Although Grandmère and Aunt Ngoan occasionally complained about living in such a busy district, too far from Chinatown where they did most of the grocery shopping, Xuan was grateful for the Latin Quarter. It certainly wasn't the wealthiest area in the city (where the Bourdains lived) and they had their fair burden of tourists (especially in the summer), but there were excellent schools, libraries, and hospitals. The Bourdains had helped Xuan's father locate his apartment in the building, where the whole family now lived, years before the real estate values and rental prices went up. They considered the building home, despite its leaky pipes and ant infestations every spring. Whenever Xuan's father would mention the possibility of buying a house in the suburbs, the family members would ask: What about their church? The Vietnamese Community Center? What about Dr. Robin?

Dr. Robin was his mother's best psychiatrist. She wasn't her favorite—that was Dr. Henri, whose solution to every setback was new medication, and who could always make her laugh. Dr. Robin hardly smiled and could not be intimidated or flattered by his mother, which helped tremendously. She was the first psychiatrist to recommend in-patient treatment. Xuan was twelve during Trinh's first hospitalization. The psychiatric ward was actually located in their arrondissement—a five-minute walk from the apartment house. And while Xuan wasn't allowed to visit during his mother's treatments, Grandmère would walk him and Cam to the hospital and stand under the window of his mother's room.

"What a nice location," Grandmère said. "She gets to look out this window all the time and see these pretty flower beds. Aren't we jealous?"

They waved to the dark window, three mittened hands in the gray air, even though they couldn't see anyone or anything inside it. But Grandmère assured them that his mother was there, waving back and growing healthier. When Trinh returned home six weeks later, Xuan told her about their window visits.

"You were there?" Xuan's mother said, noticing him for the first time, though she'd been home for hours. He could see the black pupils in her brown eyes as she gazed at him, so dark and deep that he finally stepped back. "Then why didn't you come get me?" As his father pulled him away to another room, Xuan saw that both her hands had curled into fists.

His mother had returned last week from her most recent treatment and she appeared significantly calmer—no spells, no crying fits, no inappropriate confessions . . . not yet anyway. There was no point in getting overexcited. It would take more time to determine if the results would last. The day before she was released, Xuan's father had asked if he wanted to move into his grandparents' apartment downstairs to minimize distractions before the bac. But Xuan didn't see the benefit. After so many years living in the apartment house, he knew how ineffective a locked door was to his mother. If she wanted him to hear her, to pay attention to her, a different floor wasn't going to matter.

Can humanity be envisaged without religion?

Xuan usually enjoyed the Sunday breaks from studying, when his family attended Mass in the morning and then prepared for an elaborate family lunch. He'd stopped believing years ago, but the predictable, comforting rituals of the service, the psalms and gospels, the kneeling and recitation of prayers, revitalized him for studying on Monday. But as the weeks before the bac thinned, he found himself reviewing facts and theories in his head during the homily, imagining logarithm equations scrolling across the altar as he stood in line for communion. When he looked at other students from his class in the church, he envied how calm and bored they appeared.

His mother wasn't with them. She hadn't been for several years. His dad didn't think she should attend until she felt healthier, a vague status, but his mother had easily agreed. He was right to be cautious. The last time she attended Mass, she stood up during the Eucharist and accused the priest of diluting the wine. Another reason that Mass had become discreetly relaxing for Xuan—he was free to think only of his concerns.

After Mass, while Xuan's father and Uncle Phung chatted with some acquaintances, and Grandmère and Aunt Ngoan nagged Cam about the sleeveless dress she had chosen to wear that morning, Xuan walked with Grandpère to their favorite bench near the fountain. Grandpère pulled out two cigarettes and handed one to Xuan.

"I remember taking the bac," Grandpère said, fumbling for the lighter in his other suit pocket. "Did you know I chose Spanish as my foreign language? Of course, I can't remember any of it now . . . and if I'd known Sanh and his family would go to America, I would have learned English. . . . Are you learning English?"

"Yes, Grandpère," Xuan said, taking the lighter from him to prepare the cigarettes.

"Good, good," Grandpère said. "We must acclimate to the changing world, right, Xuan?"

"Yes, Grandpère."

A year ago, on another Sunday at church, Xuan noticed Grandpère's attention shifting to the Saint Jeanne de Lestonnac statue, on the opposite side of the altar. When his grandfather failed to recite the Our Father along with the rest of the congregation, Xuan gently nudged him on his side. Grandpère turned to him, but his eyes wouldn't focus, his gaze arching upward to the angels sleeping on the ceiling, and Xuan realized, as everyone else kneeled to the pews, that his grandfather was having a stroke.

The doctors diagnosed it as a minor stroke, and determined no significant consequences, beyond a slight tremor in his right arm that one had to observe closely to notice. He continued volunteering at the Vietnamese Community Center and still bickered with Grandmère. That morning, in his crocheted hat and navy blue suit, Hung Truong looked healthier and stronger than most of the elder French men in their congregation. He only allowed himself one cigarette a week since the stroke, always after Sunday Mass.

Amid the crowd of neatly combed heads and stylish hats, Xuan recognized his father and uncle talking to the Bourdains. The four of them turned, smiling and nodding, and Xuan politely reciprocated. Though their families had ended their weekly Sunday brunches years ago after his mother's breakdown in Lourdes, they remained on friendly terms. They hadn't seen the Bourdains for several weeks, which meant they'd probably returned from another holiday. After shaking hands with his father and uncle, the Bourdains started walking toward the bench.

Up close, Xuan could tell the Bourdains were aging—graying in Émilie's hair, wrinkles around the elder Michel's eyes and lips. Not as thin as they once were. But these were still subtler, gentler aging adjustments compared to Xuan's parents. Xuan's father lost more weight with each year, his bony shoulders protruding through his sweaters and dress shirts. And his mother, a woman who once regularly attracted the stares of French men on the metro, now looked older than Aunt Ngoan.

After exchanging pleasantries with Grandpère about the weather and church service, the elder Michel turned his attention to Xuan.

"So, young man, studying hard?"

"I'm trying," Xuan said. He stuffed his hands in his pockets, keenly aware of his slouching posture, a habit since he was very young.

"You know, you should really give Petit Michel a call," Monsieur Bourdain said. "He is very busy—we hardly see him ourselves—but he must have some advice for you. And isn't your cousin also taking the bac this year?"

Xuan nodded, looking past Monsieur Bourdain, where a few feet away, Cam expertly avoided his gaze and turned to chat with Grandmère.

"Fantastic," Monsieur Bourdain said. "You children grow up too fast. I'll have Petit Michel call you."

"We really should all get together again soon," Émilie Bourdain said, a phrase the Truongs had learned in the last few years signified only politeness, nothing more. "When we return from Morocco next month, perhaps. It is so busy this time of year."

Several minutes after the Bourdains' departure, the Truong women approached Grandpère's bench. Grandmère and Aunt Ngoan had their arms linked, though it wasn't cold.

"You just missed the Bourdains," Grandpère said, dropping his cigarette and grinding it into the cobblestone.

"Isn't that a shame?" Grandmère asked. Aunt Ngoan smiled, tugging on Grandmère's arm.

"Don't be impudent," Grandpère said. "We owe them our respect. They were our sponsors."

"Petit Michel is going to call us," Xuan said, looking at Cam.

Her face appeared stricken for a moment. "Why?" she whispered.

"Ungrateful girl," Grandpère said, though his tone was playful. "To tutor you and Xuan for the bac. Can't you see how kindly the Bourdains are? Still helping us this way?"

"Ah," Cam said, nodding, finally meeting her cousin's eyes. "That's very kind."

Must political action be guided by the knowledge of history?

"It's casual," Cam said, rubbing her eraser along the edge of her textbook. "There's no need to involve the families."

"Afraid they'll start planning the wedding?" Xuan asked.

Cam stabbed the eraser into her cousin's palm. They sat at a table in the east wing of the library, shoulder to shoulder, reviewing history dates in Xuan's notebook. "Mother would kill me first, then claim it was to preserve my honor."

Xuan tipped his head up to the ceiling, squinting at the overhead lights, fuzzy, yellow, and swallowed a yawn. He knew he shouldn't care. His cousin did whatever she wanted, despite Aunt Ngoan's best efforts and Uncle Phung's tepid gestures to make peace. (*Why couldn't you be a boy?* Aunt Ngoan's question raged through the house. *A boy would never cause this much trouble.*) Their occasional battles made Xuan feel better about his mother's own disturbances in the apartment house. Noise within the family was ignored, quietly forgiven, then forgotten.

"It could be worse," Cam said. "You could be seeing Michel."

"I'm not sure my parents would notice," Xuan said.

Cam rubbed her eyes. They fell into another silence as they absorbed countries, wars, peace treaties, and dates. Xuan already had these memorized, but patiently waited for Cam, knowing how annoyed she became when he turned the page too quickly.

"Nineteen fifty-four. The final withdrawal of French military from Indochine," Cam read aloud. "And then the history of Vietnam simply ends for the French. Interesting, huh?"

"Well, we are covering French colonial history," Xuan said, turning the page, ready for the next decade.

"But not even a mention of 1975?" Cam asked. "The Fall of Saigon? When their beloved colony is finally free of all foreign conquerors?"

"We were barely a year old. Why does it matter to you now?"

"I think I can remember it," Cam said, her head slowly nodding, entranced by the olive-green face clock on the opposite wall of the library.

"No," Xuan said, biting down the side of his tongue to keep from grimacing. "I don't think you can."

"You're not the only Truong with a visual memory," Cam said.

"Photographic," Xuan corrected. "And you cannot remember events from when we were that young, it's impossible."

Cam turned her chair to face him, her eyes lit with fanciful delusion. "It was hot that day, really hot. The adults wouldn't open a window. Our mothers kept us upstairs because the front door kept opening and slamming shut. It would shake the entire house. Even though the windows were locked, we could still hear people on the streets . . . and sirens. We weren't sure if they were from the Communists or the South Vietnamese police . . . And someone shot out the kitchen window. No one got hurt, but it made Grandmère cry—"

"Our parents have told us this story," Xuan said.

"Why don't you believe me?" Cam looked irritated, folding her legs up to her chest and wrapping her arms around them. "It was an important day in our lives. This is what I can recall."

"I don't think it works that way," he said. "Like you said, I have an excellent memory and I can hardly remember any of our years in Vietnam."

"You're saying you don't remember playing soccer in the park?" Cam asked. Her arms flapped in the air as she spoke, and Xuan feared one of her erratic hands would strike him. "Or our next-door neighbors and how they turned out to be Viet Minh? Or when they took my father and Uncle Sanh away to the reeducation camps and we didn't see them for two years? You don't remember any of that?"

Xuan shook his head. "I'm not trying to be a jerk," he said. "But this happened before we could barely speak."

"If that's true," Cam said, "then I feel sorry for you. Those memories mean more than any of these ridiculous dates we're going to be tested on. All this information will be gone the minute the bac is over. But Vietnam? That was where we began. What are you looking at?"

Cam turned and glared back at a group of disapproving classmates at an adjacent table. During their conversation, her voice had spilled beyond their own table. Their classmates quickly reverted to their books, but exhaled dramatically. When Cam returned to face her cousin, Xuan's eyes had refocused on the study materials, his shoulders curved toward his notebook, like a turtle. He wouldn't look up again for several hours.

Is being free not encountering any obstacles?

On the day they were supposed to return to Paris, Xuan's mother suggested they take one last walk to the grotto in the morning. Xuan's mother promised him it wouldn't take long. She only wanted to recite a rosary before leaving. Although Xuan would have liked to stay behind with Petit Michel and Cam, he didn't want his mother to walk by herself.

Other morning worshippers sat throughout the grotto. Xuan tried his best to follow each prayer with the beads on his rosary. His mother, though, appeared deep in her own meditations, her rosary tangled between her tightened knuckles. It felt much colder than the day before.

He'd been hoping to go to an amusement park or a petting farm in the countryside. Instead, they had come to Mass for three days.

"We can be cured, too," his mother had whispered to him on the train ride to Lourdes. "We can be washed clean."

"But I just took a bath yesterday," Xuan had said.

"I'm talking about the soul," she said. "We're not pure inside. When we take our baths at Lourdes, we can have all the wretchedness of our pasts cleansed away."

The baths didn't seem that special to Xuan. The water had felt cold and the volunteers appeared curt and perfunctory in their miracle-assistance. Xuan had imagined lots of candlelight and choral music, like his first communion, but it felt more like taking a rinse in a stark gray pool house, with no diving board waiting outside. Afterward, his mother said she could feel the water's effect in her veins. Xuan had squeezed his thin arms and pretended that he could, too.

Xuan looked up to the dark skies. Not even a hint of sun.

During their last Hail Mary, a woman screamed from the front row. People stood. Xuan stood, too. He stepped closer to where the people gathered and saw an old man lying on the ground, wedged between the pews. Yellow vomit dotted the front of his navy coat. His body was convulsing.

A woman cradled the old man's head in her lap, her screams filling the normally tranquil grotto. People yelled in several languages for an ambulance. One person demanded they take the old man to the baths. His mother.

Xuan watched as she pushed her way to the center of the turmoil. "Baths," she said again in Vietnamese, making several gestures for washing and pointing next door to the baths. Finally, she remembered her French: "He needs to wash in the holy water!"

A man and a woman in dark blue uniforms rushed to the grotto carrying medical equipment. Everyone stepped out of their way. Xuan pulled his mother back from the crowd, still yelling about the holy water to the paramedics.

It started to sprinkle. As the paramedics began to take the body away, Xuan realized his mother was no longer standing next to him. He looked around the grotto, which was emptying out. His mother knelt in the front pew, her eyes and lips pressed shut.

"They should have listened to me," his mom said when Xuan sat next to her. When she opened her eyes, she did not look sad, but proud. "They have no one to blame but themselves."

Xuan stared at his mother. She seemed so much smaller kneeling in the pew, no bigger than a child. "Mom . . ."

"But it's not too late," she said, reclasping her hands and bending her head. "We can still pray. Mary can still save him."

"Mommy," Xuan tried again. "He's dead."

She shook her head, refusing to listen. "No, Xuan. He needs your prayers. You can't give up on your faith."

"This isn't about faith," Xuan cried. "This is a fact. He's dead."

"You're wrong," Trinh said, her voice shaking. "Mary protects all her children."

"No, she doesn't," Xuan yelled. "You always said that, but she never did. She didn't protect us in Vietnam and she didn't protect you in the camps."

There. He had said it. The one thing he knew could stop any conversation, what he wasn't allowed to share with anyone, not Grandmère, not Grandpère, not his father, and before this moment, not even his mother.

Before she could respond, Xuan turned and walked away. He couldn't look at her face. When he heard his mother calling out to him, Xuan ignored her, his walk breaking into a run. It felt good, his small steps quickening, the breeze and slight drizzle of rain cooling his face. His mother's voice faded but Xuan continued to soar—free, invulnerable—until a group of tourists emerging unexpectedly from a gift shop ended his flight. A misstep on wet cobblestone brought Xuan to the ground. His damp hands immediately reached for his ankle, which was throbbing already with sharp pain.

He tried not to cry. It made his ankle feel even worse. He angrily wiped his face and put his hands on the ground to push himself up. The drizzle plumped into rain and Xuan stared at the drops on his arms. It was just water. It had no magical powers. Xuan should have known better. If the Lourdes water really had healing properties, more people would know about it. Diseases wouldn't exist. The old man would survive. His mother would go back to normal. But none of these things would happen. If anything, Lourdes had made his mother worse.

Is language only good for communicating?

Xuan quietly unlocked the apartment door's three deadbolts, unnecessary since the main building's door was locked as well, but it made his mother feel safer. The lights were already off, his parents asleep. Xuan was accustomed to walking through their apartment in the dark. He passed through the living room to the kitchen, where a small square of Swiss chocolate glittered on the counter, his father's favorite token of affection, a reliable welcome-home present after a late night of studying.

Xuan allowed the treat to melt on his tongue for several seconds, then chewed away at the inlaid walnuts. He'd been having problems sleeping lately and a glass of milk before bed was often helpful. As he closed the cupboard, his mother's face appeared where the dark space had been. Her eyes were clear and bright in the empty kitchen.

"You look like you're about to cry," she said.

"I was just startled," Xuan said, feeling for the counter to balance himself, his ears pounding. "I wasn't expecting you."

His mother watched as he finished his glass of milk, then poured himself another glass. She wore her bathrobe, a bright green fuzzy robe his father had gotten for her years ago. When she was nervous, she liked to twist the sleeves of the robe. She did it now. Her hair was streaked with gray and her eyes looked heavy and yellow. She was thirty-six years old.

"You've been avoiding me," his mother said. "I can tell, and I don't know what I did wrong."

"You did nothing wrong. I've just been studying, that's all. You know how important the bac is."

She looked doubtful. Xuan's mother only knew how important it was because everyone kept telling her so. But she didn't believe much that she was told. And in the last few years, she had even begun doubting Xuan.

"Your father is putting too much pressure on you," she said. "He and Father Truong talk about you when you are not here. The bac is only a test. You're not required to take it."

"Well, if I want a good job, I do."

"You are the smartest boy in the world. You don't need a test to prove that. Why do you let this family control you?"

"I want to take the bac," Xuan said.

"We can leave, you know," she said. "I couldn't before, but you're old enough now. We can go and live away from this family."

"Mother, this is our family," he said sharply.

"I'm your family," she said. "Not them. Did they protect you when it was really important?"

"Mom . . ." How could he stop her? He could never prevent her from talking. It happened like this every time. She needed to talk, he had to listen, and then she would collapse right in front of him, a tragic marionette, and every time, he would feel responsible, because he knew better, because he should have stopped her so many times before.

This time she could sense his dread. The fingers on her right hand curled up on her bathrobe sleeve, released, and then curled again.

"Don't you realize I can only talk to you? Only you can understand. You were there."

She'd said these words to him before. When he was in junior high, he shattered a dinner plate on the floor to make her stop. Now, he merely gripped his milk glass so tightly he thought it could break in his hands.

"Mom," he said, breathing deeply to calm himself. "I think we both need to go to sleep."

His mother brought a hand to her mouth and lightly bit the inside of her wrist. Her eyes traveled up to the ceiling and when they returned to Xuan, they narrowed slightly. She offered no indication of shame. "Okay," she said.

How can we determine the gravity of a mistake?

The first time it happened, Xuan had been sleeping. Walking back to their tent from dinner, Xuan leaned heavily against his mother's leg. He wanted her to carry him, but she said it was too far and he was too heavy. At five years old, he was no longer a baby like his cousin Lum. He was so tired that he crumpled onto their sleeping mat with his sandals on. She must have forgotten to pull them off of his feet, because when he awoke, that was the first thing he realized, feeling the bits of sand and grit between his toes and rubber sandals. And then he heard the grunting, soft but steady and unpleasant. He smelled the unfamiliar odor of another body in their tent.

He slowly sat up, rubbing his eyes. With his hands, he patted around the bamboo mat, seeking his mother, but instead felt a thick, hairy leg beside him. Instinctively, he dug his fingers into the damp, unfamiliar limb. A large hand quickly slapped his grip away, followed by a louder grunt.

His mother's voice, strained but firm: "Xuan, go back to sleep."

He turned back on the mat, curled into a snail, but instead of closing his eyes, he stared at the corner of the tent. Though it was dark, he could make out their shadows from the moonlight. Three other Malay guards sat on the floor. When one of them caught Xuan staring, he smiled broadly, nudging the guard sitting next to him. Xuan turned again, burying his face into the mat, scraping his cheeks against the fraying bamboo.

It was probably only several minutes, but it was also his first realization about how long time could last when he didn't want to be somewhere. He feared breathing too loudly. When the guard finally rolled off his mother, she pointed to the door with a shaky hand, and though it wasn't cold, Xuan pulled up the thin blanket around him, occasionally allowing one eye to peek out.

"What about me?" one of the guards asked, the only one, Xuan eventually learned, who spoke broken Vietnamese.

"Tomorrow," his mother said. "My child is awake."

The grinning guard in the back spoke up, barking in Malay.

The three men exchanged smiles. Then: "My friend likes your boy."

Xuan turned his head back to the wall, facing away from the men. He shouldn't have looked at them. But his mother wrapped a protective arm over him, pulling the blanket more securely over his head.

"Do whatever you want with me," she said. "If you touch him, I will tell anyone who will listen what you've done to him and they will slit your throats."

The guard translated to his friends. Xuan couldn't see their facial expressions, but he heard a few snickers and shuffling around. They knew she was right. A woman crying rape, the camp officers would have blamed her—certainly she had seduced them—and said that she deserved it. But the guards couldn't claim the same about a small boy.

Xuan chewed away at his bottom lip, his fingers rubbing between the blanket. Finally, the tent flap flipped up and the four men were gone.

When Xuan's mother pulled the blanket off his head, she had tears in her eyes. She smeared her fingers across Xuan's face, combing back his ocean-salted hair.

"Are you all right, dear one? Did those big men scare you?"

Xuan nodded.

"It's fine now," she said, still frantically raking his hair, smoothing her thumbs against his eyebrows. "You just pretend to be asleep the next time that happens, okay?" She hugged him, cooing *my baby, my baby*, but Xuan pulled away, his face puckering. The guards' sweat and saliva had imprinted themselves on his mother's skin, in her hair. She did not smell like his mother, but sour and unfamiliar.

Was this her memory or his? He felt it was his—he could see, taste, hear, and feel the hopelessness of that night . . . or was it because his mother had reminded him of every detail for so many years? He supposed it didn't matter if it was her memory or his. On certain days, when Xuan sat on the metro or walked in a city alley, he could smell the distinct, pungent perspiration of the guards and his stomach would identify it immediately, undeniably. It rendered him senseless, temporarily disorienting him, so he'd miss his stop or lose his sense of direction. A person could not invent that sort of memory.

Do ethical problems have perfect solutions? Are fairness and unfairness only conventions?

Xuan blinked at the questions, which blurred when he first looked at them. He reread the words and realized the essay prompts were not in the cursive handwriting of his study notebook, but typewritten on official examination paper. His eyes wandered. He was surrounded by his classmates, their faces low, their shoulders hunched over as they wrote. On his right, several rows behind him, he saw Cam, wearing her reading glasses, her hair in braids, also intensely absorbed in her bac booklet.

Hearing a throat clearing from the front of the room Xuan lifted his head. Professor Arnaud glared at him from her desk, an index finger held to the corner of her right eye. Xuan returned to gaze at the exam booklet sitting before him. These questions looked familiar. He'd seen previous versions of them in his study guides and had prepared sample answers months ago. For the ethics question, he could quote from Kant's three critiques or *Confessions of Saint Augustine*, or for the fairness prompt, he could cite Auguste Comte's philosophy of positivism.

He checked his watch and bit his bottom lip. Two hours had passed, and not a mark written, no notes, no sentences. Xuan again discreetly tilted his head to the left, then the right, and realized most of his classmates were possibly on their fifth or sixth page of argumentation.

The last two hours of his life had disappeared, but it was even difficult to recall the past few days and weeks. He remembered studying with Cam. He remembered coming home that night and talking to his mother. After that, he'd gone to bed. After that, the timeline became fuzzy. No images or sounds conjured in his head like they always had before, events out of order, his photographic memory suddenly broken, leaving only an empty gray space.

A page rustle snapped in his ears. To his left, a classmate had turned to her last essay page. There was no more time. Xuan gripped his hands on the desk, planting both feet on the floor. Reminding himself he only needed to answer one, Xuan slowly reread the questions, patiently waiting for his thoughts to settle, for the sentences to follow. He felt an enormous temptation to grab his head and smash it against the desk, rebooting his memory, ending this uncharacteristic malaise. Instead, he recalled a relaxation technique his father used on his mother during panic attacks, attempting to release tension from every segment of the body, toes to head. Toes, calves, thighs, butt, stomach, chest, shoulders, neck, head. Head.

He picked up his pencil and began to write.

Why do we want to be free?

Few people remained outside when Xuan, the last to turn in his exam, emerged from the classroom. Grandpère stood in the school yard, waiting for him. He held an unlit cigarette, even though today wasn't Sunday. Cam had probably grown impatient and left ahead of them. That was fine. He didn't need to go over the answers he probably missed.

It was a bright, beautiful day. The season of the bac had begun and by tomorrow, the philosophy questions would make their annual appearance in the papers. Approaching his grandfather, Xuan realized the two of them now stood at near equal height.

"Are you hungry?" Grandpère asked, offering his lighter to Xuan.

"I'm tired," Xuan admitted. "I only want to go home."

He lit the cigarette and watched his grandfather puff, then hand it to Xuan. He inhaled, exhaled, enjoying the breaths.

"I remember taking the bac," Grandpère said. "Did you know I chose Spanish as my foreign language? Of course I can't remember any of it now . . . if I'd known Sanh and his family would go to America, I would have learned English. . . . Are you learning English?"

Xuan regarded him carefully, but his grandfather's face looked serious, waiting for an answer.

"Yes," Xuan said. "I told you I was taking English."

"Good, good," Grandpère said, nodding, as he took back the cigarette. "We must acclimate to the changing world, right, Xuan?"

Xuan pushed the breath through his lips. "Yes, Grandpère."

At the front of their apartment house, Grandpère stopped in front of the birdbath, empty and sad-looking in winter, but this sunny afternoon it contained a shallow pool of water and one sparrow perched at the edge. Like the rest of the family, he usually passed by it with only a cursory glance, but this afternoon, he leaned over the concrete washbasin with interest, until the bird flapped away.

"How long has this been here, Xuan? Did your father recently buy this?"

"No Grandpère," Xuan said. "It's always been here."

"I don't think so," Grandpère said. "I would have noticed before."

Perhaps it had only been a long afternoon. Memories are hard to quantify and impossible to reason with. People forget all the time and then the past returns, unexpectedly, disturbing the present. Perhaps philosophers could afford to ask questions, to delight in the inconsistencies and contradictions. Not Xuan. The philosophy portion of the bac had ended. He had other subjects to study.

1981

Kim-Ly Vo
Ho Chi Minh City, Vietnam

. . . *Both children were born at inconvenient times. Strangers gazed at me with pity, disappointment, even contempt. In Vietnam, pregnant with Lum, I was breeding another mouth to feed, robbing other children of precious food. In America, pregnant with Cherry, I was securing my American residency status, leeching off a welfare system I hadn't contributed to.*

Their opinions did not matter. I was happy when Lum was born. Even though I had every right to be miserable—my husband was in the prison camp, and my in-laws were insufferable—all I had to do was hold my precious son and my anxieties floated away.

I expected a similar feeling to come over me with the second child. Is it because the children have such different temperaments? I should be more understanding, since I was your third. I know what it's like not to be first. But Lum was never such a demanding child. He hardly cried. He slept so easily next to me. Not Cherry. Nothing I do satisfies her. Even now, she is crying again. I've nursed her, changed her diaper. What else does she want? I can't hold her forever.

I now realize how correct you were about raising daughters. That is why I believe Cherry must be my last child. I can't risk having another girl. I know how hard it was to have sisters. Cherry is lucky—a brother will always

protect her. I love my sisters, but I will always regret our callous competitiveness. It's hard enough to be a woman. I can't wish that kind of life on her, not
here. It would be too much. . . .

Tuyet Truong
Tustin, California, USA

❧ *Chapter Six*

CHERRY

S O UNCLE BAO CHEATED ON AUNTIE TRI. AGAIN. THE NEWS had reenergized her mother on a lazy Sunday night when Cherry expected to have the first floor of the house to herself. Her mother scooted across the kitchen floor in her chenille slippers, clicking her acrylic nails along the granite kitchen counter, the phone wedged between her ear and shoulder. Though already dressed in her pajamas, she'd forgotten to remove her gold hoop earrings, and they shook with fury.

"Who saw them?" she asked Auntie Hien.

Duyen had seen them, she'd told Cherry so the night before, but instead of interrupting, passing on the gossip that fueled her mother's conversations, Cherry turned the page of her American history text-book, where Burr was initiating the ill-fated duel with Hamilton.

Typically, when Uncle Bao got caught straying, Auntie Tri packed a weekend bag and drove Linh to stay with Cherry or with Duyen's family.

Auntie Tri would circle phone numbers in the yellow pages for divorce lawyers, occasionally calling to inquire about rates. She'd complain about what a useless bastard she'd married, his lack of ambition toward any practical job, and about how his plan to return to singing was little more than pathetic chatter, since his voice had degenerated from all his drinking and smoking—and if she had to do it again, she'd marry that halitosis-plagued, yet sweet, businessman who courted her when she was still in high school. Within a few days, Uncle Bao would show up, and after several hours of tears and screaming, he'd take the family he swore he loved and respected back home. Once, he even karaoke-serenaded Auntie Tri without any sense of irony. While that overture remained a family favorite, it still recycled the same tired accusations and promises, like a bad Vietnamese soap opera, and it surprised Cherry that no one else had grown weary talking about it.

Cherry disliked gossip, and her family was full of it. What was wrong with communication and honesty? Without other people's problems, her family would have nothing to say to one another. And Cherry's mother, still homesick for Little Saigon, needed to talk.

The garage door opened and Cherry looked up. Her brother entered, cradling a tall vase of purple tulips. Lum balanced them on the kitchen counter in front of their mother, who kissed his cheek in gratitude, while continuing her conversation. Lum turned and handed his sister a single yellow gerbera daisy, Cherry's favorite flower.

"Who was it this time?" Cherry asked, tucking the daisy into her textbook as a bookmark.

"Former fiancée," Lum said. "She asked me to tell him she's changing her phone number."

Cherry's brother worked part-time as a delivery boy for a flower shop in Little Saigon, and often brought home the rejected orders at the end of the day. Ex-girlfriends, former wives, and even pissed-off mothers, refused to sign for the most exquisite flower arrangements; their consistent anger and resentment kept the otherwise sterile house fragrant and beautiful. Their mother could count on several fresh floral arrangements a week.

Lum walked to the refrigerator and pulled out a dinner their mother had set aside. He popped it in the microwave and took a seat next to Cherry. She edged away, and he deliberately moved closer.

"We're meeting at Quynh's to watch a movie," he said. "Wanna come?"

It was tempting. She'd been cooped up in the house all day, listening to their parents bicker. Their only day off together in the week and they spent it arguing.

"I have school tomorrow."

"So what?" he said. "Haven't you been good enough all weekend?"

"But it's already eight o'clock."

"I'll get you back early." Lum stood to retrieve his dish from the microwave.

"Promise?"

He smiled as he pulled the plastic wrap from the bowl, the steam rushing to his face. "Whenever you want."

While their mother only nodded when she saw them leaving, their father stepped in front of Lum's car before he could pull out of the driveway. A pile of shrubs and branches that he'd been gathering from the front yard all afternoon lay by the side of the house.

"You said you were going to help me this evening," their father said to Lum. "Trash pickup is tomorrow."

"Sorry, I forgot," Lum said. "Just leave it. I'll do it in the morning."

Their father shook his head. "You won't wake up in time. You never do."

"I said I was sorry," Lum said, tapping his foot on the brake so the car jerked forward a little. "Do you want me to do it now?"

Their father waved his hand, turning to his pile of greenery. The back of his T-shirt was dark with perspiration. "Never mind. Go play with your friends."

They turned off the cul-de-sac, passing neighbors who likewise were collecting the week's garbage, garden waste, and recyclables. The subdivision wasn't even a year old, so the houses and landscaping still felt brochure-quality fresh, with artfully arranged trees dividing the roads, the smoothly paved sidewalks retaining their sparkly grains. The week they moved in, Lum deliberately spit his gum on the sidewalk at the end of the driveway and ground it in with his heel. The next morning, they couldn't find his gum stain. Cherry was pretty sure their mother had scraped it off. Cherry looked over at Lum. He was still scowling.

"So what movie are we watching?" she asked, once they'd merged onto the freeway.

"He knows I just got back from work," Lum said. "Why isn't that enough for him?"

"You did say you'd help him," Cherry reminded him. All afternoon, while Cherry finished an essay for her English class, she watched their father bend over the flower beds and strain for the too-tall tree branches. They hardly saw their dad during the week since his promotion at the plant as a shift manager, and when he was around on weekends, he seemed equally stressed with all the chores required to maintain the new house.

"Did he ask you to help him?" Lum asked.

"I tried," she said. "He kept telling me to go study."

"Well, he never says that to me."

"That's because he knows better." She tried to say this jokingly, but she'd never been good at teasing. Last May, after graduating from high school, Lum had been denied admission to every UC and Cal State school he had applied to. Their cousin Dat had received a Regents Scholarship to UC Irvine the previous year. Lum's girlfriend, Quynh, had the option of either attending UC Irvine or Riverside with generous financial aid. Even Linh, who only aspired to work at the family's salon because she could work any hours she wanted, had been accepted to Cal State Fullerton.

Lum promised their mother he wouldn't give up, that he'd study hard in community college and transfer to a Cal State. But instead of enrolling in the college with the high transfer rate down the street from their new house, he enrolled in the same junior college that his friends were going to. Plus, instead of reducing his hours at the florist shop, he took on more after their father refused to pay for a life-drawing class.

"The only time he notices me," Lum said, "is when I'm leaving."

"Then stop leaving," Cherry said, which thankfully elicited a smile from him.

The concrete of the freeway stretched far ahead of Lum's car. She'd forgotten how long it took to get from their home in Newport Lake to Little Saigon. In rush hour, the drive could last up to an hour, but on a Sunday evening, the lanes felt empty and vast. They arrived at Quynh's house in twenty minutes. Huy and Linh's cars were already parked in the driveway.

Quynh met them at the door. When they walked into Quynh's living room, Duyen and Linh had already annexed the couch, while Huy and Johnny lay splayed out on the shaggy carpet playing cards. Linh looked like she was about to fall off the couch, leaning so far over the side to talk with Huy and Johnny, her face nearly touching the floor.

"I thought you said you had to study," Duyen said as Cherry took a seat on the empty recliner.

"I finished," Cherry said, straining her eyes in the dim lamplight to glance over at the staircase. Lum and Quynh had already disappeared upstairs to her bedroom.

"Finally," Duyen said. "You do more work at that school than Dat does as a premed."

"I like studying," Cherry said, feeling her cheeks flush with annoyance.

"But not all the time," she said. "Not even you could like it that much." Duyen giggled, her breath sweet with alcohol. "Now if you were still at our school, you could be at the top of your class without trying so hard."

Cherry stared at her cousin's half-empty beer bottle. "Don't you have school tomorrow, too?"

"I'll write a sick note," Duyen said. "They never check anyway."

"Hey, Cherry," Linh said, sitting up. "Did you hear about Uncle Viet and Khanh?"

Cherry looked at Duyen, but she only smiled knowingly with Linh.

"They called off their engagement," her cousin sang. "One of his other girlfriends confronted him when they were out at the movies last week. Now Khanh won't take his calls."

"They'll get back together by next week," Duyen said. "They always do."

"Bet they don't," Linh said. "Because then I heard from Mommy this morning that Khanh's first husband and their daughter finally got their immigration papers accepted. So she's gonna go back to him so they can be a family again."

"Such a hypocrite," Duyen said.

"Isn't she?" Linh said, then caught the frown on Cherry's face. "What's wrong with you?"

"Nothing," Cherry lied. Duyen was playing with Linh's hair. For the last year, they'd been experimenting with hairstyles. When Cherry looked at them from behind, she couldn't tell who was who, amid their current clean blocks of black hair with identical highlights.

Duyen and Linh never used to get along this well. Since they started working at the salon, shampooing hair and sanitizing the manicure and pedicure instruments, they found more things in common: makeup, music, boys. Mostly boys. Cherry shouldn't have felt jealous. But while her brother and cousins all attended high school together, she stayed behind in middle-school hell. Her classmates didn't know what to make of her. Cherry wasn't outgoing and good at sports like Lum. Or pretty and thin like Duyen and Linh.

And she certainly hoped she wasn't like Dat: best grades in class and zero friends. Even his sister wouldn't eat lunch with him. Cherry tried to fold over her test scores when the teachers handed them back, but her classmates knew. So when her father earned his long-promised promotion at the plant and her parents could finally afford the new house they'd been coveting for months, it felt like a relief. While they claimed they were tired of the recent burglaries in the neighborhood, Cherry knew her parents' tour of the magnet high school in Newport Lake was reason enough for them to ditch their ethnic enclave. Cherry relished the fresh start, the new opportunities. She could enroll in as many AP classes and geeky academic clubs as she wanted without being compared to anyone else.

While their cousins discussed hair color and Cherry flipped through the television channels, Huy and Johnny continued their unending game of Texas Hold'em. Eventually, Lum and Quynh returned, and he joined the boys in their poker game. Ever since they were little, watching

Uncle Viet play poker at family parties, Lum and his friends had been obsessed with card games. Cherry had played it a few times, but her interest never lasted. While skill and cleverness were required, too much still depended on dumb luck.

Quynh and Duyen went outside to smoke, and since she couldn't stand watching Linh pretend to care about poker, Cherry joined them. Quynh's backyard reminded Cherry of their old yard: small, crowded, and sad. At some time, hydrangea bushes had been planted along the wire-fence borders, but they appeared in dire need of pruning, while the lawn had been left to burn out. Next door, they could hear neighborhood kids playing a night game of kickball, and grasshoppers chirping in the still warm autumn weather.

"She thinks she likes Huy," Duyen revealed as they brushed cobwebs from the patio furniture.

"Since when?" Quynh asked, her eyes hidden under layered bangs.

Duyen deeply inhaled and exhaled before answering. "Oh, who knows? He's not even her type." Duyen wouldn't elaborate. She never did, preferring simple, declarative statements without any supporting evidence. "Anyway, Linh's only doing this to piss off her dad. The loser."

"Is she really upset?" Cherry asked. Given how many times Linh's family went through this drama, her cousin should have grown used to the routine.

"I didn't tell you what she did," Duyen said, her eyes brightening. "This morning, Auntie Tri was packing to leave, like she does every time, and Linh stopped her. She told Uncle Bao it was his turn to leave. She said she was tired of him shitting up their schedules. Can you believe that?"

"Good for her," Quynh said.

"What did Auntie Tri say?" Cherry asked.

"She must have agreed with Linh because he's gone."

Quynh held up her cigarette and leaned forward. "Did you hear that?"

They listened. A footstep crunched leaves, and then another step. Duyen and Quynh both squashed their cigarettes. Cherry felt her breath shorten as the steps grew heavier, closer. A figure emerged from the side of the house.

"Jesus Christ," Duyen said, spitting into the grass. "Are you spying on us?"

"No," Dat said indignantly, stepping into the light, squinting, looking very much like the creepy stalker Cherry had expected. "Mom wants you home."

"Why didn't you just call here?"

"I tried, like three times. No one answered."

"Fine." She kicked her cigarette butt into the grass. "I need to get my purse. Stay here."

Perhaps because it was dark, Dat didn't realize he was gawking at Quynh. With his rimless eyeglasses, oversize UCI sweatshirt, khaki shorts, and slumped posture, he still didn't look old enough to attend college. A breeze rustled the trees, sending a slight chill up Cherry's arms and legs.

"How's it going?" Quynh politely asked.

"Good," Dat said, trying to casually lean one hand on Duyen's chair, which scraped forward on the concrete. "So how's o-chem? You have Manchikanti, right?"

"It's fine," Quynh said. "Didn't do so great on the last lab, so I'm going to her extra tutorial on Fridays."

"Right, I remember. I never went to those."

"Oh, yeah?"

"Well, it's just . . . I never had to."

"Oh," Quynh said, nodding. "Good for you."

"Thanks." Dat avoided looking at Cherry, probably aware that she was horrified.

Duyen returned, with Linh skipping behind her.

"How's your mom?" Dat asked.

Linh glared at him. "Fine," she said, loudly popping her gum.

"So I'll probably see you around campus?" Dat asked, looking only at Quynh.

"Sure, maybe," she said.

"We could eat together if we have the same break in between classes," Dat said, straightening his shoulders. "We probably do. I've seen you on Tuesday mornings near Tamkin Hall, but not always. You could e-mail me your class schedule, if you wanted, and I could find a good time."

"She is not sending you her schedule," Linh said, examining a chipped nail on her hand.

Duyen cleared her throat, yanking at her brother's arm. "Let's go."

"I'll see you next weekend at Lum's birthday party," Quynh said.

"Birthday party?" Dat echoed, swatting his sister's arm away, suddenly interested.

"Yeah," Quynh said, turning to look at Cherry, confused. "It is next weekend, right?" Their mother was planning a family dinner for Lum.

"Oh, right," Dat said, his dopey grin nearly nauseating Cherry. "My mom mentioned it. I only briefly forgot. Good, I'll see you there."

Lum never appeared bothered by Dat's crush on Quynh. It actually seemed to amuse him every time their cousin bumbled and stumbled around her. Quynh was the only person, aside from Grandmother Vo and his parents, Dat didn't speak down to with a sneer. Lum hardly felt threatened. Though Dat was a full year older than Lum, he was significantly shorter and scrawnier. When they were kids, Dat argued that he simply hadn't gone through his adolescent growth spurt yet, and told them they'd be sorry when he finally did. When that never arrived, he blamed his small size on not getting the proper nutrition he needed as a baby back in Vietnam, and that if he'd grown up in America, he'd certainly be as tall as Lum. But the other kids didn't care that he was short. Nor did they hold his scholastic aptitude and academic awards against him. They didn't like Dat because he was a jerk—a trait he cultivated all by himself.

"Such an idiot," Linh said, after they returned inside, interrupting the boys' round of cards and reporting on Dat's latest awkward intrusion.

"He's not that bad," Quynh said.

"You can only believe that if you're not related to him," Linh seethed. While Quynh and Cherry sat on the couch, she stretched herself out on the floor, her hair fanned across the carpet, making sure Huy could see the exposed belly between her gray tank top and jeans. Her cheeks were pink, and Cherry wasn't sure if it was from the multiple shots of Crown she reeked of, or genuine anger.

"Well, he's not worth our breath," Lum said, still concentrating on his cards.

"You remember that time when we were little and he narced on you at Grandmother's birthday party?" Linh asked.

"Linh," Cherry groaned.

"What? We were all there."

"Then we've all heard it before," Lum said.

"Not about what Uncle Chinh did after," Linh teased.

"What happened?" Huy said.

"See?" Linh said, smirking. Cherry looked away, trying not to cringe. She shouldn't have bothered. Once her cousin seized the attention of a room, nothing could shut her mouth.

"So Dat lies about Lum hitting him," Linh continued, "and Lum gets spanked, right? But what you didn't know was later that night, when Dat and his family got home, Uncle Chinh started screaming at him for being such a wimp. Like he should have defended himself against Lum, though we all know that could never happen. Next time we see him? He's got a black eye. Won't say where he got it, but we all know. His father was trying to teach him how to fight."

She began to laugh. No one joined her. Cherry watched her cousin's face flush a deeper shade of red as she hooted at the popcorn ceiling, nearly hysterical with tears. She wondered again how people could find Linh attractive. Yes, she was skinny. Yes, she had shiny, long hair. But the second she began speaking, the illusion of anything delicate, anything beautiful, shattered. At that moment, Cherry couldn't imagine anyone, or anything else, uglier than her.

The house had been dusted and swept, with day-old floral arrangements prominently displayed in each room. Clusters of blue and yellow balloons bobbed along the stair banisters. As the birthday boy, Lum wore the light-blue button-down shirt their mother had picked out the previous weekend, and he allowed her to usher him from room to room for a not-so-spontaneous circuit of chitchat.

While their father was responsible for replenishing the buffet table,

Cherry answered the front door and refreshed guests' drinks. Most of the guests arrived on time and the dishes her mother and aunties had prepared were warm and savory. Every time she passed Grandmother Vo, she'd ask if Cherry knew Dat's whereabouts.

"Maybe he's not coming," Cherry finally said, picking up her barely touched papaya salad. "Maybe he had to study."

Grandmother impatiently shook her head, like she'd given the wrong answer. "Your cousin would never disregard a family function."

When Cherry approached Lum and their mother, they were talking with the Ngos, a couple who had recently opened a dentistry practice in the old mini-mall complex where their mom used to work. When Cherry approached them, Mr. Ngo was explaining what an easy work schedule he had with his own practice.

"If I am tired and I need the morning off, I know she can help me out," Mr. Ngo said, affectionately squeezing his wife's shoulder. "Working with family has many benefits."

"Dentistry school is not too long, is it?" their mother asked.

"It's four years, just like medical school," Cherry said.

Her mother shot Cherry an exasperated look. "But not as difficult, right?" she asked, oblivious to her offense. "Cherry is book smart, but Lum? More like me, more practical smart. Learns quick on his feet through experience."

"You still need to pass the exams," Mrs. Ngo said.

"Lum always had such nice teeth. I never had to remind him to brush and floss every day, not like his sister. Show them your teeth, sweetie."

Lum offered up a demonstration, and Mrs. Ngo complimented his bite, which their mother gloated never needed to be corrected with braces.

The front door opened and Dat stepped in. Instead of greeting them, he walked directly to the dining room where his parents were getting second helpings at the buffet. After Dat whispered in their ears, Auntie Hien screamed, while Uncle Chinh's face widened into a rare smile. Conversations around the house quieted, as all curious gazes fixated on Dat.

"What's wrong?" Grandmother demanded from across the room.

Auntie Hien could barely stand still, clapping her hands like a little girl. "Tell them, darling."

Dat looked around the room, his chin nearly raised to the ceiling. The chandelier above him glittered like a crown on his head. "I won a research fellowship at the National Institutes of Health for the summer."

"In Washington, D.C.," Uncle Chinh broke in. "They only select one student from UCI each year. And not even every year!"

"So prestigious," Auntie Hien said, nodding in agreement. "Any student who has this fellowship will have his pick of medical schools."

"That's not always true," Dat said, smiling sheepishly. "But it's often the case."

The guests crowded around him to offer their congratulations. Even Grandmother Vo called him over to her seat to give him a hug.

"Sorry," Dat said when Lum shook his hand. "I didn't mean to take any attention away from your party."

"I don't care," Lum said. "It's great news."

Cherry walked into the kitchen, where she helped her dad load the dishwasher and put out the plates for cake and ice cream. They could hear her mother setting up the karaoke machine in the living room. Typically, Uncle Bao set up the karaoke machine, but since he and Auntie Tri were still fighting, he hadn't been invited.

"Did your brother call Grandmère?" her father asked as they dried the dessert forks with some dishrags. She'd called earlier that afternoon, when Lum was out picking up ice bags.

"Not yet," Cherry said.

"Tell him not to forget," he said. "She wanted him to talk to Grandpère, too. He was having a good day today. Who knows how he will be tomorrow?" He sadly shook his head and continued to rub the forks dry.

Cherry wished their father could tell Lum himself, but they'd gotten into an argument that morning when Lum was opening his presents over breakfast. Their father had bought Lum a graphing calculator.

"The man at the store said it's good for chemistry, calculus, biology," their father proudly said, as Lum turned the box over in his hands. "Top of the line."

"I'm not even taking premed classes," Lum said, handing it back to him. "Couldn't you have asked me before wasting your money?"

"You say no to foreign-language classes," their father said, "and no to literature classes. And now you refuse to take science? Why are we even paying for you to go to school?"

Their mother sent Lum off to the grocery store to pick up extra ice. She then made Cherry's father promise not to talk to Lum for the rest of the night.

"You want me to be happy today?" their mother told him. "You leave my son alone."

So he did. Their father and Lum barely looked at each other all evening and were always on the opposite ends of the room. Even when Lum blew out his candles on the birthday cake, their father stood in the doorway of the dining room, looking more like one of the polite acquaintances than a proud father.

After the cake was served, many of the guests left, but their mother's relatives and coworkers from the salon stayed behind to watch a Vietnamese movie. The kids loitered in the backyard, trying to organize carpools to Huy's house for a poker game arranged in Lum's honor. Cherry felt worn out, but her cousins threatened to make fun of her if she stayed in on another Saturday night. Duyen looked over and caught her brother lurking behind the screen door.

"What do you want?" she asked.

"Is there room for another player?" Dat asked, half of his face hidden behind the doorframe.

"Are you kidding?" Linh asked, but Lum and Huy exchanged glances and smiled.

"It's a five-hundred-dollar buy-in," Huy said. "Cash only."

"I can go to an ATM," Dat said.

"Sure then," Lum said. "Of course." He even offered Dat a ride in his car, leaving Cherry to ride with Linh and Duyen.

"What is your brother up to?" Linh asked as they walked through the house to the front door.

"Who knows?" Duyen said. "Hey, I didn't realize they had to cough up so much dough. Cherry, did you know that?"

Cherry shook her head. She hadn't realized Lum had that much cash to spare.

They said good night to their mothers, who were rehashing the evening's events and munching on egg rolls before the movie. Cherry's mother reminded her to come home early since she had an academic decathlon competition the next day.

As they walked down the driveway, a parked car across the street turned its lights on. Duyen put her hand up to peer at the familiar vehicle.

"Linh, it's your dad."

Perhaps it was because of his old singing career in Saigon, but Uncle Bao had always prided himself on his appearance: gel-sculpted hair, fitted shirts, and polished shoes. Even though he worked as an auto mechanic, his nails were always clean and trimmed, his face free of grease. Tonight, he wore a pair of loose-fitting sweats and a faded T-shirt. And he smelled. French fries, cigarettes, and body odor. Cherry looked past him at his car, and recognized Linh's ratty old Care Bears sleeping bag in the backseat. A pillow and several bags of fried shrimp chips were stuffed in the back window.

"I'll see you guys later," Linh said, only looking at her father, his eyes large and pleading.

"But you're giving us a ride," Duyen said.

"Go with Johnny," Linh snapped.

"Uncle Bao is so pathetic," Duyen whispered as they buckled into the backseat of Johnny's car. "I can't believe he had the guts to show up."

"He did wait for the party to end," Cherry said.

"Can you believe he's sleeping in his car?" Duyen asked, bopping to the thumping bass from the car speakers. "Linh must feel so humiliated."

Huy's poker party was larger than Cherry expected. She knew he'd been organizing these games for some time, but she'd assumed it was just four or five friends around the kitchen table. Instead, cars lined up around the block—Cherry counted more than were at Lum's birthday party. Plenty of guys she'd never seen before, some of them as old as their parents, sauntered around Huy's front yard. They brought along foldout card tables, metal briefcases full of poker chips, and six-packs of beer.

Lum, Quynh, and Dat arrived a few minutes later. Lum had untucked his dress shirt, already looking more at home at Huy's than he had at their parents' house. Dat was trying his best to look casual, but was clearly freaked about the cash he carried, obsessively patting his jacket pocket with his right hand. As the players exchanged their cash for chips, Cherry leaned against her brother's shoulder.

"What money are you using?" Cherry asked, chewing on her jagged thumbnail.

"Birthday money," he replied.

"All of it?"

Lum laughed as he held a stack of chips between his thumb and middle finger. "Don't worry, Cherry. I'm careful."

The poker party split into a collection of smaller games throughout the house. Dat and Lum ended up at the same table in Huy's bedroom. The girls set up their foldout chairs a respectable distance from the table. Once the deal was called and blinds thrown, everyone knew to be quiet.

Cherry's only previous poker-viewing experiences were Uncle Viet's games, before he decided to quit (or before Grandmother Vo forced him to). Those games were much more interesting to watch. At Huy's house, no one shouted or groaned at the flop. No praying or cursing. These players only muttered their calls and folds. Even when someone won a hand, he simply swept his arm to collect the chips.

Quynh returned from the kitchen and handed Duyen another beer and Cherry a glass of tap water. Between hands, Quynh would replenish the players' drinks and empty out the cereal bowls they were using for ashtrays. She did this so naturally, Cherry wondered how long she'd been tending to these games, how long Lum had been playing in them.

To pass the time, Cherry observed the players, studying their faces to determine how successful their bluffs were. The skill level was disappointing. For all their seriousness, no one even attempted to read each other's tics, leading to lousy bets and lost opportunities. Huy, the host, couldn't hide his smirk if he had any pair. Another boy slumped his shoulders at every bad hand. But the worst—for possibly the first time in his life—was Dat, indecisive when it was his turn, and petulant when he lost. Given his competitors, Cherry's brother, who held the only decent poker face at the table, had no problem taking control of the game, though his winnings were small. Cherry got the feeling he was holding back.

While Huy dealt the next hand, Linh appeared in the doorway. Her eyes were pink, her mascara smeared.

"Is this where the party is?" she asked, smiling, leaning against the doorframe.

"Shhhh," one of the players said automatically, glaring at her.

"Huy?" Linh said, taking another step inside. "Did that jerk just shush me?"

Some of the players groaned, putting down their cards, leaning back into their chairs. Huy took a sip from his glass, sharing an exasperated glance with Lum.

"Excuse me?" Linh said, waving her hands above her head. "Hello? I'm still here."

"Linh," Huy finally said, still barely looking at her. "We're in the middle of a round. Can it wait?"

Duyen stood and blocked Linh from walking farther into the room. "Why don't we go outside?" Duyen suggested. "It's boring here anyway."

Before Linh could answer, Duyen had successfully pushed her out to the hallway. Cherry and Quynh could still hear Linh yelling, her angry words muffled through the wall.

"She looked really upset," Quynh said. "Maybe we should go help."

Cherry shrugged her shoulders. If they went out there, the three of them rushing to tend to Linh's outburst, she'd only grow more hysterical. Sometimes Linh calmed down if she realized she didn't have an audience. "Duyen can deal with her."

Settling her head against Quynh's shoulder, Cherry watched another hand. She'd always admired Quynh, someone people considered both smart and pretty, a pairing no one in their family had ever managed.

"Did you know," Quynh whispered, "that Dat spent three hours helping me memorize biochemistry formulas last week?"

Cherry took a breath, trying to imagine Dat doing something so selfless. "Really?"

"He didn't have to."

"He probably wanted to," she said. "He'll be with you any way he can."

Quynh sighed. "He wants to be friends, with all of us. He told me so."

"And you believed him?"

Her smile was vague. "He thought your brother would respect him if he played."

Cherry snorted. "Why?"

"Because I suggested it." Quynh sighed. "Maybe it was a stupid idea."

Cherry peered over at the table, at the meager pile of chips in front of her cousin. While she surmised that Lum was leading the table, Cherry hadn't considered that Dat could be in last place, though it was clear why. The more he lost, the worse his calls became, his chip pile dwindling.

"Can I buy more chips?" Dat asked. "You know I'm good for it."

Huy started counting out chips. "How much do you want? A hundred?"

"I'll have five hundred again."

Huy and Lum exchanged a glance.

"I saw that," Dat snapped, wiping his sweaty forehead with the heel of his free hand. "I know what I'm doing. Just give me what I asked."

Once Dat received the chips, Huy dealt the cards. Some of the players swiftly folded. Huy revealed the flop. The rest of the players folded, leaving only Lum and Dat. Their cousin called Lum's bet and raised him a hundred. Lum raised it another hundred. Sickeningly, Dat did it again, committing the ridiculous move of the most desperate player, pushing all of his chips in. Well over a thousand dollars in the pot. The other players smirked at one another, enjoying the suicidal spectacle, waiting for the river card.

Quynh leaned forward in her seat, elbows on her knees, fingers pressed to her lips. Cherry wanted to say something to Lum, to get him to stop this, but she only sat back, her breath in her throat. She could already imagine Auntie Hien and Uncle Chinh's expressions of outrage, Grandmother Vo's withering glares of recrimination, her own mother's shame.

How could you let this happen? she'd say, not to Lum, not to Dat, not to anyone but Cherry. Only Cherry.

Lum stared at his cards, slowly chewing on his lip. "I fold," he finally said, setting his cards down.

And with that, the air returned to the room. The other players began to chuckle. Huy pushed the chips to Dat, but Cherry's cousin put his hand out.

"What are you doing?" Dat asked. "You're not even going to wait for the river?"

Lum shook his head.

"Let me see your hand," Dat said, reaching across the table.

Lum was faster, pulling his cards away, slipping them back with the rest of the cards that Huy slid over to him. "No."

The other players lost interest, pushing away from the table, milling out of the room for a cigarette break. Quynh and Cherry stood and walked up to the table.

"C'mon," Huy said quietly, resting a hand on Dat's shoulder. "You played a good game."

Dat shrugged Huy's hand off. "Don't touch me," he said. He looked back at Cherry's brother. "Did you just set me up?"

"How did I set you up?" Lum asked. "You won."

"Did you let me win?" Dat asked. "Are you pitying me?"

"Dat," Quynh said hesitantly.

Dat turned to her sharply, glowering. "Did you put him up to this?"

"Dat," Quynh said again, her voice more insistent.

"Listen," Lum quietly said, his eyes occasionally glancing at the door. "I know you've been helping Quynh study and I appreciate it. I'm just looking out for you, okay, cousin?" His words sounded sincere; even his delivery evoked generosity. But Cherry only had to look at the smile on his face. He was enjoying this.

"No," Dat said. "Not okay. I was helping your girlfriend because she clearly needed the help."

"Hey," Cherry interrupted.

"Shut up," Dat said, pointing a finger at her, before turning to look at Lum and Quynh. "But I don't need help. Certainly not from you."

"Maybe you should go," Huy said. While they'd been arguing, he'd counted out Dat's chips and replaced them with a short pile of bills.

Dat's face had grown red and moist. As he leaned forward to gather his money, the collected perspiration from his forehead sprinkled the table. His hands trembled with frustration as he stuffed the bills deep into his jacket pocket. When he finally looked up at them, his eyes appeared full of hate.

"I could report you, you know," he said. "It's illegal to gamble, and you're underage."

"Dat," Lum said, no longer able to hide his grin, "you asked to come here, remember? You asked for this."

They all silently watched as Dat took several deep breaths, zipped up his jacket, and walked out of the room. Cherry wanted to say something to Lum, but the rest of the players had returned. Quynh gathered some empty beer bottles and left the room. Cherry followed her.

In the kitchen, Quynh dumped the spent bottles into the sink and then pulled out a clean glass from the cupboard to pour herself some tap water. Cherry leaned against the counter, her eyes glazing over the dust and crumbs on the floor.

"Did you know he was going to do that?" Cherry asked.

"No," Quynh said, after taking a long drink. "I had no idea."

"Lum should have just let him lose," Cherry said, shaking her head in disgust.

"That would have just embarrassed Dat. Your brother wanted to humiliate him."

"Wait," Cherry said, confused. "Whose side are you on?"

Quynh stared at the glass in her hands. "There shouldn't be sides."

"You're defending Dat. How can you do that after what he said to you?"

"He didn't mean it," Quynh said. "You can't get mad at someone if they don't understand what they're doing."

"Yes, you can. He's not stupid. He knows how to hurt people. He always has."

"But he didn't," Quynh said. "Your brother did. Dat was reaching out to your brother, and Lum threw it in his face."

"Or maybe Lum recognized Dat was bullshitting."

Quynh shook her head. "I should have handled this better. I could have stopped this."

The piercing crash of shattered glass reverberated throughout the house. They both jumped, Quynh grabbing for Cherry's arm. A car alarm erupted, followed by shouting. Cherry recognized one of the voices, the pitch, the near shrill. People hustled down the stairs and out of the house.

When they ran outside, they saw the sparkly shards of glass scattered across Huy's driveway. The car alarm from Huy's Toyota Corolla continued to wail, while the guys from the poker game gawked at the gaping hole where the car's rear windshield used to be. On the sidewalk, Linh continued to hurl beer bottles from the recycling bin at the car and garage door. Duyen pleaded with her to stop.

Huy pushed past Cherry's shoulder. He pulled at Linh's hair once he saw the damage, incensed. "You crazy bitch!" he screamed. "What is wrong with you?"

Linh tossed another bottle. It broke near Huy's feet. "What is wrong with me?" Linh asked. "What is wrong with you?"

The distraction was enough for Duyen and Quynh to grab hold of Linh from either side. While Linh and Huy continued to yell obscenities at each other, Cherry ran behind them, pulling the half-emptied recycling bin away. With both hands, she dragged it back to the side of the house.

Eventually, Lum and Johnny pulled Huy back into the house, while Duyen and Quynh forced Linh to sit on the sidewalk, trying to calm her down.

"He didn't even ask," Linh wailed. "He doesn't even care what happened to me."

"Tell us," Quynh pleaded, as Cherry warily stood a few feet from them. Duyen and Quynh were patting Linh's hair and stroking her arms. "Tell us what happened."

Does it even matter what she said? How she rationalized this destructive, indulgent temper tantrum? Of course, it was about her parents, how they embarrassed each other, how they mortified her—and after all of it, they went home together, like they always did, like they always would. Linh took full advantage of her makeshift stage on the driveway, strangers from the party her unwilling audience, the streetlamp her inadequate spotlight. She cried, she raged, she screamed. She screamed some more.

"Why can't they just divorce each other and get it over with?" Linh asked. "Why drag me into it? Why make me miserable, too?"

Cherry couldn't help it. She couldn't keep quiet any longer. "Didn't you just drag Huy into it?" she asked.

Linh looked up, realizing for the first time that Cherry was there. "What?" she asked.

"Look at what you did to his car," Cherry said, "because you were upset with your parents?"

"Cherry," Duyen said. "This isn't the right time—"

"Are you kidding me?" Linh said, standing, her eyes furious.

"No," Cherry said, struggling to maintain her balance, placing one hand on the mailbox for support. Someone had to tell her cousin the truth. "You say you don't want your parents exposing all their secrets, yet you do the same thing. You can't keep anything to yourself. You have to embarrass all of us, too."

"Why don't we go home?" Quynh asked, pulling at Linh's arm. "You can stay at my house tonight—"

"Do you realize how much I could say, but don't?" Linh asked, stumbling closer to Cherry. "To protect the family's little baby? Who doesn't know shit?"

"Linh," Duyen said, wincing. "Don't."

"You're the one who should be embarrassed," Linh screamed, inches from Cherry's face. "You think my parents are shameful? Do you even know what yours have done? To us? To our entire family?"

Duyen now stood by Cherry's side. Her cousin had eased Cherry's grip from the mailbox, making her feel untethered, and vulnerable. Quynh had managed to pull Linh away, but her cousin still edged forward at them, her arms flailing. Linh had been in fights before. Cherry hadn't, but she wasn't scared. In fact, she wanted Linh to slip from Quynh's grasp and reach her.

"You act like you know everything," Linh sobbed, "and you have no idea."

"What don't I know?" Cherry asked. "Tell me."

"Your mother? She was the whore of Vung Tau."

Cherry blinked at her cousin's mascara-streaked face. "You're a dirty liar," she said, turning away.

"And you're a fat pig."

"Stop!" Duyen cried, near tears. "Just shut up, both of you."

"Go ask your mother who she was engaged to before your dad." Linh's voice had calmed, no longer hysterical. She sounded pleased with herself. "How many men she was stringing along."

All these eyes on Cherry, waiting, watching, expecting her to collapse, to fall apart. Instead of responding to her cousin, instead of looking back at any of them, she turned and walked away. Along the sidewalk, one foot in front of another, moderate, medium-size steps, trying to press out her rage, her frustration with every step, until she approached the intersection. It didn't work. She was still trembling.

The light was red. Don't walk. Cherry stood there, blinking at the sign, until she felt a hand on her shoulder. For a moment, she imagined— hoped—it was her brother's. But the hand was too small, too smooth. Lum was probably still inside, oblivious, uninterested, in her humiliation. It was a warm, sympathetic squeeze, but Cherry still stepped forward, letting Duyen's hand slip off her.

"Do you believe her?" Cherry asked.

Her cousin didn't answer. Together, they watched the traffic at the intersection, slow, sparse. A light-brown SUV turned on its left hand blinker, waiting to turn on their street. When it did, the halogen headlights washed brightly into their tired eyes, until they couldn't see anything else.

1985

Cuc Bui
Paris, France

... *God has blessed our family with so much. I pray every day that we are worthy of His gifts. I was afraid my sons would die in prison camp, and they survived. I feared our families would never escape the Communists, but the Lord was watching over us, and the boat captains agreed to my proposal. We were strangers in this beautiful cold country, but God provided us with our guardian angels, the Bourdains.*

They have no reason to offer such kindness, yet they do. Monsieur Bourdain is the man I aspired to be in Vietnam. I gave up this dream long ago. Perhaps Yen will one day reach his status. He is doing very well at the law firm. But poor Phung, so like his mother in heart and head. Fortunately, he is not smart enough ever to understand my disappointment. He is grateful only for his wife and daughter, content with his small life, which relieves me.

I look forward to every visit we have with the Bourdains, because I know they are busy people. They do so much for the community, and their bright young son excels at his studies. I am proud to report that Xuan is also doing very well in his schooling, and Cam is performing capably. The three of them, friends since childhood, almost siblings. I hope they will remain close all their lives, long after their grandparents and parents have passed.

Hung Truong
Paris, France

❧ *Chapter Seven*

CAM

PARIS, FRANCE, 1994

C AM HELD THE LAST MERINGUE MUSHROOM IN THE AIR, attempting to locate its proper place on the *bûche de Noël*. The sugary confection already felt soft between her fingers, threatening to melt. The Christmas yule log had cooled to an ideal temperature, the frosting buffed, the detailed piping painstakingly sculpted. She simply needed to find a free space for the last piece of decoration and her hours of work would finally end, but her eyes could not settle upon the correct location. A good patisserie knew how to finish and walk away. But Cam, in only her second year of culinary school, had not yet mastered this skill.

"You're not dressed yet?" her mother asked.

Reluctantly, Cam tore her eyes away to look at her parents, already in their church clothes, standing at the door.

"The buttercream took longer to set than I expected," she said. "I can meet you at the church."

Her mother nodded at the *bûche de Noël* with the same detachment she exhibited for all of Cam's desserts. "It looks like you're done now. We can wait a few minutes."

Cam struggled not to exhale too loudly. Christmas Eve was hardly a good time for another argument with her mother, especially this year. "You don't want to lose your seats. I can catch up with you. I don't mind."

Her fingers tensed around the cake pan as her parents conferred with each other. Finally, her father shrugged his shoulders and her mother nodded.

"We'll ask Xuan to wait for you," she said.

It annoyed Cam that her mother felt she needed an escort for the eight-minute walk to the church. Once the front door shut, Cam's attention returned to the task at hand. Of all the pastries and desserts she'd prepared in the past two years, this was not a favorite of hers. So many hours spent mixing the flour, preparing the buttercream, meticulously dragging a fork over the frosted log, sprinkling the almonds, and finally placing the meringue mushrooms, and it still looked like every *bûche de Noël* she'd seen: an artfully decorated piece of poop.

It didn't matter. She hadn't spent most of her Christmas Eve preparing the holiday dessert for herself, but for the Bourdains. And though almost every member of her family (including Grandmère) suggested she simply go down the street and buy one of the dozens of *bûches de Noël* available at every patisserie, Cam needed to make it herself. Her teachers at the culinary institute were right: once you knew what was involved in creating something, you could trust no one but yourself for its successful outcome.

Cam's mother found this perfectionist attitude tiresome. She thought desserts were a waste of time, and couldn't understand why, if Cam had to reject a perfectly decent history program at the Sorbonne for culinary school, she couldn't at least have picked an emphasis that was practical?

"I like desserts," Cam tried to explain. "They make people happy."

"Happy?" her mother echoed, her face aghast as the word dropped from her mouth. "Do you think if you went back to Vietnam and baked a lavender torte for some starving orphans who need protein and vegetables they'd be happy?"

Cam actually believed they would, but it was pointless to argue with her mother. She could never win. Her father never had, which was why he'd given up long ago. How could she explain that it was actually the difficulty in patisserie that excited her? The precision of using scales and measurements, maintaining oven temperatures, and respecting quality ingredients? There was something immensely satisfying in overcoming so many obstacles to successfully create a pastry. One minute mistake and the cream puffs deflate or the dough toughens. A finished product was an immense accomplishment, something patrons would never consider when passing a gleaming glass case of fruit tarts and croissants on their walks to work.

The elusive spot on the cake emerged, taunting Cam with its obvious existence all this time. She dropped the confection in place, pulled off her apron, and walked to her bedroom to change into the dress and shawl she'd laid out on her bed. As she finished pulling up her hair, she heard the wooden floors in the living room groan with her cousin's arrival.

"I'm almost done," Cam called out.

"You've been saying that all day," Xuan said, with sleepy cheerfulness in his voice. Fresh from another catnap, he was enjoying one of the few holiday breaks Lycée Henri-IV offered its preparatory students. Xuan was in the middle of the intense CPGE courses for admission into the leading engineering *grande école* in the country, like Michel before him. But unlike Michel, he didn't have expensive tutors guiding him through the preparatory courses. Michel was honest about how he got in, a trait she found admirable. He never apologized for who he was, to Cam or to anyone.

Cam walked to the living room as she hooked in her earrings. Xuan wore a bright-blue knit cap Grandmère had made for him years ago. It made him look like he was twelve, but he didn't care. He yawned, scratched at his elbow, and glanced at the yule log.

"Nice work," he said. The family's beloved genius, Xuan still had trouble seeing food beyond the practical application of a brioche stuffed in his mouth so his stomach wouldn't growl during his eighth hour of studying, but at least he was trying.

"It's good practice," Cam said. "I spend this much time on all of my desserts."

Xuan looked at her doubtfully, but let it go. "Do you think they're going to taste it?"

"If they do, they won't be disappointed."

He nodded. "Grandpère is walking with us."

"He didn't want to drive?"

"He said he wanted to walk. He wouldn't leave his bedroom. Grandmère finally gave up. She told him to freeze for all she cared."

Downstairs in Grandpère's apartment, he'd forgotten the argument and wondered where Grandmère was.

"She's meeting us at the church," Xuan said, as he helped him put on his winter coat.

"But why would she leave without me? Why wouldn't she ask me?"

"She probably just forgot," Cam said. It was easier to lie than to further confuse him.

"I'm going to have to talk to your grandmère," he said, carefully fitting the black fedora hat to his head. "I hope you, Cam, will be more respectful of your husband when you marry."

"I'll try."

"Try! Do you hear that, Xuan? Why are there so many bossy women in this family? So insolent to their husbands. At least your mother has learned to be more obedient, isn't that right?"

Eight months ago, Cam had returned home from a weekend pastry seminar in Lyon to a smiling, chatty Aunt Trinh helping her mother julienne vegetables for Sunday dinner. Cam assumed this was one of her aunt's temporary upswings due to a change in medication, but instead, the balance prevailed. She started going out again, and several months ago she had returned to attending church. This was the first Midnight Mass and *réveillon* celebration Aunt Trinh felt well enough to attend in years.

Xuan refused to discuss his mother's recovery with Cam, which wasn't so unusual since he kept most of his thoughts to himself anyway. Cam had long ago developed a patient persistence in order to learn anything intimate about her cousin, such as Xuan's boyfriend Jean, one of his classmates from Lycée Henri-IV. Cam understood why her cousin would want to keep this quiet from their family—they had enough to deal with—but she did long for the day when Xuan could finally think of himself first.

Outside, Grandpère automatically reached for Cam's hand as they crossed the street. She linked arms with him and passed the basket holding the *bûche de Noël* to Xuan. Cam thought it was unfortunate that her affection for Grandpère had increased due to the solid, irrefutable fact that he was sick. Before his Alzheimer's diagnosis, Cam had openly, loudly preferred Grandmère. Her grandmère, so sweet and patient, made sure everyone in the family was warm, properly nourished, and comfortable, while her grandpère, she remembered even as a small child, was grumpy, surly, and always sniping at Grandmère. But what Cam found most unforgivable was his unabashed preference for Xuan as a grandchild, just because he was a boy.

"But why does that matter?" Cam had asked her father when she was little. "Isn't being a girl good, too?" Her mother and aunt were girls, and so was Grandmère.

"Grandpère grew up with different values in Vietnam," he'd said. "He loves you, too, but he shows it differently."

But because Grandpère was the head of their family, the difference scraped at her heart. At church and Vietnamese community events, Grandpère made sure to introduce his smart, studious grandson Xuan before anyone else, even Grandmère. He hardly ever addressed Cam directly. Most of the time, he'd bark at Grandmère or Cam's mother to control that crazy girl—the one who wouldn't sit still in church or wandered off during their walks around the 13th Arrondissement—before she embarrassed their entire family.

After Grandpère forgot about a teakettle he left burning on the stove one afternoon, Grandmère didn't want to leave him home alone. Cam, her mother, and Aunt Trinh took turns spending time with Grandpère. Once an avid reader and letter writer, Grandpère would ask Cam to read to him from the newspaper and her cookbooks. Though she knew it was because of his memory loss, Cam enjoyed her grandpère's rapt attention and questions. Unlike her mother and aunt, she never tired of answering them, no matter how many times he repeated himself.

The church had already filled to capacity by the time they entered, full of regulars and the lapsed who attended Mass only for Christmas and Easter. Cam noticed there was only room for two other people in her family's pew. Cam's mother waved at them. She would pressure them to squeeze in—dismissive of the twice-a-year worshippers invading their pew. That wouldn't be comfortable for anyone, especially considering how hot the church already felt with so many bodies inside. Up on the second floor, where the choir also sat, Cam knew there'd be more room.

"You take Grandpère," Cam said, placing his hand into Xuan's. "I'll go stand in the balcony."

"Should we bother finding you afterward?" Xuan asked.

She ignored him and made her way through the crowded aisles and up the carpeted spiral staircase. People stood anywhere they could: slumping against the walls, sitting on the staircase, crowding around the archways. The balcony was not that different, but behind the choir, she saw him. His wool coat lay on the pew, saving her seat.

Pulling off her glove, she reached for his hand, and marveled at how cool it felt despite the stuffiness in the room. Michel turned his head and smiled at her.

"Merry Christmas, Cammie," he said.

"Merry Christmas."

She and Michel had bumped into each other at a bookstore in the Marais. She was looking for a birthday present for her American cousin Cherry and he was browsing for used copies of a Derrida he needed for class. They hadn't spoken in years, though they still saw each other at church and the Bourdains' annual Christmas *réveillon*. Michel took Cam to a brasserie for a drink and they ended up spending the night together.

Cam remembered the first time she saw Michel, or Petit Michel, as they called him back then. His hair was so blond it almost appeared white, and Cam—freshly arrived from Vietnam, where the only hair she ever saw resembled her own—was amazed that hair could be so bright, like angels' hair.

Not everyone thought so. "That child looks like a ghost," Cam's mother commented in Vietnamese. "How can he be so pale?"

Though only a year older than Xuan and Cam, Petit Michel was the leader when the children played together. He told them what toys they could touch, and his favorites that they could not. When bored, Xuan and Cam would devise tricks to convince Petit Michel that some toys were actually more popular at their school playground than his electronic games, which confused and frustrated the baby-faced Bourdain.

"How would you know?" Petit Michel asked. "Did they even have toys in your country?"

"We had toys," Xuan said defensively. "We just couldn't bring them over on the boat."

"They weren't that great then," Petit Michel said. "My parents taught me to take care of my stuff."

Xuan called Petit Michel a pain, but Cam thought he was funny. She didn't mind his bossy manner, because she could be bossy right back. There was nothing wrong with stating what you wanted. If more people did that, such as her grandmère or her father, there would be less misunderstanding, less unhappiness.

As they grew older, Petit Michel lost interest in his toys and allowed Xuan and Cam to play with more of them. When Petit Michel turned ten and decided he preferred reading, he put most of his toys in boxes and gave them to the Truongs. For Cam, he personally handed over his frayed Babar the Elephant, which she kept on her bed for years.

After meeting him one night over drinks, her friends criticized Petit Michel as morose, bland, but Cam believed there was great potential behind his aloof silences and indifferent cigarette drags. He simply needed time to understand what she already did. Her tenacity would work in her favor, as it had their first night together, when she pushed her way through his apartment, undressing him and herself, assuring him that no one in their families had to know about them, not yet anyway.

* * *

The Bourdains' annual *réveillon* was always a lavish feast. After Midnight Mass, the family opened its home to fellow parishioners to eat, drink, and eat again until dawn. It was the only night of the year Cam's family ever stayed out past ten o'clock, though by two in the morning, most of them could be found dozing in one of the upstairs bedrooms. As children, Cam and Xuan relished the challenge of staying up the entire night, running around the Bourdains' spacious house, playing tag, and eating oysters and foie gras until their tummies ached. They never had opportunities to eat these French delicacies at home, and even now, when Cam ate oysters at a café with friends, they never tasted as salty fresh as the ones she remembered slurping off a cocktail napkin at a Bourdain *réveillon*.

Madame Bourdain spared no expense in decorating and catering for her biggest party of the season, her Christmas trees and nativity scenes growing more elaborate every year. This year, the Bourdains displayed their decorative masterpiece outdoors. Guests walked past and marveled at the life-size crèche in the pruned-back rose gardens.

"What is that supposed to be?" Grandpère asked, as the family stared up at the monstrous concrete statues draped in gold and silver twinkle lights.

"It's the birth of Jesus Christ," Cam said. "I mean, a re-creation."

"It's a spectacle," Aunt Trinh said, looking both horrified and fascinated.

"It's not that bad," Uncle Yen said.

"They only get more ridiculous," Cam's mother said. "Remember the actors they hired to play the wandering wise men last year? They had too much wine and started heckling the guests."

"Maybe next year Madame Bourdain will rent an orphan to play baby Jesus," Xuan said, smiling innocently at Cam's chilly glare.

After Mass, Cam and Michel had separated to find their families in the tangled church crowd, agreeing to meet after dinner. Cam's mother regarded her suspiciously after hearing her story about sitting up with the choir during mass. Now, she looked at everything and everyone at the party with annoyance.

Yet, Cam continued to smile, cooing with Aunt Trinh over the lush mistletoe draping the front doorway and the massive silver fir Christmas tree in the candlelit ivy-and-berry-trimmed atrium. Stationed by the front door, Monsieur Bourdain, wearing a fluffy red-and-white Santa hat, rang a jingle bell, and reminded the children to drop their shoes by the fireplace. Cam's mother would not ruin this evening for her. At the end of the night, hopefully even she would be happy for her.

In the spirit of a community feast, the Bourdains invited guests to bring treats for the dessert table. When Madame posted the sign-up sheet on the church community bulletin board in early November, Michel suggested Cam bake one of the requested yule logs.

"It's my father's favorite," he said. "He's always complaining that the *bûches de Noël* we buy are so sloppy. He'd like your attention to detail."

While the family searched for their table in the dining room, Cam walked through the parlor, where the caterers continued adding to the buffet. Stopping at the dessert table, Cam opened the basket and felt relieved to find that her yule log hadn't been damaged in its travels. She lifted the cake and placed it on one of the last empty silver platters. Surrounded by poorly crafted tarts, imprecise petite fours, and lumpy sugar cakes in the shape of baby Jesus, Cam's *bûche de Noël* brilliantly stood out as an artistic achievement.

Although it was time to walk away from her creation, Cam lingered at the table, adjusting the yule log's placement, watching as other parishioners deposited their desserts and left for the dining room. She wasn't sure what she expected. Of course, the Bourdains had to greet and entertain their guests, but how were Michel's parents supposed to know that this was her *bûche de Noël*, and not one of the other careless yule logs that littered the table?

When Cam had started culinary school, she and her mother had battled over kitchen space and ingredients, with her mother always winning because she made food the family could actually eat. Her father tried to sample Cam's projects out of politeness, but no one in her family had much of a sweet tooth. Cam began spending more and more time at Michel's apartment, only two blocks from her school, where she had an entire kitchen to herself. She explained to her parents that she'd found practice space at the school's kitchens. Michel tasted and approved of all of her baking projects, perhaps a little too much.

"Is Petit Michel gaining weight?" Grandmère asked in Vietnamese, as Cam took a seat between her and Grandpère.

"No," Cam quickly said, then hesitated. "I don't think so."

"Look at him," Grandmère said, brazenly pointing to where the Bourdains sat, at a small bistro table in the midst of several long banquet tables surrounding it like a star. Michel stood next to his father, lifting a flute of champagne to his mouth. They had their suit jackets off, the elder merrily wearing his Santa hat and the son in a green elf stocking cap. "His belly hangs over his belt just like his father's. If he's not careful, we won't be able to tell the two Michels apart!"

Cam's mother hooted at this, while Aunt Trinh managed a faint smile. Her eyes occasionally surveyed the crowded dining room, always drifting toward the exit. Cam's mother and Grandmère had made sure Aunt Trinh sat between them, so she wouldn't have to speak to any strangers.

On the other side of the table, Xuan and his father read over the blessing Uncle Yen planned to read. Every year, the Bourdains asked a close friend to propose the Christmas blessing, which usually consisted of thanking the family for their generosity and kindness over the years. Cam felt confident her uncle's blessing would be no different. Uncle Yen's law firm still considered Monsieur Bourdain's publishing house its biggest client.

Grandpère placed his hand on Cam's. He already looked exhausted, his eyes avoiding the sparkly votives on the table. "Aren't you supposed to be sitting at the children's table in the other room?"

"No, Grandpère," she said. "We're big enough that Xuan and I can sit with the adults now."

"Oh?" He looked delighted. "You two are growing up so fast."

After the initial welcome from Monsieur Bourdain, he called for Uncle Yen to give his blessing.

"Make sure to speak up, dear Yen," Monsieur Bourdain reminded him, with a wagging finger. "Your voice is so soft, and we want everyone to hear you."

Xuan rolled his eyes, but only Cam noticed. Everyone else still had their hands obediently folded in prayer, eyes expectantly watching Yen Truong. She could tell that her uncle, unaccustomed to public speaking, was nervous, unconsciously folding and refolding the sheet of paper in front of him, adjusting his reading glasses on his nose.

"The Bourdains have always been giving people, and I experienced this firsthand when they helped save my family. While I was still a law student, our beloved Vietnam was conquered by the Communists. When my wife, son, parents, and my brother's family managed to escape to Malaysia, the Bourdains, through much hard work and personal expense, sponsored their immigration to France. Their generosity still amazes me. They have certainly become part of the Truong family. We thank God for their existence and their continuing work for the Lord. Bless their family's good health. May God bless this meal they have provided for all of us."

The dining room filled with soft murmurs of agreement. While the string quartet in the center of the room began its first piece, the catering staff filed in to offer the first course: lobster bisque and iced oysters with lemon wedges.

"It was a beautiful toast," Xuan assured his father as the room filled with polite slurping and the string quartet's version of "Silent Night."

"Yes," Cam's mother said, after taking the smallest sip of the bisque off her spoon. "I didn't realize they saved our lives. Thank you for reminding everyone."

"Ngoan," Cam's father said, sighing.

"We all know they're not your favorite people," Uncle Yen said. "But we are in their house, and we are eating their food. You can be discreet for one night."

"How am I being indiscreet?"

"They did sponsor us," Aunt Trinh said, looking confused. "Yen was only telling the truth."

"Ngoan realizes this," Cam's father said. "She didn't mean any harm, Yen."

"You don't need to defend me," Cam's mother said.

"What have they done to you?" Uncle Yen whispered furiously, leaning forward, nearly spitting in his soup. "They are godparents to our children—"

"That wasn't really our choice—"

"Who sponsored their catechism classes? Who bought Cam her communion dress? They have only been kind to us."

"Are you convinced of that?" she asked.

Cam tucked the linen napkin under Grandpère's chin, thankful that he paid no attention to the argument, listening instead to the quartet playing nearby.

"Did you ever see the water puppet show in Hanoi?" he asked her.

Cam shook her head before tasting the bisque: creamy, good temperature, too much pepper.

"One day, I'll take you to see it. You, Xuan, and Lum would enjoy it so much. Where is Lum?"

"He's in America," Cam said, "with his parents and his sister."

"When did he go there?"

"Years ago, Grandpère." Tilting her neck, she watched Michel silently eat with his parents. They'd finished their bisque and now focused on the oysters.

They'd agreed to meet in his bedroom when the seated dinner ended and guests mingled around the house enjoying flutes of champagne, mugs of cider, and cheese platters. The children rushed to the family room, gathering around the indoor Christmas tree to find candies and chocolates from Père Noel in their shoes. The Truongs meandered throughout the house, Cam's mother and Aunt Trinh watching the children in the family room, while the men and Grandmère walked outside to the courtyard to gawk again at the life-size crèche.

Cam stood on the staircase, watching Michel and his mother talk to a couple in the corner of the parlor. She caught his eye several times, and he discreetly nodded in her direction. When it looked like the conversation was at last ending, Cam slowly wandered up the stairs. No one paid attention to her.

Resting her elbow on the door handle, she gently pushed, and sneaked inside the bedroom. Still holding a drink with one hand, Cam reached around for the light switch. As the room filled with the soft glow of a tableside lamp, her eyes scanned the four walls. Since their relationship began, Cam had only spent time in Michel's apartment, which maintained the tastefully detached aesthetic of his mother. It reminded Cam of a hotel. She'd assumed Michel was too busy studying to change anything around, so she'd occasionally bring a bouquet of flowers for the dining room table or intentionally leave a puddle of clothes in the bedroom. But even this bedroom lacked any personal touches, and easily could have been mistaken for one of the Bourdains' immaculately prepared guest rooms. Her only recognition of Michel was his overnight bag sitting next to a mahogany chest of drawers.

The door opened and Cam turned around. Michel pulled off his elf cap, placed it on the table next to the lamp, and slipped his arms around her waist.

"Merry Christmas, Cammie," he said, touching his nose with hers.

She kissed him briefly before pulling away. "Are they coming up?"

"Father is still playing Père Noel," he said. "I'll go down in a few minutes and tell them we have good news to share." His arms around her tightened, momentarily lifting her off the floor. "You still feel tiny."

"Then we talk to my parents," Cam reminded him. "Remember? You have to formally ask my father and Grandpère, even if he gets confused. It's tradition."

"I remember." He smiled and kissed her again.

His breath smelled of brandy. "Don't drink any more," she said. "I don't want us to forget anything tonight."

"It's sweet that you worry. It's beautiful." His blond hair felt silky between her fingers. He was combing his hair forward lately, worried that he'd inherited his father's hairline. Once or twice he had expressed the desire to shave all his hair off, but Cam had discouraged it.

He wanted to lie down for a little bit, to rest before fetching his parents. The bed felt so soft and warm. Not as springy as her bed at home, the bed she'd known since they moved to France. The mattress enveloped their bodies like fresh, silky marzipan. After so many hours on her feet, Cam sighed contentedly, listening to the music and chattering through the floor.

"We can't fall asleep," Cam said, struggling through a yawn.

"We won't," he said.

A few minutes passed. She could feel his breath on her neck, moist and steady. "I'm scared," she said.

He didn't answer initially and she feared he'd dozed off. "You don't have to be scared. Everybody loves a wedding," he said.

She wasn't sure what time it was when Michel got up. After putting a throw blanket around her, he said he was going to get his parents. He kissed her on the forehead, promising to return in a few minutes.

Tucking a strand of hair behind her ear, she listened, listened, listened for his knock. Although she wanted to get up before then, rearrange her hair, make herself as presentable and perfect as her yule log (which had better still be there when they returned downstairs to celebrate), the plumpness of the pillows and the caress of the blanket were too inviting.

Cammie Bourdain. Camille Bourdain. Camille wasn't her given name, but it could change on the marriage certificate; simply an extension of four letters, her fulfilled identity. It sounded better to her than Cam Bourdain. She never really liked her name, which pronounced in a certain way meant orange, an alternative her mother enjoyed because she had an orange tree behind her childhood home in Vietnam. Cam promised herself that her child would bear a name she could be proud of, one chosen with the care and affection of both parents.

The knock on the door was loud and continuous. Cam pulled herself up, realizing she had no idea how much time had passed. She couldn't find a clock on the cerulean walls or mahogany wood furniture. Smoothing her hair and straightening the sleep rumples from her dress, she walked to the door and, after vigorously shaking her head, opened it.

Cam's mother glared at her. She had her synthetic fur jacket on. "What are you doing? This isn't a guest room."

"Really?" She fought the urge to slam the door. Michel and his parents would be there any moment.

"Where have you been? I've been looking for you."

After peering down both sides of the hall, Cam pulled her mother into the room. "I've only been up here a little while."

"A little while? It's four o'clock."

Cam rubbed at the corner of her eye with a knuckle, careful not to disturb her eye makeup. Michel's elf cap was gone from the table. He must have put it back on before he left. "No, it's not."

Her mother offered her wristwatch. Cam turned and looked out the window. Still an indigo night. No different from when she first came upstairs.

"We're leaving," Cam's mother said. "Grandpère wants to sleep in his own bed."

"No," Cam said, shaking her head, shaking off the drowsiness she still felt. "I have to stay."

"Why?" Her mother was searching her face. "Do you think he's going to come back up here? Cam, he's been downstairs drinking with his parents for the last hour."

She stared at her mother. "Wait . . ."

"I'm not stupid, Cam." Leaning forward, she hissed, "You aren't stupid, either. Do you really think he's going to marry you?"

She took a few steps back until her legs bumped against the bed. Cam sat. "No. You don't understand. You don't know the whole story."

"I do. And you are not going to embarrass this family. We are going home."

Just as her mother had managed to pull her off the bed, Cam saw Michel and his parents in the doorway. Her face relaxed into a smile. With the men in their holiday hats and Madame Bourdain's jingle bell necklace, they looked like a Christmas miracle.

"Are you all right, darling?" Madame Bourdain asked, trying to hide her surprise of finding the women in her son's bedroom. "Too much champagne?"

"She's fine," Cam's mother said.

"Cammie?" Michel asked, looking concerned.

"Who is Cammie?" Cam's mother asked.

"Mother," Cam said, pushing her hand away, but her mother refastened her grip.

"What is going on?" Monsieur Bourdain loudly asked, his face looking pinched and ruddy, but all Cam could focus on was his furry hat. "Michel, why did you bring us up here?"

Although the bedroom was large, it suddenly felt very small for five people standing around the bed, which still looked rumpled from Cam's nap. Realizing everyone's eyes lay on him, Michel's own could not settle—flitting between his parents and Cam. He straightened his back, his telltale technique to appear confident, but this time, Cam did not find it charming. Standing next to his much taller father, he looked like a weaker, fainter version of Monsieur Bourdain.

"We have something we want to tell you," Michel finally said.

Monsieur Bourdain shook his head. "No, son," he said, the joy of Père Noel trailing out of his voice. "Let's talk about this first."

"That's what we're trying to do," Michel said.

"I mean privately," he said, looking scornfully at Cam and her mother. He turned and left the room.

"Where is your father going?" Madame Bourdain asked.

"Michel," Cam said, but he was already following his father out of the room.

Madame Bourdain offered a weak smile, reverting to her role as hostess. "Excuse me," she said.

They'd been in the room for less than a minute, Cam realized. She looked up at her mother, who no longer appeared angry but pitying, perhaps even satisfied. It was so hard to tell with her.

"I think we should leave," Cam's mother said.

Wanting to speak, Cam could only nod in response. Her mother led her by the hand out of the room. The walls were bending. She wanted to throw up.

Downstairs in the parlor, Cam saw her *bûche de Noël* still sitting on its silver platter, untouched, ignored. A few guests still nibbled on cheese and drank champagne, while the Bourdains stood in the corner, whispering, shoulders touching.

She felt her mother's hand on her shoulder, pushing her forward.

"I'm right here," she said softly, and together, in synchronized step, they walked across the room.

"You are not getting married," Monsieur Bourdain declared as Cam and her mother approached the family.

"We have to," Michel said. "And you will accept it."

The Bourdains reluctantly stepped back to regard Cam and her mother. While Madame Bourdain gazed nervously at Cam, Michel's father wouldn't even look at her.

"Is she pregnant?" he asked. "Were you stupid enough to impregnate her?"

Cam felt her knees lock. Her mother turned to her, her nails digging into Cam's wrist. She wouldn't meet her mother's eyes, wouldn't speak.

The younger Bourdain didn't say anything, his arms crossed in front of him, staring at the shiny marble floor, like a child awaiting punishment.

Madame Bourdain pulled on her husband's shirtsleeve, the jingle-bell necklace tinkling with her urgency. "Please, Michel, this is not the time."

It was too late. Guests meandered around them, oblivious about their discussion, cheerily munching on the endless array of treats. Cam didn't mind the strangers, whose opinions mattered little to her, but then she saw her grandparents, Xuan, and the rest of her family. They had their coats and scarves on, bundled up like carolers.

Monsieur Bourdain finally turned to Cam, his eyes cold and thin. "Are you telling the truth? Are you really pregnant?"

Though Cam could feel her mother's nails digging even deeper into her arm, close to breaking skin, Cam could only look at her Michel. Why wasn't he meeting her eyes? Why wouldn't he answer his father? When her voice refused to release, Monsieur Bourdain spun around, looking for someone, anyone who could answer him.

"Monsieur Truong," Monsieur Bourdain said, walking up to Grand-père, whose arm was linked with Aunt Trinh's. "Did you know anything about this?"

"Excuse me?" Grandpère asked, smiling, not understanding.

"Michel," Uncle Yen said, trying to touch the man's shoulder, "what is the problem?" But Monsieur Bourdain angrily shrugged his hand off.

"Your granddaughter," Monsieur Bourdain said, nearly standing over Grandpère, shaking with fury. "She has trapped my son by claiming she is pregnant. Did you know about this? Is this what you teach your grandchildren?"

"She's my daughter," Cam's father said, stepping forward between Monsieur Bourdain and Grandpère.

"Will you take responsibility then for ruining my son's life? Because Petit Michel would never do this intentionally."

"Did he say that?" Phung calmly asked.

"It is obvious to anyone."

"Are you saying my daughter forced herself on your son?"

"We have taught him better than this," Monsieur Bourdain retorted, his face as red as his ridiculous hat. "He wouldn't have touched your daughter unless she provoked him."

"Shut up!" Aunt Trinh barked. "Leave her alone! Why can't you leave her alone?"

Her words echoed throughout the parlor, clear and sharp. Monsieur Bourdain staggered backward, looking at their entire family as if they were diseased.

While Uncle Yen tried to calm Monsieur Bourdain and Xuan tended to his mother, Grandpère shook his head, his eyes shiny with tears. "What has happened to Cam?" he asked Grandmère in Vietnamese. "She is only a child. How can he be so angry with a child?"

Cam didn't know if she should walk ahead of her family or behind, which was more discreet, and which would humiliate them less. Her father made the decision for her, putting her coat over her shoulders, and walking alongside her. She eagerly leaned into his support, wanting to fold herself into this comfort, this acceptance, forever. As they walked past Petit Michel, she felt the grief bloom in her chest, and turned her head away from him.

"I am very sorry," Madame Bourdain said as the Truongs walked out the front door. "I don't know what to say."

They passed the enormous crèche, still brightly lit, the fake animals and people crouching over the manger. The twinkle lights cast an orange glow over the statues, the animals and shepherds, the wise men, Joseph and Mary.

In the car, Cam allowed her mother to hold her until she asked, "What have you done? What have you done to us?"

It took Michel eight days to try to contact her. The morning after the New Year holiday, he called and a few hours later, came by the apartment. It was the first time a Bourdain had ever visited a Truong. Cam pretended she was asleep. Each time he returned, Xuan or her father would send him away with an excuse: she was tired, sick, shopping, napping. He left letters in carefully sealed wheat-colored envelopes. Cam's father stacked them in a neat pile on the dining room table next to the napkin basket, where they stayed until Cam finally asked her mother to throw them away.

In late January, Michel finally found her between classes. She was turning a corner after leaving a test kitchen, adjusting a flour measurement in her head, when she felt a hand enclose her elbow.

His clean, freshly shaven face startled her. His eyes did not appear swollen from tears or lack of sleep. His complexion looked as tan as if he'd returned from a holiday. He explained his parents had gone to their apartment in Marseille after the *réveillon*, a family tradition. His mother had begged him to go with them.

"I'm sure that must have been hard for you," Cam said, busying her hands with the button loops of her coat.

Michel ignored this. "I still want to marry you. I still want our baby." He spoke very proudly, like he'd been practicing and wanted his words to bear significance. "My father has calmed down. He regrets how we all behaved, but he's willing to listen to our plans."

"What plans?"

"I just said them. Getting married. Raising the baby together."

Cam shook her head.

"You don't want to get married?"

She shook her head again. Her toes felt cold. They were standing outside, but Cam didn't want to suggest they go sit somewhere to-gether.

"You don't want the baby?"

She watched the shock spread across his face. A brief moment of calm surrounded her, like a flower petal settling onto the ground.

"It's an innocent child, you know," he said, raising his chin. "What you'll be doing is a mortal sin. Can you live with that?"

He was deliberately trying to provoke her, just like her mother had. But she wouldn't react to his manipulations. She simply shrugged her shoulders, surprised how easy this felt for her, now that she knew she didn't love him.

"This is serious, Cam. If you do this, then we can't be together. My parents can't forgive you for killing their grandchild."

"It's not theirs," she said.

"Are you doing this out of revenge?" Michel asked. His lips briefly puffed out, and Cam recognized that face from when they were chil-dren, an expression she and Xuan secretly called the Petit Prince pout. "I thought you were smarter than this."

"I can be very dumb sometimes."

When she'd learned she was pregnant, she wasn't happy about it until she told Michel. He was the one who said they should keep it, he was the one who thought they should get married. He planned to move her into his apartment, where they would have room for a baby, where she could still be close to school, and their parents could help take care of the child. It all sounded so possible and lovely. It wasn't until the *réveillon* that she realized what a fantasy it was. They simply had been wasting each other's time.

Her mother tried to convince her otherwise. After returning home from the Bourdains, her mother encouraged Cam to wait until she heard from Petit Michel before deciding anything. Now that he was her poten-tial grandchild's father, perhaps he deserved a chance to explain himself.

"I don't know," Cam admitted.

"He will call you tomorrow," her mother said determinedly. "He will, because he loves you."

Her mother's fantasy, as desperate as it sounded, seemed so possible that night. Its sheer, unexpected optimism helped calm her to sleep. The sun was beginning to rise. They'd all sleep in until the afternoon, and then wake up for a late lunch and to open Christmas presents. And if her mother was correct, Michel would call. Apologize. Fix everything. Fulfill his promise. She'd give him his present. After all, Christmas miracles did not come from God, but from people; decent, sweet people who loved you.

Cam's appointment was scheduled for the following Thursday. Xuan had already agreed to accompany her.

But this was taking too long. "If you want," she said, "you could tell them I miscarried, that God took the baby away." She took a breath, surprised at how bitter she sounded. This wasn't how she intended it at all. "Or you can tell them the truth. I don't care."

"I could stop you, you know," he said, stepping forward, squaring his shoulders. If anyone had seen them, they'd think they were about to kiss. "I can be cruel, too."

"But you won't," she said, turning her face up to look at him. The blood was rushing to her head, and her limbs felt like they were floating away. "We're going to leave each other alone."

1982

Kim-Ly Vo
Ho Chi Minh City, Vietnam

. . . *Mother, do you remember, when we were younger, how the neighbors would criticize us for walking around in our bathing suits or inviting our male friends to the house? How instead of sequestering us in the house all day, like those Catholic zealots, you permitted us girls to enjoy ourselves like the boys did? They do that here in America, and no one objects. At the elementary school near our apartment, boys and girls play sports and games and are treated equally. Children are not given predetermined destinies. Instead, the teachers encourage the parents to allow the children to pursue their own interests and strengths, whatever they may be. At first, I found this freedom refreshing, but now, I can see its drawbacks.*

Lum has adjusted so well. His English is excellent (he even helps me with the occasional translation at the bank or grocery store), and although most Vietnamese boys are short compared to the Americans, he measures the tallest in his class. He must have inherited those genes from our family, perhaps our father. Sanh, as you will see when you are with us, is short, even for a Vietnamese man. Lum is so well liked by everyone. I predict he will make an excellent lawyer or businessman, or even a politician!

Cherry is smart and clever—sometimes, I'm afraid too much for her own good. Unlike Vietnamese teachers who encourage humility, her nursery school

teachers praise her, to the point that the child believes these compliments too readily. I try not to spoil her, Mother, but I cannot stop Sanh from doing so. If I discipline my daughter, she hardly listens, always turning to her father as if he is her only parent. She treats me like a servant.

Is this how I acted around you as a child? If so, please know I have learned my lesson. It is true, Cherry is still young. Perhaps this is just temporary. I hope so. . . .

Tuyet Truong
Westminster, California, USA

~~ *Chapter Eight*

KIM-LY

SINCE BA LIEM'S SLIP IN THE BATHTUB A FEW MONTHS ago, her psychic abilities could predict the last two numbers in the California SuperLotto. Kim-Ly had been suspicious, but she couldn't deny her friend's uncanny skill, consistent almost three out of every four drawings. For the opportunity to earn millions of dollars, these were not terrible odds.

"They float inside my head only a few seconds before. Too bad it doesn't come earlier, huh?" Ba Liem giggled. "Then we could be rich."

Kim-Ly believed it could. SuperLotto occurred twice a week. Every Wednesday, Kim-Ly and the twins convened at her family's beauty salon where they watched the selection of white rubber balls bounce and twirl in a gleaming glass case until they rolled out in a clean, tantalizing row. As Kim-Ly's eyes caressed the number combination that could yield a lucky someone permanent financial security, she would chide herself for not selecting those numbers. Of course, there would be a 12 in this week's drawing. There hadn't been a 12 in three weeks. She'd record the numbers in her small crocodile skin notebook and study them at night, determined to decipher the lottery's mystery.

Only Kim-Ly and Ba Liem's twin sister Ba Nhanh knew of the fortune-teller's recent intuition and they planned to keep it that way. While they agreed to share any substantial winnings, they didn't want to tip off any selfish, greedy relatives or friends who could suddenly decide they loved them again. So until they devised the strategy to capitalize on Ba Liem's talent, they discreetly studied the lottery drawing every week, each buying one ticket, just in case.

SuperLotto only cost a dollar for each game, but still some of Kim-Ly's children, even grandchildren, felt compelled to criticize.

"Do you know the odds of winning the lottery?" her granddaughter Cherry once asked. "Of even winning your dollar back?"

"Are they any better than surviving a war?" Kim-Ly retorted, holding her lottery ticket close to her chest, over her heart.

Most of the time, the twins and Kim-Ly sat in peace in the waiting lounge. Midweek, the mall was never crowded, with most people still at work or at home with their children. But this afternoon their concentration was interrupted by hooligans.

Her underachiever grandson Lum and his friends had the gall to take up all of the chairs in the waiting lounge. Unless they were getting their hair cut (which some needed), she didn't understand why they took up such valuable seating space, smudging their greasy fingerprints on the gossip magazines and newspapers with their careless perusing. Couldn't they hang out in the food court with the rest of the smokers? Lum once again flaunted his irresponsibility, allowing his friends to harass his dying grandmother.

"Boys, let your elders sit down," Lum's mother, Tuyet, said, as she sorted through a drawer of nail files and cotton balls. She turned to Kim-Ly. "And you're not dying. You have high blood pressure."

"Severely high blood pressure," Kim-Ly muttered, pulling her shawl around her shoulders.

Two peroxide blondies entered the salon and pointed to the pedicure stations. Tuyet nodded and turned to her mother. "Be nice," she said, wagging the emery board in Kim-Ly's face.

Waiting until her daughter walked out of earshot, Kim-Ly whispered to the twins, "Since when do we pay respect to children?"

"Ridiculous," Ba Liem agreed. "This is your beauty salon. They have to be nice to us."

The women grinned at each other as they took their usual seats, not even acknowledging the boys' meek bows of respect. While three of the deadbeats hid behind gossip magazines, Lum unabashedly returned eye contact and smiled.

"So what are you doing this afternoon?" Kim-Ly asked her grandson. "It must be something special to take time off from school."

"It's spring break, Grandmother," Lum said, his shoulders slouched over like a common laborer.

"You can still study," Kim-Ly said. "Extra time to review materials."

"Thank you, Grandmother," Lum muttered, suddenly very interested in the television. Ba Nhanh was clutching the remote control, trying to find the channel for the lottery. "I studied everything last night so I'm taking a break today. But I appreciate your advice."

She knew he was lying. Even economics majors at anyone-can-enroll community colleges had other coursework to study. A person could never finish studying. And he believed he could be a businessman? Kim-Ly wanted to press the issue, but her granddaughter Linh and her friend Quynh wandered in. They wore skimpy tank tops and low-waisted jeans. While Quynh obediently greeted Kim-Ly and the twins, her own granddaughter brazenly passed by her to kiss her boyfriend Huy on the cheek.

"How are you feeling, Ba Vo?" Quynh asked, straightening Kim-Ly's scarf.

"My throat is so dry." Kim-Ly wheezed softly to demonstrate. "Could you get me some water?"

Quynh squeezed Kim-Ly's hand and left for the water cooler at the back of the salon. Kim-Ly's eyes wandered to her daughter still serving the blondies. While Tuyet scrambled to scrub both of the customers' callused heels, one of the blondies in the massage chairs met eyes with Kim-Ly, then quickly looked away.

"Hi, Grandmother," Linh finally remembered, still not moving from Huy's lap.

Kim-Ly shifted her scrutiny to her granddaughter. Linh's mother was busy twisting curlers into a customer's hair, or else Kim-Ly hoped she'd scold her daughter for her whorish behavior. After registering Kim-Ly's lengthy look of disapproval, Linh slid off her boyfriend's lap and into the chair next to his. Quynh returned with a paper cup of cold water.

"How are your parents?" Kim-Ly asked, accepting the refreshing drink. "Are they doing well?"

"They're very busy," Quynh said, taking a seat next to Lum, who immediately put his arm around her. "They always are this time of year."

"Then I'm sure you must be helping them around the house a lot," Kim-Ly said, leaning forward in her chair. "Looking after your brothers?"

"Yes," Quynh said. "Of course."

"It's starting," Ba Nhanh said, poking the remote control into Kim-Ly's side.

Kim-Ly pulled her freshly purchased lottery ticket from her purse, holding the top with one thumb and the bottom with another. The twins did the same. As they waited for the orange-tanned host to announce the numbers, Kim-Ly noticed Lum and his friends plucking their own lottery tickets from their pockets.

"What is this?" she demanded. "Are you making fun of us?"

"The jackpot is up to 120 million," one deadbeat said. "It's on the news."

The older women exchanged grave glances. Wouldn't that be terribly ironic? For one of these naïve newbies to win over a dedicated player? Lum held his lottery ticket next to his grandmother's.

"Look at that," Lum said. "We have two numbers in common. Think it's in our blood?"

Kim-Ly ignored him, her eyes returning to the television. While the mandolin music trilled and her daughters chatted with customers, Kim-Ly and the rest of the ticket holders remained silent as the numbers filled the screen.

Her hopes were promptly dashed. She was out by the third number. Most of the boys had tossed their tickets as well. But Ba Liem held on to hers, biting her lip in concentration. Only the elder women noticed, the young ones chattering among themselves. Kim-Ly's body tensed. What if Ba Liem won? How could they contain their triumph?

When the final number appeared, Ba Liem placed her ticket back in her purse. "Too bad," she said, looking at her sister and Kim-Ly. "Maybe next time. I'm hungry. Where should we go?"

"There's that new *cha ca* restaurant downstairs," Ba Nhanh said.

Kim-Ly shook her head, sniffing in distaste. "Don't go there. The owner is a rat."

"How so?"

"Don't you remember? I lent him money for his first restaurant that went bankrupt. Then the fool asked me for another loan, as if I'd forget. When I refused, he called me terrible names."

"Awful," Ba Liem said. "What about some *banh cuon* across the street? They said they'd give us a discount if I read the owner's palm."

"Let's go," Ba Nhanh said. "I haven't eaten anything since lunch."

"I can't go anyway," Kim-Ly said. "I'm waiting for Dat. We're going to see the doctor again. I've been feeling faint, you know."

The twins cooed in sympathy. "Our poor friend," Ba Liem said.

"Does this mean you won't be able to come to Las Vegas with us next weekend?" Ba Nhanh asked.

The twins had returned only last month from one of their weekends in Las Vegas, taking one of those free buses the casinos sent over to Little Saigon every Friday morning. It was supposed to be a good deal: free transportation, deeply discounted rooms only minutes from the Strip, and a book of coupon vouchers for buffet meals. Kim-Ly was suspicious. Nothing, especially in America, was free.

But the twins came back with such enviable stories about the different foods they'd tasted and the free shows they'd watched on the "glamorous strip." Casino strip, not strip mall. And during their last visit, Ba

Liem realized her intuition applied to the daily bingo games held at the smaller casinos on the Strip. Suddenly, Las Vegas did not seem so terrible. Except for a few insufferable drives to San Diego and San Francisco, Kim-Ly had never been outside of Little Saigon since arriving to America.

"I'm still considering it," Kim-Ly said. "What was the name of the bus company again?"

"Tommy Luck or Bonny Luck, or something," Ba Liem said. "Who cares? It's free!"

Kim-Ly was still determining how to tell her children about this trip. They were so concerned about her health and complicated medication regimen. Of course, as an adult she could do whatever she wanted, but she didn't wish to needlessly worry her children.

Dat arrived not long after the twins left, exactly on time, hands gripped around the shoulder straps of his gray nylon book bag. He obediently greeted his elders in the salon, then stared at his dawdling cousins and their friends.

"What's going on, cousin?" Lum asked.

Dat shrugged, looking down at the shiny floor, littered with dirt and hair. The boys had never gotten along. Kim-Ly blamed it on their mothers' competitiveness, which she'd encouraged when they were younger, never believing it could grow so petty.

"Nothing," Dat said. "What are you doing?"

"That's not true," Quynh said. "Your sister told me you won the President's Award. Congratulations."

Dat blinked at her for a moment. Sighing, Kim-Ly bumped his elbow with her bag.

"Thanks," Dat finally said. "It was a statewide essay competition. I'm the first biology major to ever win."

The other boys weren't listening, looking over their shoulders at the clock on the wall and exchanging glances. Linh rudely snapped her chewing gum.

"That's great," Quynh said. "Your parents must be so happy."

"Of course they are," Lum said insincerely, his arm still looped around Quynh. "Good luck."

"Hey, I'm up for a big award, too," Huy said. Linh sat back in his lap again. "Worst attendance in World History. Think they'll give me scholarship money for that?"

The children laughed, all except for Quynh and Dat. Dat's cheeks flushed red, but he was too dignified to respond to such childishness. Kim-Ly quickly gathered her bag and scarf to stand, taking her grandson's arm. As they walked out of the salon and descended the escalator, they could still hear laughter echoing throughout the mall. Or perhaps that came from the children in the arcade on the third floor. No matter.

Dat remained silent in the car. Kim-Ly adjusted her seat and secured her seatbelt, impressed with how clean and pine-scent fresh her grandson kept his car. Kim-Ly had contributed a significant sum to help his parents buy the used Honda for Dat's high school graduation gift, and he was clearly grateful. After Viet's abrupt move to Houston six months ago, Dat had dutifully stepped in as Kim-Ly's driver and companion to her doctor's appointments.

"They're a little rambunctious," Kim-Ly said. "Your cousins and their friends. But they are harmless. They need discipline."

"They encourage each other's laziness," Dat said when they stopped at a red light. "Quynh was on the honor roll in high school, but now she's always at the bottom of the grading curve. She doesn't even care. If she only spent time with other people who took studying seriously . . ."

While her grandson looked rather stoic behind his sunglasses, his fingernails dug circles into the steering wheel. "She's a smart girl," Kim-Ly said. "She will realize."

"She loves Lum," Dat said. "She always has. I know he's my cousin, but he drags her down. She'll never get anywhere with him."

"They're children," Kim-Ly said. "Their affection is not serious. She will grow out of this crush and become more ambitious with her life. Do not worry, Dat."

Dat looked at his grandmother, his chapped lips slightly parted in surprise. "I'm not worried about them. I have a lot of other things to think about. You know how hard I study. You know how much I work."

"Of course I do," Kim-Ly said soothingly. "It is so kind of you to think of others."

At the clinic, Dat stayed in the examination room to translate, even though the hospital provided a medical interpreter. Kim-Ly never trusted translators to tell her everything because they were not family. The nurse checked Kim-Ly's blood pressure and found it still elevated. Kim-Ly and Dat listened to the doctor's recommendations to monitor her diet, perform moderate exercise, and limit alcohol consumption. After consulting the most recent blood tests, the doctor prescribed another medication.

After waiting half an hour at the pharmacy, they finally returned home with the new prescription. Alone in her room, Kim-Ly pulled out her new medication and held the orange bottle under the bedside lamp. She rattled it and unscrewed the cap, watching as the little yellow tablets spilled neatly across her rosewood nightstand, over the edge, and under her bed.

Whenever the doctors or her grandchildren would bring up the potential consequences of high blood pressure, she had to laugh. How could they guarantee that if she took this yellow pill in the morning and that blue pill at night that her quality of life would increase by 15 percent? Unlike playing the lottery, which was all gain and tiny loss, a person's survival could not be determined by odds. If bad things were going to happen, they would happen. The pirates did not care if your boat had a 65 percent chance to reach Malaysia unscathed. They would threaten and pillage you anyway.

There were nearly forty people on their fishing junk, and though Kim-Ly had complained that their family had been shoved into the undesirable middle section, with no quick access to pee or vomit off the side of the boat, she realized when the pirates appeared how fortunate they were to be protected by so many bodies. Everyone knew who they were, what they wanted, when they saw the boat creeping up the horizon, hours earlier.

There were only six of them. Six Thai pirates versus forty Vietnamese refugees. Logic dictated that the Vietnamese could simply overpower six thieves whose only weapons were dull fishing knives and rusty razor blades. Yet so many of her boat companions threw over their valuables, hysterically weeping for mercy. Their cowardice incensed Kim-Ly. The pirates hadn't even bothered to jump onto their junk, sluggishly circling the boat, and gathering their unearned spoils like monks collecting donations at temple. This was the laziest pirate attack Kim-Ly could imagine.

Odds had nothing to do with the volume and clarity of her scream. When the pirates drew near enough that she could see the moles on their faces and smell the stench of their ragged clothes, she reached her mouth up to the sky and with all the breath in her lungs, she wailed and wailed and wailed. Kim-Ly wasn't even sure what she was saying, if words uttered from her throat or nonsensical, guttural moans. But when she felt her son Viet grab her face, press his forehead against hers, and she was finally calm enough to look around the boat, Kim-Ly realized that it had worked. The pirates had left. The rest of the refugees stared at her, frightened or impressed, she wasn't sure. They said nothing for hours. They simply listened to the waves, dreading the appearance of another boat, but armed with the security of Kim-Ly's shattering, powerful siren.

Later, the other passengers would say the pirates were too lethargic to bother jumping on the boat to slash Kim-Ly's throat. They'd gotten what they wanted and had left. Kim-Ly felt these ungrateful dissenters had missed the point. If someone were going to take something from her, she wouldn't allow it to happen quietly.

Years later, her children would still have to wake her from these screams. The pressure of Viet's or another child's hands around her shoulders, the soggy texture of the sweat and tear-stained sheets, the warmth of the bed, these sensations returned her to America. She was not on a boat. She was not falling into an ocean. There was no need to shout.

On Sundays after the salon closed, her daughters stayed late to disinfect the pedicure tubs and sinks, clean the mirrors, and mop the floors. They also caught up with Vietnamese soap operas, touched up one another's roots, and tried to convince Kim-Ly to consider letting them color her hair. But Kim-Ly only wanted to watch the soap operas and scolded her daughters for such childish vanity. She'd grown to admire her increasing white strands and hoped she'd live long enough to have an entire mane of stunning white hair.

That night, the girls were too busy looking up American names to bother Kim-Ly. Middle daughter Tuyet had recently changed her legal name to Tanya. She said she'd grown tired of hearing Americans butcher her name.

"Tanyaaahh," Kim-Ly said when her daughter showed her the new driver's license. "Taaahhh-nnyahhhh."

It sounded unnatural. The name Tanya belonged to one of those big-foot blondies who visited the salon, not to the tiny middle-age Vietnamese woman painting their nails. But of course, this was the daughter who named her own child after a fruit.

Hien and Tri didn't think the name change was so strange, and consequently, were following their sister's example, like mindless ducks, as they always did. Just look at their newest hair color: spicy nutmeg, another fancy way to say brown. Copycats. So while Tuyet/Tanya scrubbed the pedicure tubs with smelly chemicals, Tri hunched over Hien's hair roots, cheerily counting the new white hairs she found as she touched them up.

"What about Helen?" her eldest daughter asked, dog-earing a page from the name book. "It's similar to Hien."

"It sounds old," Tri said, pulling back Hien's hair part to reach the roots in the front. "It's a retired woman's name."

"Those women used to be young, too," Hien said. "I like the sound of it. Helen of Troy, like that movie on television last year."

"Do you know why I gave you that name? Because it was your grandmother's. Your father and I wanted to honor her memory. And now you want to change it to some character from a movie?"

"I'm not replacing your name, Mother," Hien said. "I'm just adding an American one."

"If I'd known we'd be in America forever, I would have named Linh differently," Tri said as she wrapped her sister's hair in a stained orange towel. "Maybe Jessica or Amanda. American teachers treat students differently if they can pronounce their names. They don't judge them as harshly. That's why Cherry does so well."

"That is ridiculous," Kim-Ly said. "What about Dat? He does very well and no one is calling him Dan or David."

"Do you know how much he has to work for it?" Hien said. "He studies harder than any other student in his classes. It's not easy for him."

"And that is because he is Vietnamese? Listen to you girls, victimizing yourselves all over again. This is not wartime. Why do you worry so much about the Americans' opinions of you? Do you really think they are thinking about you so much?"

"Viet is changing his name," Tuyet/Tanya said.

"No, he isn't." Kim-Ly would know if her last surviving son would do such a thing.

"Yes, he is," she said. "Ask him the next time he calls. He wants to be called Victor now."

Kim-Ly didn't reply. Viet suddenly felt even farther away from her. She hadn't realized that was possible. After he decided to move away, ostensibly to be closer to that trashy girlfriend and her bastard children, Kim-Ly was unable to leave her bedroom for a week. Viet had been too polite to reveal his true reasons for leaving: he'd grown tired of listening to his mother's advice about limiting his card playing, and pursuing a law or business degree instead. Though he nodded and pretended to agree, Kim-Ly knew her words were not as valuable as her deposits in their joint checking account. Now, he only called her to ask for an increase in his monthly stipend, or to promise once again that he was just weeks away from settling into his new home and inviting Kim-Ly out for a visit.

"We live in America now," the former Hien said. "We're not ever going back to Vietnam, you said so yourself."

"That doesn't mean you forget who you once were," Kim-Ly said. "A name is your identity. You're going to regret it. And I hope I don't live to see that."

No one responded. Perhaps she'd made her point, but more likely they'd grown weary of arguing with her. Their eyes traveled to the television, where the vapid lead characters from the latest Vietnamese soap opera were arguing about a scandalous conversation between the husband and the maid. Kim-Ly despised how fascinating she still found these shows. Illegally imported, they always revolved around family woes. No one ever mentioned a world outside the home, nothing political or historical. If any outsider tried to understand her people from these soaps, instead of those atrocious American films, they would think the war had never happened. That the Vietnamese were pretty, self-absorbed elitists instead, not so different from Americans themselves.

The girls were talking about an academic debate that Cherry had qualified for. Her granddaughter participated in some school-related event every weekend. This one was in La Jolla. Tuyet/Tanya wanted to make it a family outing and go to SeaWorld.

"I can't," Kim-Ly said. "I'm going to Vegas."

Her daughters all stared at her, with that stunned expression they had inherited from their father.

"Are you crazy?" Tuyet/Tanya asked.

"How are you going to get there?" chimed Hien/Helen.

"Who's going to make sure you take your medication?" Tri asked.

Kim-Ly was prepared. She would take the Johnny Luck Resort and Casino Complimentary Luxury Coach to Las Vegas with her dearest friends Ba Liem and Ba Nhanh. They planned to stay for three days and two nights. She was perfectly capable of administering her own medication as she always had been. And no, she was not crazy, simply bored. She needed a vacation.

"This might be okay," Tuyet/Tanya said, more to her sisters than to Kim-Ly. "Lum will be in Las Vegas that weekend for a school project. His business class is taking a tour of a resort construction. He can keep an eye on her."

"School project!" hooted Kim-Ly. "You believed that?"

"Why are you going there?" Tri asked suspiciously.

"We're going to see a free show. And to go window shopping."

The girls exchanged a knowing glance.

"Don't worry," Kim-Ly sneered. "I won't be taking any of the family money. I have been saving my own. It isn't related to the salon in any way. We have all learned from that misunderstanding, haven't we?"

That lovely reminder was enough. Kim-Ly would finally be leaving the state of California with her friends. She only had to agree, several times, that she'd call and meet up with Lum once in the morning and once in the evening for the duration of her trip. They put Lum's number in her purse, her suitcase, and in both pockets of her cardigan. If Lum didn't hear from her, the daughters warned, they'd drive to Vegas and find her.

"Why build a city here?" Kim-Ly asked as they stepped off the bus and the dry heat punched her in the face. She couldn't believe how much dead land stretched between Orange County and Las Vegas. While her native country was lush with jungles, rivers, rice paddies, and beaches, this landscape could only cough up rocks, weeds, and lots and lots of clay.

"Ahh, but why not?" Ba Liem replied, looking absurd in the oversize plastic sunglasses the resort stuck in every seat pocket. "This is the American Way, Ba Kim-Ly. Arrive broke on Friday, leave rich on Sunday."

For most people, it was likely the other way around. But they didn't have a psychic by their side. The bus had driven down the Strip for the virgin patrons to ooh and ahh at the lights and fountains, but their hotel was actually ten minutes away from the main strip in the suburb of Henderson. They dropped their bags in their hotel room and cooed at the floral wallpaper, two double beds jammed against the windows, ashtrays on every surface. After washing up in the cramped bathroom with tissue-thin towels, they eagerly took the elevator to the hotel's casino floor.

Kim-Ly was glad to be standing between the twins. Everywhere there were stroke-inducing neon signs, singing and dinging slot machines, and people smoking. And women in tiny outfits with doily napkins on their heads, trying to talk to her. Ba Nhanh explained they were taking drink orders.

"Free?" Kim-Ly asked, and then instructed Ba Nhanh to order her a gin and tonic.

As they wandered the casino floor, surveying the slot machines and gaming tables, Kim-Ly realized she hadn't accounted for the fact that most of the inhabitants of Las Vegas would be speaking to her in English. It was an easy thing to forget living in Little Saigon where everyone spoke Vietnamese. Kim-Ly's English was limited to the essentials: *Hello, Good-bye, Yes, No, Sorry, Thank you, Restroom.* How could she learn enough to play bingo?

"You only have to look at the numbers they show on the screen," Ba Liem assured her. "And we'll be with you."

It turned out most of the players in the Johnny Luck Bingo Parlor were Vietnamese anyway, or at least Asian. As soon as they sat in the plush chairs and brightly colored tables, another doily waitress came by.

"Another gin and tonic water," Kim-Ly said, and after a look from Ba Nhanh, she added, "that last one was very weak."

The bingo dealer, a tall Chinese woman with frizzy hair, announced the bingo rules in English, Vietnamese, and several other languages. As a casino employee handed out bingo cards and sponge-tipped daubers, Kim-Ly was surprised by how much a pack of cards cost, and even more surprised at how many packs her friends purchased. This wasn't like their dollar games of SuperLotto.

"You have to increase your odds with the number of cards," Ba Liem explained. "Trust me. We've watched how people win at this. You can never win from just one pack."

Kim-Ly reluctantly purchased a second pack. The twins spread their cards across the table, uncapped their daubers, and ordered another round of drinks. The waitress also brought complimentary bowls of peanuts and pretzels to their table.

"And remember," Ba Liem said, "you have to scream 'bingo' really loud here. If you don't and they hear someone else say it before you, you lose."

"We've seen fights over it," Ba Nhanh whispered. "In this very casino."

After only twenty minutes and twelve numbers on the wall screen, a man in the back bingoed. The twins were right. You did have to scream, and he certainly did. Kim-Ly couldn't tell if he was in pain or joy. They watched as the winner danced up the aisle to collect his prize. Kim-Ly realized why she preferred California SuperLotto. It was cheaper, and she didn't have to watch the winning bastard skip away with money that should be hers. She also began to suspect the cards were fixed. Kim-Ly couldn't control what number patterns she bought and she had to work fast to mark the called numbers with the dauber. Kim-Ly's eyes were not as sharp as they once were. With SuperLotto, the rules were simpler and fairer. The Lotto didn't punish the slow.

After several hours, Kim-Ly grew bored. She'd depleted nearly half of her leisure money that day, and at the rate they were going, she wouldn't have enough for dinner.

"Aren't you hungry?" Kim-Ly asked the twins, whose eyes studied the bingo wall with the intensity of cats stalking prey. "All I've had are those drinks and I feel dizzy."

"They'll bring food to the table," Ba Nhanh said. "All we have to do is ask."

"What do they have? I can't read their menu. Can you tell me if they have anything I could eat?" Kim-Ly felt a sudden pang for the food court at the mall in Little Saigon. Though she complained that some of the vendors skimped on meat in the noodle dishes, at least she could depend on ordering something she knew. What if they only had pizza and hamburgers?

The twins were not listening. They'd purchased another round of cards and were busy setting up their games. If Kim-Ly didn't buy another set of cards, she'd have to wait at least another hour for them to finish. Like almost every other player in the bingo parlor, their rear ends seemed intent on remaining parked in those cushy velour seats.

"I'm calling Lum," Kim-Ly said, standing from the table. "My grandson will worry. I'm supposed to take my medication."

Kim-Ly wandered out of the bingo parlor onto the casino floor. She recognized many of the people sitting at the slots from hours earlier. Two young men her grandsons' age bumped into her from behind with tall plastic cups of beer. They mumbled apologies and continued to push and laugh at each other.

Turning the corner, Kim-Ly squinted through the bright lights and saw Viet emerging from behind an island of slot machines. When she called out and waved to him, the man turned and walked away. Kim-Ly lowered her hand and pulled her purse closer. She felt conspicuous in her dark-green *ao dai* and purple cardigan. She fished into her pocket for Lum's number and located a pay phone near the public restrooms.

"Come quick," Kim-Ly said when she recognized her grandson's voice on the line. "They'll kick me out if I'm not gambling."

"They won't kick you out," Lum said. But he must have believed her. He was there in under fifteen minutes, along with his hooligans. This time Kim-Ly was comforted by their loud, boisterous presence. She held on to her grandson's elbow for support, which he allowed, and the rest of the boys surrounded them like a protective tortoise shell.

"I want to try one of those buffets," she said. "I have discounts." She waved the coupon book that the bus driver had handed them earlier that day.

"There's one at our hotel," Lum said. "Where are Ba Nhanh and Ba Liem?"

"They have your number. They can find us later."

The nighttime sky looked dusty from the particle lights of the neon-tangled strip. Lum and his friends drove her to what looked like an Egyptian pyramid from the outside but was just a regular casino and hotel on the inside. The buffet restaurant, while not nearly as scintillating as it appeared in the posters and televisions around the hotel, did have all-you-can-eat shrimp and lobster tails. Dissatisfied with the greasy lo mein noodles and dried-out fried rice offered in the Chinese food station, Kim-Ly filled two dinner plates with seafood, butter, and cocktail sauce.

"So how much money have you lost?" Lum's friend Huy asked, as they settled down to their massive meals. The boys had rejected the seafood, instead feasting upon thick cuts of prime rib, baked potatoes, spaghetti piles, and pizza slices.

"It's my money," Kim-Ly said. "I do with it what I want." She put down her fork. "And so do you boys, apparently. School project? Are your parents that dumb?"

While the boys nervously laughed, Lum sniffed the air, like someone had passed gas. His eyes focused on his grandmother. "Have you been drinking?"

Kim-Ly plucked a shrimp from her plate and chomped down, tail included.

"You've been gambling *and* drinking?" Lum asked. "What about your medication?"

"The doctor said a drink or two was permitted."

"Mom asked me to look after you," Lum said. "If anything happens, guess who they're going to yell at?"

"I'm fine," Kim-Ly retorted. "No one will think badly of you because I wanted to have one drink on my vacation."

"She's right, Lum," Huy said. "Listen, she doesn't tell on us, you won't tell on her, right?" And to prove his point, when the server passed by to take their drink orders, Huy added a glass of wine for Ba Vo to their several pitchers of beer. "Wine is supposed to be good for the heart, right?"

"Correct," Kim-Ly said. "And I'll overlook how you must have obtained that false driver's license." Lum still looked cranky, so she reached over with her fork and pronged his arm. "But I appreciate your concern. It's nice to finally see your thoughtfulness. Family should watch out for each other."

"Yeah?" Lum asked, looking unconvinced.

"How do you think you got that job at the Vans' flower shop?" Kim-Ly said, unable to suppress a giggle. "Your mother asked me to call in a favor. The Vans have benefited for years from my generosity."

Her laughter must have been infectious, because the boys tittered, all except Lum, who studied his plate, clenching his jaw.

"Why don't you tell us, Ba Vo?" Huy said. "How many businesses in Little Saigon have you loaned money to? How many have you shut down?"

Kim-Ly shrugged, inciting more laughter. She could have told them the truth, that those businesses had sunk themselves, and her mistake was to invest in them in the first place. She knew there were people in Little Saigon who spoke ill of her, but they were too shortsighted to consider the whole picture. She could loan these aspiring entrepreneurs the money, but not the smarts to succeed. They should have felt grateful for the opportunity and resources she had given them.

For most of her meals, Kim-Ly ate with family or the twins. If her grandson were ever present at a birthday dinner or Tet celebration, he usually sat at the other end of the table with his sister. Kim-Ly took this opportunity to notice what her grandson consumed (lean meat, broccoli, pizza slice) and didn't (fatty meat, onions, even the beer, since he was the designated driver). She found it useful to see him interacting with his friends in an environment less aggravating than the salon. Though she still believed that they were wasting their potential with too much leisure, she did find some of their interaction sweet and sincere. They shared their dishes and refilled each other's mugs. Kim-Ly only wished Lum could treat his own cousin Dat in this manner.

For dessert, they licked cones of vanilla soft-serve ice cream. When they returned to their table, Kim-Ly noticed her grandson was missing.

"Where is Lum?" she asked. "Did he get lost?"

His friend Huy and another boy were shaking their heads and bumping shoulders.

"What's wrong?" Kim-Ly said.

Huy shook his head again. "He's calling Quynh—again . . . I bet he's gonna ask her soon."

Some of the other guys hushed him, looking uncertainly at Kim-Ly.

"What?" Huy said. "It's true. You know they talk about it. We all know that."

"You're kids," Kim-Ly said. "You're not even finished with school yet."

"Well, you can do anything you want in America," he said.

"Shut up, Huy," one of the hooligans said, leaning over to stuff a bread roll in the inebriated boy's mouth. "So much beer in you, gotta absorb some of it before you say some more crazy."

"But Ba Vo, don't you like Quynh?" Huy asked.

"I think she's a nice girl, very obedient and smart," Kim-Ly said.

"But I'd want my grandson to have a good job and salary if he were going to marry her. She deserves that."

"He's doing all right, Ba Vo," one of the boys said. "He'll probably make more money than all of us."

"How's that?" she asked. "His mother tells me his grades. They're not that impressive."

"Have you seen him playing cards?" They all started to laugh. When Lum returned to the table, they changed the subject. As her grandson talked to his friends and playfully stole a broccoli floret off Huy's plate, she tried to analyze his face, but his image blurred no matter how much she squinted, and in the soft yellow light of the restaurant, she felt she could barely see him at all.

Poker. She knew her husband and friends played back in Saigon, and that her sons used to play with their American business clients. Viêt ran a poker game when he still lived in Orange County. Early in her marriage, before the children were born, she occasionally sat in on one of her husband's games and was surprised to discover how well she read other people's faces and took away their chips. But she was smart enough to realize when to walk away and not lose any money. To understand it was just a game. Card playing indulged such a male vanity. So when the boys drove her back to her hotel, she asked them inside to play at one of the Johnny Luck tables.

"I don't know," Lum said, staring warily at his grandmother.

"Come on," Huy said, drunker than he was during dinner. "The blinds are probably tiny here. It'll be good practice."

While the boys fanned through the poker tables, Kim-Ly returned to the bingo parlor, and found the twins sitting where she left them.

"Have you moved?" she asked. "Don't you need to use the restroom?"

The twins waited until the bingo dealer announced a mandatory break in the game. "That's why you should only snack and not drink during bingo," Ba Liem said. "While you were off with your grandson, you missed an exciting moment."

"Very exciting," Ba Nhanh echoed.

"Did you win?" Kim-Ly asked.

"Almost," Ba Liem said. "I was feeling the premonition again and had four numbers in a row . . . but then some old Filipino in the front row called it. The ruckus ruined my concentration."

Kim-Ly sat in her old seat, but waved off the eager casino employee who offered her a card pack. "We have more important things to discuss." She told them about her conversation with the boys and Lum's plan to trap Quynh in an early marriage.

"They're just children!" Ba Liem said.

"Didn't you want Dat to marry Quynh?" Ba Nhanh asked.

"That's beside the point," Kim-Ly said. "I don't think these kids have any idea what responsibility comes with marriage. I'm afraid if I say anything to his mother, she'll try to encourage the boy. She did the same thing, you remember, eloping without my permission."

"Many young people elope in Las Vegas," Ba Nhanh said, nodding knowingly.

"Quynh isn't even here," Ba Liem said, swatting her sister's arm.

Kim-Ly wanted to chat more with her friends, but the ringing bell indicated the break had ended and the twins returned to their obsession. It was disappointing. She had such hopes for her first vacation without her children. The brochures she'd read about Las Vegas promised shows, restaurants, street performers, and so many thrills, she'd likely pass out. But the twins and the rest of their bus travelers felt content sitting in a bingo parlor that didn't even have windows.

After half an hour of watching the twins lurch over their bingo cards, clucking in disappointment, and Ba Liem's forehead scrunching as her intuition neared, Kim-Ly left. Wandering the casino floor, making sure to skirt the walls of the room and avoid intimidating groups of boisterous gamblers, Kim-Ly realized that her delinquent grandson and his friends had provided her better company on this vacation. She secretly hoped they hadn't left.

It took some time to find them. While she'd wandered the poker tables on the main floor, she finally spotted one of the boys through the glass windows of an enclosed room of the hotel. When the tall black guard tried to block her entrance at the velvet rope, she yelled at him for his impudence, but he couldn't understand her. Luckily, Huy heard her from across the room, stepped into the feud, and after a short exchange in English, the guard let her in.

"Why were you hiding from me?" she asked.

"We found a tournament," Huy said. The players in the glass room looked as crazed as the twins in the bingo parlor.

"And why aren't you playing?" Kim-Ly asked.

"I'm already out. We're just waiting on Lum and the other guys."

Barred from sitting near the active tables, Huy led Kim-Ly to a corner reserved for the losers and nonplayers, where they enjoyed hot appetizers and refreshments. Because they were complimentary, Kim-Ly determined that another gin and tonic couldn't hurt, especially if she had snacks with it.

Lum and the rest of the boys sprawled at different tables. Kim-Ly wondered if this was a part of their strategy. All the men at Lum's table looked much older than him. Most were smoking and their clothes looked wrinkled and ill-fitting. This had to happen to many gamblers. They became so concerned with their game they lost all perspective on their appearance. Lum, on the other hand, just looked like a little boy.

Kim-Ly turned to Huy. "Lum looks scared. Is he in trouble?"

Huy shook his head, not even turning in Lum's direction. "Nah, he's good."

She analyzed the chips on the table. Lum's pile looked comparable to those sitting next to him, but not nearly as large as the chip pile of the heavyset man with the cowboy hat and sunglasses. Cowboy clearly seemed to be intimidating the others. He grunted and used his thumbs a lot to indicate his wishes to the dealer. Only Lum and another player seemed relaxed and willing to stay in the rounds.

Lum's chips dwindled. He'd challenged Cowboy in two consecutive hands and lost. Kim-Ly felt torn between wanting him kicked out so they could leave, and wanting him to prevail over the fat bastard. His face expressed no worry as he patiently moved his chips and held his cards with the utmost aplomb. It was the same confident expression Viet always wore whenever he assured his mother he'd pay back her small loan, that she only needed to have faith in him.

On the other side of the table, Cowboy smirked, his mustache twitching, his left index finger caressing a white chip. He was going to beat her grandson, she felt sure of it. Kim-Ly wished she could see Lum's cards. The poker room appeared friendly with complimentary drinks and food, luxurious chairs, and pretty girls, but it was a trap. All of them were lured to this hotel built in America's wasteland just to take away their money. Cowboy probably worked for the casino. Perhaps he was Johnny Luck. Narrowing her eyes, she realized Cowboy had blurred until he became one orange, flaming mass. She put down her perspiring drink.

"Are you all right, Ba Vo?" Huy asked.

She couldn't say anything. She could only hear her heartbeat thumping louder and faster, reverberating to the top of her skull and crashing to the bottom of her stomach. Clutching her hands to her chest, she tried to quiet it, and looked down at her purple cardigan, covered with the crumbs of all those tiny quiches and minitoasts. Her heart grew louder, faster, higher, hotter, until Kim-Ly couldn't stand it any longer. She stretched her neck back, her eyes confronted by the orange lights shining from the ceiling, filling her line of vision, and she screamed.

She didn't remember closing her mouth, collapsing to the floor, her head cushioned by the rose plush casino carpet. What she could recall was Viet's face above her as her eyes blinked open.

"Don't leave me," she pleaded. "You know I am not well. I need you."

Viet sighed, unmoved. "You're going to be fine, Mother. You'll always be fine."

When she blinked again, Kim-Ly realized it was Lum's face hovering over her. He was crying. A man and a woman in white uniforms had wrapped something tight around her arm and were shining tiny flashlights into her face. The stethoscope chilled her skin. They were asking her all sorts of questions and the boys were quickly shouting their translations. If she could see them, hear them, feel her hands and feet. Kim-Ly ignored all their questions, turned her head until she could see her grandson, and asked to go home.

"Do you want to go to a hospital? Do you want to see a doctor?"

She shook her head. "I want to go home."

Kim-Ly didn't know what happened with the poker game and she didn't want to ask. The other boys stayed behind.

"We don't have to tell anyone," Kim-Ly said, pacing her voice to sound friendly, gentle. "Your mother and aunties would only worry."

"Maybe they should." The lights of an oncoming car briefly illuminated his angry, tight face. "They checked your purse, Grandmother. You didn't have your medication on you. Why is that?"

"I must have left it in another bag."

"You can't do that, Grandmother. Do you realize you could have died tonight?"

"Pills can't keep me from dying."

"Are you kidding?" Lum whipped his head to stare at her. "After complaining to Mom that I don't take you to your doctor's appointments?"

"You don't."

"Because you always want Dat to take you."

"Is this what it's about?" Kim-Ly asked, pouncing on the opportunity to deflect. "You should not let your jealousy control you this way."

"Trust me, Grandmother, I'm not jealous of Dat."

They fell silent for many miles. Kim-Ly looked out the window to a casino that the twins had pointed out on the ride into Vegas, nestled on the California–Nevada border. One step over and gambling was illegal. One step back and the money was yours to lose.

"Did you know I was never allowed to hold you as a baby?" she said. "Your mother was very cruel to me. If you're not allowed to hold your grandson, how can you ever know him? I may understand Dat better, but that is not my fault."

"I know you disowned us, Grandmother," he said.

"Oh, that's ridiculous," Kim-Ly said. "Your mother takes everything so literally."

"She told me about the American officer," Lum said. "You tried to force her to marry him instead of my father just so you could make a business deal."

"Is that what she told you?" Kim-Ly said with a snort. "Then you really are as stupid as Dat says."

She expected her grandson to deny her provocation, to defend himself. He remained silent as he switched lanes to pass another car. Kim-Ly furtively watched him, the tightness in his cheekbones, the squinting in his eyes. She wondered if he was sincerely wounded by her words.

"I believe her," he finally said. "I know what you're capable of. It shouldn't surprise me, given how you and Uncle Thang made money back in Vietnam."

"We never sold anything illegal! Your mother never understood the family business." The pressure returned to her chest. "Do you want your mother to know how you mistreated me tonight? The activities you participated in?"

Her grandson had the insolence to smile. "You can't leave anyone alone," he said. "Not those poor people you give loans to and not your family. You meddle and meddle, and make things worse. You drive Uncle Viet away because you refused to see his children. You destroy lives. I don't have to stick around and let you do that to me."

Looking over at him, the oncoming traffic manipulating the lights and shadows across his face, he appeared menacing, deranged. "You should not speak to your mother this way," Kim-Ly said, loudly, forcefully.

He turned to her, his eyes thinning, focusing, seeing her. "I am not your son."

They returned to her home at Hien and Chinh's at nearly two in the morning. Lum walked her to the front steps and after she unlocked the door, left without saying good-bye. At breakfast the next day, Hien told her that someone in Huntington Beach had won the SuperLotto jackpot while she'd been in Vegas. A lawyer's housewife who clearly didn't need the money had bought the ticket on a whim.

The family sipped on asparagus and crabmeat soup and said nothing about Kim-Ly's early return. When Dat stood to leave for the library, Kim-Ly pressed his hand to stay. She waited until Dat's sister and parents had left the table to tell her grandson everything; the false driver's licenses, the drinking, the gambling, even Lum's foolish plans to propose to Quynh. Dat didn't seem surprised. He listened to what she said, never interrupting, and they both sighed at the trouble Lum had fallen in.

"You have to help your cousin. He's not smart enough to help himself. He'll say anything to hide his addiction. He'll even say I am not well."

Dat slowly nodded, pushing up the bridge of his eyeglasses with his pointer finger. "I'm glad you confided in me, Grandmother. I promise you, we will help him. He will not disgrace this family."

"I trust you, Dat," Kim-Ly said, smiling and patting his shoulder. "I know you will fix this."

At such a crucial moment in her family's life, Kim-Ly felt grateful to have a family member she could rely on. Although she knew some of her family considered her rigid, even impossible, Kim-Ly set high standards for their own good. She wanted the best for them. To see Lum throw his life away because he overestimated his intelligence, because he trusted those he should not, was all too familiar. The world could be cruel to the weak and slow-witted. Just look at what happened to Viet. She had loved her son too much to help him properly. Such suffering would not continue down her lineage. Lum's parents couldn't see it. Neither could his sister. Only Kim-Ly could. So she and Dat would help him. Lum would never know it, but they would rescue his future.

1986

Cuc Bui
Paris, France

. . . *I received a postcard from my grandchildren in America the other day. They had taken a vacation to Mexico, which they can drive to by car. Lum and Cherry say they have been swimming at the beach and visiting street fairs. How exciting for them.*

While I'm aware they sent that card out of respect, I can't help but feel offended. Wouldn't you? If they have free time from school, shouldn't they be visiting their grandpère? I can't imagine what Mexico has to offer over their family. They have a beach in California. But how often can they see us?

I do not blame them. They are too young to understand. But their parents, their father, he is the one who disappoints me. I know I tried my best with my boys, but it still pains me to watch how my youngest turned out. Not as smart as Yen, not as loyal as Phung. Always bowing down to that serpent of a wife, who has always hated us, even when we cared for her when her family kicked her out to the streets. She dares to blame us for our family's separation. An aberration of a human being, I shall never say or write her name again.

This was Sanh's choice. He has no one to blame but himself. While I am of the mind that men should choose their own wives, his choice has never made sense to me. Now he must suffer for it for the rest of his life. . . .

Hung Truong
Paris, France

❧ *Chapter Nine*

HOA

HOA REALIZED HER GRANDDAUGHTER WAS TROUBLED the first night she arrived. Cherry acted cranky, distracted. Her appetite, which Hoa remembered as healthy, enthusiastic for her grandmère's cooking, was poor. Hoa understood this was typical adolescent behavior—she'd seen it with both Xuan and Cam—but unlike her cousins, Cherry accepted no comfort from her grandmère. Her hug at the airport was brief and perfunctory, and conversation at her welcome dinner felt awkward and forced. Cherry excused herself early that evening, claiming to be exhausted. Later that night, Hoa sneaked into the study where Cherry was sleeping to make sure her blankets were covering her properly. After adjusting her pillow, Hoa fought the impulse to kiss those chubby cheeks and delicate eyebrows. It was hard to believe she was already a young woman. And Hoa had only spent a handful of days with her in that short lifetime.

Hoa knew she shouldn't push herself on her granddaughter—that she should give her time to recover from the plane ride, and space to re-acquaint herself with her relatives—but she couldn't help her eagerness. She had three weeks with her granddaughter. Three weeks. Cherry had come alone to Paris this summer, without her parents and without her brother, Lum, who claimed he had to work. This was the second year in a row that Hoa had not seen her grandson.

The next morning, Cherry walked with Cam to her patisserie in the Marais, and returned with a book of postcards she purchased from a street vendor along the Seine. While Hoa picked up the living room and folded laundry, Cherry worked for over half an hour on one post-card, her tight, square handwriting nearly impossible to read when Hoa passed by and casually peered over her shoulder. While Cherry was feeding Grandpère lunch in his bedroom, Hoa sat on the sofa and wist-fully stared at the card from across the living room. She could not in-vade her granddaughter's privacy. She tried to focus on her crocheting.

"Why don't you tell me what is bothering you?" Hoa finally asked when Cherry returned from the bedroom with an empty bowl and spoon. "What can you put in writing that you can't say to me?"

"You're the one who taught me to write letters," Cherry said. "Some-times they can be more intimate than talking. You can say more."

After depositing the dishes in the kitchen, she walked to the sofa and sat next to Hoa, who was crocheting a blanket. "I've kept all of your letters," Cherry said. "I read them when I miss you."

Though she recognized her granddaughter's strategy, Hoa allowed herself to be swayed. "So you are writing to a friend?" Hoa asked, smil-ing. "A boyfriend?"

Cherry's face flushed pink. "No, just my cousin."

"Oh," Hoa said, immediately regretting the assumption.

"You don't have to feel sorry for me," Cherry said. "I probably wouldn't have time for one, even if someone were interested."

Hoa smiled again, relieved. "Relationships when you are too young can cause a lot of waste in your heart."

"Did you have boyfriends when you were my age?"

"The only young men I knew besides your grandpère were family. We did not socialize like you and your cousins do now." She sometimes felt grateful for this. She did not enjoy watching Cam suffer these last few years, and disliked how the Bourdains snubbed their family every Sunday at Mass, all due to Petit Michel's callousness. She hated how secretive Xuan acted with his own relationships, never bringing anyone home, only discussing his studies. Neither of them showed any inclination toward a marriage anytime soon. Perhaps Xuan and Cam could use some guidance. True, Hoa had reservations against arranged marriages after her own, which was why her two younger sons chose their own wives. But finding a partner, a suitable partner, especially in a country like France, could be a lonely prospect.

Cherry fingered the crocheted yarn in Hoa's lap. "Did you ever write letters to Grandpère? He was asking for his mail during lunch."

Hoa managed not to cringe. "I've been with him every day since I was seventeen years old. We never needed to write letters."

"Aunt Trinh said she never saved Uncle Yen's letters."

Hoa remained silent as Cherry continued to play with the stitching.

"I guess it's not like she wants to remember that time or anything," Cherry said.

"No," Hoa tentatively admitted. "None of us——"

"Lan!" Hung screamed from the bedroom.

"Who's Lan?" Cherry asked.

"One of our servants back in Vietnam," Hoa said, pushing the knitting needles off her lap.

They could smell feces before entering the room. Hung sat up in bed, his face red and sweaty. He stared at them for a second. Hoa wasn't sure if he would scream again or burst into tears.

"I'm sorry," Cherry said. "I asked him after his lunch. He said he didn't need to go."

"That's okay, darling," Hoa said. "There are laundered sheets in the hall closet." When her granddaughter left, Hoa strode to his bedside and pulled his sheets away. He'd gotten it everywhere. They'd have to wash the blankets and duvet cover.

"If you keep humiliating yourself like this, you're going to drive all our family away," Hoa said, peeling the soiled clothes from his thin limbs. She wrapped them into a ball and dumped them in the hamper.

"Where are my letters?" Hung asked as she buttoned him into a fresh pajama top. "Why are you hiding them?"

With Hung incontinent, she'd moved her single bed out of the bedroom to sleep in the study. He didn't like her near his desk, though he rarely used it anymore.

"No one writes to you," Hoa said, closing the top button, though in the past he complained it restricted his breathing. "All of your friends are dead."

"You're lying."

"Why would I lie?" Hoa asked tiredly, pulling an adult-size diaper from the top drawer of his dresser.

"I'm not wearing that," Hung said with dismay.

"You are." Hoa easily fended off his protesting hands and pulled the diaper around his legs to fit firmly around his seat. One of the few benefits of Hung's ailment: now she was physically stronger than he was.

Lan. She lived with them back in their old house in Nha Trang. The younger sister of another servant, Lan was sixteen and had only stayed for several months before leaving for school. Hoa barely remembered her name until she found it in the letters. She should have realized how odd it was for a servant to have enough money to go away to school. For someone so young, the girl was shamelessly overdramatic, even if these were love letters—always thanking Hung for his patronage, effusing about the literature and criticism she read in school, expressing how she missed and craved his opinions on her poetry. Some of the poems sounded charming, Hoa had to admit, in a youthful kind of way, but their naïveté and optimism were grating, often unbearable to read through to the end. Love that transcends war and time? Devotion of a thousand suns? Hoa thought Hung had better taste than that. Hung and Lan apparently had met several times during Hung's business trips to Saigon. After recording the dates of their correspondence and meetings in her journal, Hoa stacked Lan's letters into a small pile and returned them to Hung's box in his desk. She wedged the box between old issues of Vietnamese newspapers, where none of the children would ever find them.

When the doctors first diagnosed his condition as Alzheimer's, Hung's moods seemed to soften. He smiled more. He picked fewer fights with his sons and teased the grandchildren at the dinner table. But Hoa received no such benefit. Although his eyes brightened around the children, the changing trees in autumn, or a foolish news segment on television, the enchantment dissolved when his gaze found Hoa. Something deeply embedded in his disintegrating brain clicked over, reminding him how he'd treated her, how he should always treat her. At best, he tolerated or ignored her. At worst, his tantrums revealed how much he'd regressed.

The first time Hoa bathed Hung in the washtub (it had been several weeks since his last bath and the smell had become unbearable), he'd smacked her in the face so hard—drawing blood—they were afraid he'd broken her nose.

"What are you doing?" Phung yelled, stepping between his parents. His voice sounded so threatening in their tiny bathroom that even Hoa felt fearful.

"I can bathe myself," Hung insisted, sullenly cowering behind the toilet, naked. "I'm a grown man."

"You *do* need her help," Phung said. "You can't hit her, Father, not ever again."

While they argued, Hoa turned her back to prepare the bathwater, initially twisting the knobs to find a good balance of hot and cold, then slowly, subtly, closing the hot faucet until the temperature cooled short of comfortable. Hung submerged in the water, his face grimacing in pain, pulling his knees to his chest, his skin puckering with goose bumps, until Hoa finally relented, and turned the hot water on again to mix with his bath.

Hoa wondered if Hung's illness was not a tragedy, but rather, nature's way of correcting their relationship. With his memory fading, finally,

finally, her home would be under her own control. She would decide what they would eat for breakfast, lunch, and dinner, without his approval. She could contribute to conversations with the children and grandchildren without Hung telling her to shut up. With Hung silenced, she could finally utilize her voice.

"What does he remember?" Cherry had asked one afternoon after returning from a shopping trip with Aunt Trinh. Hoa was washing lettuce leaves in the kitchen while Cherry set the table for dinner.

"It is different every day," Hoa said. "Sometimes he can only remember when your daddy and uncles were little boys in Nha Trang. Other days, he asks for one of your cousin's cakes."

Her granddaughter stopped in front of one spot at the dining table, chopsticks still in hand. "What if one day his memory doesn't come back?"

"That may happen," Hoa admitted.

"I guess there are some things worth forgetting," she said.

"You speak like you've lived long enough to regret things," Hoa said, a soft smile on her face.

"I was thinking about Auntie Trinh," her granddaughter said. "She told me about Pulau."

Hoa turned off the water, the leaves shaking in her wet hands. Cherry looked at her expectantly.

"What did she tell you?" Hoa asked.

"Enough," Cherry said.

The expression on her granddaughter's face baffled Hoa. Was it horror? Sympathy? Blame? If it were Cam or Xuan's face, Hoa would have known immediately. The ambiguity in a face that should have been familiar disconcerted Hoa. Before she could look deeper, Cherry turned her back to finish dressing the table. Such a simple motion, and the moment slipped away.

"She asked me," Trinh said, when Hoa found a moment alone with her that evening. "I wasn't going to lie to her."

The grandchildren had gone out to listen to music with some of Xuan's friends from school. Trinh had brought up the laundry from the basement to fold clothes before going to sleep.

"But she is so young," Hoa said.

"She is sixteen," Trinh said, almost laughing as she smoothed out a crease from a clean pillowcase. "I was with Yen by her age."

"Cherry is different," Hoa said. "She wasn't born in Vietnam. We don't know what her parents have told her."

"I don't think it's much," Trinh said, "or she wouldn't be asking me."

Hoa's grasp on Hung's sock tightened, imagining the two of them confiding in each other, sharing such secrets on their outings away from the apartment house, away from Hoa. "You need to be careful," she said.

But of course, her daughter-in-law only chuckled. "If she wants to talk, I'm going to talk. Look what happened to me when I didn't. Aren't things better when we are finally truthful?"

That was debatable. Since confessing all to Yen, to the rest of the family, at her therapist's prompting, Trinh had no choice but to believe that her life was better. Yet, not much changed. Yen, who had always been devoted to her, stayed true to his marriage vows, but Xuan, the poor boy, who had never recovered from all he'd seen his mother endure, remained wary, distant, suspicious. Trinh pretended it didn't bother her, but Hoa knew she felt hurt. Hoa hoped such an estrangement would never split her from one of her sons. Even with Sanh far away, she sought comfort in her freedom to pick up the phone and call him whenever she wanted, as he often reminded her to do. Perhaps she should call him tonight, and ask about Cherry, if there was anything Hoa should know, if there was anything she could do. But that could just needlessly worry her son. Hoa didn't want that. She wanted this to be a good visit for Cherry. She wanted her to come back.

Hoa rarely had the privilege of an afternoon out with her sons, and this excursion was not for pleasure. The tour of a nursing home in a suburb outside the city, was only to look, nothing else. The facilities, swathed in bright shades of violet and yellow, were brochure-worthy. There were fresh flowers in every room. Every floor sparkled with color-coordinated nurses and orderlies and smiling, rose-smelling patients. Yen tried to persuade her to call them residents. These were the residents' bedrooms and this was an assisted-care home, not a hospital. After researching all the facilities in the area, Yen found that this one offered the best services for patients with Alzheimer's. Best of all, they had multilingual staffers, including several physicians and orderlies who spoke Vietnamese.

"Ngoan heard about this place at the community center," Phung said. "They have other Vietnamese residents so he can make friends."

"We'll be able to visit him anytime we want," Yen said. "They even have an extra bed in each room for family to stay overnight."

"How is that different from our apartment?" Hoa asked. "Where I can sleep in my own bed and not have to take a train every morning?"

"Because there are medical professionals here who can tend to Father," Yen said. "Instead of waking up every two hours to change his sheets or check his blood pressure, you can have your life back."

Hoa stopped in front of a bright pink vase of flowers and pulled out a stray wilting lily. "And do what?"

"Whatever you want," Phung said. "We all agree you deserve that."

"That's very kind," she said, placing the dead flower on the counter for a custodian to find. "But this isn't like your wife's illness. He isn't a danger to himself, he just needs my help. I can take care of your father."

They walked past a common lounge, where several residents were playing card games or reading. One older Vietnamese woman sat in a wheelchair, staring at the television, but not really watching. Her hair bun was not tied properly, likely arranged by a careless nurse. Hoa noticed the woman had slight, but obvious tremors.

"I remember her," Phung said. "Didn't she used to work at the community center?"

"That's Ba Cuc," Yen said. "Should we say hello?"

"No," Hoa said, suddenly afraid. "She will be embarrassed. Let's go home."

Her sons still wanted to take away some brochures, in case their father's condition worsened, in case Hoa changed her mind. Returning home, they discovered that Hung had barricaded himself in Hoa's bedroom and wouldn't let anyone in. How he mustered the strength to hold the door against three grown women, she had no idea. After listening to several of Hoa's healthy threats through the door, he allowed her in. He wore only a gray T-shirt and green boxer shorts. Her knitting basket was upended, needles and yarn strewn across the room. His desk drawers were pulled open, paper, pens, and photographs littering the floor.

"Where did you go?" Hung asked. "Why did you leave me alone?"

"You weren't alone," Hoa said. "Our granddaughter and daughters-in-law were with you."

"You can never leave me," Hung said. "This is your obligation."

"I know." She waited until he was calm enough to walk him back to his bedroom, where he sat in his reading chair. Hoa put a *Paris Match* magazine in front of him.

"I want my letters" Hung said. "I saw them."

"No, you didn't," Hoa said, licking her thumb and smoothing some cowlicks in his hair. "They're all gone."

There was another girl, actually a woman this time, named Ngoc. Her letters were a bit harder to decipher since Hoa couldn't read French, and Ngoc seemed to sprinkle many of the colonial phrases in with the native to flaunt her bilingual education. Hoa thought it a bit pretentious, but supposed Hung found that alluring. Why Hoa even bothered to read the letters instead of immediately tossing them like the others was the discovery that Ngoc knew their sons by name, their interests and strengths, and even deigned to give Hung advice on the children's education. In one especially urgent letter, Ngoc recommended a law school in Paris for the "talented, but distracted Yen." After several discreet conversations with her son and grandson, Hoa realized that it was indeed the same university Yen had been recruited for years ago, the scholarship that had taken him away from their family, and eventually led all of them to France.

July 14, Sunday, Bastille Day, and even the Truongs were celebrating. Xuan planned to march with his school in the televised annual military parade on the Champs-Élysées. It was the school's most prestigious honor for its students, and Xuan had been looking forward to this moment for weeks. Hoa had to iron her grandson's uniform several times to ensure the seams fell straight and the hemlines hung properly.

Since Hung couldn't be left home alone, Cam's parents volunteered to stay behind. Hoa hadn't walked along the Champs-Élysées in years. Yen bought several crepes from a street vendor to munch on while they waited for the parade. They found a viewing space on an intersection under the Arc de Triomphe, which would allow them to see Xuan and the rest of the cadets from several angles, but also provided no protection from the summer sun.

Hoa strained against the partitioned rope to find her grandson. Trinh and Cherry jumped up and down, waving, pointing, but she couldn't find him. Finally, as the cadets marched past their section, Xuan's face emerged from the masses, jubilant, winking, thrilled. It lasted the briefest of seconds, Hoa beaming at her grandson, and then he was off again, marching past the rest of the Parisians along the Champs-Élysées.

Cherry only had a week left before she returned to America, and during her time in France, she'd spent most of her days with Trinh. Hoa couldn't really blame her granddaughter. How could she expect a teenager to sit in an apartment all day, when she could be shopping or exploring the city with her younger, more exciting aunt? Hoa still had every evening with her granddaughter. She reminded herself of this whenever she felt annoyed at their shared laughter or whispers at the dinner table.

At least they had this day together. Hoa resolved to make more efforts with Cherry. Perhaps she could ask Trinh or Ngoan to watch Hung one afternoon, so she and Cherry could go out together.

An arm wrapped around her waist, disturbing her thoughts. Cam put her head on her grandmère's shoulder. Hoa smiled. Though her feet hurt, the sun still shone in her eyes, and their neighbors' cigarette smoke made her cough, Hoa did feel content. Everyone's faces tilted to the sky watching the French Acrobatic Patrol perform its flypast. She remembered watching this on television for years, but it felt more impressive, and noisier, in person. Although she was not French, she imagined

Xuan and Cam's futures, their children's futures, in this country, and the neat trails of smoke made her feel irrationally optimistic.

After the parade, Xuan caught up with the family to take pictures in front of the Arc. Sunburned, exhausted, he beamed joyfully from the day's excitement. They were all supposed to walk home together, but Xuan invited his father to meet up with his schoolmates for a drink at a brasserie. The men promised to be home in time for dinner.

Trinh noisily wept as the women walked home. It seemed the woman had been crying all day. Hoa looked over in disdain, as both Cam and Cherry comforted their aunt, whispering words of assurance.

"He didn't even ask me to come," Trinh said, sobbing into Cherry's hair. "He doesn't need his mother."

"Maybe only men were invited," Cam said, soothingly. "He would never intentionally leave you out."

Trinh emphatically shook her head. "Something is broken between us. It has been for a long time, I just couldn't believe it. I should not be surprised. This family is cursed."

They stopped at an intersection, waiting for the crosswalk. Hoa turned to look at her daughter-in-law, whose face was streaked with fresh tears. "What are you saying?" Hoa asked.

"We're cursed," Trinh repeated. "We have been since we left Vietnam."

The light turned green, the walking man flashed, and the women crossed the street with the rest of the parade watchers. Everyone was eager to return home for their Bastille celebration dinners. Cam had stepped back in order to walk with Hoa, but Cherry remained at her aunt's side. This was supposed to be a day when families came together. Instead, they were once again tending to one of Trinh's moods. Hoa wondered if the time would ever come when Trinh wouldn't ruin another holiday.

"Girls, we still need some limes and peanuts for the dinner," Hoa said, pulling out some bills from her handbag and handing them to Cam. "Your auntie and I will meet you at home."

Hoa waited until the girls had rounded the corner before turning to her daughter-in-law. "I want you to stop all this nonsense about a family curse," she said, offering Trinh one of her handkerchiefs. "You are upsetting everyone."

"I'm only saying what they already feel," Trinh said, accepting the silk handkerchief and dabbing the corners of her eyes. "We should stop pretending."

"No one is pretending! This is all in your head."

"Really? My assault in the camps? Father's dementia? How Phung can't keep a job, or how Cam had to abort the Bourdains' baby? Coincidental misfortunes, all in one family?"

"It is life," Hoa said. "Everyone suffers. We are not special."

They reached the apartment house. Trinh stopped in front of the garden, kneeling into the soil to pinch some blooms from the basil stalks. When she turned to reach the front door, Hoa stood in the doorway.

"Did you tell Cherry all of this?" Hoa asked.

"She already knows," Trinh said. "We are not the only ones suffering. Poor Lum is paying for it, too."

"How?"

"You need to ask Cherry," Trinh said. "I will not betray her confidence."

Hoa stared at Trinh. Her tears had dried. Trinh now looked serene, calm. "I have only been supportive of you," Hoa said. "All these years, I have treated you as my own daughter."

"I believe you," Trinh said, nodding. "But if you want to know why your granddaughter is so sad, you need to ask her."

Hoa didn't have much time or energy to consider Trinh's words once they entered the house. There were too many tasks and people in the way to think of anything other than ensuring that Hung was bathed and dressed, the nice plates and silverware were set on the table, and that the dishes were warm when everyone was ready to sit down. Xuan was so unusually relaxed and chatty when he arrived home, even Trinh swallowed back her insecurities. They talked of pleasant things. Cam prepared Xuan's favorite dessert, a mixed berry tart.

Hoa resolved to speak to Cherry the next morning. There was no need to ruin such a lovely evening, and they were exhausted from all the sun, food, and wine. Once Hoa finished putting away the last of the good dishes in the cupboard, she put a kettle of tea on the stove. She looked for Cherry in the living room, and saw that the study door was closed. When she opened it, she found Cherry sitting at Hung's desk. The drawer was pulled out. Atop the desk, small stacks of letters and envelopes surrounded Hung's upended box. Cherry held one of the letters in her hands. Her forehead was creased in concentration.

"What are you doing?" Hoa asked, stepping into the room and closing the door behind her.

Cherry looked up, her eyes wide, but unalarmed. Unashamed. "I was looking for stamps."

Hoa crossed the room as quickly as she could, snatching the letter from Cherry's hands, grabbing as many from the desk as she could, pulling them into her arms. A few pages slipped from her hold, and cascaded to the wooden floor.

"These are private letters," Hoa said, trying to cram them back inside the box, but in her panicked haste, she crinkled and ripped some of the pages. She tried to squeeze the box lid shut, but it kept popping open, bloated with more pages than Hoa could remember.

"It takes me twice as long to read Vietnamese as English," Cherry said. She hadn't moved from her seat, though Hoa was now pacing the room. "And I can barely read French. Can you?"

Hoa turned to look at her granddaughter. "You shouldn't have done this," she whispered.

"Why not?" Cherry asked. "It's okay. I know what it's like to be disappointed by someone you love."

"You don't understand," Hoa said. Dizzy, she sank to the bed, her hand groping for the pillow, finding it, hugging it to her chest.

"Then tell me," Cherry said, walking over to sit next to Hoa on the bed, "because I've watched you work and care for this man from morning to night."

"This man is your grandpère," Hoa said. "You should only have good memories of him."

"You're not even angry," Cherry said, disappointment shading her voice.

Hoa sighed. "It's been many years. Some day, you'll understand what I mean."

"But you're still suffering," Cherry said. "Why do you still let him hurt you? Because he's family? Why do we have to love them more than they love us?"

She observed her granddaughter's face, contorted in frustration. Young Cherry, not even seventeen, eyes dull from a lack of sleep, shoulders slumped with the burden of other people's problems. How could her parents let this happen to her? How could Hoa? She released the pillow, and reached over, resting a palm over her granddaughter's jittery fingers. "Are you talking about Lum?"

Cherry jerked her hand back. "No."

"Your auntie mentioned your brother. You know you can tell your grandmère anything."

"There's nothing to tell," Cherry said, pulling back, standing. "Please, Grandmère, you don't need to worry about us."

Hoa watched Cherry carefully as she wandered back to the desk, waiting, hoping she would change her mind. It sometimes worked with her sons and Xuan, and often with Cam. If she was patient enough, if she endured enough silence, they would realize she was trustworthy. They would confide in her, knowing she would keep their secrets safe.

But Cherry refused to look up, avoiding any eye contact, any connection, with her grandmère, her gaze lingering on Hung's box of letters.

Hoa reached again for the pillow. Perhaps it was different with American grandchildren. How could Hoa expect such trust when she herself could not reveal her own secrets? The letters loomed between them, taunting Hoa. Uncertain, ashamed, she did not want to make a mistake.

"I love you," Hoa said. "I love you and your brother so much. I think about you always."

"I know, Grandmère," Cherry said, looking up, and the softest, vaguest of smiles appeared. "We do, too."

* * *

After Cherry's departure, the apartment felt quiet. Hoa arranged Hung in the living room to watch television while she changed the linens and scrubbed the bathroom. That only took an hour, so Hoa decided to clean the kitchen stove and floors. Then she cleaned the inside of the refrigerator, tossing out anything that smelled spoiled or felt soft. Looking at the clock, she felt dismayed to find still an hour until lunchtime, when her daughters-in-law planned to stop by to eat with them. Hoa took a seat next to Hung and picked up her crochet needles.

Hung remained silent, absorbed in a soap opera he never would have watched a year ago. Now, he found the television program full of exaggerated gestures and screaming confrontations captivating. Sometimes, her curiosity got the better of her and Hoa would ask him what was happening. The characters' arguments usually involved love affairs, swindling, kidnappings, and stolen inheritances. It bemused Hoa that Hung always rooted for the naïve victims, who whined and cried over constantly being deceived by loved ones. Usually, he talked back to the television, yelling at the characters over their predictable, disastrous choices. But this morning he sat and silently took the drama inside of him, hardly reacting to their problems.

"Who is being bad today?" Hoa asked.

Hung thought for a moment and then pointed when a careless, young blond boy in an argyle sweater and short shorts sauntered onto the screen. "He is evil," he said. "He is tricking his family."

"And who is being good?"

After several seconds, he shook his head.

"No one is being good? That's a shame."

Ngoan returned from the community center and Trinh walked downstairs to prepare for lunch. The women usually didn't go out of their way to join Hoa and Hung for such a routine meal, but Hoa suspected they wanted the house to feel less lonely after Cherry's departure. Hoa appreciated their good will.

Hoa left Hung to his soap opera to help the women with lunch preparations, which were simply a matter of reheating several dishes and steaming rice, since they still had so much food left over from the weekend Bastille dinner. When Hoa returned to the living room to call Hung to lunch, she realized he'd left the couch with the television still on. She checked his bedroom, the bathroom, and the office.

"Ngoan, Trinh," Hoa said, returning to the living room, noticing the door ajar. "Did you leave the front door open?"

Both women said no. Hoa opened the door and peeked down the hall, where she saw the building's front door was open as well. Still wearing her slippers, Hoa padded outside, looking down both sides of the street. To her relief, she saw Hung at the corner, still in his pajamas, staring at another apartment building.

"What are you doing?" she asked when she reached his side. "You cannot leave the house by yourself. You could get lost."

Hung turned to her with wet eyes. "I can't find the house."

"You just left it."

"No," Hung said, once again peering up at the apartment building in front of him. "I know what my house looks like."

"We live here now," Hoa said, hooking her arm around his. "We live in France. Now we have to go inside. Lunch is ready."

"What are you talking about?" Hung shook off her arm, suddenly angry. "I know where I live."

Trinh had walked outside to follow her, and Hoa waved for help. Pedestrians brushed past them, one bumping into Hoa's shoulder. Hoa held on to Hung's pajama sleeve as tightly as possible.

"You are causing trouble," Hoa said. "The food is going to get cold."

"You are not my wife," Hung screamed when Trinh grabbed his other arm. Together, they dragged him back to their apartment building, while he hollered, kicked, and spat. "You are evil women. I do not know you. My family would not treat me this way."

After Hung hurled his rice bowl against the wall during lunch, shattering Cam's framed diploma from culinary school, Hoa and his daughters-in-law carried him back to his room. Although he kicked and flailed on the bed for several minutes, Hung eventually tired himself out and fell asleep.

"Are you sure you don't want to reconsider the nursing facility in

Neuilly?" Ngoan asked when Hoa returned from the bathroom. They'd already swept up the rice and broken bowl from the floor. "We could talk to the Buis about how their mother likes it."

"Who is their mother?" Hoa asked, serving herself some soup. "I think we saw her there. Does she have Parkinson's disease?"

"Yes," Ngoan said. "That's Ba Cuc. But she liked people calling her Audrey because her mother was French. No one ever did, though."

"Audrey," Hoa echoed, the name suddenly sounding very familiar. She could see the name before her, printed in letters, in loopy scribbled handwriting.

"Don't you remember?" Ngoan asked. "Ba Cuc and her family were on the boat with us. She was the widow, just she and her children. They stayed at Pulau, too, but left for Paris a few months ahead of us."

"She brought all those canned sardines on the boat," Trinh said. "I can't believe I almost forgot that. Those sardines saved our lives."

"I don't know," Hoa said, staring at her soup, her breath collapsing as the woman's face, young and old, bloomed together, in her mind.

These were the letters she could not read. They were all in French—in tiny, tiny cursive script—and they made up almost half of Hung's precious collection. They were still disheveled from Cherry's reading a few days ago. She hadn't had the opportunity to reorganize, but with her daughters-in-law's unwitting help this afternoon, she was ready to burn the letters on the stove.

Hoa remembered seeing her at the community center. She coordinated the French tutoring services for the young refugee children. Cam and Xuan had both enrolled in those classes. Hoa could not recall ever seeing her husband with the slut, even in passing conversation. But Hoa never spent as much time at the community center as Hung. She had preferred her sanctuary in their apartment, and he apparently wanted to be elsewhere, which was fine by her.

She had been confused when Hung returned to their home in Saigon and confessed that he only purchased enough seats for their family. Hoa had seen the amount of gold Hung had hidden in his clothes and it seemed enough to purchase the entire boat. Sanh's wife, Tuyet, was dev-astated. She had already told her mother and siblings about the planned escape. Hung scolded her for telling them before he'd even bought their seats. He claimed he never promised her anything. He also reminded her that the Truongs were now her family, not the Vos. While Hoa felt badly for her daughter-in-law, she had to admit she also felt leery of Tuyet's devotion to a mother who had disowned her for marrying their son. Hung was correct: they didn't owe this cruel family anything.

But even they didn't deserve this, being passed over for Hung's mistress and her bastards. It didn't matter if he felt disdain for the Vos. Could Hung have imagined the ramifications? That by leaving Tuyet's family behind, they'd lose their youngest son and grandchildren to America?

Trinh was correct. Their family was cursed. They'd broken their promise, left the Vos behind. They'd never been the same since.

The letters lay heavy in her tired hands. She wondered if he still thought it had been worth it. While the correspondence with the other women seemed superficial and immature, Hoa could not pass the same judgment on these letters written in French. She could only imagine what their affair had meant to them if it had survived a war, a refugee camp, and a new country. It reminded her of those terrible soap operas.

Hoa wanted these answers, despite the way it made her heart tighten and her breath catch. But there was no way to know. She couldn't read French. She couldn't ask Hung or any of her children to translate. She could only hope Cherry could forget them.

Standing over the lit stove, Hoa imagined these letters burning up, purging her sanctuary of the filth her husband had brought in, the sordid details that had taken Sanh and her grandchildren away from her. But her hand would not complete the action her heart willed. She stood there, watching the blue-and-orange flames flicker. When finally, her arm ached over the tension, she turned away, placing the letters on the kitchen counter.

Stealing these letters had initially felt like a triumph. Though she scoured his desk drawers and the top of his closet, she never could find his journals; she suspected he'd destroyed them when he realized he was growing ill. But somehow he couldn't bear to get rid of these precious letters. They were enough. The information of his past would be hers, just as his knowledge slipped away. After all these years, she believed she'd earned it.

But the discovery did not make her stronger. Even with his mind half gone, Hung still won. The words would haunt her for the rest of her life, whether they burned or not. Because while he was allowed to forget everything he'd done, she had no choice but to remember.

"What are you making?" Hung asked, wandering out of his bedroom, sniffing at the air. "When are we having lunch?"

"We already had lunch," Hoa said, tucking the letters into the cutlery drawer.

Hung looked pained, but she firmly maintained his gaze. "I'm still hungry."

"You'll have to wait until dinner."

"I know that we don't live in Vietnam anymore," he said softly, the closest he could come to apologizing. It was impossible to know what he remembered of the last few hours, of the last several days.

"Good," Hoa said. "Do you want to watch your program?"

He nodded and walked over to the couch. Hoa turned on the television. Another soap opera, different characters, similar storylines.

"Where is Cherry?" he asked.

"She left this morning." Hoa approached the window and looked outside, where the trees, sidewalks, and cars gleamed harsh and bright in the sunlight. It would be several hours before her sons and grandchildren returned home.

"Oh," he said. "When will she come back?"

"She's not coming back," Hoa said, drawing one of the window shades to soften the rays of the afternoon light.

"Oh," he said again. He was not paying much attention. The commercial had ended and the program's opening credits began.

"You were wrong," Hoa said. "You thought Sanh and his family would follow us to France. You thought that you could have everyone around you, your sons, your mistress. But you made a foolish, stupid choice."

Hung looked askance at her, annoyed. "Why are you yelling?"

"One seat," Hoa said, struggling to keep her voice level, "you could have offered Tuyet's mother one seat, but you had to give them all to Ba Cuc? Because her family was so much more important? So worth destroying mine?"

He straightened his shoulders, looking directly in her eyes. "I honor my obligations, woman."

The way he said it, his tone, sounded clearer and sharper than Hoa had remembered for a long time. She narrowed her eyes, aware she was talking to her true husband now. "What about the obligations to your own children?"

"I wasn't going to leave my daughters behind."

She rolled her eyes. "You don't have any daughters."

"I promised their mother I would protect them. They suffered enough without me."

Hoa stared at him, a knot of dread uncoiling in her stomach. "What family are you talking about?"

Hung blinked a few times, then returned his gaze to the television. "I told Audrey you would never understand."

But Hoa did. Finally, after all these years. She slowly walked in front of the television, blocking his view, forcing him to look at her. Her old Hung didn't even flinch, cold and imperious as she remembered. So many wives would have cherished such an opportunity to reconnect with their demented husbands, a precious moment of clarity. Hoa could only hope this was their last true conversation.

"Did you talk to her about me?"

His features softened in an expression that was completely foreign to her. "We discuss everything together."

Why did this surprise her? Even when she thought he had been rendered powerless, when she finally had achieved the upper hand, Hung could find another way to cut into her.

"But you don't have her now," Hoa reminded him. "Ba Cuc is dead."

Hung's face blanched.

"She is. Soon, you will be, too. And then I'll be the only one left."

Hung didn't answer, turning his head, as if distracted.

"No one else is going to know. I wouldn't ever wish that on any of our children. Do you understand me, Hung? This beautiful sacrifice of yours? It will die with you. But me and my boys? We'll go on. We'll survive in spite of you."

He did not look at her. Hung was choosing not to listen. Hoa stepped out of the television's way, and watched her husband's eyes brighten at the sight of his soap opera. Within seconds, he was engrossed in the made-up people's problems, a faint smile tugging on his dried lips.

Hoa walked to the sofa, pulled out her knitting needles and sat next to her husband, struggling to relax her breathing because, as she reminded herself, there was no purpose in getting upset over this man. Nothing would change and it could never be improved. His mind was leaving both of them, and she didn't want to interrupt its departure.

"Who is being bad today?" she asked, untangling the yarn in her lap.

After staring at the screen for a minute, Hung remembered the story-line, the characters, and he pointed.

1987

Cuc Bui
Paris, France

. . . *I do not see much purpose in reevaluating past decisions. For the most part, I think I have done well for my family. I protected and cared for them as best I could. But I am only a man. Life does not always present us with ideal circumstances. Our beloved country is a great example. When I think of our countrymen still suffering under those Godless heathens, I feel full of shame.*

They did not choose poverty. Not only were they born without resources or schooling, now they must watch as the wealthiest, most educated people flee the country. I cannot imagine their frustration. So I cannot presume to judge any decision they make to survive. When we hear about the corruption and bribery plaguing the new government, it should be no surprise to any of us. What choice do they have?

While our generation was expected to marry under our parents' wishes, our children and grandchildren are not required to build their lives around such an obsolete tradition. Why couldn't this more liberated thinking have been an option for us, only a generation earlier? Seeing all the couples openly kissing and strolling along the Seine, even at the food market, I envy their youth, their freedom.

I have honored my wife in every obligation. I have performed all the duties required of me. I do not regret your companionship. It helped me survive

my marriage. And as you've told me before—and it comforts me to no
end—it has helped you survive. . . .

Hung Truong
Paris, France

∂ℓ Chapter Ten

CHERRY

C HERRY COULD HEAR HER FATHER'S BELLOWING THROUGH the thick carpet and insulated walls. She turned up the volume, the music of *Faust* strumming over her father's frustration. The CD, a present from her cousin Xuan, was her most effective study aid. After listening to several hours of *Faust*'s violins, she'd memorized three pages of conjugated verbs and could recite them without prompting. Cherry tested herself twice, then pulled off her earphones. Her father continued to rant, but other voices had joined in, her brother's, then her mother's.

Someone stomped across the ceramic tile hallway. The side garage door slammed, the house shuddering in response. Lum's car.

Cherry jumped off the bed, swung her door open, and ran down the stairs. "Wait!" she cried, pushing past her father in the kitchen to reach the garage. By the time she ran out, her brother's car had already pulled out of the driveway, the garage door noisily closing.

"What's wrong?" her father asked.

"Lum was supposed to drive me to school this morning," she said.

"It's Saturday."

"We're meeting for a history-class project."

"Tuyet!" her father called out to the living room, where his wife stood by the front window next to her plastic cherry blossom tree, her arms crossed in front of her. "Can you take her?"

"Why can't you?" her mother asked, barefoot, still dressed in velour pajamas, her unwashed hair and her reading glasses on.

"The electrician will be here soon," he said. "Do you want to talk to him about the wiring?"

"Fine," her mother said, walking into the kitchen and picking up the keys from the counter. She appraised Cherry: up, down. "Don't you think it's time you learned how to drive?"

"Don't pressure her," her father said. "She will learn when she's ready."

Then Cherry remembered. "My books are in Lum's car." Her mother loudly sighed. "I thought he was taking me."

"You cannot rely on him anymore, okay?" her father said. "From now on, Mommy and I will take care of your rides."

"What is the matter with you?" her mother asked. "You drove him away. Isn't that enough? You don't need to attack him in front of his sister."

Her father looked at Cherry. "Do you know how much money he has left?"

Cherry shrugged, her gaze scouring the kitchen floor, dust bunnies gathering in the corners. Only Lum knew how much. Last week, their father found another requested credit card application—triggering another interrogation, another blowout—which ended with their mother crying and their father dramatically tearing up the Visa envelope. Lum didn't even flinch. Her father rarely came home in time to pick up the mail, and Cherry suspected Lum was hiding other cards.

"Why don't you know this?" Cherry's mother pressed, now eager to turn on her. "You're his sister."

"You could ask him, too," she pointed out, but her voice felt weak. It always did when she tried to argue with her mother.

"He's destroying his credit," her father said. "Who knows if he's tapped into our cards as well—"

"This isn't about you," her mother interrupted. "I don't care about our credit."

"If you want to keep your house, you will."

They stared each other down. Cherry slunk away from the kitchen, leaving her parents to what they did best: yell at each other, blame each other.

"Where are you going?" her mother asked, following Cherry to the staircase. "Do you think you're too busy to help your family?"

"I'm getting my bag," Cherry said, her hand reaching for the stair rail, trying not to cringe as her mother moved toward her.

"Leave her alone," her father said. "She doesn't know anything."

Her mother spun around. "She's so devoted to her own studies, she has no time to help her brother." She turned back to Cherry. "Have you forgotten how Lum took care of you?"

"Daddy," she pleaded, walking up the stairs.

"Ignore Mommy," he said.

Safely behind her door, Cherry turned the stereo back on, and softly, deeply exhaled. She no longer cared if she made it to the history group on time.

"Do you think you're so much better than him?" her mother bellowed through the closed door. "Better than us?"

Instead of responding, Cherry twisted up the volume. But there was not enough music, no decibel level to match her mother's rage.

For so long they all wanted to believe Lum, especially their mother: it was just a game, a hobby. But over the last two years, he'd grown sloppy, tired of concealing something he was proud of. If his grades weren't that great, so what? The president's honor roll didn't offer the rewards of a royal flush.

Lum had flunked out of his classes and the junior college had placed him on academic probation. Instead of trying to salvage his GPA by making up his failed courses, Lum took the summer off and worked full-time at the flower shop. Their father didn't even ask if he wanted to go to France. He claimed he didn't want his relatives to see what had become of his son. Lum asked if that was why he and their mother had stopped going years earlier.

Perhaps it wouldn't have mattered if Lum were actually as good as he believed. But he'd grown cocky, finding more games around town, taking trips with his friends to Vegas, and his losing streaks grew far more frequent than his wins. Eventually, any money he'd earned from playing dried up. He started borrowing, first from Huy and Johnny, then from these new friends he was making at these parties. He even asked Cherry.

Lum promised the loans would only last a short while—to earn back his losses. Cherry's college savings halved, then quartered, until hardly anything remained. Cherry couldn't believe she'd just let it happen. When the bank statement arrived in the mail, their parents read the pathetic balance.

While their father threatened to kick him out of the house, their mother sprinkled Gamblers Anonymous brochures around the house, and clipped articles on gambling addictions to tape to the refrigerator and Lum's bedroom door. She even invited a priest home one night for dinner, a recent refugee from Vietnam. At the dinner table, their mother reminded Lum that he was baptized as a baby, and could still be redeemed. Cherry concentrated on chewing her food, too embarrassed to even look in the direction of poor, clueless Father Tung. Lum skipped out early that night, saying he was meeting up with Quynh for dessert. They all knew where he was going.

"What can I do?" her mother asked Father Tung, ignoring her husband's stern, exasperated looks. "I'll do anything."

"You can pray for him," Father Tung said. "You all can."

"And he'll get better?" her mother said, fiercely gazing at their dinner guest. "Can you swear on your savior?"

He didn't answer, struggling to swallow the last shreds of pork stuck in his throat.

Her mother sat back after a minute of silence, looking disgusted. "Then what good is your God?"

* * *

Walking to the school parking lot, Cherry spotted Lum's car in the fire lane. His blinkers were not turned on. She looked behind to see if anyone from her project group was around. Not that they knew anything about her brother.

"Sorry," Lum said, a sheepish smile on his face when Cherry opened the passenger door, a gush of air-conditioning greeting her. "At least I remembered to pick you up."

"Thanks," she said, falling into the bucket seat, slamming the door hard.

"I called home when I realized," he said.

"What were you doing, anyway?" she asked. "I didn't think you had to work today."

"I was with Dat."

"Dat?"

"He knows a good poker club in Tustin."

"Oh, yeah?" Cherry asked, pulling out her sunglasses from the front pocket of her backpack.

"It's not what you think," he said. "College students play poker, too. This is a good one. Lots of rich boy investors. That's why the returns are so big."

"Since when does he want to help you out?"

"I think he's serious," Lum said, pulling off his hat and laying it on the dashboard. His hair was growing long, hanging over his eyes.

Dat had heard that Lum was out of money and wanted to offer him a deal. Dat would bankroll Lum in this new poker club in exchange for playing under his supervision. When Lum asked why he wanted to help, Dat said he didn't want Lum's gambling to ruin their family's name. If Lum listened to his advice, he could use the cash advance to earn his way out of debt.

"What happens next?" Cherry asked.

"What do you mean?"

"When you go through his money and can't pay him back?"

"I didn't tell you this so you could shit on me," Lum said, his upper lip curling. "I know this is my last chance."

"Or you could stop right now, and work it off," she reminded him. "Mom and Dad said they'd help."

"I don't want their money."

"You'll pay them back, like any other responsible person would. You don't need to break the law."

"You sound like Dad," Lum said. "Do you know how long that would take? You want me to work like a slave like Mom and Dad have all these years. And for what?"

Cherry glared at her brother. "You mean the house that they love?"

"The bank owns the house," Lum said. "In one hand, I could make enough to earn out my loans and clear three months of their mortgage payments."

"When was the last time you won?" she asked.

His arrogant, self-assured smile faded. His eyes resumed the frostiness she'd grown to despise over the last two years.

"There used to be a time when I didn't have to convince you to believe in me," Lum said.

She exhaled sharply, straightening her shoulders. "Maybe I'm growing up."

"No," Lum said. "That's not it."

They looked out of their respective windows, silent, the rest of the ride home.

Dat's offer was not news to Cherry. A week earlier, her cousin and Grandmother Vo had dropped by the house in the middle of the day. Only Cherry was home. At first, the visit appeared impulsive, since Grandmother's physician had relocated to a clinic in Irvine, and she often liked to stop by the house unexpectedly. The three of them sat in the living room, Grandmother in Sanh's suede chair, Cherry and her cousin on opposite ends of the sofa, sipping on the jasmine tea Cherry had taken as long as possible to prepare.

"Do you want me to call my mother?" Cherry asked. "She's not supposed to be home until five."

"We came to visit you, child," her grandmother said.

They looked at her expectantly. "For what?" she asked.

"Your brother," she said, sighing loudly, wrapping her spearmint-colored scarf around her wrist, once, twice. "What else would I be talking about?"

Since Cherry and Lum's parents had proven incapable, Grandmother felt obliged to clean up the family's reputation.

Cherry sat silently as they outlined their plan. Dat found a poker club, a circuit populated by wealthy undergrads from the local UCs and small colleges like Chapman. The club held their games after hours at a popular tea shop in Westminster. The club typically lured college kids in, allowed them to win for a while, then slowly but surely, leeched their winnings, and eventually their bank account balances, away.

A fixed game wasn't a shocking system. Cherry was sure Lum had seen it done before, maybe even participated in a scam or two himself. But Grandmother and Dat were counting on Lum's ego to do him in. When he was gambling, he believed he was smarter than any system, any person. He thought he could beat the house, a gambling addict's fatal flaw.

Dat met one of the club's members, Thinh, through a classmate. Dat would pay Thinh on the side to make sure Lum didn't win. Lum would run up a large enough debt that Dat would then claim to be unable to cover. When Lum couldn't pony up the money, the house would scare Lum out of ever playing in Orange County again.

"How are they going to scare him?" Cherry asked.

"They're not allowed to touch him," Grandmother Vo said, explaining that part of Thinh's payment included protection for Lum.

"And you just believe them?"

"They're getting paid for it," Grandmother said. "These boys aren't stupid when it comes to money." She overturned her teacup, indicating she needed a refill.

In the kitchen, waiting for the teakettle to boil, Cherry listened to her cousin and grandmother chat about her doctor's appointment earlier that day.

Some people may have been surprised that grandmothers were capable of saying such things, concocting such schemes. But Grandmother Vo, if you believed the rumors, ran a black-market operation with some American officers in Saigon (*How do you think she could afford that house as a widow?* Linh once reminded Cherry). There were plenty of Little Saigon business owners who either worshipped or despised her, depending on how much money they owed her. As she talked, she sipped on her tea, adjusting her scarf. Blackmail, extortion, she spoke about these actions as naturally as she complained about the weather or her heart condition.

"Why are you telling me this?" Cherry asked, returning with the teapot.

"I knew you'd be suspicious of Dat offering to help your brother," Grandmother said. "You're a smart girl, smarter than your mother. The only way to help him is to scare him straight. He needs us. He needs you."

Cherry shot them a doubtful look as she poured their tea. "What am I supposed to do?"

"This plan to rescue your brother is delicate, with a lot of my money at stake. If you suspect that Lum is catching on, you must tell Dat."

"Not you?" Cherry asked.

"Dat is now responsible," Grandmother said, sitting back into the sofa cushion. "I only provide the funds. I want nothing more to do with it. I have enough to worry about with my failing health." She wheezed into her scarf.

"What if I say no?" Cherry asked, crossing her arms.

Grandmother looked unimpressed. "You're not stupid, child. I know you. We have sat by and watched Lum humiliate our family for far too long. But this is no longer about family honor. When gamblers become desperate, they will turn to anyone for cash. That is dangerous."

"He wouldn't do that."

"Are you kidding?" Dat cried. "He probably already has."

"Dat," Grandmother warned. "We are all on the same side here."

Her cousin shook his head at Cherry. "I don't understand you," Dat said. "Don't you want him to be better?"

"Of course she does," Grandmother said. "She loves her brother. She knows this is best for him."

Cherry bristled. This was not her brother. The night before, after realizing her ATM card was missing, and after searching the house for it, she had confronted him. He hadn't even looked apologetic. The Lum she knew would have recognized the hurt in her face and would have wanted to fix it, because he once loved her, and once cared about what she thought. He was no longer that person. Cherry was tired of defending him, tired of being disappointed in him, tired of being angry, tired of being tired. Grandmother and Dat were merely speeding things along to their logical, inevitable conclusion. In losing everything, Lum could finally be her brother again.

"Okay," Cherry said.

Once Dat introduced Lum to the new poker club, they became inseparable. These two boys who wanted nothing to do with each other as children now called each other on the phone every night. Cherry would come home from school and find Dat, Lum, and Quynh watching a movie or eating takeout in the family room.

This new friendship became the family's preferred topic of conversation. Dat's parents loudly worried about the possible corruption of their precious firstborn, while Cherry's mother hoped some of Dat's strong work ethic could rub off on Lum.

Inexplicably, the plan seemed to be working. From what Dat told her in discreet phone calls, they were settling in at the new poker club— a few wins to keep Lum interested, enough losses to rack up a reliable debt. With new funding, Lum's confidence had returned: he whistled throughout the house, cheerily chatting on the phone to Quynh or Dat, saying nothing to Cherry; he was still sore over his sister's lack of faith in him. She longed to fast forward to the next stage of the scheme, when the lucky hands, Grandmother's money, and her brother's smug smirks would dry up for good.

"And you never listen in on their conversations?" Linh asked as she drove them to Duyen's house one Saturday afternoon. Linh and

Duyen had finished their morning shift at the salon and were dropping by Duyen's place to pick up sweatshirts and snacks before going to the beach.

"No," Cherry said.

"Aren't you curious?" Linh said. "What could Lum and Dat possibly say to each other every night?"

"Mommy changed the PIN on Dat's bank account," Duyen said, then shrugged when Cherry turned to look at her in the backseat. "She doesn't want what happened to you to happen to him."

"You still think he's trying to swindle Dat," Linh said.

"What else could he want?" Duyen said, slurping on her milkshake.

"Duyen," Cherry groaned.

"Sorry," Duyen said. "But you know it's true."

"Huy told me he saw them outside the science library the other day," Linh said. "Maybe Dat is turning your brother around."

"Did he say hello?" Cherry asked. Months had passed, but it still unsettled her not to see Lum's oldest friend around. He was one of the saddest casualties of Lum's stupid addiction.

"He still says he's not talking to Lum until Lum pays him back," Linh said. She shrugged at Cherry's frown. "It's a lot of money. People don't forget stuff like that."

When they turned on Duyen's street, they found a silver Lexus sitting in front of the house, the engine still running. As they pulled up, the tinted driver's side window rolled down and a Vietnamese man with spiky hair and mirrored sunglasses poked his head out. He looked at them for a moment, ducked back in, and the window promptly rolled up.

"Weird," Linh said, then glanced over at Duyen. "An old boyfriend?"

"I don't think so," she said, after looking the car over.

"I'll find out," Cherry said, hopping out of Linh's car. Her heart pounding, she approached the silver Lexus and tapped the window. Hip-hop music vibrated through her fingers. "Hello?" she asked, praying it wasn't one of the poker-club members. "Can I help you?"

It took a minute for the driver to turn down his music and lower his window. The upholstery reeked of cigarette smoke. He grinned at her.

Cherry realized he wasn't a man, but a boy, maybe twenty, twenty-one. He grinned at her. "Is this Dat Le's house?" he asked.

She paused for a moment, hoping that her cousins couldn't hear. "Who are you?"

He mimicked her pause. "Just a friend."

"I'm his cousin. I know you aren't his friend."

The boy laughed, almost wheezing. "Ah, you're Lum's little sister, the smart one."

"Dat's not home," Cherry said.

"Well, he and Lum told me to meet them here. So I think I'll just wait."

Duyen stepped out of the car, joining Cherry. "Who are you?" she asked, tilting her head. "Have I seen you before?"

"Ah," the guy said, leering at Cherry's slender cousin. "You must be the beauty queen."

"Want me to call the cops?" Linh yelled.

"Ladies," the stranger said, ignoring her, slapping his steering wheel with the palm of his hand. "I promise you I'm no intruder. I'm just waiting on a meeting with friends, okay?" His grin returned. "And here they are."

The girls backed away from the car as the boy stepped out. He wasn't that tall, actually a little scrawny, with a pointy jawline and sloped shoulders. He looked more intimidating sitting in his car. He dressed all in black, his jeans noticeably more faded than his shirt and jacket.

"This is your new friend?" Duyen asked, after Dat, Lum, and Quynh joined them on the driveway. "I'm so impressed."

"This is a private meeting," Dat said, clearing his throat. "Why don't you girls just go inside?"

"Do you hear yourself?" Duyen said. "Since when do you take meetings?"

"Duyen, it's okay," Quynh said, but she still had her sunglasses on, and the tight smile on her face did not feel reassuring.

"Yes, it is okay," the boy agreed, pulling off his sunglasses. "It's a beautiful day, and these are some lovely ladies."

Cherry pulled at Duyen's arm, following Linh into the house. Lum hadn't even looked at her.

Once inside, they ran up to Duyen's room where her window had a good view of the driveway. Duyen carefully slid the window open as they sat beneath it on the floor. Several minutes passed.

"Can you hear anything?" Duyen finally whispered.

"No," Cherry said. She pulled two of the venetian blinds open with her fingers to look. Although she recognized that they spoke Vietnamese, Cherry couldn't hear their words. Dat made large gestures with his arms, while Lum stood eerily still, his arms crossed.

"You know who that is, don't you?" Linh said, pulling a teddy bear from Duyen's bed to use as a pillow.

"Who?" Duyen said.

"That's Bac Luong's youngest son, I remembered when Lum said his name. Grandmother loaned his dad the money to open up a restaurant, but he couldn't pay the rent."

Cherry glanced at her cousin. "What happened?"

"They had to close down, and then the family moved to New Orleans."

"I guess not all of them," Duyen said. "I wonder how he can afford a Lexus."

"He must be in a gang."

"No, he's not," Cherry cried.

Linh and Duyen looked at her suspiciously. "How would you know?" Duyen asked.

"I just don't believe it. Lum would never associate with anyone like that."

"You mean Lum only plays with nice gamblers?" Linh asked.

"He isn't a criminal." Cherry watched as they exchanged one of their secret glances. "He *isn't*."

"I hope you're right," Duyen said. "Because this doesn't just affect Lum."

"Then why don't you ask *your* brother?" Cherry said.

But Cherry was worried, too, and Linh's observations lingered with her the rest of the afternoon.

When Lum smiled at her during dinner that evening and asked about her classes, Cherry asked him about his new friend. Even in front of their parents, his smile didn't waver.

"Thinh?" he said. "He works at a hotel where we make deliveries."

"Vietnamese?" their mother asked, brightening. "What's his last name?"

"I don't remember," Lum said.

"Well, he must be making a lot of money at the hotel," Cherry said, reaching over the table for seconds of the lemongrass chicken. "That's a really expensive car he's driving."

Lum's face still didn't crack. "Thinh is in guest services. He works the reservation desk."

"That's great," their father said. "Maybe he can help you get a job there."

Lum squirmed in his seat. "I'm not sure it works that way."

"How do you know if you don't try?" their father asked. "If I hadn't kept looking for better opportunities, I'd still be a custodian."

"A custodian isn't a bad job," Lum muttered.

Their father laughed. "Unless you have a family to feed. Unless you want to have a house. You can do better than delivering flowers."

"I know I can do better," Lum said, his voice thickening, his good mood dissipated.

"By working hard," their mother interrupted, putting a hand on Lum's clenched fingers. "By being a good boy. No card playing, right?"

"Right," Lum said, glancing briefly at the perfectly filed fingernails tap tapping on his fist. "No card playing."

Later that night, Cherry called Dat. He answered on the first ring. Dat promised that Lum was already close to reaching his debt limit with the poker club. Thinh had dropped by to warn Lum that next week's Tet tournament was his last chance.

"Then they'll throw him out," Dat said, "Blacklist him from playing in any other club in Orange County. It'll be over."

"And they're going to make sure he loses?" Cherry asked. "They can do that?"

"Of course," Dat said with a scoff. "They're practically professionals. We've already put up the money for the game."

The assurance in his voice unnerved her. "Do you know who this Thinh guy really is?"

When Dat didn't reply, Cherry relayed what Linh had told her. Cherry could hear Dat's shallow breathing.

"That was a long time ago," he said finally. "So what?"

"So what?" Cherry repeated furiously. "So maybe he isn't a huge fan of our grandmother?"

"I approached Thinh. He's never met Grandmother."

"You don't think he could have figured it out?"

"I have all the details worked out," Dat said. "Thinh is not in control. I am."

"Why are you doing this?" she asked. "I know Grandmother's reasons, but you don't even like Lum."

"He's family," Dat said, sounding offended. "Lum just needs to learn his lesson."

"What lesson?"

"That this isn't the proper way to succeed. That you can't cheat. It takes hard work."

"You mean, he needs to be more like you?"

"I'm sick of him dragging everyone down around him. She deserves better."

"She?" Cherry repeated. He was silent. "You mean Quynh? Are you doing this to impress her?"

"You know, I've taken hours away from my valuable personal time to help your brother. I'm not going to apologize for who I am. And you're not so different from me, you know."

"Yes, I am," Cherry said.

"Oh, really? Why did you agree to Grandmother's plan? Because you were thinking of yourself. He emptied your bank account. He probably has gotten into your parents' accounts, too. You know college isn't cheap, Cherry. Don't pretend you don't."

His accusations stuck in her head as she brushed her teeth, washed her face, and prepared for bed. Were she and Dat so different? They

to his wife. "Well, here is your American son. Selfish, disrespectful, practically unemployable except as a delivery boy and nickel gambler—"

"Sanh!" their mother said.

Her brother stood. "Thanks for the plane ticket. I'll just cash it out."

"Lum," their mother said.

"Enjoy your little family reunion," he said, slipping his arms into his jacket. "I'm sure you won't even miss me."

While Cherry and her father sat at the table in silence, Lum stormed through the house, their mother following him, entreating him to stay. He ignored her, grabbing his keys, slamming the garage door. As he started his car engine, Cherry could hear her mother sobbing through the garage walls.

Cherry's mother returned to the table. When her father tried to take her hand, Tuyet slapped it away. "Have you forgotten how to speak?" she asked, glaring at her daughter.

"Me?" Cherry asked. "What did you want me to say?"

"Something," her mother said. "You could have said something."

The Tet Festival in Little Saigon was the only outdoor event their extended family bothered to attend regularly. Other holidays, Halloween, Valentine's Day, Fourth of July, were barely acknowledged. If it wasn't Christmas, Cherry's parents considered it an American excuse to not work. But Lunar New Year was the glorious annual exception, an opportunity for the entire community to boast its local pride.

The festival took place at the high school's athletic fields, and over the years, had grown larger and more elaborate, with a stage for a talent show, and a petting zoo with ducks, chickens, and piglets. Children sang folk songs, Vietnamese veterans marched in formation, and everyone chewed on overpriced scallion-seared corncobs and tart papaya salads in Styrofoam cups. During Tet, Grandmother Vo voluntarily walked outside for more than an hour, though always with her sun umbrella.

This year, Duyen had the idea for the salon to host a booth in the community section of the fair. She thought they could give discounted hand and foot massages to raise money for an orphanage in Vietnam. Cherry's mother and aunts encouraged the idea—such good publicity for the salon—and Duyen was put in charge of organizing it. Duyen took out an ad in the festival program, calling the event "One Hundred Hands and Feet for the Children." She enlisted Linh to coordinate the massages, and Quynh and Cherry to facilitate the appointments and to collect money.

The night before Tet, the girls met at the beauty salon to fold flyers and to make signs. The salon smelled of bleach and Exotica, Duyen and Linh's latest perfume. The television played an old episode of a *Paris By Night* show. Linh couldn't find any other videos to play in the salon. Cherry hid a chemistry book under a stack of flyers, stealing peeks when she could.

"Do you know how wretched people's feet are going to smell after walking around all day at the fair?" Linh asked, shaking her magic marker to eke out more ink. "Why can't it just be 'One Hundred Hands for the Children'?"

"We already agreed to give foot massages in the program," Duyen said. "And I'll do the feet if you're so picky. I give better massages anyway."

As she folded flyers, Quynh kept turning around, supposedly to look at the television, which hung next to the wall clock. Then she would check her cell phone. She hadn't gone with Lum and Dat to the Tet poker tournament. Quynh was usually so good at looking calm, even when Lum was losing, stubborn in her faith in him. Cherry hoped when it was all over and done she'd stay with him. Cherry didn't know if Lum could handle losing Quynh, too.

Quynh wandered off to pick up some drinks, but after ten minutes, Duyen delegated Cherry to go fetch her. Cherry found Quynh in the food court, sitting next to the water fountain in front of the stage, where they used to hold the annual beauty pageants and local variety shows. For Tet, the business association had stocked the fountain full of fresh goldfish. Most of them would die within a few months, but for now, the water glittered with bursts of gold and silver. When Cherry was little, she used to count them, charting how many survived each day. The last one would hold on for a week or so, swimming alone, until it, too, floated to the surface. Cherry always pitied the last goldfish—imagining its loneliness, its anxiety. Quynh sat in the white plastic chair, staring at the bubbles from the waterfall.

"You can call Lum," Cherry suggested, pulling up a chair next to her. "They must take a break, right?"

Her brother's girlfriend reached over to flick the water gently, and six fish immediately scattered from her disturbance. "You know I love your brother."

"Yeah," Cherry said cautiously.

"But if I know he's doing something wrong," Quynh said, "something dangerous, I should say something, right?"

Cherry leaned forward. "Tell me," she said.

Quynh's eyes remained transfixed on the goldfish as she confessed how Lum had learned about Dat's plan. He'd known for several weeks. Lum had approached Thinh one afternoon when Dat wasn't around to inquire about a loan. Feeling guilty about borrowing so much of Dat's money, Lum wanted to pay him back and start a separate line of credit with the poker club. Thinh then assured Lum that his cousin had plenty of funds—both to bankroll his playing and to pay the club to control Lum's game.

As Quynh continued, Cherry struggled to listen, but her heartbeat was growing louder, crowding out everything else. Her arms and legs had stiffened, her fingers clenching the chair. Lum wanted to confront Dat, but Thinh talked him out of it. He said he liked Lum and wanted to help him out. Thinh thought the two of them could team up, squeeze Dat for even more cash, and split the money.

It would culminate at the Tet Tournament. While Dat expected Lum to lose early on and for the club to finally kick them out, Thinh would instead offer Lum another buy-in. He'd then continue to lose his bets, anteing up more, far beyond what Dat had already arranged with Thinh. Dat could try to stop it, but could he really stand up to Thinh and the rest of the poker club? And at the end of the night, when the house was looking to settle, they'd remind Dat that he was responsible for Lum's debts. Every penny.

Cherry closed her eyes, imagining across town the panic Dat must have been feeling. "What if Dat doesn't have the money?" she asked.

"They're going to beat him up," Quynh said sadly, almost matter-of-factly. "It's what Dat was planning for Lum."

"That's not true," Cherry said.

"It is," Quynh said, shaking her head. "I didn't want to believe it, either, but Thinh had Lum listen to a voice mail Dat left on his cell phone."

"Oh God," Cherry said.

"I tried to convince your brother to hold them off," Quynh said. "They might give Dat a few hours to leave and collect the money, but I'm scared. Lum thinks he can trust Thinh, but you met the guy. He's a punk. What if he's trying to scam both of them?"

"We have to warn Dat."

"It's too late, it's already happening."

"They promised me they weren't going to touch Lum," Cherry said, breathing deeply, trying to calm her voice. "They promised."

Quynh tilted her head, looking at Cherry. "Who is *they*?"

Cherry took in a breath, saying nothing.

"You already knew," Quynh said.

Cherry finally nodded.

Quynh slapped the plastic table next to them with both of her hands. Hard. "Who else?" she demanded.

"It wasn't my idea."

"Say it."

She looked to the floor. "Dat's getting the money from Grandmother Vo."

Quynh sat back in her chair, blinking.

"I wanted him to stop," Cherry said. "We all did."

"I should have known," Quynh said. "Dat never would have done this on his own. Of course your grandmother was using him."

Cherry wiped the tears from her eyes again and looked at her watch.

She didn't know how long the game was, or even where it was taking place. "I need to find them."

"No!" Quynh yelled, standing, holding up her hand, looking revolted. "No. I will tell Lum. You stay here. You don't do anything until I tell you, okay?"

"One Hundred Hands and Feet for the Children" grew a line around the corner, edging out the popular kissing and karaoke booths at the festival. Everyone, from little girls to grandmothers and even high school boys, waited their turn, fanning themselves with the discount coupon flyers. The allure of cheap foot rubs was too good for fairgoers to resist.

Cherry worked the registration table, trying to remember the occasional smile. She couldn't have her mother or cousins asking her any questions. Not yet. She hardly slept last night, waiting for Lum to come home, which he never did. Cherry had called Lum and Quynh, but neither had called her back. She tried Dat's cell phone, but he never picked up. So instead, she sat at her family's festival booth, scanning the crowds, bracing to find one of their familiar faces.

"Can't we cut off the line?" Linh complained, as yet another sweaty pair of feet slipped out of its sandals into her swollen hands. "I bet we've rubbed at least two hundred hands and feet by now."

"We are honoring every coupon," Duyen said. "We have a reputation to uphold."

"But I'm tired," Linh whined, reaching for another squirt of the lavender-scented lotion, a fragrance Cherry had come to revile.

Around lunchtime, Cherry spotted Lum standing a few feet from the booth. Cherry frantically waved, but he shook his head, holding two fingers to his lips, and walked away.

"I need to pee," Cherry said, putting down her stack of coupons and standing.

"Well, hurry back," Linh hollered. "And could you get us some more soda?"

She'd lost him in the crowd. Festival attendance had reached its peak.

Cherry passed through the cultural village, where children pawed at the farm animals in the petting zoo and families posed in front of the blossoming plants, and the food booths, where even the aroma of char-broiled pork and spicy rice noodles could not distract her. The game vendors heckled that for only one dollar she could toss a ring and win a giant stuffed cow to celebrate the Year of the Ox. Cherry even circled the charity booths.

She finally found Lum in the second row of seats at the cultural stage, his arms spread across the chair backs like he was sunbathing, watching a group of children perform a traditional folk dance routine. There weren't many people in the audience, only proud parents shouting encouragement and taking photographs. The back rows were sparsely filled with sunbathing teenagers, loudly talking throughout the show. Her mother made her perform in one of these Tet dance groups when Cherry was six. She'd cried so hard during the show that her mother agreed afterward she never had to do it again.

Lum didn't look up when Cherry stood in front of him, his eyes following the performers. A picked-over plate of noodles sat in the chair next to him. She picked up the soggy plate and sat, facing her brother. A toothpick dangled between Lum's teeth.

"Where is Dat?"

"Oh, that's funny," he said, picking a scallion from his teeth. "I was going to ask you the same thing."

Cherry looked around the audience. "Do you know if he's safe?"

Her brother finally looked over at her for a moment, his eyes wide, mocking. "I had no idea you had so much concern for our cousin."

"You have to call Thinh and his boys off of Dat."

"Why? If he thought this was the perfect lesson for me, I'm sure he can learn from it, too."

"Dat isn't like you—"

"What are you saying? That I deserved it?"

"No," Cherry said, struggling to still her hands in her lap.

"Let's not worry about him for a moment, okay? Why don't we talk about you? Because I am curious to know how my perfect little sister could tear herself away from school long enough to betray me."

Cherry closed her eyes. "I wanted to help—"

"Help me!" Lum laughed, loud enough that a father in the row in front of them turned to give a disapproving glare. "Because our family is so good at that, right?"

Cherry cringed. "Fine," she said. "That doesn't mean siccing these goons on Dat is the answer."

"He owes us money."

"It was never yours."

"I disagree," Lum said. "I worked very hard to earn that money. I smiled and talked with that idiot even though he lied to my face every day. I watched him drool over my girlfriend. I let Grandmother and Dat believe they were conning me. I played to lose, which I never do."

"Lum, if you do this, if you hurt Dat, the family will never forgive you. Not even Mom."

"Do you think that matters to me anymore?"

"It should. They may have set it up, but you did it. You chose to take Dat's money and you chose to double-cross him. Who are you? Stealing money with a gangster? That's not the Lum I know."

"You think I'm the only one who's changed?" Lum shifted in his seat, to look at her. "We used to make fun of Dat. Now you two are so much alike it makes me sick."

The grass below them started to blur. She rested a hand on the folding chair in front of them. Cherry and Lum had never talked to each other like this before. But they both must have known that it was time. It had been a long time coming.

"Maybe I understand how he feels," Cherry said. "You didn't just take money from Dat and Grandmother Vo. Remember?"

"I told you I was going to pay you back."

"It's not about the money," Cherry said, shaking her head sadly, tiredly. "I want to trust you, Lum, but you've made it impossible. Every time, you'd make me look like a fool. You've made us all look like fools. You think I betrayed you? You did it first, Lum."

The dancers curtsied and scampered off the stage, to the sound of scattered applause. A group of little kids in karate *gi* shuffled onto the stage.

"Don't worry anymore, sister," Lum said. "Once I get my share, this will all be over."

"What does that mean?"

He stood, looking down on his sister, his upper lip curling. "It means you won't have to worry about Dumb Lum anymore."

"You're leaving?" Cherry asked, but he didn't answer. He began walking away. She followed. "Lum," she kept saying, trying to keep up with him as they weaved through the people traffic and lines at the food booths. Cherry bumped into a few shoulders, ignoring the occasional protest or dirty look. "Where are you going? Why do you even need all that money, anyway? To prove a point?"

"No," Lum said, spinning around to face her. "To get away from all of you."

It lasted only a second. Lum turned and walked away, until he became another dark head in the crowd. But his expression seared into Cherry's memory, this face she used to know better than her own. Lum's flawlessly composed mask he'd maintained for so long had crumbled. He looked honest for the first time in years. And in that moment, Cherry could read him perfectly, what he thought, what he felt: he hated her.

When Cherry returned, she found Quynh at the registration table in her family's booth, taking coupons from patrons in line.

"Where have you been?" Duyen yelled from the back of the tent.

Cherry sat next to Quynh, waving at one impatient customer to hand over his coupon.

"He's out in his car in the parking lot," Quynh said quietly.

"You brought him here?"

"He wants to talk to you."

"What happened?"

Quynh had arrived at the end of the tournament, when Thinh and his boys were preparing to take Dat outside. Quynh stopped them, and she and Lum had it out over Dat. She believed that Dat must have been tricked by Grandmother Vo. Lum was pretty sure he hadn't been. That was why he never bothered telling Quynh about Grandmother Vo's involvement—he knew she'd take Dat's side. Furious, Quynh demanded that Lum let her leave with Dat to give him time to get the money from Grandmother. Thinh and the club agreed to the extension, provided Dat deliver the outstanding debt to Thinh's apartment the next morning. But Dat never showed up.

"Why doesn't he just go to Grandmother and get the money?"

"He's freaked out. He's scared your grandmother will be mad at him."

"He's more afraid of her than gang members?"

"Just go talk to him," Quynh said, looking behind at Cherry's cousins, who were eyeing them suspiciously. "I'll take care of the line. He's parked in front of the library."

Dat lay curled under a sun-bleached blanket in the backseat of his Honda. Cherry slammed her hand against the window. The doors unlocked and quickly relocked after she slipped into the driver's seat. She glared at him through the rearview mirror.

"You have to leave," Cherry said. "Lum is here."

Dat poked his head above the blanket. He looked terrible: bloodshot eyes, rumpled hair and clothes.

"I can't ask Grandmother," Dat said, his voice hoarse. "You have to."

"Why me?" Cherry cried.

"She told me I could only spend up to $10,000 on your brother. How am I supposed to tell her they now want $20,000 more? She pays my college tuition, Cherry."

"They are going to hurt you, you idiot," Cherry said. "Your good friend Thinh is going to make sure of that."

"How was I supposed to know?"

"Because I warned you about that creep!"

"If you knew so much, then why didn't you tell your brother?"

"You're blaming me . . . for trusting you?"

"I had no idea how sick your brother was," Dat said with a sneer. "That he'd turn on his own cousin. I admit now, I was clearly out out my element. I'm not a hoodlum. I just want to be a doctor."

Gripping her hands on the steering wheel, she imagined shoving Dat's face in it. A shiny car pulled in front of their parking space, sitting idle, blocking them in. Cherry squinted at the familiar vehicle and real-ized. Thinh's Lexus.

"Dat," she quietly said. "Where are your keys?"

"Why?" he asked, but balanced the keys on her shoulder anyway.

She fumbled them into the ignition, but it was too late. The Lexus emptied, Thinh and one guy coming to the driver's side, and two others along the passenger side. They were surrounded. Thinh cheerfully rapped on Cherry's window. Taking a breath, Cherry rolled the window down a few safe inches, trying to ignore the pounding in her heart, the whim-pers from the back seat.

"Hello, Little Sister!" Thinh said. "Is Dat home?"

"We're going to get the money right now," Cherry said, "if you'd just move your car, please."

"That's so good to hear," Thinh said, "but we'd still like a private word with Dat."

"Why?"

"Well, because we already did him a favor last night and he needs to pay up for that one. No more freebies."

"You can trust me," Cherry said, staring at Thinh unwaveringly in the eye. She had to appear confident, unafraid. "I will get you the money."

"I'd believe that," Thinh said, "if you were anyone else but Ba Vo's granddaughter."

"Listen," Cherry said, feigning a look of sympathy, when all she wanted to do was roll up the window and drive over his body. "I know what she did to your father. I'm very sorry about that."

"What are you sorry about?" Thinh asked, his smile fading. "The fact that she bankrupted him? Or that she then made sure that no one would give him another loan for a restaurant? Not even clear across the country in Louisiana?"

"I don't know about that—"

"Right," Thinh said. "Your grandmother wasn't so eager to tell you about my lowly family, right? How my father couldn't even find work as a dishwasher?" Thinh leaned over the car, his face pressed against the opening in the window. He exhaled tobacco breath into Cherry's face. "You know he shot himself? After my mom left him? Did your grandmother ever share that story with you?"

"I'm sorry," Cherry said, fighting the tears. "But Dat and I . . . we're not responsible for that."

"Are you kidding? She stole from my family so you can have your nice cars, your pretty houses. So, yeah, you *do* owe me. A lot more than the money. But I'll take what I can get for now."

Before he could reach his hand through the window, as Cherry prepared to scream, a tall figure, waving his hands into the air, yelled from across the parking lot. Cherry exhaled. Her brother. A look of concern spread across his face.

"Wait right here," Thinh said, pointing a finger at Cherry, his bright, frightening smile reappearing. "We're not done."

Lum jogged up to Thinh's car, as the four boys met him. They stood together in front of the Lexus, the group of five, a perverse team huddle. Cherry despised how comfortable they seemed with one another, how Thinh casually slung his arm around Lum like they were family.

"We have to get out of here," Dat whispered, his sobs vibrating throughout the car.

So those punks got to stand there and decide their fate? And she and Dat were just supposed to sit and wait for their decree? Thinh looked over at their car and seemed to nod in understanding. Cherry leaned back in her seat, short breaths flaring through her nostrils. She was tired of not acting, tired of sitting when everyone else was standing, and still getting blamed for everything, by everyone. They wanted Little Sister to do something? To act?

Cherry glanced around their space—surrounded on both sides by cars, but there was the curb, the library walkway. As her eyes returned to the guys absorbed in conversation, her fingers settled over the car keys in the ignition.

Once she started the engine, she jolted the car into reverse, pressing hard on the gas so they could stumble up on the curb. As the boys turned to look at them, Cherry wrestled to get the car into forward drive and slammed on the accelerator, driving over the library flower beds. A giggle bubbled out of her. She couldn't help it. She'd never driven an automatic transmission, much less a manual, before.

"Go!" Dat screamed, sounding both terrified and thrilled. "Go, go!"

This is where her perfect narration falls apart, where others have to take over the story for her. Her memories of the rest of that afternoon exist only in flashes. Cherry does not trust these fragments. They contain perspectives that have been fed to her after the fact, and perhaps they are not her own at all, just other people's opinions, insistent truths.

Linh had watched it happen. She'd been waiting for Huy at the entrance to give him one of their family's festival passes. She heard people yelling near the library, then saw Dat's car lurching through the flower beds, tumbling toward the parking lot. While two of the boys had jumped into Thinh's silver Lexus, Thinh and one other guy were struggling with Lum. Thinh knocked Lum to the ground.

Linh didn't see the gun—she'd only heard it . . . followed by the sound of Dat's car window shattering. The car slammed into an oncoming minivan. Linh began to scream. The Lexus's passenger window closed and the car accelerated around the accident, knocking into two parked cars. It paused long enough for Thinh and his friend to jump in before peeling out of the parking lot. By the time Linh stumbled to the car, Lum had already pulled Cherry out to the ground. There was blood on her shirt, on Lum, on the car upholstery, on the concrete. When Linh opened the rear door, she found an unconscious Dat sprawled across the backseat. She gingerly searched his body for any bleeding, any injuries, finding nothing. The paramedics later confirmed that he'd simply fainted.

When Duyen first heard the shot, she thought a car engine had misfired, until groups of people started running toward the parking lot. Heightened voices soon mingled with sirens. It took a good fifteen minutes for one of Duyen's ex-boyfriends to reach their family's booth to tell them that Cherry, Dat, and Lum had been in a shooting.

Their parents said Lum refused to talk to anyone when the crowds descended, only following the paramedics as they lifted Cherry onto the gurney. Even with their father and Uncle Chinh yelling in his face, Lum didn't react. When one paramedic attempted to check his body for injuries, Linh said Lum reacted so violently—thrashing his arms and legs—that he had to be restrained.

At the ER, questioned by the police, Lum accepted the blame. He never mentioned Dat, Grandmother, or Cherry. It was simply a disagreement with Thinh, a game gone sour between former friends. Disgusted, their father demanded Uncle Bao and Auntie Tri take him home. He also wasn't to be left alone, in case he tried to run off. Auntie Tri said she didn't have to worry about that. Once they arrived at his parents' home, he went to his room, not even coming out when Quynh came by to see him.

Back at the hospital, one of the nurses gave Cherry's mother a sedative, while her father signed release forms. Doctors explained that the bullet had punctured her liver, her bowel, and possibly other organs. They didn't know it then, but she would require a series of surgeries over several weeks to repair the internal damage. Months later, Cherry would go back to talk to the doctors, requesting to see her diagnoses, X-rays, and charts. Explaining that she wanted to be a surgeon one day, Cherry would come to understand the long, arduous process it took to heal her body.

Cherry's first memory was a conversation that happened a month later, though her family swore she'd wakened earlier, and had even had entire conversations with them. She awoke to her mother sitting next to her, reading a magazine. After calling for the doctor, Tuyet returned to the bed, looking at Cherry with teary, maternal eyes. Caressing her greasy, neglected hair and rough skin, her mother said Cherry already looked better.

"What time is it?" Cherry asked, her throat still dry. "Where's Lum?"

She wouldn't answer her daughter's questions until the doctor on call had been paged to the room. The doctor shone a tiny flashlight into her eyes and ears, and measured her heartbeat. The nurse checked her blood pressure and monitored her fluids. Their gestures were warm but professional, while her mother stood by the window, examining her nails. Once the doctor assured Tuyet that she was healthy enough to talk, her mother closed the door and pulled her seat next to Cherry's bed.

The good news: they caught the shooter and his accomplices. Enough witnesses and affidavits had been collected that the prosecution was confident the defense would accept their terms and plead no contest. Thinh and his boys turned on one another at the police station. The shooter claimed the gun had fired off accidentally, that it was only supposed to scare them.

Grandmother Vo arranged to pay off Lum's gambling debts. Cherry's mother never said if that included the money Lum and Thinh had scammed at the Tet Tournament. Cherry wasn't going to ask. There was also no mention of Dat or Grandmother's plan. Cherry's mother still didn't know. The family had come together through this hardship, taking turns at the hospital to sit with her, covering one another's shifts at the salon, making potluck meals to share at her parents' home.

Cherry kept looking at the door as her mother spoke, wondering why she wasn't calling her father or Lum to come over.

Finally, her mother said it. "Daddy is in France."

"With Lum?" Cherry asked. "They left without us?"

Tuyet avoided looking at her daughter, her hands smoothing the folds of the bedsheets, and tucking the loose fabric under the mattress, while she told Cherry that Grandpère had passed away two days earlier. Cherry wasn't surprised: Grandpère had been ill for years. According to Tuyet, two weeks after Cherry's accident, Uncle Phung had called, warning them Grandpère had contracted a virus and had been admitted into the hospital. His immune system was already fragile, and the doctors didn't expect him to survive his pneumonia.

"You haven't said anything about Lum," Cherry reminded her. "Where is he?"

It was one of those rare times Cherry would recall her mother ever looking afraid. She couldn't even look at her while she spoke about him. The day after the police closed the investigation, only a week ago, their parents put Lum on a plane for Ho Chi Minh City. Her mother claimed it was temporary, six months at most, enough time for Lum to reevaluate his behavior and, though her mother didn't say it, for gossip to settle around Little Saigon.

"What happened to France?" Cherry asked.

Her mother shook her head. "Grandmère doesn't need another burden. Your daddy talked to his aunt and uncle in Saigon. They remembered Lum from when he was a baby and were willing to help."

Cherry stared at her mother, determining if she was serious. "You sent him to Vietnam?"

"Vietnam was our home," her mother said. "Lum can get better there."

She claimed Lum wanted to go. Their father thought Vietnam could reshape his perspective, remind him of his humble roots, so when he returned to America, to them, he could have a fresh start. It sounded so redemptive and inspiring. They probably shamed him, guilted him into leaving. No one can force you from your home unless they make you believe you didn't deserve to be there.

Cherry lay back on the bed, aware of the stitches in her abdomen, trying her best to turn away, looking out the window into the hospital parking lot.

"Don't be ungrateful," her mother said. "Daddy was prepared to disown Lum. I had to beg him to compromise. We couldn't lose both our children."

"I'm still here," Cherry pointed out.

"I know," her mother said softly, her face looking even sadder. "You don't think this hurts me? To send my only son away?"

"You didn't have to," Cherry said, thinking of Grandmother Vo and Dat, wondering where they were, how they'd managed to stay so silent, so innocent. How different this all could have been if she'd awakened earlier.

"This is the only way we can bring him back to us," her mother said. "Give me six months, and this will be over."

Her mother turned away, trying to regain her composure, her chest and shoulders heaving with every breath. Cherry watched silently, the words on her lips, but what good were they now? It was done. She'd slept through all of it. Grandpère was dead, her father was gone, and so was her brother. Her mother was all Cherry had. She imagined how easily Tuyet would turn on her when she realized Cherry was partly responsible. Cherry couldn't admit anything now, not yet. It would only enrage her mother, upset the entire family. Grandmother Vo and Dat could easily deny it. Who would they believe? What would her admission do but harm?

Six months. Maybe her mother was right. They could wait six months. She'd be wrong, they'd both be wrong, but that realization wouldn't occur, not fully, until the first six months had come and passed. And another. And another. But for that afternoon, in that moment, Cherry had to believe her mother. She had no other choice.

1983

Kim-Ly Vo
Ho Chi Minh City, Vietnam

. . . I know I have tried to explain to you why I believed I had to marry Sanh instead of Officer Anderson. You don't ever address my excuses in your letters, and I understand you find it hard to believe me. I have no one to blame except myself. I keep trying to talk about it because I am still trying to understand it. How can you explain such a terrible mistake? Perhaps the only thing to do is seek forgiveness.

When you told me Officer Anderson wanted to marry me, all I could see was his liver spots, his white hair, the way he breathed so loudly through his mouth at dinner. I couldn't imagine us together. I still can't. Do you think he is still alive? I doubted very much, at his age, he would ever want to be a father.

Looking at my children now, I can't imagine not being a mother. That afternoon, when you left me at work, I saw my future ahead of me and I became frightened. Despite all the harmless flirting my sisters and I engaged in, we had never really considered a man we wanted to marry. I'd thought about Thao, but you had never approved of him, and rightly so. After we separated, as everyone knows, he went off and married that whore Lanh. I couldn't believe my only other option was Officer Anderson. It was a death sentence. I needed to find a way to save myself.

Sanh was my boss. He was educated, well spoken, and his family was respected. Not the handsomest man, but is that really important? I did not love him, but I knew he loved me already, and having that without even trying for it is an advantage. I did not doubt that he would make a good husband and father.

Of course, now I understand that even making a practical decision can have unimaginable consequences. I didn't feel I had any other choice. Sanh and I may have our problems, but I still must believe he will be a good provider for my children, and for you when you finally join us. . . .

Tuyet Truong
Westminster, California, USA

✑ *Chapter Eleven*

SANH

A S THE WHITE BANDANNA SLIPPED FROM HIS FOREHEAD, Sanh was grateful for the distraction. He bowed his head to adjust the mourning cloth—wiping beads of sweat from his forehead, tucking the fabric behind his ears—as his family dutifully continued the rosary. Sanh hadn't recited the prayer in years, but doubted if anyone noticed. All eyes focused on his father's casket, lavishly adorned in yellow and red roses, while Sanh's returned to his weeping, careless son.

Sanh and Lum should have sat next to each other as the youngest son and grandson of the deceased. But the family had wisely separated father and son, with Sanh between his brothers, and his mother sitting with Lum on the opposite end of the pew. If anyone from the funeral had looked upon them now, they'd assume that Lum was the saddest mourner, the filial grandson; he must have cherished his grandpère so.

Sanh knew the truth. His fingers involuntarily curled at the sound of every sob, every word Lum uttered in accordance with the prayers he knew nothing about.

After two long flights, with several delays and a few hurried calls home to check on Cherry's condition, Sanh had arrived on his parents' doorstep. His mother had opened the door to their apartment with a tentative smile, then opened the door further to reveal Lum, sitting in his grandfather's armchair. Stunned, Sanh allowed his mother to pull him inside, past his brothers and sisters-in-law who were naïvely chatting with Lum, into his father's former bedroom, where the air felt thick and heavy with incense.

Sanh had told his mother why he and Tuyet sent Lum to Vietnam. She clearly hadn't shared the news with the others. He'd wanted to save his mother from the horrific details of Cherry's attack, but Sanh now realized that had been a mistake. If she'd been privy to the traumatic specifics, the circumstances her grandson created that nearly killed her granddaughter, she never would have arranged for Lum to leave Vietnam after only a week, and without his parents' permission, to attend Grandpère's funeral.

"He arrived yesterday," his mother said, sitting on the bed beside him. She looked more tired and frailer than he remembered from his last visit, which admittedly, had been several years ago. "He has been very upset."

"About what?" Sanh asked.

His mother looked at him disapprovingly. "He needs to say goodbye, too."

"You could have told me. You could have asked."

"There was no time. You had enough to worry about."

He stared at the closed door, imagining his son on the other side, his body unmarred, his mind, for the most part, intact. "Mother," Sanh said, "he is the reason for all of my worries."

"Sanh," his mother said, "your father would have wanted the two of you reunited today."

"It's too soon," Sanh said. "I'm not ready, and he isn't, either—"

"It is the perfect time," his mother said. "I just want my family to be together. For this one day. Please? Let me take care of both you and Lum."

Sanh sighed. "And who's going to take care of you?"

Hoa reached over to hold his hand, squeezing it. "It has been too long since we were last together. Let us comfort each other."

After the service, Sanh wanted to rest his head for only a few minutes, but his father's bedroom had become a regular stop on the mourning tour. With a polite knock and whispered apology, friends walked reverently around the small room, touching his father's belongings, pretending they understood what Hung must have suffered. Sanh wished they could finish the formalities, deposit their bereavement gifts of food and flowers on the table, and leave him alone.

Just as Sanh had fallen into a deep nap, another knock. His mother slipped in, closing the door behind her.

"Monsieur and Madame Bourdain are here," she whispered.

"I thought Yen said they weren't coming," Sanh said.

"I need a few minutes," his mother said. "If I go out there too soon, I might say something regrettable."

"You're the widow," Sanh reminded her. "You can say anything you want."

His mother smiled for the first time since he arrived, and Sanh's mood lifted at the sight of her familiar tiny, dark teeth. "Perhaps this is my opportunity? I can finally tell them what a careless son they raised? How we only invited them out of politeness?" She pulled up a chair and sat next to the bed. "I wish you could stay longer."

"I do, too," he said. "But I need to get back to Tuyet and Cherry."

"It would be a shame if you left without speaking to him."

"Mother," Sanh said with a sigh.

"Lum is suffering—"

"He feels guilty," Sanh said. "There's nothing I can say to relieve him of that."

"You sent your son away."

"You sent Yen away," Sanh reminded her, though he wished such fortunate options as law school existed for his son.

"That was different. We were afraid he was going to get enlisted."

"Then it's not different. Lum was in danger, too, if he stayed in America. He needs time away from us. From me."

"He needs his family," his mother said.

"I'm sorry," Sanh said, shaking his head.

"Lum made a terrible mistake. He knows that."

"I don't think so. Not yet."

"Sanh," his mother said, sitting back, her face pinched in reproach. "You are his father. What has happened to you?"

LITTLE SAIGON, CALIFORNIA, 1980

Until they moved to America, Sanh never realized how rarely he spent time alone with his son. Someone was always around who wanted to hold or tend to Lum: his mother, one of his sisters-in-law. So on their first flight out of Malaysia, Sanh was surprised when Tuyet plopped the child into his lap and excused herself. Sanh had held Lum before, but usually when the boy was asleep and pliable. On the hot and stuffy airplane, Lum squirmed in Sanh's stiff arms, pulling away and kicking. Lifting his head up, the little boy released a frustrated wail, red-faced, eyes dripping with tears.

Tuyet returned from the lavatory scowling, and scooped the child up from Sanh's feeble grasp. "I could hear him from the back of the plane," she hissed. "Can't you settle your own son?" And then, as if to prove the point, she rocked him against her chest until Lum fell asleep. "When the second child comes, I'm going to need your help. You can't rely on your family doing everything for you anymore."

Sanh tried. During their orientation sessions, he and Tuyet took turns watching Lum while they attended English language classes and applied for jobs and housing assistance. But again, Vietnamese refugees surrounded them, only too happy to hold Lum whenever Sanh felt tired.

The refugee services found them a one-bedroom apartment in the small town of Tustin. Sanh was astonished by how empty the place felt, even with the several "Welcome to Your First Home" boxes—blankets, pillows, toilet paper, some mismatched cookware and silverware, bowls and plates—and quiet. While Sanh inflated the air mattress in the bedroom, a volunteer from the Vietnamese Catholic Charities center arrived with two bags of groceries. Sanh paused, lingering by the bedroom door as the woman offered to have the charity truck bring over some donated secondhand furniture.

"No, thank you," Tuyet said. "I'm not Catholic." Finally apart from her religious in-laws, she said this with relish, no longer having to pretend as she had when Sanh's parents insisted Lum be baptized.

"You don't need to be Catholic," the volunteer said.

"We don't intend to convert to Catholicism, so don't expect that, either. Thank you for the food, but you don't need to come again."

As Sanh walked out to the living room, Tuyet closed the front door.

"She was trying to be nice," he said.

"I'm tired of handouts," she said. "It's demeaning."

Living on their own, without parents, Sanh finally understood how crucial practicality was in a wife and mother. Husbands and fathers were supposed to be the stubborn, unyielding ones. Yet in America, Tuyet revealed herself to be just as obstinate and proud as his father. When Tuyet and Lum fell asleep after a lunch of bologna sandwiches and sweetened rice milk, Sanh found the address for the Catholic charity on a flyer in one of the grocery bags and after consulting a map, made the twenty-minute walk.

The volunteer he spoke with was kind and she arranged to have the charity truck drop off a used sofa and dining room set the next day when Sanh knew Tuyet would be away for a sewing class at the refugee resource center. He would tell her they were from another assistance agency.

"Do you have a job yet?" the volunteer asked. Noticing Sanh's embarrassment, she continued, "Because we have some open positions. Would you like to apply? It would help us out tremendously. If we don't fill these jobs, they won't continue to offer them to us."

"I had some interviews at the resource center," Sanh said hesitantly. "But I haven't heard anything yet."

"What did you do in Vietnam?" the volunteer said, sorting through a folder.

"I worked in the foreign ministry," Sanh said, sitting up. "Press relations. I can speak and translate in three other languages."

"You can speak English fluently?" The volunteer jotted a note on the yellow pad in front of her. "Would you be interested in working at a school?"

SAIGON, VIETNAM, 1974

He never expected more out of his job than what he received. Sanh edited and translated press releases for the Foreign Ministry, enjoying a decent salary, regular hours, and enough responsibility that it didn't appear he had avoided enlistment. Even so, Sanh worked diligently. He took his assignments seriously, translating the ministry's announcements into English, French, and Spanish, often staying behind at the office when his coworkers had left for a drink at one of the hotel bars.

He'd received a promotion, of sorts, and an assistant to help with fact checking. Though she wore too much makeup and her perfume irritated his sinuses, especially on humid days, Tuyet performed capably. Every morning, he could expect to find the assignment sheets and contact lists collated on his desk. Though she couldn't help with the translations, she showed an eagerness to acquire a working knowledge of the languages, taking home English or French dictionaries when she left the office.

A naval officer picked her up every afternoon at four o'clock. Tuyet made sure to have her work finished by the time her boyfriend arrived because he did not like to wait. One time, Tuyet was on another floor, gathering a needed signature, and the officer stood by her desk in his stark white uniform. The officer refused the seat Sanh offered, barely looking at him.

"He's a jerk," his colleague Cung said, after the pair had left one afternoon. "You should ask her to work late one night. Steal her away." He grinned when Sanh frowned at him. "How else are you going to get a wife? We worry about you, Sanh."

He did not feel sure he loved Tuyet until the day her mother arrived, interrupting their morning debriefing to yank her out of his office. Until that moment, it never occurred to Sanh that she had a family, someone who could push her around. She had always seemed so independent, opinionated, unafraid to disagree with him or his colleagues during staff meetings. Sanh understood how Tuyet's mother, an older, haughtier version of Tuyet, wearing a turquoise blue *ao dai* and large sunglasses, could make a person cower.

When Tuyet returned, her eyes were swollen. She asked if she could speak to Sanh privately. He invited her into his office, closing the door. Her mother was trying to marry her off to some seventy-year-old American officer who leered at her and her sisters like they were prostitutes.

"He is a terrible man," Tuyet said, "but he doesn't compare to my mother." According to Tuyet, her mother ran an opium den, working primarily with Americans. Tuyet's oldest brother, Thang, ran most of the operations, but her mother made all the decisions. With the Communists looming, she wanted to sell her daughter to one of her former clients to get out of Vietnam.

"She kicked me out of our home," Tuyet said. "I either marry this man or I have nowhere else to go."

"What about your boyfriend?" Sanh asked.

"Thao?" she said, looking surprised. "He's only a friend. His wife and I were classmates in primary school." Tuyet wiped her eyes, looking slightly embarrassed. Sanh wasn't sure what he was supposed to do. Walk around his desk and hold her hand? It seemed inappropriate, though he longed to comfort her.

"Do you live with your family?" Tuyet asked.

"Yes," he said.

"But you're not married. You don't have a girlfriend or fiancée."

"No."

Her eyes lifted, so beautiful, intelligent, admiring. They met his. "Do you want to marry me?"

The elementary school did not need to fill a teaching position, the vice principal explained. Teachers in America needed certification. Sanh would require several years of schooling for that. When Sanh explained he'd earned his university diploma with honors in Vietnam, the vice principal, Mr. Gaines, a normally unamused man, smiled.

"This is an interview for a custodial position," he reminded Sanh. "Carlos can train you. He is excellent with new hires."

The head custodian was a chubby Guatemalan with a laugh that carried across the schoolyard. He offered to share his sandwich and fruit when he realized Sanh hadn't brought a lunch. He was delighted Sanh spoke fluent Spanish and teased his accent, promising to correct his European pronunciations. Carlos had arrived in the States twelve years earlier and had four children of his own, but they did not attend this school. "Not the same district," he said. "Besides, I wouldn't want my kids to see how these children act. Very spoiled. No manners."

During the seven-hour school session, Sanh covered the lower division east wing, mopping and stocking bathrooms and tidying hallways and corridors. After the three o'clock school bell, he was permitted to enter the classrooms, where he emptied the metal trash cans, gathered crumpled paper and stray pencils from the coat closets, and pried off fresh chewing gum from underneath the desks. While restocking the boys' bathroom, he smelled something rank, approached the fourth stall, and saw someone had missed the toilet while defecating. Glad that Carlos and the other custodians were cleaning the other wings, Sanh tensed his fingers around the stall door, slamming his forehead into it so he would not cry.

When he arrived home, Tuyet was annoyed that he'd forgotten to pick up a package of vermicelli noodles at the Chinese grocery store near the school. "I guess we'll just eat rice again tonight," she said, throwing open the kitchen cabinets, searching for the rice cooker, "even though it took me hours to make the broth. But who cares what I do all day?"

Sitting on the floor, Sanh watched as Lum turned the pages of his coloring book, pointing to the green and blue crayon markings on a pair of skunks. When his son tried to put an orange crayon into his mouth, Sanh gently pulled it away from his face and back toward the coloring book. He tried not to take Tuyet's mood personally. All day, she'd been trying to sew a bag of blouses, some work she picked up from Mrs.

Nguyen, another refugee who lived down the hall who convinced her it was easy money. Having never sewn much before, Tuyet had already ruined the stitching in two blouses, which would be deducted from her pay.

"I don't think I should stay at the school," Sanh said. "I think I can find something better."

"It's a starter job," Tuyet said, measuring rice into the cooker. "After a few months, you can ask for a promotion to teach in the classroom."

"It doesn't work that way," Sanh said. "Carlos has been there for almost five years and he still cleans toilets."

"Carlos doesn't have a college degree like you do," Tuyet said. "We need to be patient. You prove yourself, they'll reward you. Did you go to the refugee center to ask about the sponsorship forms?"

"When was I going to do that?"

"You know we have to file those papers soon. I wrote to my mother weeks ago."

"I'll go tomorrow," he promised, closing his eyes, suddenly aware of his aching shoulders and calves. He leaned forward, trying to stretch his cramped spine.

She didn't answer him. Silence gave way to the sound of the simmering soup pot, the water faucet turning on and off, and the occasional padding of Tuyet's slippers on the linoleum kitchen floor. Sanh extended his legs in the living room, watching as Lum tried again to eat his crayon.

"No," Sanh firmly said, pulling the crayon away from his son's face.

"Carrot," Lum said in English, pointing again to his coloring book, where an upright bunny was munching on the vegetable.

"Yes," Sanh replied in English. "Carrot, here. But this is a crayon. You can't eat a crayon."

Only four years old and Lum's English was catching up with his Vietnamese. His son had been attending English courses at the refugee resource center for the past month, and Sanh found his pronunciation so articulate, so precocious, he wanted to call his mother in France. Maybe Lum would take after his father and find languages more addictive than science or mathematics. But Sanh could only call France on Sundays, and even then he only had ten minutes. Overwhelmed with how much he needed to say, he often said very little, hoping, praying that his silence could somehow express how much he missed them.

That night, his family did their best to help Tuyet feel comfortable. At dinner, his mother asked about Tuyet's favorite dish, and promised to pick up the ingredients from the market the next morning. Trinh and Ngoan offered some of their clothing to Tuyet until she could arrange for her belongings to arrive. Even Sanh's father deigned a polite smile and occasional nod when they spoke of their plans for a quiet, simple wedding ceremony.

While the women helped clean up dinner, Sanh joined his father in the alley for a cigarette. The scent of fresh magnolia flowers from his mother's window box mingled with rotting garbage in the dumpster.

"This should be a relief to your mother," his father said. "Those matchmakers had branded you an eternal bachelor."

Sanh ignored the insinuation. His parents had hired two matchmakers, both family friends. But after four awkward dinners, with four different, but equally shallow girls who expected Sanh to look and act like his older brothers, Sanh declared that he'd tired of matchmaking.

"She's smarter than anyone you could have found for me," Sanh retorted.

"I don't doubt that," Hung said. "She is very, very smart."

Sanh glared at him. "What is that supposed to mean?"

Hung exhaled a long drag and cocked his head. "She's not in love with you." He said it with such cheerfulness, such a lack of surprise, that Sanh had to look away.

"You don't know her," Sanh said. "You haven't even spoken to her."

"Am I wrong?" Hung asked. "You know I'm not. Why not admit it to your father, if no one else?"

He knew his father was goading him into an argument. It was something he often did, and Sanh fell for it almost every time. Unlike Yen, who enjoyed debating and never took it personally, or Phung, whom their father usually avoided, Hung's deliberate remarks often burrowed into Sanh's memory, keeping him awake and brooding long after everyone in the house had fallen asleep.

"Are you going to oppose the marriage?" Sanh asked.

"When this could be your only shot?" Hung smiled. "No. This is your choice. Perhaps you will surprise me."

There were times Sanh didn't mind the job, especially when he, Carlos, and the other custodians sat on the basketball courts and shared a cigarette, or when he had a few minutes during the classroom sweeps to peruse the books that Lum and his younger sibling would read and learn from one day. During their weekly call from France, Sanh's father had requested that if the second child was a boy, his name be Etienne. As for a girl, his research continued. Sanh suspected his father chose the name to remind him they should be in France. Thoughts of the new baby lifted Sanh's spirits.

He dreaded lunch duty most. Sanh found the students' young, petulant voices grating, their slang and garbling of their birth language offensive. It frustrated him that some children would mock his accent when walking past him, believing their English to be superior. He hoped to teach Lum and his younger sibling to articulate, to take pride in every word they spoke. The earlier lunch hour for the lower division grades was not as irritating as the later hour with the older children, who were noisier, rowdier, and deliberately messier.

As Sanh tied up two garbage bags, he saw Carlos on the other side of the cafeteria leaning over to pick up a milk carton from the floor. But before he straightened up, a crumpled lunch sack sailed across the room, bouncing off Carlos's hip. When Carlos looked up, trying to determine where the bag came from, only titters came from a table full of fifth-graders. Carlos resumed picking up the stray trash, but Sanh was watching. Only a few seconds later, a boy stood at the table, a bag in his hands, his forearms creating a graceful arc, similar, Sanh recognized, to throwing a basketball. When the boy released the sack into the air, which brushed past Carlos's elbow, Sanh had already crossed the cafeteria.

He hadn't really thought about what he would do or say after reaching the snickering boys, but he did feel immense satisfaction watching their faces tense in terror as he grabbed the back of the boy's shirt.

"What is wrong with you?" Sanh screamed, refusing to let go of the boy's shirt collar as he attempted to squirm out of his grip. "Do you treat your brother this way? Your father?"

Carlos would later tell him that the other boys and girls yelled at Sanh to let go, that their cries had alerted the teacher chaperones on duty, who should have been watching the brats in the first place. But what surprised Sanh was that his attempts to talk to the boy had not even been understood, that of all the languages Sanh could speak, the one he chose was Vietnamese. Gibberish to these American school kids. Ching-chong crazy talk.

In America, the vice principal said, adults could not touch students in a threatening manner, even for disciplinary purposes. It was against the law. Because Sanh was a new refugee, because of all the hardships he and his family had endured from the war and relocation, because he clearly did not understand the rules of his new country, the school would release him from his duties quietly, without alerting the school board. They would talk to the boy's parents and hopefully persuade them to understand. Carlos gave him a ride home after he cleaned out his personal locker and surrendered his school keys and identification card.

"My brother works for the water company," Carlos said. "I'll ask him if he knows of any work." He patted Sanh's arm, and Sanh regretted no longer having work hours to spend with his new friend.

When he stepped into the apartment four hours early, he braced himself for Tuyet to bark at him. Instead, he found the apartment empty, a basket of clean laundry in the middle of the living room. Sanh checked the calendar. Lum's language preschool and Tuyet's sewing class did not meet today. He looked inside the refrigerator: plenty of food.

Sanh sat in the living room and turned on the television, waiting, and taking down the toll-free numbers of the technical college commercials that flashed across the screen. When Tuyet walked in two hours later, holding Lum's hand, a man was with them, walking closely behind.

"You remember Thao," Tuyet said, a hand on her hip, sighing irritably, maybe from the heat, or the pregnancy. Four weeks from full term, Tuyet grew weary walking anywhere with her large belly and swollen feet. "He gave us a ride to the grocery store."

Lum reached his arms for Sanh, who obligingly picked him up. Lum's hands felt sticky and he smelled like cherries.

The former naval officer remained as unfriendly as Sanh remembered. He'd recently arrived in the States. His wife and two daughters still lived in Vietnam. When Tuyet asked him to stay for dinner, he declined, saying he needed to go back to his sister's apartment. They lived in Westminster, north of Tustin, where he said other refugees had been placed. After Thao left, Sanh wanted to know how they had run into each other again, but before he could ask, she interrogated him first.

She could have taken it worse. No screaming or tearing off to the bedroom. No angry outburst, which made him feel even more terrible. Instead, she sank into the crooked dining room chair, the one Sanh had promised to fix days ago. Tuyet put a hand on the package of diapers she purchased that afternoon. Should she return these?

"No," Sanh said, letting a squirming Lum down to patter to the television. He walked over to sit next to his wife. "We need the diapers."

"What about my mother? What about sponsoring my family? You promised we'd take care of them now, Sanh."

His wife did not cry easily. She hadn't cried when they reunited after his two years in the reeducation prison, or on their boat to Malaysia when they lost direction for three days and believed they'd starve to death. The only time he remembered his wife breaking down happened the day before their escape from Saigon, when they learned Sanh's father could not buy enough seats to bring Tuyet's mother and siblings with them. She couldn't bring herself to tell her mother in person, even when Sanh offered to go with her. The same despondent expression colored her face now. She wiped her nose on her blouse sleeve while one of Lum's cartoon characters happily sang from the living room.

"I'm going to the refugee resource center tomorrow," Sanh said. "And Carlos said his brother may know of something. I'll find another job. We also have my mother's jewelry. We could try to sell the pieces if we really need money."

"I wish my mother was here," Tuyet said, her lower lip jutting out.

"What would she know that we don't? This country will be new to her, too."

She shook her head, half-smiling in that secretive manner of hers. "You don't know. My mother knows how to find money."

"I can take care of us," he said. "I will."

Sanh and Tuyet's two-month wedding anniversary marked the start of monsoon season. And the Communists infiltrating the south. As high-ranking government officials fled for Thailand or Taiwan, Sanh spent his last days at the ministry with his coworkers shredding documents. Phung returned home with dispiriting reports of South Vietnamese soldiers dropping their weapons and fleeing. Refugees from the countryside already blotted the streets, setting up tents and camps on every available meter of sidewalk. Sanh's mother and the servants stockpiled water and rice. No one knew how long the electricity and water would stay on after the Communists entered the city.

Rocket attacks, so terrifying on the first night, quickly integrated into the city chorus of thunder from the monsoon season. Abiding by the twenty-four-hour curfew, the family remained inside, Hung compulsively locking and relocking all their doors and windows. The children stayed upstairs with their grandmother.

As Phung was adjusting the radio to listen for news reports, a bullet shattered the kitchen window, spraying glass across the wooden dining table and floor. Trinh and Ngoan screamed, running up the stairs to the children. After waiting a few minutes to make sure no additional gunshots followed, Sanh crept into the kitchen, and peered out the window. The alley was empty, but a few other windows down the street had been blown out as well.

Phung had promised to deliver a message to a fellow officer's family, and Sanh agreed to go to Tuyet's family's home to make sure everyone was safe. Hoa didn't want them to leave, but Phung was determined to honor his friend's last request. Tuyet gave Sanh a small envelope to give to her mother. "This goes only to her," she said. "Don't let anyone else in the family take it from you."

Sanh and Phung accessed alleys to cross the city. Phung led, compulsively changing their route according to the changes in the steady thumping of gunshots and mortar fire. So distracted by the chaos around them—like the small boy rooting through the purse of a mangled bargirl on the sidewalk—Sanh probably would have walked right into a sniper's line of fire.

Many of the house numbers had been hidden or destroyed, but finally Sanh found the Vos' address. Though the exterior had been vandalized with spray paint and the garden was littered with trash, its former grandeur was evident. While Phung walked across the street, trying to find his friend's house, Sanh walked up the broken brick path to his wife's former home.

After he knocked on the front door several times, a faint voice inside asked who he was.

"I'm Sanh Truong," he said. "Tuyet's husband."

The door cracked opened. A tall, thin man with a mustache and longish hair peered out. From Tuyet's photographs, Sanh recognized Thang, Tuyet's older brother, the one who ran the family drug business. The man looked him up and down. "So you're the fool," he said.

"Your brother-in-law," Sanh said.

The man shrugged. Such a casual gesture, yet it made Sanh want to strike him in the face.

"Tuyet wanted to make sure you were all right," Sanh said, suddenly incensed that he wasted all this time battling the crowds across the city, risking injury, for this ingrate.

"Oh, you can tell dear sister we are doing just fine," Thang said. "She shouldn't concern herself with us anymore."

"I'll let her know," Sanh said. As he angrily turned to leave, he remembered Tuyet's letter in his pocket. When he looked back at the door, he saw that Thang was still watching him, an unsettling smirk on his face, until an M-16 spraying bullets nearby startled both of them. But when Sanh took a step toward the house, Thang shut the door. Sanh ran down the block and found Phung on the next street.

A few blocks ahead, a crowd had swarmed and was looting a row of stores. A mother and daughter dragged a twin mattress down the street. As he followed Phung, Sanh tore open the envelope. Tuyet's letter was short and barely legible, unlike the clean handwriting he remembered when she transcribed notes at the ministry.

Phung stopped in front of a deserted grocery store where a naked toddler wept beside a burning garbage can. Kneeling at the boy's side, Phung asked where his family was, but the boy only continued to sob. Sanh held the letter up to his face.

Please accept my humblest apologies for my betrayal and deceit. I made a grave mistake marrying against your wishes. You are my first family, the only one I shall honor, and I will do anything I can to earn your forgiveness.

A teenage girl ran up to them, grabbing the hand of the little boy and dragging him away. Phung turned to Sanh, who threw the letter into the burning trashcan.

"What was that?" Phung asked as they ran down the street, avoiding a broken bicycle in the middle of the intersection.

"Nothing important," Sanh said.

The waiting room at the refugee resource center was full of mostly Vietnamese men, a few with their children. Lum kept shaking his sandals off, dangling them from his toes, before flinging the shoes across the room, under the folding chairs onto the gummy, hair-infested floor. Though Sanh roughly scolded him each time, Lum considered it a game until his father finally forced the boy to sit in his lap, which didn't please Lum at all. He whined for his mother, and elbowed his father in the chest.

"Where is his mother?" the man sitting next to him asked. He had on a baseball cap and a toothpick dangling from his teeth.

"Cosmetology seminar," Sanh said. "It lasts all day." It was the only reason he agreed to watch Lum, after a wall-bending screaming match with Tuyet. She had to take notes and practice hand massages and manicures, while Sanh only had to wait at the resource center, again, applying for jobs he'd never get, again. To stop the neighbors from stomping on their ceiling, Sanh finally relented.

"You're kinder to your wife than I am," the man said. "We have four kids and they go where she goes. Usually she leaves them at her sister's."

"We don't have any family here yet," Sanh said.

"Lucky you," the man said.

He hadn't mentioned anything to his parents about losing his job, only listened as they talked about Yen's apartment in the Latin Quarter, the Chinatown district that had a decent amount of Vietnamese vegetables and groceries, how the kids could already speak conversational French to their parents. Though Lum's articulation was impressive, he was lazy about practicing his vocabulary, in part because Tuyet continued to speak to him in Vietnamese.

Last week, Sanh had thought it made sense to apply only for jobs that required one bus route, no longer than a half hour. That way, he could stay closer to home in case Tuyet went into labor. But this morning, Sanh applied for every position posted on the job announcements boards along the hallway, from Fullerton to Laguna Beach: administrative, custodial, technical, manual. If he could get an interview, if he could only talk to someone, he could explain why he needed the job, why he would never mess up again.

"My wife is going to have our second child," Sanh told the employment counselor, as he did every time. His eyes avoided the stacks of other applications on Mr. Stoops's desk. "She is very worried about our finances."

"There are many refugees looking for work," Mr. Stoops said. "We have to be patient."

"I don't think my wife has any more patience," Sanh admitted, remembering how Tuyet locked herself in the bathroom the night before.

The fight had begun after Sanh decided he wouldn't pawn his mother's jewelry, arguing it was more important to preserve it for their children.

Tuyet insulted the jewelry, calling it worthless anyway, throwing it in his face before retreating to the bathroom. Through the closed door, she threatened to leave him if he didn't get a job in another week; she could find another man to take care of her and the children.

The counselor looked up from his paperwork, his deeply tanned face concerned. "Is there a domestic situation we need to discuss?" he asked.

"We have tempers," Sanh admitted, his voice soft, though the counselor's door was closed off from the waiting room. "Both of us. It can be stressful."

On the floor, playing with one of the brochures from the waiting room, Lum looked at the counselor and back at Sanh. "Mommy's mad," he said in Vietnamese.

"Yes," Sanh agreed, "Mommy was mad last night."

Sanh had pounded on the bathroom door that night, demanding she open it. Lum curled up on the air mattress in the bedroom, weeping that he needed to use the toilet, yet Tuyet had refused to listen to either of them.

"What are you going to do?" Tuyet's voice had taunted him through the door. "Are you going to hit me? Are you finally going to act like a man?"

"Mr. Truong," Mr. Stoops said, leaning his elbows on the desk. "Domestic violence is a serious offense in America. We do not hit our wives or children. It's against the law."

Sanh had taken the soiled bed sheets and Lum's clothing to the laundry machine in the building's basement; they only had the one set. When he returned to the apartment, Tuyet was telling Lum a bedtime story Ngoan used to recite to the children back in Vietnam. At the end of it, Tuyet glared at Sanh as if he were intruding.

"I'm not hitting my wife," Sanh said, offended at the counselor's suggestion.

"There are other ways to resolve disagreements," Mr. Stoops said. "We have marriage counseling classes here twice a week. I can have the social worker call you and your wife tonight to talk about it."

They had lain in bed last night looking at the popcorn ceiling instead of each other. When Lum began to snore softly, she said after the baby was born, she and the children were going to move out. Thao recently rented his own apartment, and it had an extra bedroom. One of her instructors at cosmetology school said she could work at her nail salon. Sanh could go to France, to live with the family he truly cared about. She'd find another father for the children.

"They're my children," Sanh said.

"You're such a fool," Tuyet said. "Have you ever looked at Lum?"

He drew a breath, digging his fingers into his thin pillow.

"You're lying," Sanh said. "You'll say anything right now." But after she fell asleep, Sanh examined Lum's resting face, and thought of Thao. He recalled the man's high forehead and lean body standing next to Lum's own gangly figure, so different from Sanh's compact stature. Lum was only a toddler, not fully formed. Still sleeping, Lum stretched his arms, patting Sanh's chest, a familiar gesture that Sanh usually took to mean the boy was having a bad dream. Instead of comforting him, as he would have last night, Sanh softly pushed the boy's shoulder and turned him to face his mother.

Mr. Stoops agreed to follow up on his job applications and promised to call within a week. After returning from the refugee resource center, Sanh prepared a lunch of instant ramen noodles with a raw egg mixed in. Lum complained of the orange and green flakes floating at the top of his Styrofoam cup.

"They're vegetables," Sanh said, between bites of noodles. "They're good for you."

"Mommy always takes them out for me," Lum said, sullenly poking at the cup with his chopsticks.

"Speak to me in English," Sanh said. "You have to practice."

"I want something else," Lum said stubbornly in Vietnamese, slamming the cup on the dining room table. The Styrofoam cup cracked in his tiny grasp, and the noodles and broth broke through, gushing off the table and splattering the carpet.

Before Sanh could lunge for him, Lum scrambled out of his seat and ran for the bathroom, nearly falling as he turned the bedroom corner. Lum had already slammed and locked the door by the time Sanh caught up with him.

"Open this door," Sanh screamed, pounding on the cheap wood with the palm of his hand. "Open it now!"

There was no answer on the other side, no taunting, no chiding, just short gasping breaths.

"I'm going to count to ten," Sanh yelled, slamming the door again with his hand. It vibrated against the hinges. "And if you don't unlock this door, I will kill you. Do you hear me? I will. I am your father!"

He had never said anything like that before. He'd never felt so angry, remembering how only twelve hours earlier, he had been yelling at the same door, at another family member who should have respected him. But once he spoke the words, he felt compelled to count, loudly, steadily, until he reached eight, and the doorknob turned, the door slowly swinging open.

Lum's hooded eyes, eyes that belonged to Tuyet, were large and puffy, tears streaking his cheeks. His red-and-blue striped shirt and gray shorts were dark with soup stains. He crossed his arms in front of him, already bracing his small chest. It occurred to Sanh that he'd never seen his son cry so much until they moved to America.

When Sanh stepped through the door, the boy recoiled, covering his head and neck with his arms. Sanh wrapped his hands around Lum's tense shoulders, turning the boy, and walked him out of the bathroom.

From under the kitchen sink, Sanh found several dishrags and the wastebasket, and brought them to the dining table. Together, they picked up the cold noodles from the table and floor, and sopped up as much broth from the carpet as they could. When Lum tried to dangle a dusty noodle into his mouth, Sanh pulled it away.

They pressed the rags into the carpet, using all their might. "Does it still smell?" Sanh asked, burying his nose in the carpet's dark spots. Cocking his head to the side, he saw Lum's face split into a joyful grin. He called his father a silly puppy. Sanh kissed the top of the boy's head, trying to shut out the words he screamed only a few minutes earlier. Children. They forgave and forgot so easily.

*　*　*

Like others in their neighborhood, their father thought it best to register early, to appear compliant and to appeal to the Communists' sympathy, or at least to their sense of efficiency. Anyone affiliated with the former regime or the American occupation was required to enroll in the reeducation program to assimilate to the new Vietnamese government. Completing the program promised access to state benefits, such as official status in the party and food rations for their new lives in the unified country.

Of course, whisperings and suspicions abounded. A family down the street revealed themselves as Viet Minh, which had stunned the neighborhood. Spies living alongside them all this time? But Hung, Phung, and Sanh had discussed the prospect of trying to escape the country on unreliable boats or rafts, and it had seemed dangerous and foolish. They had Cam and Xuan to think of, too young for such a risky journey. And the new government was promising reunification. One country. Forgiveness, forgiveness. At the time, it didn't seem naïve to believe in these words, not when they had few other choices.

At registration, officers informed them that the program would take place in a training facility only a few hours from Saigon, and that it would be brief. They should bring enough food, pens, paper, and clothing to last ten days. Higher-ranked officials would be gone for a month.

Tuyet hadn't looked frightened or nervous when they kissed goodbye. In fact, Sanh couldn't recall her looking more beautiful and optimistic, and he was impatient for the ten days to finish so he could return home. This last image of Tuyet was likely embellished during his time away, but it also could have been the glow of her yet unknown pregnancy. She promised to take care of the other women and children. She talked of opening their own business to help support the family once he returned from the program.

As their cadres determined their reeducation progress unsatisfactory, the brothers' sentences stretched longer and longer. It pained Sanh to count the days on the calendar he and Phung had drawn with the pens and paper (they never ended up using them for anything official) and hid under their cots. In a suspicious gesture of humanity, the brothers were allowed to share a tent, along with four other men. They worked fourteen hour days of hard labor. Their tent mates were especially sympathetic to Sanh, the youngest, who'd never spent time in the countryside before, and endured in grueling succession dehydration, heat sickness, and malaria.

Years later, his children would ask Sanh to describe the reeducation camps to them. The word *camp* was not a proper translation. Nor the word *reeducation*. The two put together compounded a lie that still tasted vile in Sanh's mouth. They had been in prison. The regime's refusal to use the correct term only further demonstrated its hypocrisy.

Since he could see no benefit in frightening the children and generating needless nightmares, he kept the facts simple: their work unit was in charge of digging wells and latrines the first year, planting crops the next. After two years of labor, written confessions and sworn allegiances to the new government, he and Uncle Phung were released. Sanh assured Lum and Cherry that they only signed those documents to get back to their family. By that time, Lum had already celebrated his first birthday and needed his father.

When Sanh found out Lum had been born, he'd only known about Tuyet's pregnancy for a few weeks. It took months for mail to arrive to their work unit, and Sanh suspected the cadres delayed screening their letters longer than necessary to antagonize more work out of them. Hoa wrote that Tuyet had given birth to a healthy boy, nearly seven pounds, the quickest delivery of all the grandchildren. Their father had given his third grandchild the name Lum, which meant lush forest, a jungle, the very debris the Communists ordered Sanh to destroy every day.

Sanh had burst into tears upon reading the letter, his brother and tent mates quietly celebrating with stolen beer from the mess hall. The men shared tales of their own children's births and encouraged Sanh to express his hopes for his new son's fortune. Since the guards frowned upon prayer, Buddhist or Catholic, Sanh whispered these expectations. A father had the right to predict his son's success. Phung assured him they would remember Sanh's hopes for the rest of their lives, praying for Lum's destiny to follow Sanh's wishes.

* * *

In America, a father was allowed, even expected, to witness his child's birth. As long as he sterilized his hands and wore proper garments, he could stand alongside the doctor and nurses in the delivery room. He could even cut the umbilical cord.

Tuyet didn't like this Western custom. She didn't wish to feel vulnerable in front of Sanh, especially when they were barely on speaking terms. The nurse warned Sanh that husbands found it difficult to watch their wives endure so much pain, but he promised he would not leave Tuyet's side for even a restroom break. Whatever happened between him and Tuyet—whether she left him, or he left her—he would not miss his child's birth.

What she didn't know—what he wasn't sure he wanted her to know— was that while she was at her last cosmetology seminar, he had received and accepted a job offer at the water treatment plant. Carlos's brother had arranged for the interview, and the executive manager who hired Sanh told him he'd served in the Vietnamese war and held nothing against his people or his country.

"That's not my country anymore," Sanh replied as he shook the man's hand.

"Course not," the manager said. "You're going to be an American soon. And I know from experience you new Americans make the best employees."

Sanh would give the job six months, but as soon as he made enough to afford airfare to France—as soon as the new baby could travel—he planned to take his legitimate child back to his family. Tuyet and Lum could stay in America. She could work on getting her drug-dealing mother and criminal siblings to America on her own. And if she wanted her second child back, she could buy her own ticket to Paris and try to find them.

Sanh's father finally found a daughter's name: Cherie. In French, it meant "darling, dear one." Cherie Truong. It signified the promise of new affection and love. Sanh thought it was a much better choice than Lum had been.

"I thought I should come out there with the new baby next month," Sanh said.

"So soon?" his father asked. "What about Tuyet and Lum?"

"They'll be fine," Sanh said. When his father didn't respond, he pushed forward. "Maybe we could stay out there for a while, see if I can find a job there."

"Are you having problems with money?" Hung asked.

"No, I just thought—"

"So your wife was wrong about America," Hung said. "And you want to punish her by leaving her and Lum there alone?"

"I thought you wanted the family together," Sanh said, trying to control the anger creeping into his voice. He glanced up to where Tuyet and Lum were obliviously washing dishes in the kitchen.

"You chose your family," Hung said coldly. "No son of mine will ever run away from his responsibilities. Not even you."

On a late Wednesday night, Tuyet's labor contractions began. After a few hours, Sanh called the Nguyens, who had agreed to give them a ride to the hospital.

Lum held on to his father's hand as Sanh was trying to leave the car. The hospital orderly was already helping Tuyet into a wheelchair.

"I want to come, too," Lum said, his arm snaking around Sanh's elbow, trying to lock in his grip. "Don't leave me."

"You need to go home with the Nguyens," Sanh said, peeling his son's arms away from him. "I'll come get you after the baby is born."

"Promise?"

Sanh impatiently glanced into Lum's tearful, expectant eyes. "Yes."

In the delivery room, a nurse noticed Sanh fidgeting and asked if this was his first child's birth. He said yes, then no, then yes again.

The doctor explained that the baby was face up, the wrong position. Tuyet screamed obscenities in Vietnamese. She asked for her mother, for her sisters, for Trinh. Sanh stood next to her, providing ice chips and blotting her forehead with the wet hand towel when the nurse prompted him. Tuyet stared at him after swallowing one of the ice chips.

"I'm going to die," she moaned unhappily.

"No, you're not," Sanh said, trying to concentrate on her face instead of the rags of blood the nurses kept taking away.

"You have to take care of our children," she said. "You know that, don't you? I was only angry before. You are a good man, Sanh. It's why I chose you."

"You're not going to die," he repeated. But even as he said it, her words slid inside his ears, traveling down his body, paralyzing him with the possibility of her prediction.

She looked so weak. Sanh now understood why in Vietnam, fathers customarily left the room. He'd never felt more impotent—it was worse than leaving for America on their own, worse than getting fired at the elementary school. Standing there with his useless hand towel and ice chips, which Tuyet waved away, Sanh realized how irrelevant he was. If he couldn't save his own wife, he didn't deserve her.

His father had been right. Tuyet was his family. Her face crumpled through every painful contraction, yet she turned to Sanh with eyes full of trust, fear, and love. Sanh realized no other woman would ever look at him that way. Yes, they had hurt each other. And lied to each other. But they'd chosen this life together. They'd abandoned their families to make this new one. If Tuyet could possibly die to give him this child, the least he could do was give her, give their family, all he had.

A final push from Tuyet and the baby emerged. A girl, covered in blood and meconium, howled to the ceiling. Sanh stared at this creature in wonder, then back at Tuyet, who was panting, perspiring, face contorted, very much alive.

After cutting the umbilical cord and watching the nurses bathe the child, Sanh asked to hold the baby first. He would always be grateful for that privilege, and would cherish those exclusive minutes for the rest of his life. The infant's eyes were still closed, a small mat of black hair on her head. Her complexion radiated a furious blush, which the doctor assured him indicated robust health. Such a healthy girl. His baby girl.

"What are you going to name her?" a nurse asked as he cooed at his new daughter.

"Cherie," Sanh said softly, still distracted by her tiny hand that refused to uncurl.

"Cherry? Like the fruit?" the nurse asked. "That's so pretty, a beautiful fresh cherry."

Sanh turned and looked at the nurse, who was completing the birth charts. "Yes," he said, smiling, allowing the American word to turn over in his head. "Cherry."

PARIS, FRANCE, 1997

With all three apartments opened to bereavement guests, Sanh and Lum managed to remain on different floors during the funeral reception. Most of the family had gathered in the ground apartment, ushering out the final visitors. Weary of the prolonged good-byes, Sanh wandered upstairs to Yen's apartment to begin cleaning up. He found his son hovering around the dining room table, sweeping up crumbs from the tablecloth. His son's hair appeared longer, but Sanh wondered if that was even possible. How different could he really look after only a few weeks away?

The night of the accident, after leaving Cherry at the hospital, Sanh and Tuyet came home to find that Lum had set out all seven of his credit cards, his driver's license, checkbooks, and bank account information on the kitchen counter. Sanh saw that his devastated son blamed himself entirely. But while Tuyet could still embrace the boy, Sanh was not ready to comfort, to forgive, not while Cherry still lay in the hospital.

Many of Tuyet's relatives lived in Orange County. Sending Lum to his Uncle Viet in Texas, another gambler, was asking for further trouble. France was out of the question. His relatives had enough to deal with. His uncle and aunt Tran in Saigon were decent, compassionate people. Sanh remembered how frustrated his father had been at their refusal to escape with them, but the Trans had been determined to make their lives in the new regime. Their sons already buried from the war, the Trans didn't want to be far from their graves. When Sanh called his uncle, he kept the details of Lum's transgressions brief and vague. The Trans did not press for details. They promised to care for Lum as their own son.

Sanh approached the dining table, and picked up some crumpled linen napkins. Lum looked up, blowing his hair away with a puff of his breath. He and his sister both did that.

"Thank you for letting me stay," Lum said, his voice devoid of the arrogance that had contaminated him for the last two years. Sanh willed himself to breathe. His heart rate had not accelerated, his head felt clear. Perhaps it was the appropriate time to talk.

"You should thank Grandmère," Sanh said.

"How is Cherry?" Lum asked, helping his father gather the empty plates into a stack.

"She's recovering." At the sight of his son's relieved smile, Sanh immediately regretted the admission. "That doesn't change anything."

"I know," Lum quickly said. "Believe me." He looked so vulnerable, so much like his mother, that Sanh's shoulders momentarily relaxed.

"Have they been treating you well?" Sanh asked.

"Granduncle and Grandaunt? They've been very gracious."

Sanh nodded, as he followed Lum into the kitchen with an armful of glasses. "I'm glad."

"But it's not home," Lum said. He eased his pile of dishes into the sink and turned to face his father. "It's not where I'm supposed to be."

Sanh winced. "Lum, we agreed: six months."

"You agreed. It's been two weeks, the longest two weeks of my life."

"And ours. You're supposed to be thinking about what you've done."

"I have," Lum said. "All I do is wait for you or someone from home to call. All I think about is my sister, and how I'm not there to help her, when I'm the one that caused all of this—"

"What do you think you can do?" Sanh asked. "You're not a doctor. You can't heal her. You barely graduated from high school—"

Lum closed his eyes. "I talked to Bac Van. He said I could come back to the flower shop. I can go right from the airport, if you want."

Sanh shook his head. "It's not about the money. You know that."

"I want to help. Let me prove to you that I can."

"I told you, the best thing you can do right now is to stay away."

"How is that helping? Does it only help you, so you don't have to look at me?"

The floor creaked, and Sanh and Lum turned to see Madame Bourdain standing in the living room. "Excuse me," she mumbled, her eyes trailing the floor. "We're leaving, and I needed my purse."

They silently watched as she found her bag on the sofa, and hurried out of the apartment, high heels clicking as she walked away.

"We can't go back," Sanh said softly. "You can't make this better, at least not right now."

"I can. You just won't let me."

"It's too late. I told you, the best thing you can do is to leave us alone."

Sanh left Lum in the kitchen. His mother was waiting for him in the living room, a grave look on her face. Sanh hadn't heard her coming in. Had she passed Madame Bourdain? Had the nosy woman warned his mother?

"He is not a monster," Hoa said, following Sanh out the door. "He is your son."

"Cherry could have died," Sanh quietly reminded her. They descended a flight of stairs to the middle floor, and he opened the door to his parents' apartment.

"But she didn't," Hoa said. "I know my grandson. He will never let anything like that happen again."

"You weren't there," he said, walking toward the closet. "You don't know."

"You have always been hard on him," Hoa said, as he dug out his coat. "This is not how you treat your child."

"I'm trying to protect my children," he said, slipping his arms into the jacket. The sleeves felt too loose. Inhaling sharply, he realized he'd grabbed Lum's by mistake. He quickly shrugged it off.

"Where are you going?" she asked, when he finally buttoned his own coat.

"I need to walk," Sanh said.

As he opened the front door, his mother reached for his other hand. Sanh paused. "You don't have to be like him," she said. "Your father could never forgive, but you are better than him. I have faith in you."

Sanh didn't respond. As he descended the last set of stairs, Sanh noticed the door to the ground apartment had closed. He imagined his brothers and their families inside, relieved from all the guests, yet still grieving the loss of their father, taking comfort in each other. Sanh unlatched the front door and stepped outside.

The spring air felt cool, soothing on his face. He breathed deeply, allowing the air to fill his lungs, relieving the tightness in his chest. For a Sunday afternoon, the neighborhood felt unusually quiet, which Sanh welcomed. He didn't know where to begin walking, but it didn't matter. The freedom to turn any corner, cross any street, felt invigorating. Sanh loosened his tie, a pale yellow tie which all the men had donned for the funeral. It was a Truong tradition.

He found himself in an open-air market. At one stall, a mother and daughter sold large bouquets of lilies and tulips in shades of pink, violet, and white. He found an empty bench and sat, watching as the mother and daughter smiled and chatted with patrons. The two women shared more than the same hair color and cheekbones. Their facial expressions and body language mirrored each other so harmoniously; coexisting in elegant synchronization.

What would have happened if they'd moved to France all those years ago? Would Tuyet, Lum, and Cherry be sitting in the house with the rest of the Truongs, healthier, happier, safer? Sanh had promised to do better for his children. Yet, Lum's life was in shambles, and even Cherry, with her AP classes and college potential, seemed lost and unhappy. Despite all their intentions and efforts, Sanh and Tuyet had failed their children. He couldn't really blame Tuyet: her father had died when she was young, and her mother was a monster. And though Hung had been a difficult father, at least Sanh had his mother.

Hoa. Beloved, nurturing, long-suffering. And naïve. A mother during wartime, she only knew how to protect and forgive. Sanh didn't know how to explain to his mother that raising children in peacetime possessed its own difficulties, ones no one could have adequately prepared him for.

Despite their argument this afternoon, Sanh could recognize that Lum was already changing. His posture was no longer haughty and defensive. He listened when his father spoke. When Lum's addiction was at its worst, no one could reach him. But today, Sanh realized his words held influence over his son. They finally mattered.

Between the flowers, a man with a yellow tie walked away. Sanh sat up. For a moment, he wondered if his son was near. Perhaps Lum had decided on a walk as well, to clear his head. Maybe he was sitting in a park, or strolling through one of the public gardens in the neighborhood, or even walking through this market. Sanh could find him. He could then explain to Lum, outside of the claustrophobic confines of the Truong house, that just because he couldn't come home yet didn't mean his family had deserted him. It was just too soon. If Lum came home now, his opportunity to change, to improve, would disappear. He needed distance and time away from the evidence of his temptations and failures. Returning now would endanger any of the progress that two weeks had already yielded. Sanh loved him too much to let that happen.

Of course, hearing this would be difficult, but Sanh would find the right words to persuade Lum. He had to. If Sanh was ever going to be a true father to Lum, they'd have to make this sacrifice together. This was not a punishment. This was their redemption.

1984

Kim-Ly Vo
Galang Island, Indonesia

Wonderful news. The paperwork has been approved by immigration services. In a month, you will be joining us here in sunny, beautiful California!

We cannot wait for your arrival. The children are excited to finally meet their cousins, aunts, uncles, and especially you, their grandmother. You will see much of my beloved father in Lum. And I look forward to your help in raising Cherry. She needs you, most of all.

Next week, we are moving into a house to prepare for your arrival. It was a bank foreclosure—a very good deal. We will be within walking distance of Vietnamese grocery stores, and pho *and* banh cuon *restaurants. It will be like Saigon before the war. I think you will find it better than Saigon ever was.*

Our years of suffering are soon coming to an end. They have taught me a valuable lesson: families are not supposed to be separated. While our circumstances were dictated by war, we are free to do as we choose in America. Our family shall never be apart again.

Tuyet Truong
Westminster, California, USA

⚬ Chapter Twelve

CHERRY

SAIGON, 2002

THE BABY LOOKS LIKE GRANDPÈRE. WHICH MEANS HE resembles Lum, but given the arched hairline, the scrutinizing, alert eyes, the way he already grabs fistfuls of anything within his reach, Cherry can only see her grandfather. Frequently, obsessively, she reaches over to pinch Anh's chubby feet. His reaction is delightfully predictable: a squeal, a gummy grin, a frenzy of leg pumps. Anh is wily, even at seven months. Though he cannot yet crawl, he wriggles and twists in Cam's embrace, determined to see and touch what he pleases, a trait, her cousin Xuan predicts, clearly inherited from the Truong family.

"He's doomed," Xuan says, a ghost of a smile on his face. "He'll never be satisfied with anything in life."

Lying back on the floor, Cherry realizes that her cousins liked being in the old house. They want to say good-bye. She lifts her head to find Xuan still tracing his eyes over the ceiling. Cam and Anh's cooing echoes off the bare walls and floors. Cherry attempts to follow Xuan's gaze, wondering what he is seeing, imagining. When nothing comes to her, her eyes wander back to her cousin's face, which is growing more and more into Uncle Yen's—noble, aloof, even unfriendly when he isn't smiling. And while Cam has evolved into an attractive blend of her parents, her breezy gestures and mannerisms all point to her mother. Cherry wonders who she reminds people of. It disconcerts her, how their looks, even their words, can seem merely reminders of their parents. She already hates that her voice can reach the breathless frenzy of her mother's animated demeanor.

Her cousins brought a package from Grandmère when they arrived in Saigon. That evening, Cherry opened the box to find a lavender-and-cream crocheted blanket and a rubber-banded pack of letters. Grandmère had attached a note, explaining that the letters once belonged to Grandpère, and that they had been returned from the mistress's family after Ba Cuc's death. Grandmère didn't want them—hadn't even looked at them—but perhaps Cherry did. Stunned, Cherry folded up the note, replaced the rubber band, and buried the letters at the bottom of her bag.

A sticky hand clamps down on her shoulder. Anh beams at her, softly patting her face, and the letters, the expensive airfare, and marathon flight feel far away. She isn't sure how it is possible for one tiny person to fill her with such calm and happiness. She doesn't ever remember feeling such peace, and it makes her dread the day when she must fly back to California. Just one week before her medical school orientation.

Xuan and Cam scheduled their trip with Cherry's return departure in mind. Upon hearing that the Trans planned to sell the Truongs' old house, Xuan and Cam knew this was their last chance to visit their childhood home. After a week in the city, they planned to travel through central and northern Vietnam until reaching Hai Phong, the hometown of Grandmère's ancestors. They wanted Cherry to come with them. Lum agreed before Cherry had a chance to decline.

"As much as I know you enjoy watching Anh sleep, eat, and spit up all day," Lum said, "you're still young. You need to get out of this house."

Lum and Tham's choice for the baby's given name came from the

Trans, whose first son was named Anh. For a middle name, they chose Hung to honor Grandpère, but Cherry's parents still grumbled over the choice. They raised Lum for over twenty years. Why weren't they consulted beforehand? Despite this show of disrespect, Cherry's parents sent over six care packages of diapers, baby bottles, and swaddling blankets. They want to visit, but have to wait until their father retires from the plant in November.

"Maybe I'll move back," Xuan murmurs, breaking the silence. His cousins look over at him, skeptically. "Lum did it; why can't I? They could probably use another engineer."

"You're not leaving me," Cam says, as Anh lunges over to rake his chubby fingers across the floor.

"Then come, too," Xuan suggests.

Cherry shares a raised eyebrow with Cam. Her cousin shakes her head. "He's in mourning. His boyfriend broke up with him and now he thinks he needs a continent between them."

"This has nothing to do with Stephan," Xuan says.

"He was married," Cam reminds him. "He was never going to leave his wife and family for you."

Xuan catches Cherry's eyes widening. "They're separated," he explains. "She lives in Madrid."

"I'm glad he dumped you," Cam says. "You never would have ended it. But that's another Truong flaw. We love the wrong people and everyone suffers."

"I haven't," Cherry admitted.

"You're protecting your heart," Cam says, patting her head. "That's a good thing."

"Not always," Xuan says.

"Show me the evidence, Monsieur Truong," Cam says. "My relationships, yours, they've all combusted."

"Two examples! What about Lum and Tham?"

"They're not married yet."

"You're a pessimist."

"Our family should go back to arranged marriages."

"Those don't work out, either," Xuan says.

"Grandpère married the right woman," Cam says. "It's the wrong one who caused so much pain."

"It's not Ba Cuc's fault," he says.

"Don't defend her," Cam says, sounding annoyed. "Grandmère raised you, too."

Xuan turns over on his stomach to look at Cherry. "You knew, right?"

"Yes," Cherry admits. "I wasn't sure you did."

"We all suspected," Cam says, "but then the woman's family had to come over to our house after she died, bringing back all of this stuff he'd given to her. It was awful."

"Grandmère couldn't get out of bed for a week," Xuan says. "It was like Grandpère dying all over again."

"I didn't know that," Cherry says sadly.

Cherry turns over to stand, while her cousins talk. She reaches into her messenger bag, pretending to look for her phone, but digs deeper until her hands feel the bundles of letters at the bottom. Her head tilts back to look at her cousins, engrossed in a peek-a-boo game with Anh, their gestures in complete sync. Her cousins' closeness continues to amaze her, more like siblings than she and Lum ever were. When they talk, they unwittingly blend their Vietnamese with French, speaking so quickly, that Cherry cannot always keep up. Cherry's fingers tighten over the envelopes, listening to their chatter, as she debates, considers.

"I think I hear Lum's truck," Xuan says.

Her hands still clutching her bag, Cherry walks to the window. Indeed, Lum is double-parked in front of the house. He stands in front of it, cupping his hands over his eyes to shield them from the sun. She smiles, reaching out one hand to press against the recently washed window, unreasonably happy to see him.

NEWPORT LAKE, 2001

She lasted three months during her first trip to Vietnam before her parents' guilt-laden phone calls brought her back to California. Cherry knew they wouldn't forgive her if she missed Christmas with them. Her father cried at the airport gate when he saw her. Her mother made obvious efforts to keep her happy: cooking her favorite dishes, letting her sleep in as long as she wanted. But her mother was unaccustomed to her being home all the time, not at school or volunteering—a lazy Cherry, someone who read magazines in the living room when Tuyet wanted to watch television, or finished the last of the tangerines without replacing them. Tuyet kept asking if Cherry wanted to drive to UC Irvine or try to speak with someone at the medical school.

"It's too late," Cherry said. "I've already deferred."

"But you've always been good about catching up with schoolwork. Remember after the accident?"

"I don't want to catch up," she said. "I'm fine with the year off."

Her mother didn't believe her. When the salon's receptionist quit on short notice, Cherry took over daily duties at the front desk. Her mother loudly declared to her sisters that it was only temporary, until Cherry found an internship at a health clinic or lab.

"We didn't invest four years of college for you to answer phones," Tuyet said. When she wasn't pestering Cherry about medical school, her mother wanted to know all about Lum's fiancée: her family, education, work prospects, whether she was tricking Lum to try to get to America. "But if that brings him back to us, fine," she said, while they cleaned out expired cosmetic products at the salon. "They can divorce after a few years and she will have a visa. And we will have our son."

"They're having a baby," Cherry said, pulling out another tray of half-empty nail polish bottles to dust.

Her mother winced, still adjusting to the news of becoming a grandmother, though she had had weeks to process the information. "Times are different," she said. "If they are not happy in a marriage, why should they stay together?"

"Why are you and Dad still together?" Cherry asked.

"Don't be crass," she said, picking up each bottle to clean individually.

"Then why did you say you regretted marrying him?"

"I never said that!" her mother cried. "Daddy and I are happy. Is this why you left? Because Daddy and I were arguing?"

"No."

"Then what is it?" she asked, her eyes so intent that Cherry instinctively leaned back. "You can tell me."

But when Cherry opened her mouth, no words emerged. Not yet. The days she spent at home watching her parents' quiet routine of meals, television, and early bedtime, reminded Cherry why they kept quiet for so long, how increasingly necessary these silences had become. Her father's forgetfulness had worsened in the months she'd been away. He was working shorter days at the plant and spoke often of accepting the early retirement package his boss had offered. Her mother had quietly taken over most of the household duties, but said nothing to Cherry about it. Another topic they couldn't discuss. Her father's remaining household chore was the gardening, which he took pleasure in, spending long hours in the backyard tending his rosebushes.

Cherry's mother finally managed to announce Lum's news to the relatives, though with some creative editing: she claimed that Lum and Tham had already married, and were so in love and eager to start a family that they already had plans to conceive a child. (*Just let me do it this way*, Cherry's mother had said after catching her disapproving frown. *I know what I'm doing. What harm can come? They're in Vietnam.*)

The relatives dutifully exclaimed their happiness at the news, and in her benevolence, Cherry's mother decided to throw a California reception for the newlyweds. So what if the guests of honor couldn't attend? Or didn't even know about it? Their parents could collect the gifts for them. And they would need the wedding money to help with the baby.

Their mother put down a deposit at a Chinese seafood banquet hall in Garden Grove. Since she didn't have a wedding picture, she improvised with a candid shot from Cherry's trip, taken during a walk along the Saigon River. Her mother asked the clerk at the photo shop to blow up the picture, airbrush the smog from the boats, and crop out Tham's belly. After enlarging the picture to near life size, she bought a bright-gold picture frame. The picture sat on their dining room table for a week before the reception, so Cherry would occasionally startle when passing it.

Though their mother wanted to invite more people, hoping to beat Dat and Quynh's 300-plus reception attendance, their father held firm that the guest list stay under 200. Cherry's mother requested she wear her red *ao dai* at the reception, along with Duyen and Linh, as if they were bridesmaids just arriving from the imaginary ceremony. Her mother grew obstinate over the smallest details—fighting with the banquet manager over the appetizer choices and refining the song list with the band daily. Her moods worsened as the reception neared.

"Just humor Mommy," Cherry's father pleaded the morning of the reception, after her mother barked for her to call the florist again. "She will be better after this day is over."

Bold red tablecloths and matching roses decorated each table of the ballroom. The Vietnamese variety band that had played for Quynh and Dat's wedding—the one Cherry's mother believed was exceptionally talented, and worth the inflated fee—had already set up their instruments on the stage and were performing a microphone check.

Since only Cherry had ever met the lovely bride, the guests congratulated her and expected her to intuit her new sister-in-law's thoughts about the marriage. Of course, Tham was thrilled. She loves Lum very much. She is eager to meet the rest of the relatives. Oh yes, she cannot wait to start a family. Hopefully it will happen soon!

Cherry's smile endured until dinner. She sat at the honored table next to Grandmother Vo, who wore her blue velvet *ao dai*. Dat and Quynh arrived late, during the shark fin soup appetizer, weaving through the tables to find their places. Quynh had also dressed in a red *ao dai*. Cherry hadn't seen them since leaving the country before their wedding.

After dinner, the banquet hall's floor manager projected a slideshow onto the wall above the buffet tables. Cherry's mother coordinated pictures of Lum growing up to his favorite Vietnamese music, three old love songs, played on a loop. Some of the pictures Cherry barely recognized, the sepia-toned photographs taken when their family lived in Vietnam and Malaysia. Tham only showed up in the last few frames, all pictures Cherry had taken in Vietnam. When the lights turned back on, Cherry noticed her mother grasping her father's hand on top of the table, tears shining in both of their eyes.

The MC and band returned to the stage, entreating guests to join them on the dance floor. Linh dragged Huy to dance. She believed her longtime boyfriend planned to propose soon. Duyen danced with one of Dat's colleagues, a pediatrics medical resident. Cherry sat at the table with her parents and grandmother, continuing to greet and accept gifts from people she'd never met. With the lights dimmed and while no one was looking, Cherry unfastened the top two side snaps of her constrictive *ao dai*, indulging in the luxury of breathing after so many hours.

Dat finally found Cherry in the hallway, stepping from behind a ficus plant and surprising her as she came out of the restroom.

"So, how is Lum?"

"Jesus," Cherry said, putting a hand on her chest. "He's fine."

She and her cousin silently watched as guests took calls on their cell phones or passed them to reach the restrooms.

"It all worked out, didn't it?" Dat asked. "Quynh and myself, and now Lum and . . ."

"Tham," Cherry said, rolling her eyes.

"Right. We've all been through so much, but we survived. We prevailed."

"Yes," Cherry said, nodding. "Especially with the family sending Lum off. That worked out perfectly for you."

Dat snorted. "When are you going to let it go? There's a reason some of us succeeded here, and others didn't. Maybe Lum never should have left Vietnam in the first place. Maybe he's where he belongs."

"Well, then I hope we all get what we deserve," Cherry said. "Especially you."

"We've all gotten over it," Dat said, tilting his head. "Except you. You're the only one. If you think you need to talk to a professional, I could help you find someone reputable."

His face was serious. Before she could respond, a tipsy Duyen wandered over, her head bopping to the samba music, pulling Cherry away to complain about the pediatric resident's body odor. Once they returned to the table, Cherry spied Dat whispering something into Quynh's ear, and the couple quietly left during her mother's final toast of the evening.

After the guests had departed, the rest of their relatives packed the minivan with leftover floral centerpieces, food trays, and the wedding presents, though most guests had observed custom and simply left money envelopes for the newlyweds. At home, Cherry's mother displayed the roses on every available counter and tabletop space available. Cherry knew in a few days they'd start to wilt and darken, and that her mother would wait until the last possible moment to trash them. She missed having flowers in the house. While her father went to bed, exhausted from the day's events, her mother stayed in the living room to organize the presents. Around two in the morning, Cherry noticed the lights were still on from under her bedroom door. She wandered out of her room and found her mother sitting on the living room floor, still in her lilac *ao dai*, reading each wedding card and filing every check and cash gift into a manila folder. Early the next morning, her mother left for the bank to deposit the money into a savings account she'd opened under Lum's name.

A week after the reception, Grandmother Vo called. Unfortunately, Cherry picked up.

"Come over," she said. "I need help with my closets."

"I'm busy," Cherry said. Just because she was unemployed and not in school, her grandmother thought she had nothing better to do. This afternoon she and Duyen planned to go to the beach.

"Your mother just told me you were watching television," Grandmother said. "And bring over some *banh cuon* from that deli on Magnolia. I'm hungry."

Though her closets really did need a thorough cleanout, Cherry suspected she also felt lonely. Without anywhere to go during the day, Grandmother wore a long-sleeved oatmeal blouse and simple black pants. She didn't bother tying up her hair, and her thin gray mane hung past her knees. Since Ba Nhanh's stroke, she no longer spent much time with the twins; most of her days consisted of television and nagging telephone calls to her children. She didn't like sitting at the salon because she tired easily and had no convenient place to nap. But she did miss talking to people, talking at people.

After she finished her lunch, though Cherry was still eating hers, Grandmother seized her opportunity. "Your mother is concerned about you."

Cherry swallowed her bite of food and looked at her grandmother with dread.

"We thought you'd be different," she continued. "You finally had everything: brains, looks, an education—and what do you do? You run away like your brother. Very disappointing."

Cherry lowered her chopsticks. "Lum didn't run away."

"Then where is he?" Grandmother asked. "Not one phone call to his grandmother on her birthday or for Tet celebration. He's become as disrespectful as your mother."

"Why would he want to talk to you?"

Grandmother smiled rarely, so it startled Cherry to see her lacquered teeth. "You think you're so smart. I try to help my grandchildren, and somehow, I am the villain. Why are you blaming your cousin? You know better than that. He may be smart at medicine, but didn't this show us how inept he is at deception?"

Even in screwing up their lives, Dat somehow managed to look good.

"You should have stayed out of it, too," Cherry said. "It's because of you that Thinh came after us. You ruined his family." As soon as the words left her lips, Cherry felt breathless, bracing for Grandmother Vo's reaction. But what could Grandmother do? Tell on her? Let her explain to her mother.

"So melodramatic," Grandmother sneered. "Is it my fault his father couldn't manage a business? Is it my fault that boy overreacted?"

"He took revenge on your grandchildren," Cherry said. "You can't deny that."

"It was unfortunate," Grandmother admitted, her face softening. "But I've taken responsibility. Who took care of Lum's debts? Who paid the deductibles for your hospital bills and physical therapy? You think I don't care, but I have always provided for you."

"And Lum? Did you provide for him?"

"What did he lose?" Grandmother asked. "He has a wife and a career now, two things he could never achieve with gambling." She smirked at

Cherry's look of disbelief. "Why are we talking about him? The only person I am concerned with now is you. I thought you'd recovered from your accident, that it hadn't affected your brains, but maybe not."

"Don't worry about me, Grandma," Cherry said.

"I worry," she said, shaking her head. "You think acting out like Lum is going to make your mother love you more? It's not."

"What?" Cherry cried. "That's crazy."

"It is crazy," Grandmother agreed, nodding adamantly. "But you see, you couldn't even rebel with any sense of conviction. Back here within months. It makes you look insincere."

"That's not why I left," Cherry said.

"Are you sure?" Grandmother asked. "You've done everything you can to be an obedient daughter to your mother. Best grades, best behavior. Yet, she devoted all her love to the boy who only gave his family grief. Why shouldn't you try and see if acting badly could work for you?"

"My mother loves both of us," she said. "She's not like you."

Grandmother laughed. "That is a child's perspective. Some day, Cherry, when you are a mother, you will realize. Motherhood does not turn you into some benevolent goddess. We have the same flaws we were born with. The difference between your mother and me? At least I can admit my faults."

Grandmother had tired of talking. She needed a nap. While she snoozed on Uncle Bao's recliner in the living room, Cherry approached the task of her closet. After three hours of sorting through yards of untouched mothball-pungent *ao dais* and fabric, Cherry found three thick wads of letters buried deep in one of her trunks, underneath a pile of decade-old Vietnamese newspapers. They were all from Cherry's mother, written to her grandmother when she was still in Vietnam and the refugee camp, sealed shut, never opened. She didn't know if Grandmother Vo had any idea these letters still existed—she had instructed Cherry to throw away any contents she couldn't sell to the consignment shop. So Cherry stuffed the letters in her tote bag, making sure to dust and polish the trunk before Grandmother woke up and walked into her bedroom to check on her progress.

After leaving Grandmother's, Cherry drove to a tree-shaded spot in the nearby park and rolled down her window. After gently unsealing the earliest postmarked envelope, she unfolded the aged letter. For the next hour, she did this for every envelope; unfolding, reading, rereading, refolding, until they once again sat in collated piles in the passenger seat, as if no one had ever read them. But she had. She had read, effectively memorized, every letter.

Although Cherry recognized her mother's controlled, precise language, she did not sound like herself. Instead, she came off simpering, self-pitying, phony. The first batch of letters chronicled her years in the refugee camps, her complaints of the living quarters, the food, her in-laws, her husband. The first mention of Cherry came in the form of a sick stomach and burdensome fatigue, and Tuyet's dread of a possible pregnancy. The second and third batches of letters were from America. The contents were not surprising. She tried to remind herself of this. Still.

Cherry supposed her mother was being completely honest. The papers felt flimsy, crushable, between Cherry's fingers. She could easily crumple up her mother's unfair opinions, these impossible expectations. Looking at the dates of the letters, Cherry couldn't have been more than two or three years old, barely speaking age, yet her mother already expressed how Cherry disappointed her, how she aggravated her.

A good daughter would return these letters to her mother, but then again her mother probably would have been angry with Cherry for taking them. And Cherry wanted to keep them. After digesting these words—feeling how they scratched at her pride, her heart—Cherry realized that they no longer belonged to her mother.

Cherry pulled up in the driveway of her parents' house and sat there for several minutes, the engine still running. Her father finally came out the front door, waved, and went back inside. Cherry stashed the bundle of letters under her seat, making sure to lock all the doors.

Her parents sat in the dining room, balancing their checkbook, the bills and checks spread across the table. This ritual occurred every month, on one of the rare afternoons her parents were both at home. Cherry had many memories of walking in on her parents arguing over one of her mother's impulsive Nordstrom purchases or the insufficiency of her father's paycheck. Most of the time, Cherry would walk straight past the dining room to reach the stairs for her bedroom, but this afternoon, she stood in front of the table of bills, waiting for her mother to look up.

"How was Grandmother?" her mother asked, tearing open one of the envelopes with her index nail.

"She's fine," Cherry said. "Her closets were a mess."

Her mother finally glanced up, her eyes impatient, shameless. "That's it?" she asked.

"What else?"

"Don't play coy," she said, pushing back her hair, recently trimmed and colored by Auntie Tri. "Since you won't listen to your own parents, we were hoping she'd talk some sense into you."

"I guess I'm more difficult than you thought."

"Cherry," her father said, a warning in his voice.

"What was she supposed to convince me about?" Cherry asked, her gaze on her mother unflinching. "That wasn't clear."

"We want you to stop wasting your life," her mother said. "You spend every day watching TV or going to the beach with your cousins. Do you think your father and I are going to support you forever?"

"I said I was going back to school next year."

"Why should we believe you? I've seen this happen to my clients' children. We are trying to protect you—"

"Right," Cherry said, laughing.

Her mother's eyes flashed, her chin rising, and Cherry fell silent. She knew what the look meant.

"There is nothing worse," her mother said, her voice still calm, but tightly controlled, "than carrying regret. It weighs on you for a very long time."

"What do you regret?" Cherry asked. "What did you do that makes you hate your life so much?"

"I don't hate my life."

"You're lying." Cherry stomped her sandaled foot on the tiled floor, the clack echoing throughout the house. She didn't care if she looked like a petulant child. "I know you," she continued, her voice trembling.

She needed to sound strong at this moment. She needed to believe in her words. "I know how you really feel."

"Cherry!" her father cried, standing between the two women, even though her mother still sat at the table. Perhaps it was enough that he blocked their view of each other. "What is the matter with you? Your mother and I are concerned. You've been so depressed."

"I will not feel sorry for her anymore," Cherry's mother seethed, wiping tears from her eyes. "She has had every opportunity a child could want. I never imagined she could turn out to be so selfish and spoiled—"

"Maybe you should have sent me away instead," Cherry said.

"I knew she would be like this," her mother said, looking at Sanh. "Just like your father! He never cared who he hurt, and neither does she."

"Stop blaming them," Cherry said. "It's always someone else's fault, isn't it? It's never you. You never do anything wrong."

"Please," her father said. "You are both emotional right now—"

"I want to go back to Vietnam," Cherry whispered.

"Oh, God," her mother sounded like she was both laughing and moaning. "Well, if that's what you want, then go. You always get what you want, eventually. I'm tired of fighting you."

"Go upstairs," her father said to Cherry.

Cherry looked over at her father for the first time that afternoon. He'd taken off his reading glasses. His hair, gray at the temples for so many years, now appeared whiter than she remembered. In his hands, he had shredded a bill envelope into slivers of paper. His exhausted, red-rimmed eyes pleaded with her.

Imagining the letters still in her car, realizing what she knew that they didn't know, Cherry turned and walked upstairs.

SAIGON, 2002

In the cavernous new house, the Trans' furniture looks outdated and small. While Cam and Cherry unpack boxes around Anh's crib—another gift from the absentee grandparents—Tham and Grandaunt Tran compile a list of fabrics and shades for dressing the windows and open doorways. Lum screws lightbulbs into the fixtures and the chandelier in the atrium. Xuan and Granduncle hold the ladder.

To celebrate, Lum takes them out for a seafood dinner in the Cholon district, a restaurant he regularly frequents with his foreign clients. The server shows them to a spacious round table on the second floor beneath several ceiling fans.

Lum insists that everyone order a dish. Steamed whole catfish, giant crab legs, black bean clams, salt and pepper prawns, deep fried tofu squares, corn and coconut fritters, fragrant gingered bok choy, and garlic broccoli overfill the table until they have enough food for a party twice their size. They maneuver teacups and plates to keep dishes from falling. Tham mashes chunks of catfish into broth and rice with her chopsticks and patiently feeds it to Anh. Cherry eats more than she has in days.

After dinner, they walk to the nearby outdoor market so Grandaunt can pick up fresh vegetables for lunch and dinner tomorrow. While the rest of the family filters through the market, Lum and Cherry take Anh to a mango cart near the west entrance. Despite the gorging, Lum still needs dessert. Anh grabs a piece of fresh mango from his father's fingers, and Lum allows him a nibble. The air feels tight and smoky around them, the sky swirling sherbet pollution clouds. Across the street, a group of school children practices a marching routine. They wear identical haircuts and outfits, and Cherry can easily imagine Anh one day chanting and strutting with them.

On her first night back in Saigon, Cherry had shown her brother pictures of his California wedding reception, unsure if Tham should see them, if she would be offended. As he flipped through the photos, laughing, he called for Tham to come into the room, and they giggled at all the flowers and decorations for their make-believe wedding.

Cherry pulled the pictures away after Lum started mocking the MC's bouffant hair. "Mom worked really hard on this reception," she said, holding the photographs to her chest.

Lum's forehead creased, his smile fading. "I know that. I'm not laughing at her."

He tried to make up for it, complimenting the cake and exclaiming that he couldn't wait to read the cards from all the guests. But it was too late. He probably thought she was overreacting, and perhaps she was; this was exactly the sort of thing they would have laughed about before.

After they find some plastic chairs under a shaded tree on the outskirts of the market, Cherry pulls out two letters and places them on the table. Lum settles Anh into his lap and then lifts up one of the letters.

"Haven't we moved on to e-mails?" he asks.

"They're not from me."

He opens the first one, reads a few lines and puts it down. He glances at the other letter and sets it aside as well.

"Where did you get these?" he asks.

"Grandmère gave me Grandpère's letters," Cherry says.

"And what about Mom's?"

"I found hers in Grandmother Vo's closet a few months ago. A whole box of them. She was going to throw them away."

"So that's what made you think you could take them?"

"Yes," Cherry says, sitting back, frowning. "I thought you'd be happy to see them."

Lum shakes his head. The look on his face is strange. "Why?"

"Excuse me?"

"Why are you walking around Saigon, in ninety-degree weather, carrying pounds of letters that don't belong to you?"

Cherry stares at him. "You're mad?"

"This isn't like you," he says, shifting Anh to his other knee.

"How would you know?" she asks. "Maybe this is me. Maybe, unlike the rest of you, I want to understand."

"Understand what?"

"Why we keep hurting each other. Why none of us can stop."

"Do you really think you can learn that through some old letters?"

She thinks of her afternoon conversation with Xuan and Cam, and wonders if Lum knew, wondering if he should know. "They're all I have," she says.

Baby Anh snatches the ripe fruit, delightedly squishing the mango in his fist, the bright pulpy juices dribbling between his fingers. Lum reaches over to dab them with a paper napkin.

"That's not true," Lum murmured, looking up at Cherry. "You have me."

Later that night, while everyone else is ready to sleep, exhausted from the day's events, Anh will not cooperate. Perhaps unsettled by the central air-conditioning from his new home, he wails in his crib. Tham tries everything. She nurses him, rocks him, coos songs to him. Finally, Lum offers to take the baby on a stroll around the block. Cherry, still writing postcards in the living room of boxes, offers to walk with them. They pull out the bassinet stroller their parents sent, too bulky to use in most of the city streets, but a perfect fit in this new neighborhood.

Though they are the only occupants on the block, the gaslight streetlamps cast a warm glow on the sidewalk and fresh asphalt—so much energy burning for only one house. If it weren't for the humidity, Cherry could easily imagine herself in Orange County. She watches the long shadows they create, and attempts to step on her own. Lum adjusts the shade of the bassinet several times, attempting to find the angle that will lull Anh to sleep, but it is useless: the little boy chatters softly, enjoying his midnight ride.

"He really does look like Grandpère," Cherry says.

"Maybe," Lum says, pulling the shade down. "You know the last time I saw Grandpère, he thought I was Dad?"

"Really?"

"He yelled at me," Lum says. "That's when I realized he thought I was someone else. He asked me if I was still married to that bitch of a woman. Grandmère had to lock him in his room. She asked me not to say anything."

Cherry peers up at her brother. "That's your last memory of him?"

"I know. But at least he couldn't remember it, right? A few hours later, he let me take him out for a walk in the gardens."

"But we're not sure," Cherry points out. "We'd like to think all he remembers are happy and pretty things, but we don't know."

"I'd like to think he had some peace," Lum says.

"Do you think it's better that way?" Cherry asks. "Having the worst memories erased? Or would you want to know all of it?"

"I don't know," Lum admits. "I think you have to make sense of whatever you have."

Cherry gazes at her nephew's small, still feet. He is finally asleep. They have reached Lum's house, but instead of strolling up the walkway, they make another loop around the block.

"I've been thinking," Lum says, his voice slow and thoughtful, "Mom wrote that letter a long time ago, before she even knew who you were going to be."

She inhales a breath of hot air. "But what if she was right?"

Once again, her mother's letters creep inside her skin, the angriest, most frustrated passages wrapping around her chest; her mother fancifully imagining a family of three, a more manageable number to care for, only one child to support—one dutiful, filial son. It was enough. It was all she wanted. And then this other child had to come along and ruin everything. If Cherry hadn't been born, things could have been different. Once her mother introduced this possibility, even in decades-old letters, Cherry imagines fulfilling her mother's wish—of disappearing, of never existing.

"She was just a scared girl back then," Lum says. "My age. She was only trying to get her mother to forgive her."

"You only read one letter," she says. "I've read all of them."

"And how do you feel?" he asks. "Is it enough? Do you feel like you know her now?"

"No," she admits, and merely uttering it, admitting it, feels both painful and exhilarating.

"See? It doesn't matter. The things our family did to each other, what we did to each other, they don't make up who you are. Our mistakes don't dictate our lives."

She looks up to the sky. "Is that why you stayed away?"

"I don't know. It was nice to only think of myself for a while, to learn who I was away from them. Maybe you don't need to move to Vietnam, but you can move on."

"I'm trying."

They leisurely round another block, listening for some time only to their footsteps. Cherry feels like she can walk this cul-de-sac for hours and never grow tired.

"She's been calling me," Lum finally says, "ever since you arrived. She asks about the baby, but really, she wants to know about you. She wants me to tell her you're coming back."

"Of course," Cherry says. "I'm all she has left."

Lum sighs. "She told me about Dad. He refuses to see a doctor. He thinks his memory is just fine."

Cherry's hand reaches for the stroller bar to balance herself. She thinks about their father, how he wept while dropping her off at the airport this last time. She'd never seen him cry more than in this past year.

"He's been talking to me, too," Lum says. "More than he ever had before. He keeps asking when I'm coming back to visit, so I said maybe over Christmas."

Was that what it took? The possibility of their father forgetting their inconvenient past? She doesn't know what to say. It is everything she has wanted and not wanted, all at once. The grief cancels out the joy cancels out the anger, so she cannot feel anything.

Cherry glances over her shoulder. The house is dark. They are still alone. "Tell me a story," she says.

"What do you want to know?"

She considers this her opportunity, and she is no longer timid.

"The afternoon at the Tet Festival," she says, "what you saw."

"Cherry . . ."

"Tell me," she says again. "I need to know how you felt. I promise that by tomorrow, I'll forget."

Lum hesitates, looking around him, even though it is the dead of night. No one else can hear him except her. Looking again at Anh, assured his son is asleep, Lum turns to his sister. Cherry feels her ears, mind, heart opening. He tells her.

HA LONG BAY, 2002

Minh Quang, the fishing junk they rented for the day tour through the caves, is large, with cabin seating for at least twenty passengers. Yet, they are only three. The family of crew members (two brothers, their wives, and four children) outnumber Cherry and her cousins. Once the junk pushes off from the dock, Xuan and Cam strip down to their swimsuits to sunbathe.

"Get out here," Cam barks from behind her sunglasses. "It's better if you lie down."

"Or I can wait for the Dramamine to kick in," Cherry says from the safety of the cabin.

"What kind of Vietnamese are you?" Xuan mocks. "It's a good thing you were born in America. You never would have survived the ride out."

Cherry checks her watch and realizes they still have nine hours before returning to land. The nausea weighs like a cloud in her chest and abdomen. She lies out on a row of seats, using her messenger bag as a pillow, listening to the chug chug of the boat engine. Cherry wishes her brother could have come with them, but there was no way he could leave Tham alone with the baby, even with the Trans' help.

Small fingers tickle through her hair. Cherry turns and one of the children, the youngest girl, smiles at her, a dimple in her left cheek. The other kids stand behind her. When Cherry sits up, the older boy points to her bag, which she obligingly opens. They touch everything, her digital camera, her Dramamine, her journal, her purple leather wallet. Cherry asks them to be gentle with the bundles of letters. She lets them take pictures of each other with the camera and promises to mail them copies. Eventually, one of their mothers yells for the children to leave their customer alone.

The boat captain hollers that they are approaching the first isle of limestone caves. The morning fog has melted off, unveiling more fishing junks around them. Cherry steps out on the deck to join her cousins, who are waving at the tourists and locals passing by. The breeze feels soft and cool. One boat is full of fraternity boys who whistle at Cam, beckoning her to come on board. She shakes her head no, then flashes them.

Once the boat anchors, Cherry eagerly steps off to join the queue leading into the caves. Inside, she and her cousins shuffle through the line, gazing at the stalagmites and stalactites and the gaudy Christmas lights draped around them. The caves must have been beautiful once—they probably still are—but the rainbow neon lights and fake water fountains remind Cherry of a bad Vietnamese pop-music video. Empty beer bottles and stray trash litter the partitioned walkway and the corners of the caves.

When the second isle offers more of the same, they request that the captain scrap the caves for the rest of the day. The captain suggests taking them to a secluded bay that none of the other junks know about for kayaking and swimming. They stop at a floating fishing village, where the wives pick up some of the most colorful fish Cherry has ever seen to cook for lunch.

As promised, the captain takes them to an empty bay of lushly forested islands and islets surrounded and shaded by larger karsts. Some of the faraway limestone islets look like giant sea turtles bubbling to the water's surface, while others resemble stony skyscrapers. Cam and Xuan race each other to the closest isle, diving off the junk without hesitation. After pulling off her tank top and shorts, Cherry stands at the edge of the boat. She stares into the water, remembering all the gasoline and refuse floating in the harbor. The first time she tried swimming in the ocean was when her parents took them to Mexico for a vacation. While the rest of her family swam through the waves, she was repulsed at how the saltwater burned at her eyes and nostrils. For the rest of the afternoon, she sat on the shoreline, waiting for her parents and Lum to return. But that was many years ago. Behind her, she can hear the children laughing. Instead of looking, Cherry closes her eyes, bends her knees and jumps.

The bay feels seductively warm, the water gliding around her bare arms and legs like a silky blanket. Cherry blinks a few times and then stretches her arms into a lazy freestyle. Her cousins wave at her from the islet, and Cherry takes her time swimming toward them, enjoying her few minutes alone, yet still in the comfort of their watchful gazes.

While Cam tries to climb up the limestone's jagged edges, Cherry and Xuan find a smooth surface to sit and watch her. Occasionally, the water laps up, splashing their feet, trickling between their toes. Xuan and Cam had wanted to come to Ha Long Bay because of Grandmère's stories. Her ancestors were once fishermen in Ha Long Bay, long before their family migrated to the south.

"What was Grandpère's funeral like?" Cherry asks. She has always regretted not attending to support Grandmère.

"It didn't rain," Xuan says, "which he would have approved of. Most of our parish was there, and his friends from the community center. Even Ba Cuc and her family were there, though we didn't realize at the time who she really was."

"How do you think they met?" Cherry asks.

"I think they knew each other in Vietnam," Xuan says. "I guess he followed her to Paris."

"Or she followed him."

He squints, leaning back on his elbows. "I guess we'll never know."

Cherry falls silent. Although she hasn't opened Grandpère's letters, she doesn't trust having them away from her, afraid that if left in Saigon, the Trans will find them, or worse, Lum will throw them out. But perhaps there is another reason she brought them on this trip. Maybe she and her cousins are meant to read them together.

"I can't really judge him," he says, the water glittering off his hair. "Not now. People do really stupid things when they think it's for love."

Cam calls out for a hand. Cherry jumps up to help her cousin with a final, slippery step over two mossy boulders. Several nicks decorate her legs, but Cam proudly grins over her accomplishment.

"Nice view?" Xuan asks.

"There isn't a bad one," she says, collapsing onto the rock, folding her scratched up knees in front of her. She looks around them, happily exhaling. "Maybe we should move here. We'll get a houseboat and float around. I'll learn to fish and Xuan can operate the boat."

"What about Cherry?" Xuan asks.

"She'll be the house doctor," Cam says, turning to rest her head in Cherry's lap. "In case any of my cooking makes us sick."

"I can barely watch over myself," Cherry says.

"You're being modest," Xuan says. "You survived one of the worst things that can happen to a person. They can't teach you that in medical school."

Cherry feels her face growing warm. "That doesn't mean I can take care of anyone."

"Yes, you can," Cam says. "Who's been holding our passports and getting us to our trains and boat rides on time? Who found the local pharmacy when Xuan got the runs in the middle of the night in Hue? You're like Grandmère. It's your nature."

"I knew it." Cherry beams at her cousins. "I should have grown up with you."

"Trust me," Cam says, closing her eyes. "It wasn't so great on our side of the ocean."

"But we could have been together."

"We're together now, right?"

"I'm going home next week. So are you."

"We don't have to," Xuan says.

"But you both have jobs," Cherry says. "I have school."

"They'll be there when we return," Cam says, opening her eyes and spotting Cherry's doubtful expression. "They *will*."

After they've had enough sun, they begin swimming back to the *Minh Quang*. There is no rush, so they float on their backs, admiring the bright blue of the cloudless, open sky. The children are out on the deck, and Cherry waves at them, thinking that lunch must be ready. They stand at the edge of the junk and one of the boys struggles with something in his arms. Cherry floats over on her stomach, treading water, trying to determine what it is. Then a flutter of papers drops from his arms and off the side of the boat. Another. And another. The children are yelling, and one of their mothers emerges on the deck. She roughly yanks at the boy's arm, pulling him back from the junk's edge. In his other hand is Cherry's camera. He was trying to take a picture of them.

The yellowed envelopes scatter across the top of the water, fanning out like schools of fish. For a brief moment, they stand out bright and clear in the jade-green bay. Xuan and Cam swim ahead of her toward the soaking letters. But Cherry can already feel them growing heavy, sinking, sinking to the bay floor.

ᴥ Acknowledgments

This book belongs to many people.

Thanks to the National Endowment for the Arts, the MacDowell Colony, Washington State University, and California College of the Arts for their support of the research and writing of this novel.

Thanks to Dorian Karchmar, for her insight and quick thinking, to Nichole Argyres, who often understood my characters and plots better than I did, and to Laura Chasen, for having the answers to any and every question that I had.

Thanks to my family and friends, who rallied me through the many versions of this book. Especially AT and Teresa Phan, Andrew and Hannah Phan, Terry and Patricia Shears, Ellen Lee, Anu Manchikanti, Sharon Ongerth, Vu Tran, Alex Kuo, Joan Burbick, and Augusta Rohrbach. To Julie Thi Underhill, for her beautiful pictures and the elegant redesign of my Web site.

And to my life partner, Matt Shears. Your compassion and wisdom is laced throughout these chapters, which you have read and reread for the last seven years. I am honored to share my life, children, and writing with you.